OF

DECEIT

AND

SNOW

ASHLEY W. SLAUGHTER

OF DECEIT AND SNOW
Book Two of THE CROWNED CHRONICLES

Library of Congress Cataloging-in-Publication Data
Name: Slaughter, Ashley W., author
Title: Of Deceit and Snow / Ashley W. Slaughter.
Description: First edition. | Santa Rita, GU: AWS Writing, 2022.
Identifiers: LCCN 2022916058 | ISBN (hardcover) 978-1-7369638-3-8 |
ISBN (paperback) 978-1-7369638-4-5 | ISBN (ebook) 978-1-7369638-5-2

First edition, November 2022

Edited by Gina Kammer
Cover Design by Lena Yang
Published by AWS Writing

For more information, visit ashleywslaughter.com

BOOK TWO OF
THE CROWNED CHRONICLES

OF
DECEIT
AND
SNOW

ASHLEY W. SLAUGHTER

A MAGIAN PENINSULA NOVEL

TABLE OF CONTENTS

FOR EVERY WOMAN
WHO HAS EVER FELT TRAPPED—
YOUR VICTORY IS COMING

OF

DECEIT

AND

SNOW

BOOK TWO OF
THE CROWNED CHRONICLES

A MAGIAN PENINSULA NOVEL

2

CHAPTER ONE

THE LAST TIME my mind took me to the woods, it'd been a good thing. A much-needed escape from my prison of Tarasynian walls.

Not this time.

This time, my breath came quick. My heart pounded painfully against my ribs. Shadows taunted the corners of my vision.

My beating heart morphed into beating hooves. Shadows became flashes of hunters riding through snowy evergreen trees. The horse beneath me glided through the forest at a blistering speed, but I had little idea where I was. I was too focused on outrunning my hunting party.

But my prey wasn't an elk or a wildcat or a fox. No. It was something invisible, yet so tangible I could taste it on my tongue as it stretched toward me through the evergreens. The robust, full-bodied earthiness of home. My kingdom. My people.

But just as fervently as I reached for my kingdom, I too was pursued. A beast I'd come to know all too well was hot on my heels.

As I caught my first hopeful glimpse of the low-lying Beryl Foothills of home through the dense trees, an armored hand caught my billowing cloak. I turned sharply and found myself face to face with my beast's deep blue, red-flecked eyes—

I hardly registered the book slipping through my fingers. The cover slapped shut on the floor. I struggled to rein in my ragged breaths, my hand clenched at the base of my throat. I looked down at my feet, safely planted on the stone floor of my rooms, but my heart continued to race against the pounding of hooves. I still felt the cold of the frozen forest in my lungs.

I shuddered violently against the cold. I tried to shake my head free of the panic, but to my body, my captor was still so close.

The walls—were they closing in? No, they weren't walls anymore. They were dense evergreen trees. I felt scrapes of branches against my face, heard the rush of water from a nearby stream.

You are not on horseback, Rose, I told myself. *You are not in the woods of Tarasyn. You are not outrunning anyone.*

Then, most painfully: *You are not anywhere close to home.*

But it'd *felt* like I was.

Then the world tilted, and the corners of my vision blackened.

No, no, no. Not again. Gryffin would be walking through my door any moment.

I shot shakily to my feet and grabbed hold of the nearest branch—no, it was my windowsill. *Windowsill,* Rose.

I heard a muffled voice in the distance, full of concern. "Your Grace?"

As soon as the door opened, I would bolt.

I would. I would do it this time. I had to get home.

But in my mind, there was no door. Only thick woods.

But I *heard* it, the lock of the door releasing and the creak of the hinges. I took a step in that direction, then another.

"Rosemary?" A hand reached for me, and it was a familiar hand, rugged and calloused from too many long nights of riding. My heart sang.

Zeke.

"What's wrong with her?" I heard him demand, but it was not Zeke's voice.

I reeled away from him and fell into a thick patch of bushes—no, a person. Two people. My chambermaids.

"Your Grace, come. Sit here."

And as much as I wanted to fight, as much as I knew I needed to get through that door, my body followed the gentle instruction of my chambermaids. My eyes closed as I lay back, and a cold cloth found my forehead.

"Has she been this way all morning?"

"No, Your Majesty. I-I'm not sure what happened to her." The genuine concern in Cassia's voice—I could place it now, the voice of my head chambermaid—warmed my chest, and my galloping heart slowed.

Gryffin's concern, not so much. "Rosemary? Are you all right?"

I hated these bouts of panic. And this one all from a stubborn daydream that had escalated into something more. They made me feel weak when I knew I was not. They made me feel as though everything were out of my control, which, indeed, most things were.

But there was one thing I knew I *could* still control. I prepared myself to see the red-flecked gaze of my captor, and, slowly, I allowed my eyelids to flutter open as I reached for his hand.

The black ring around my vision was gone, as were the dense trees. Instead, I was back in Snowmont's guest quarters, with Gryffin and Cassia peering at me with creased brows. One of my other

- 3 -

chambermaids, Vasilie, was warming a pot of water in the fireplace.

"Gryffin?" I asked as warmly as I could.

He laid a hand on my cheek, and I fought against the urge to cringe. "Rosemary. How are you feeling?"

"Tired," I answered honestly. These episodes always wore me out, and this one was nothing like I had ever experienced.

A warm cup of tea was put into my hands, and I nodded my thanks to Vasilie.

Gryffin squeezed my hand. "What happened?"

You, I wanted to shout. *Your eyes. Your betrayal. Your ax hanging over my head.*

But I couldn't say any of that. I had a game to play. "A daydream," I responded. "I have too much time on my hands these days."

It was one of the most truthful things I could have said. Too much time to try to fill. In fact, I'd read every book on the tiny bookshelf in these rooms at least once since I'd been held here. Wait—what had I just been reading? A glance down at the book lying on the floor where I'd dropped it reminded me—ah, yes, *The Fawn and the Fanciful Frog.* Again. It was a happy little story, at least, though I'd read it three times now. Its familiarity slowed my heart to a steady trot rather than an outright gallop.

Aside from reading, I picked up weaving again—something I hadn't done since I'd been a small girl—with the help of my handmaids. I was almost finished weaving an entire square foot of blue sky. That was about twenty hours sitting at the loom. Exhilarating.

I memorized the tapestry of the elk hunt that hung upon the wall opposite the bed. Probably the source of my earlier daydream that sent me spiraling. Fourteen hunting dogs, all very large with long, wiry coats. Six men on horseback, three bay horses, two chestnut and one white. Four bows, two spears. Seven trees, twenty-three bushes.

If Gryffin didn't kill me first, my boredom and anxiety would surely do the job.

"Would you like more books then?" Gryffin asked. "I'll have some sent up. Or maybe you'd like to learn an instrument? I can have a flute made—"

Why was he so bent on keeping me merely occupied?

"I want to *leave* these rooms, Gryffin." It wasn't the first time I'd asked. After all, I'd been locked in here for an entire month.

Yes, today marked one month.

One month of no word, no suspicion of foul play, and no sign of a search party. With no correspondence from my people and with Gryffin as my only informant, I had no knowledge of what was going on outside these castle walls.

Or inside, for that matter. Playing prisoner in Tarasyn certainly wasn't the most enlightening position to be in.

I glanced at Gryffin as I massaged my temples softly, my fingertips grazed the raised scar above my left eye. That scar was yet another reminder of why I needed to get out. The woman who'd killed a Tarasynian soldier would have a difficult time gaining any citizen's respect. Even if that woman were to become their queen.

Their queen.

Another shudder ran down my spine.

I would get out of Tarasyn before that happened.

It was not as if I couldn't bear it here, however. Gryffin hadn't kept me in chains or locked in the castle's dank dungeons as I'd thought he would.

On that first night, Gryffin had led me instead to the castle's guest chambers. My arrangements were actually quite *comfortable.*

True, the guest chambers of Snowmont were in severe need of updating, seeing as they haven't welcomed guests in seventy-odd years.

But the plush chair I sat in now, with its furred cushions and wide arms, was admittedly more comfortable than any of the furniture I'd had in my own rooms in Hillstone.

The difference was that *my* rooms did not feel more constricting with each day.

Not to mention the tightly locked door.

The long silence and Gryffin's hard, narrowed eyes made me realize that I'd sounded harsh in my request, so I lowered my voice to a modest timbre. "I want to see the rest of the castle. You've always talked so highly of the work you and your brother have been doing to make improvements." That wasn't a lie either. I'd have to be committed to the asylum if I wasn't at least curious to see what lay beyond my wooden door. I squeezed his hand gently. "I'd like to see what you've done."

He looked down at our hands, and his expression softened. When he looked back up to me, there was a new twinkle in his eyes that almost disguised the red flecks. "Of course, Rosemary. Just tell me when and where, and I'll gladly show you around. You aren't a prisoner."

That was when I felt his Talent pressing to make me trust his words. A slight pressure nudged against the curves and corners of my mind. I'd grown to expect it, but that didn't mean it didn't scare me. I still didn't know what I'd done in the woods to ward off Gryffin's Talent. As a precaution, I'd started building a castle.

Anytime I felt that pressure, I immediately began laying down bricks and stones, mortaring them tightly together. I knew better than to believe I was not a prisoner. That I wasn't one misstep away from being disposed of.

One turret. One battlement. I told him what he wanted to hear. "I know, Gryffin."

He held my gaze for a moment, and slowly, I felt the pressure of Gryffin's Talent subside. He smiled. "Good. Are you hungry?"

Not in the least, I wanted to say. My stomach felt queasy more than anything, and the only thing helping was the warm tea in my hands. But before I could say anything, a castle worker from the kitchens came waltzing through my door with two plates of steaming food followed by another with a bowl heaping with fresh fruits. They placed the food with a flourish onto a little table at the foot of the hunting tapestry and left just as gracefully as they'd come in.

What a show.

What Tarasyn lacked in warmth, they made up for with their food. The meat tasted different here—*better.* I think it was altogether a bit fattier. And the fresh produce! In this frozen place? They must have had acres upon acres of greenhouses. The smell alone of the plate in front of me urged me to take a bite. So, despite my roiling insides, I dared a morsel of roasted ham.

Gryffin continued his own end of the conversation—how he'd slept the night before, how his sword practices had been going, how Roderich's memorial service had gone yesterday. I'd refused to attend the service, though it would have given me an excuse to leave these rooms. I couldn't bring myself to be around people who were mourning a man who'd threatened my kingdom and almost killed me.

Gryffin had told his people the truth—for the most part. He'd told them that Roderich had been power hungry, and that he'd gone about conquering surrounding kingdoms in a brutal, wasteful way. He'd told them honestly that *he* had killed Roderich, for Roderich had been standing over me—the love of his life, his *queen*—with his sword poised to kill.

That last part was a bit of an embellishment.

And of course, with Gryffin's Talent, there was no doubt in his subjects' minds that killing their former king was the right thing to do. There was no ill will whatsoever toward the man that had killed his own brother. They all accepted their beloved prince—their new king.

But Lecevonia would know better . . . once I made it home.

I nodded along through Gryffin's rambling while nibbling at my crisp pear, cutting myself a larger slab of ham, and tearing apart a piece of bread. Their bread was not quite as fluffy as Lecevonia's, but the plump raisins that they added were nice. The food was acceptable to my stomach after all.

Gryffin had just finished telling me of the latest on his brother Yaris, who was technically the older of the twins, when he suddenly said, "I'm going to announce our engagement to the citizens."

I froze mid-nod, and I felt another wave of panic drumming through me, my stomach pitching again.

No.

An engagement. The one thing keeping me alive, and the one thing I thought I could control. But I couldn't let it happen, not yet . . . I slowly placed my raisin-studded bread back down onto my plate and sat a bit straighter in my chair. "Gryffin, I'd . . . I'd like more time—"

Before I could venture further, Gryffin laughed. "So, she *can* still speak!"

A sigh that was a confusing mix between relief and frustration escaped me. Of course he knew how to get a response out of me. So, I began again, steeling myself to tell a lie. "Gryffin, the thought of marrying you brings me a joy I didn't know I could have. But I can't. Not yet." I practically spat my last few words, but I tried to keep my voice soft. "I don't want our marriage to start on any mistrust."

As if that were possible.

If Gryffin knew I never planned to marry him, he'd kill me. He'd killed his brother for standing in his way, and if a marriage to gain access to the Lecevonian throne hadn't been so valuable to him, he'd undoubtedly already have done the same to me. But he wouldn't, not until he was *certain* that our marriage was a lost cause.

No, I would never marry him. I knew this was a dangerous game I was playing. But I needed to give Amos more time. And Zeke and Isabele—surely, they were back from Port Della by now. So, I needed to continue to stay alive.

Gryffin looked at me with such convincing remorse that I almost believed that he felt sorry for what he'd done. Almost.

"Rosemary," he said. "You'll see that everything, from the moment I stepped foot into Lecevonia, was all for us. For our kingdoms, and *every* kingdom across the Peninsula."

"It was all for *you*." My words were sharp like shattered glass, instantly cutting through the façade I'd been so carefully holding.

From the very moment the words escaped my mouth, I regretted them, for a shadow of anger darkened my captor's features. He glared hard at me, then down at the table, the knife he'd been using clenched tightly in his white-knuckled fist.

Angering him was not what I should be doing. Showing him how disgusted I was by his actions, even less so. But I'd meant what I'd said, and he knew it. We sat in a lengthened silence, the tension across the table as taut as a bowstring.

Finally, Gryffin took a deep, shaking breath. "You're wrong." He turned his gaze up to me, and thankfully it had softened to a tired grimace. "Everything, Rosemary. The use of my Talent, my *imprisonment* in Lecevonia, Roderich's death, my bringing you here. I carried out and endured all of it with only the sake of the Peninsula in my mind."

And Thomas's death? I wanted to ask him, but I refrained. I knew my loyal guard's murder was only for Gryffin. To make his goal of getting me alone easier. Besides, he'd already told me during one of his past visits that he regretted it now. A waste of life, he'd said. That he should have just used his Talent on both of us, especially since his actions pushed *me* to see through his Talent.

He'd also admitted that his imprisonment at Hillstone had not been part of his plan. Yes, he'd known from the moment I rode through those woods that dreaded morning that his and Roderich's false assassination attempt would work flawlessly. And afterwards, when things had no longer gone according to his plan, he'd known without a doubt that his brother had been behind the attempt on my little sister's life, the one that had instead claimed our beloved Sterling. But he hadn't expected to be *caught* knowing such things.

So, he'd come up with the ridiculous lie of chasing after my heart. He had truly played me like a perfectly tuned harp, thrumming across my heartstrings with each deceptive stroke.

He told me that he'd almost lost me in the prison—that he'd felt my will slipping away from his control. I'd almost been free from his power, had my sheer stubbornness to trust him been a little weaker.

"Would you have ever told me?" I asked him abruptly.

But Gryffin hadn't been in my head, reading my thoughts. He only looked at me with puzzled eyes.

"About your Talent," I clarified.

He was quiet for a moment, weighing his response. Finally, he leaned his elbows against the table. "I hadn't truly decided. Possibly, in a less direct way. In some way to make you see it as a useful tool rather than a deceptive one."

"So you would have still lied to me," I said flatly.

He clicked his tongue in dissatisfaction. "We're only going to go in circles this morning, aren't we?"

I parted my lips, ready to let some equally snide remark fly, when a heavy knock on my door reverberated throughout the room. When neither of us acknowledged the interruption, the door opened, and a deep voice called from the hallway. "Your Majesty."

We both turned our heads to the doorframe sharply, though I did so out of reflex. I knew I wasn't the one being called for, and Gryffin was "His Majesty" now, no matter the means of how he'd obtained the title.

"What is it, Campton?" Gryffin answered gruffly.

"You're needed in your office, Your Majesty."

There was the shortest second of tense silence, as if Gryffin were deciding whether or not he was willing to shirk his duties a bit longer for the sake of winning our argument. But in the end, he was nothing if not dedicated. He nodded his head once. "I'll be there in a moment. Tell Fendrel to make himself comfortable."

The man named Campton bowed and padded away down the hallway. With a heavy sigh, Gryffin put down his fork and knife. My chambermaids immediately began clearing the plates from the table, but I kept my hands hovering over mine, signaling that I wasn't quite finished. They nodded quickly and backed away as Gryffin stood from the table. "I suppose I should let you get some rest then."

"Yes. You should." I was done playing my part this morning.

After a silent battle raging in his eyes, he lifted my hand to his lips and kissed it with surprising tenderness before letting go. "I'll see you tonight."

Then, my captor strode from my chambers, the bolt of the door's lock sliding into place behind him.

What took the most effort to acclimate myself to was the *cold.* True, my capitol city saw snow almost every winter, but the rising temperatures of spring always melted away the powder and slush. Here, the frigid crispness of the air was perpetual. I was thankful every day for the thick furs and the burning fireplace that kept me warm, but that also meant that I opted to keep my window shuttered most of the time to trap in the heat and block the most unwelcome chill. Which usually led to another round of utter tedium.

This evening, however, I kept my window open, for I refused to go another moment with only that tapestry to look at. I stayed cocooned in my brown fur blanket and let the breeze escaping from the frozen world outside nip at my cheeks.

The reason the snow clouds skirted the capitol city still evaded me, but in a way, I was grateful for it. I was always amazed by the colorful vibrance of the city. Even in the courtyard below my window, trees of blues, reds, and oranges stood out starkly against the evergreens of the forest. Sterling would have been astounded.

The sun had already set behind the low snow clouds, dinner had come and gone, and the courtyard torches in the had been set aglow by the time Gryffin returned. This time, I knew I needed to play nicer, and I looked forward to the click of the bolt and the creak of the old hinges. When he appeared through my door, I stood from my windowsill to greet him with an exuberant smile on my face.

"Hello, Gryffin."

He looked shocked for a moment, and the familiar prick of his Talent immediately dissipated.

I had to admit that my mood felt very out of place. Even my unease at the sight of him was more subdued than normal. But he'd told me that I could leave my rooms, and I was ready to hold him to his word.

As he came forward and took my hands in his, a smile of his own stretched from cheek to cheek, all traces of our earlier argument gone. "Ah, my Rosemary. Now you're looking more like yourself."

I continued to smile despite the ice settling in my veins. Truly, how would he know? The only *me* he'd known had been trapped under his Talent. But I kept my tone light to hide my thoughts. "Well, I've been thinking of your offer this morning, and I've decided."

"Oh?"

I nodded eagerly. "I'd like to go now, and I'd like to go anywhere," I said, answering his *when* and *where* stipulations. *Anywhere* did not give him a reason to say no, and I was determined to see anywhere else but this room as soon as I possibly could.

He raised his eyebrows at my response, but his unwavering smile told me all that I needed to know: he'd agree, as long as my mood stayed this happy. After a second of thought, he asked, "How about I take you to the conservatory?"

Snowmont had a conservatory? How . . . classy. Or pretentious. One of the two.

"It's something that I've been wanting to show you," he continued, "and I think you'll be impressed." His laughter shook his dark curls, which I had found charming once upon a time. He offered his arm to me, and I looped my arm through his as if it were still as natural as ever.

The release I felt as we stepped through my door was insurmountable. It was as if my lungs had just drawn a lifesaving breath after having been tightly bound for far too long. Even the narrow corridor felt freeing. I stretched my shoulders with a little hum and a roll of my head, relishing the new space.

Every candelabra along the hallway had been lit, illuminating our way. They signaled that the king was home.

For a fraction of a second, I considered my appearance. It was the first time anyone in Tarasyn would see me, aside from my guards and chambermaids. I was not really dressed to be seen by the public. At least, not to be seen as a queen. The gnarly knot of hair upon my head would have made Hazel cry.

I gathered quickly that the guest chambers must have been in the original part of the castle, for the dark stone hallways pressed together tightly beneath the low ceiling. New candelabras had been added amidst the older to give more light, but the smell was musty and dank from too many years without the sun.

"I'm sorry that this is the first you see of Snowmont," Gryffin said with a bit of chagrin. "We hadn't focused on renovating the older section. Only adding the newer."

"'We' as in you and Roderich?" I asked, doing little to hide the murderous accusation in my voice. Then I chided myself. I'd lose my new freedom before I even get to enjoy it if I couldn't keep my tone in check.

To my relief, Gryffin didn't seem phased. He even smiled. "And my other siblings, of course. They have a say too."

There was no door separating the old section of Snowmont from the new section. From the moment we stepped through the gaping entrance at the end of the corridor, it was as if I'd been dumped into a new world.

As the hallway suddenly opened into a massive room, the first thing that caught my eye was the exorbitant amount of *color*. The large stones that built the walls had been painted just as they had been on the outside, in great swaths of reds with shimmering accents of golds, and countless hues of blues, greens, and yellows. It reminded me of the stained glass nerys lily in my chapel, without the definitive shapes.

The ceiling soared above our heads, with rafters crossing over one another in complicated arrangements. From the rafters hung banners of what must have been the Tarasynian crest: a crimson sun peeking around a white mountain, embellished with green and gold grape vines around the border. I thought I heard the croaky call of a crow and shuddered. I quickly averted my eyes from the rafters and instead studied the tapestries that covered every wall.

They certainly liked their needlework in Tarasyn. I wondered absently if insulation from the cold had anything to do with it as I studied the different scenes depicted on the tapestries: another hunting party, though this time they seemed to be hunting rabbits with a pack of dogs and large red-tailed hawks; a quaint garden where two women in extravagant clothing were conversing with one another; the same women in the same garden, but with a little girl running around them with a scruffy white dog now; a regal throne room with a grand king accepting the fealty of one of his subjects. Smaller tapestries also hung above the mantle of the colossal fireplace, but I could not see what scenes those had been woven into.

The warmth emanating from the blazing fire caressed me even from a distance, which was more impressive than anything. Though, with a fireplace large enough for even my towering former guard Roger to step into with ease, I supposed it shouldn't have surprised me.

Gryffin must have seen the reluctant awe on my face, for he chuckled quietly and announced, "Snowmont's new Great Hall."

As I shrugged off the fur blanket I'd kept wrapped around my shoulders, I ran a hand over the nearest burgundy velvet couch—one of many that were spread throughout the room, all with plush rugs lying underneath them.

This was surely not what I'd expected the castle of two killers to look like.

"Come," Gryffin said, nodding his head toward the left end of the room.

As he led me across the Great Hall, I found that my earlier concern for my appearance had not been needed. Each couch and chair in this grand room was empty. No one stood by the fire's warmth. No stragglers from supper conversed around the edges of the room. Despite the heat from the fireplace, the absence of another living soul left the room feeling cold. I thought it odd—surely it was not *that* late in the evening?

We came upon a set of large, brass double doors, and Gryffin's mood lifted even higher. With a growing smile on his face and his shoulders proud, Gryffin held one of the doors open for me. I walked through, and I found myself in a glass globe.

The conservatory made me feel as if I were standing in a gigantic soap bubble that had settled onto the ground outside. The icicles on the snowy trees along the edge of the castle grounds danced and twinkled in the moonlit breeze, yet it was still *warm* inside our bubble.

Innumerable plants surrounded us, lining the cobblestone walkway that curved through the conservatory. I noticed plants of all different varieties, most of which I hadn't seen before in my life. The low-growing plants with large, plump leaves and trees bending overhead with shady fronds looked like they belonged along the lush, tropic beaches of Loche. Others were more familiar, such as roses and violets. I thought I caught the pink petals of a peony peeking from around a linden tree, bringing Sterling's kind, sun-wrinkled face to mind.

When I looked at Gryffin, he wore the smuggest look I'd ever seen. "Well?" he asked.

It was ostentatious. It was arrogant. It was domineering.

But it was beautiful.

Anyone with any appreciation for nature would have to admire the sheer amount of *life* in the room. What's more, this globe felt more alive than any dining hall and courtyard I'd experienced. These plants had the same energetic buzz as the evergreen trees out there in Tarasyn's forests had. But here, in this controlled environment, it was a little less unsettling.

Finally, I let my shoulders relax a bit in surrender. "I've never seen anything like it."

As a satisfied smile spread across Gryffin's features, an unfamiliar and starkly feminine voice suddenly spoke from behind him.

"You'll get used to it. I assure you."

"Always a ray of positivity, this one," Gryffin murmured dryly, rolling his eyes. He sidestepped, exposing the young woman who had stealthily crept up to us.

"My sister, Kathryn." He waved his hand lazily between the two of us in introduction. "Kathryn, this is Rosemary."

Even without the introduction, I would've been able to tell there was some relation. With her cascading dark curls that seemed black in the dim light and tall statuesque frame, she was the female incarnate of Gryffin. And her deep blue eyes did not have the frightening flecks of red, only the gray of the ocean's depths, holding a sharp, smiling intelligence.

Could she really be only seventeen? I recalled my sweet Isabele, her innocently wide brown eyes and shy demeanor, the timid droop of her shoulders. Surely, if Kathryn was seventeen, growing up at Snowmont had accelerated her maturity somehow. I didn't even think that I held *myself* as confidently as she did.

"What other woman would you be walking with so late in the evening?" Kathryn replied with a roll of her eyes, which instantly made me want to grin. Then, she turned a great white smile toward me. "I've been dogging my brother about letting me meet you *before* the end of civilization. And even still, this was an accident!" She shot a glare in

Gryffin's direction. "Has he even given you a proper tour of Snowmont yet?"

Before I could answer, Gryffin cleared his throat. "This was actually the first time Rosemary requested to leave her rooms."

Requested to leave my rooms? *Permitted* was the more likely the word I would use! But I held my tongue. Instead, I played along with a simple smile. "I decided it was time to see something else other than my same stone walls." And that stupid tapestry.

Kathryn studied me closely in the silence that followed, and I couldn't place the emotion that was churning in her fierce eyes. Something like doubt. Or mistrust? But surely that wasn't right. We'd hardly spoken a word to each other.

Then, as if her strange gaze had meant nothing—which maybe it hadn't—she blinked quickly and turned to her brother. "How have you kept her from me this long? The only other woman in Snowmont?" She shook her head before turning back to me, a grin pulling at one corner of her lips. "You're absolutely gorgeous. I can't believe Gryffin isn't showing you off to the entire court."

Her blatant compliment would have typically taken me by surprise, but it felt so sisterly that I smiled. I liked her.

"Well, you've met her now." Gryffin set a hand on Kathryn's shoulder. "And it's getting late. You should sleep soon, Kathryn."

By the indignant set of her eyebrows, his sister looked as if she were about to argue. But the longer she thought, her face settled into a resigned mask. "Fine," she grumbled. "But make sure she gets out of her room from time to time. I mean, really, what has he been up to, keeping you locked away for so long?" She met my eyes again, and this time they screamed a clear emotion. Understanding.

"Locked away." Interesting choice of words on her part.

Before I could think of any way to acknowledge her remark, she gently touched her hand to Gryffin's, outstretched finger to finger, a space between their palms. An old greeting and farewell among loved ones on the Peninsula. So old, in fact, that I hadn't seen it used in Lecevonia for years. Tarasyn was more traditional than I thought.

"Good night." Kathryn dipped her head to both of us and walked out of the conservatory, shoes clicking as she closed the thick door behind her.

Without her presence, the conservatory felt a little darker.

I wheeled around to face Gryffin. "I must meet with her again."

"She'd like that too," he answered with a small smile. "Tomorrow morning, I'll tell her to meet you in the Great Hall."

For the first time in over a month, I felt an inkling of gratitude toward this man.

CHAPTER TWO

SINCE ARRIVING IN Tarasyn, I'd learned three things.

The first—everyone in the kingdom knew how to dress for the cold. The furs and wool-lined dresses were a must in this frozen environment.

Second, as I learned from my chambermaids, dressing for the cold—if not solely for fashion—was actually viewed as a "poor man's" notion. Only those in poverty had no way of heating their homes, which was a fortunate yet surprisingly low number since the kingdom was only six years free from a seventy-year period of unrest.

And third, only the oldest generations cared whether or not they looked "impoverished." Everyone else dressed for comfort.

I certainly had no qualms, dressed in my dark-burgundy gown, as the warm wool pressed against my skin like a most welcome embrace. I did have my hair done with a little more care today, however. I'd asked Cassia to use her creativity to braid it into some form of regality.

And now I stood staring hard at my chamber doors. After yesterday, might I have a bit of freedom? Was it silly for me to even have the thought? With a deep breath, I strode forward and pulled at the rusted handle.

Locked. Of course.

I groaned quietly, took my seat near the window, and picked a book off the small shelf without even looking at its title. I was sure to recognize it from the first few paragraphs anyway. So I sat there, nestled into my fur blanket and eyes vacantly scanning the first page while I waited for Gryffin to release me from my prison cell.

I'd only gotten midway through the first chapter when I heard the quiet knock, the twist of the lock's bolt leaving its chamber. When Gryffin appeared through the open door, I jumped up from my seat. The book that I'd suddenly forgotten about fell to the floor with a thud.

Despite the innate dread at his arrival telling me to run, I gave him a quick kiss on the cheek and passed him to stand near the door. "Shall we?" I asked. If I kept moving quickly, I thought that perhaps I might distract myself from the disgust of touching my lips to him.

Gryffin stood wide-eyed for a moment, clearly dazed by my sudden affection, before stepping to my side and offering me his arm. "Not hungry this morning?" he asked quietly as we began walking down the narrow hallway.

I shook my head, though my stomach told me otherwise. "I'd like to see Kathryn."

He didn't press the subject any further, but I hoped that he'd have food brought to us later.

The Great Hall looked different during the day with the sunlight pouring through the ceiling-high windows and bathing the room in a cool glow. The colors on the walls seemed more subdued, more sensible. Elegant, even, if I had to admit it. I shed my blanket and began scanning the room, but there wasn't a soul in sight. Again.

Where was everyone? Why was the castle not bustling with activity?

Gryffin sidled up beside me. "Don't be surprised by Kathryn's tardiness. It's rare that she is ever on time."

A voice harumphed from the far entryway. "Rare? Is that so, brother?"

I turned my head toward the newer wing of the castle to see Kathryn wrapped in a fur cloak of her own, making her way toward us. "You really ought to give me more credit than that." The moment she was close enough, Kathryn elbowed her brother in the ribs and unfurled her cloak near the grand fireplace, exposing an exquisite blue and gold gown that would have made Hazel faint of delight.

She then turned to me with a positively gleeful smile. "Good morning, Rosemary!"

"Good mo—Oh!"

She surprised me by taking my hands in hers, and she dragged me to the nearest velvet-covered couch. As we sat, Gryffin took a seat in a chair not far away.

He wouldn't leave me unsupervised, it seemed.

Kathryn noticed it too. "You'll smother her, Gryffin."

Gryffin ignored her remark with an innocent pout of his lips before sliding a book from his vest and cracking it open to a bookmarked page. He'd come prepared to sit there for a while.

Kathryn rolled her eyes and looked back to me. "Well, tell me everything. How are you liking Tarasyn?"

Her enthusiasm made me smile, but could I be truthful? It was hard enough keeping up with my lies to Gryffin. Maybe I could spare a bit of honesty with Kathryn. Trivial honesty, anyway.

"Well," I said, keeping my laugh light, "the cold and snow are taking some getting used to. To be honest, I haven't seen much of Tarasyn other than what I see outside my window." That was true enough. I wickedly hoped Gryffin heard the disdain in my voice. "But the city looks beautiful."

She nodded excitedly. "Have you ever seen so many colors?"

Actually, yes. In Sterling's gardens. A fresh wave of homesickness threatened to raise tears, but I smiled as brightly as I could and warded them off. "Back home, wildflowers of all sorts of colors would be blooming now. My sister Clara would be bringing me bouquets of them."

Kathryn squinted at me, skeptical. "Wildflowers?"

"Yes?" I answered her question with a question.

"Without a conservatory?"

It was then that I realized just how secluded Kathryn had been here at Snowmont. Here was a girl who has seen nothing but her own icy kingdom all her life. I hadn't seen much, but at least I'd had the chance to leave Lecevonia when I was younger.

"Is Lecevonia truly very different then?" she asked. "I've only read a bit about the other kingdoms in whatever books I could find in the bare bones of our excuse of a library." She wrinkled her nose in distaste.

Ah, that was right—Gryffin had said that their resources were few.

I nodded slowly, my mind wandering back to the streets of Equos. "Very different. By this time of year, the Beryl Foothills are a sea of green grass and wildflowers."

"To see hills instead of mountains, grass instead of snow . . . It's hard to imagine." Kathryn had this dreamy look in her eyes, a look that seemed as far away from this kingdom as Loche.

I smiled lightly. "That makes two of us. Tarasyn is unlike anything I've seen before." I could already picture her bright blue eyes alight with excitement, taking in Lecevonia's green expanse. "If you do find yourself in my kingdom, I know my sisters would love to give you a tour of Equos. Maybe even Port Della, if you're lucky."

She smiled, eyes envious. "Sisters. I've always wanted a sister." She looked toward Gryffin and rolled her eyes. "Someone else to temper the thundering masculinity in this castle."

This time, I couldn't hold back my laugh. "Thundering masculinity?"

"Oh, for Haggard's sake, yes!" Kathryn leaned back into the couch and snorted loudly. "I wish no one my same fate."

Gryffin chimed in from his seat. "Oh, surely it hasn't been that terrible."

Kathryn was right—he was absolutely smothering me. Didn't he have a kingdom to run?

I nudged Kathryn's shoulder and spoke in hushed tones. "What does he do all day?"

Kathryn rolled her eyes and, side-eyeing her brother, answered just as quietly. "He's shut away in his office most of the time. There's a lot of shouting, a lot of people rushing in and out. Haggard only knows why he wanted to be king."

"Shouting?"

Her eyes turned very serious, and she lowered her voice so low that I had to lean in to hear her words. "Something about military action."

Military action!

What was happening out there?

My thoughts returned to Lecevonia, to my army, to my people. Had my kingdom made a move against Tarasyn after all? I silently thanked Amos, my general, my colonels.

Unless—it wasn't Lecevonia that opposed Gryffin? Had he set his sights on overthrowing my uncle in Somora now?

I needed to know what Kathryn knew. But in order to do that, I needed to speak with her in private, without the prying ears of Gryffin. In my mind, the beginnings of a plan took hold.

"The conservatory is very nice," I murmured, still quiet.

She locked eyes with me, her gaze puzzled by my sudden change of subject. "Yes," she answered slowly, "there are more species of plants in there than I can keep track of."

"And it seems very quiet. Especially after the sun has set." I wasn't yet sure how I'd escape my room, but I decided I'd work through that obstacle later. What I needed now was for Kathryn to read my mind. *Please understand,* I begged, keeping my eyes locked on hers.

Just the tiniest lift of her eyebrows. A widening of her eyes. A flash of comprehension.

"Absolutely," she answered. Then, suddenly speaking much more loudly, she added, "I'm also hungry! Come with me—I'm sure they're still serving breakfast in the Dining Hall."

That small gesture gave me hope that I could trust her.

We were both about to stand, but at her remark, Gryffin lifted his head. "Nonsense, I'll have food brought in here." He raised his hand and motioned to a castle worker, who had been standing quietly near the entryway to the newer section of the castle since we'd arrived.

Kathryn sighed, turning in her seat. "Gryffin, I'm sure Rosemary wants to see—"

"No."

Gryffin's stern and resolute denial surprised both of us. He waved again impatiently to the castle worker, who flitted over to his side. They exchanged whispers, and then the man hurriedly left the room.

Gryffin's fervor struck a chord in me, and I suddenly realized *why* I hadn't seen anyone else in the castle yet. Why I'd been locked away for so long, why I hadn't been introduced to Kathryn before now. Why the Great Hall had been empty both last night and this morning—a matter which he'd probably arranged himself—and why he didn't want me to go to the Dining Hall now.

He was keeping me out of sight.

As to the reason, I didn't know. But he did not want more than the strictly necessary people to see me just yet.

A moment later, as carts of food began pouring into the room, I shifted my gaze to Gryffin. He was staring at his sister, his eyes cold and annoyed. Then, he must have felt my eyes on him, for he turned his hard stare on me. His jaw softened, and a kind smile broke through his frigid expression.

In my charade, I returned the sweetest smile I could muster.

But behind my smile, I was already scheming a way out of my rooms later that night.

Gryffin had come and gone quickly. He'd said that he still had a desk-load of work to do, unfortunately, but that he'd wanted to watch the sunset with me from my window. How charming.

And, quite unfortunate for me, he'd locked the door behind him as usual.

I paced in my rooms after he'd left for what felt like an entire hour, trying to conjure up a new plan to get past that locked door.

If Zeke were here, he could pick the lock with no problem. But he was not, and he'd never taught me. My plight wouldn't be solved that easily.

My only hope would be my guard then. Which was another matter entirely.

I shot a glance toward Cassia, busying herself with brewing a cup of herbal tea for me. My other chambermaids were cleaning the fireplace, sweeping in the corner, and other odd tasks here and there. Would any of them help me? They'd never denied me anything before, but surely their allegiance was with Gryffin.

Still, I wondered if I could test that sentiment.

I stopped my pacing and turned to Cassia, feigning a yawn with my hand over my mouth. "Cassia," I began softly, "can you do something for me?"

She looked up from brewing a cup of herbal tea. "Of course, Your Majesty."

Her words made me smile—she was the only one to call me *Your Majesty* here, when Gryffin wasn't around. I took care wording my request. "I'm feeling very drained from the day. Would you and the others mind turning in early tonight?"

Her eyes turned skeptical. "Without your bath?"

I responded with a wry grin. "A night without a bath won't break me."

She pursed her lips, and I saw the suspicion enter her eyes. For good reason—a warm bath was what I looked forward to the most in this cold chamber. Cassia was too smart to overlook that little fact.

"King Gryffin is strict on the time we are to leave your room," she said slowly.

I silently cursed him and hoped Kathryn would wait—

"But I think we can make an exception for one night." The corner of Cassia's lips turned upward into a little grin, and she nodded her head toward my other chambermaids. "Come, girls. Her Majesty would like to retire for the night."

As the other girls put aside their tasks and filed out through the maid's door, I squeezed Cassia's wrist with a relieved sigh. "Thank you, Cassia. Please believe me when I say you have my utmost gratitude."

"Of course." Then, she muttered so low I almost thought I

misheard her. "I don't know why he treats you like a criminal anyhow."

Ah, so at least *she* was not oblivious to Gryffin's treatment. But before I could acknowledge her words, she slipped through the maid's door and shut it tightly behind her.

And I was alone.

After having no real privacy in weeks, this unfamiliar silence felt like a caress. I considered for a fraction of a second just staying here, relishing in the solitude. But no, I needed to talk to Kathryn. I needed to know what she knew.

So. Now for my guard.

Admittedly, I didn't know for sure which guard was outside my door for the night. I thought back to the past couple of nights, trying to recall the order in which they'd stood behind that door. My night guard was on a rotation of three men, but who had been my guard last night?

Sir Brantley? Yes, it was him.

Wait. No. He'd been the night before last. I remembered his blonde wavy hair—because it always reminded me a bit of Zeke—behind Gryffin's head in the doorway two nights ago.

Then last night must have been Sir Poole. So tonight, Sir Kreodin was standing outside my door.

Right?

Utterly confused, I decided to take a chance. I walked to my door, took a deep, encouraging breath, and knocked softly.

"Sir Kreodin?"

A pause. Too long of a pause.

Boars, I thought to myself angrily. I'd gotten it wrong.

Then, a deep, inquisitive voice answered and sent a shot of relief through me. "Yes, Your Grace?"

Great! Now what?

I needed to think fast, and the only power I currently had was—

Oh, no.

As the idea came to me, I mentally groaned and reprimanded myself for what I was about to do.

I tried to sound as demure as I possibly could. "Sir Kreodin, if I may be so bold, I believe you to be my favorite guard."

I heard the shock in his gruff chuckle. "Is that so?"

"Mhmm," I answered softly. "You are by far the kindest and the most handsome. I . . . I always find myself wanting to run my fingers through your hair." I cringed at my own words and desperately hoped that he actually had hair. I couldn't remember. "I'd like to spend more time with you, if you'll allow it."

A hesitation. "In there?"

Did I want him in here? It'd get him to unlock the door, surely, but some sense of self-preservation in me told me that having him in my rooms without my chambermaids would not be the smartest idea.

"Oh, no," I replied quickly. "My maids would surely not keep our secret. I want us to go someplace where it can . . . where it can be just us." I hoped my stammering was coming off as coy.

A longer hesitation than before. Haggard, if this did not work, Sir Kreodin would run to his king, and Gryffin would have my head.

Then, a jingling of keys. The bolt of my door's lock sliding out of its place.

My door opened, and my guard stood before me with a goofy smile on his face. He did have hair, thankfully, and quite luxurious hair at that. Sweeping red locks that rested on his shoulders.

"Where to?" he asked, eyebrows raised.

How sad that Gryffin's guards were more loyal to a pretty face than to their king. But it worked in my favor tonight.

I stepped out into the corridor and laid my hand softly on

Kreodin's forearm. I found that faux flirting with Kreodin was much easier than my ploy with Gryffin. Maybe because Kreodin didn't disgust me just by his presence.

"Close your eyes, and I'll lead you."

Kreodin was more than happy to play along, his big smile never leaving his face as he kept his eyes squeezed shut, guided by my touch. As we approached the doorway to the Great Hall, I stopped while we were still concealed in the shadows of the tight corridor.

"Now, I have a surprise for you," I said, putting all my energy into a convincing simper. I knew my success here was highly improbable, but I fervently hoped that he was feeling too wanton to think straight. "Keep your eyes closed, please. I'm going to let go, and don't open your eyes until I say so."

His gravelly laugh gave me a sense of victory—underneath the prickling displeasure of violation. I may have started this game, but his eagerness was beginning to unsettle me.

I released his arm and began to silently back away from him, toward the Great Hall. I repeated, "Keep them closed . . ." a couple of times before my voice could sound too far away. Then, as I skirted the corner through the doorway, I turned to run.

But I'd only made it a few steps before his large hand clasped my wrist.

I gasped as he pulled me back into his chest by my waist. His breath was hot and unforgiving on my neck.

"Is the surprise a game of hide and seek?" he asked, that same gravelly laugh deep in my ear. "Or maybe catch-the-queen?"

I tried to yank my hand away, but his grip was strong. "Let go of me."

But he shook his big head and held me tighter. "You said you had a surprise for me."

"You'll answer to your king if you don't let go of me." As threatening as my words were, my voice shook so violently it'd come out weak as a mouse's. Tears pricked my eyes, sprung forth from fear and anger.

He only gripped my wrist tighter and chuckled into my hair. "You can't tell him anything. You'd have to deal with his wrath too." He glanced down at me with hungry eyes. "You wanted this, didn't you?"

I glared over my shoulder at him. "Not anymore." Who did this man think he was? A man that was stronger than me, certainly.

But I hadn't snuck out of my rooms to be overtaken by a brutish boar.

Fine. I had a surprise for him.

With every ounce of my strength, I reeled my elbow back and jabbed it into his ribs. That was what Zeke would have done.

Kreodin grunted and loosened his hold around my waist, just enough for me to spin around in his arms and jerk my knee up into his groin.

I'd never had to do that before, but by the way Kreodin folded into himself, it seemed pretty effective.

His arm disappeared from around my waist with a moan of agony, and the moment he released my wrist, I ran.

My shoes padded silently across the Great Hall's rug-covered floor as I ran, and I flew through one of the heavy brass doors of the conservatory without looking behind me. I shut the door as quietly as I could and leaned against it, listening.

No footsteps. No voices.

I closed my eyes and rested my forehead against the door with an exhale. I couldn't believe I'd felt guilty for fooling the man! He was no more innocent than me. Had he been a better man and soldier—more honorable, loyal, respectful—he would not have played into my ruse in the first place.

But that didn't matter anymore. I'd done it. I'd escaped my rooms.

And what's more, Gryffin would never find out. After Cassia's display of loyalty tonight, I trusted her to keep my little infraction a secret, as well as to keep my other chambermaids in check. And surely Kreodin would never admit to leaving his post to philander with the king's woman, which only ended in a knee to the groin. He most likely would not even raise the alarm, only roam the castle halls searching for me silently.

Then, a tapping of shoes around the perimeter of the Great Hall reached me through the brass door. My eyes shot open, and I backed away, glancing around the conservatory in case I'd have to dive into the nearest plant cover.

The door on the right opened, letting in just the tiniest sliver of light, and a hand curled around the door's edges. A slender figure stepped into the darkness of the conservatory, and a second wave of relief washed over me.

Kathryn.

CHAPTER THREE

"WHAT ON EARTH is one of my brother's soldiers doing out in the halls moaning like a banshee?" Kathryn asked, rolling her eyes. Then, she saw my disheveled hair, and her eyes widened. "Oh . . . Well, a woman does what she must."

She grabbed my hand and pulled me forward. "No prying eyes or ears here. Very nice choice. But we don't have a lot of time with that crite roaming around the halls. Come, follow me."

She led me down the stone pathway through the plants, turning this way and that, and again I was amazed by the liveliness of the room, a green force humming from plant to plant. I wondered how so much energy could be contained in this globe without cracking the glass.

She stopped when we came to an alcove in the shadow of a tropical tree with lobed leaves larger than dinner plates. A lone bench was nestled beneath its branches.

The moment we sat, she turned her torso and looked at me squarely, her blue eyes burning. "Rosemary, I need you to be honest with me."

"All right," I answered slowly, caution pinching the corners of my eyes. Though I had been the one to ask her to meet with me, she'd quickly taken the reins of our conversation. She was a force of nature. I supposed that we would see just how truthful I could allow myself to be.

Her eyes never left mine. "Do you want to be here?"

Her question stunned me into silence. Kathryn wanted honesty, but already I had no idea whether or not I could give her that. My honest answer would expose the only thing keeping me alive.

What if she was under Gryffin's influence right now? Would he convince her to tell him everything I say to her? That was simply a chance I could not take.

Unless.

Kathryn narrowed her eyes. "You don't trust me." Impatience coated her tone.

"Should I?" I retaliated, harsher than I meant to.

She certainly had the same confidence as her brother.

Kathryn's eyes widened with indignation, and we sat in tense silence as we each scrutinized the other.

Her assumption had sent a bristle down my spine. Trust. That was something I refused to give easily now. And for her to think she deserved it so freely—

I took a fortifying breath.

"If I am to trust anyone here in Tarasyn," I began carefully, "I need to be given good reason to do so. I sometimes can't even trust myself, after seeing what Gryffin can do. Experiencing it . . . How can I be sure my mind is completely my own? That *your* mind is completely your own?" I gestured in her direction and shook my head. "I don't have the luxury of trusting just anyone."

Kathryn considered my words in silence, and slowly, the steel in her eyes dissipated. She chuckled without a hint of humor. "I haven't been under his influence in years. But I know what it feels like. And I know how his Talent works."

Pain stung her words, and I wondered what Gryffin had made Kathryn believe.

"I also know he's been keeping you locked in your chambers," she continued. "Do you honestly think I haven't tried to visit you already? The guards posted outside your door turn me away every time, and I know whose orders they follow."

So, she knew part of my situation already. And she was too smart, or too experienced, to be influenced by Gryffin's deception now. But where did her loyalties lie?

"You don't sound particularly fond of your brother."

She muttered a small sound of contempt. "I know that he can't be trusted. Roderich may have been maniacal, but at least he was straightforward. Gryffin, however . . . His lies upon lies make his motives unpredictable. When I learned he'd *killed* Roderich? Our own brother?" She spit on the ground. "Gryffin may be my brother, but he's not my king."

So her loyalty certainly did not lie with Gryffin. And if it was to Roderich, then her loyalty lay with him atop the nearest mountain peak. Though she hadn't sounded very fond of him either.

Maybe, after having been burned by her other family members, she was simply loyal to herself. She has been a prisoner here too, in her own way.

If I told her the truth, she could very well end my life and send our kingdoms into a full-blown war—if they weren't already. However, if there was anyone who would be helpful to have on my side in this frozen kingdom, it would be her.

I decided to take a chance.

"Gryffin captured me in the woods of Equos and brought me here with the intent of marrying me. I've been locked in the guest chambers, bored and angry, when I should be back in Lecevonia. With my people."

It felt amazingly *freeing* to tell someone what I'd been holding so rigidly inside my mind for the past month. I took a deep, revitalizing breath and exhaled, somehow stronger than I'd been just moments before.

Her blue eyes raced across my face intently before they fell to the floor. "I had a feeling. I just needed to hear it to be certain, I suppose." She lifted her gaze. "What happened then?"

What happened.

So much had happened.

"He had me fooled," I whispered. Suddenly, everything I hadn't been able to talk about seemed to roll off my tongue. "He fooled me from the moment we met. I'd truly believed that he'd wanted me, that he'd had Lecevonia's best interests at heart. He had me fooled into thinking that I cared for him, that I wanted to *marry* him! The thought of it now sickens me."

I felt so stupid as I told her all of this. There was a saying in Lecevonia, "the hen doesn't know what the wolf does." Well, I was undoubtedly the hen.

"The only thing he wants is power," Kathryn said, shaking her head. "He speaks with his silver tongue, and he coaxes good feelings out of you, and then he takes what he wants. All while you believe he means well." She glared through the conservatory's wooden doors, and I felt that glare travel through the walls, all the way to her brother's chambers.

Again, I wondered: what had he made her believe?

"How did you see through his Talent?"

"I'm still not sure," I confessed. "He killed my guard to ensure that I was alone." A familiar stab of grief tightened my chest and made it hard to breathe. Oh, Thomas. "That was when things became clear. Or . . . hazy, I suppose. It's hard to describe." Just the effort of remembering brought back the head-pounding fog of confusion.

She looked outward, toward the frosted pines. "No need. I know what you mean."

"He'd tried to convince me that my guard had tried to hurt me, but I'd known better than that." My voice had grown very quiet, just a murmur among the energetic buzz of the plants around us. "So I tried to run. Oh, Haggard, did I try to run. Then I tried to fight. But I couldn't get away before he knocked me unconscious. Next thing I know"—I faced my palms upward, my empty hands expressing my helplessness—"I'm tied up on horseback, on my way to Tarasyn. Since then, I've been keeping up a charade that I intend to marry him, one day. Otherwise, I know he'd kill me."

"Did he do that to you?" Kathryn pointed to a spot above my left brow.

It took me a moment to realize she was asking about my scar. "No, I was cut during a battle with a Tarasynian soldier."

Kathryn bit her lower lip, pity creasing her brow. "It must have been deep."

"Not really. But it did not heal well." I remembered the constant splitting open of the old wound, more than once by my altercation with Gryffin. The week and a half of traveling with no way to properly clean it hadn't helped.

"Well, did you win?" Though still filled with sympathy, her ocean blue eyes started to lighten excitedly.

The Tarasynian soldier's angry, dirt-smeared face slackening upon his death flashed in my memory, and a fresh recollection of my trauma bubbled over the rim of its carefully constructed box in my brain. "Yes," I said quietly, "I won."

Kathryn sat there, absorbing what I'd told her, her eyes again glued to the trees beyond the glass.

"Does any of this come as a surprise to you?" I asked carefully.

She answered with a quick shake of her head. "No. I— . . . I knew of his plan. I knew why he wanted to marry you. But I'd underestimated how far he would go." She snorted in disgust at her own words. "When he'd first brought you here, I thought maybe you'd wanted to come with him. Or at least *thought* you wanted to. Under his Talent, you know? Then, when your door stayed locked . . . I began to doubt. What he's doing now is wrong. You shouldn't be held here against your will."

She sounded sincere, but her words settled uncomfortably in my stomach. Even if I'd been under Gryffin's influence, I still would have been here against my will. Where was the line drawn?

Finally, she turned away from the world outside the glass and looked at me. "I was not always Gryffin's first choice for a confidante, but with Roderich gone, he started coming to me. I don't know much, but I'll tell you all I *do* know." She rested her hand in mine and squeezed it. "We don't have much time tonight, but what's most important for you to know is this."

Her eyes glinted in the low light, and suddenly I feared the next words out of her mouth before she even uttered them.

"Gryffin *can* overtake the Peninsula without you. He doesn't need you."

I felt a flash of surprised confusion cut across my face. Then dread. My voice was small when I next spoke. "He's going to kill me then."

But Kathryn shook her head. "Not yet. Marrying you would make things easier for him. It would mean there'd be no war, no deaths, no waste of supplies to get what he wants. That's why he hasn't offed you yet—because he thinks there is still a chance."

Yet. Yet. I hated this conversation. As if my fate were already sealed.

"Gryffin is resourceful," Kathryn continued. "If there is a sensible path, he's going to take it. That's why he went to Lecevonia to marry you in the first place."

Gryffin had told me this himself so many weeks ago in the woods of Lecevonia, trying to make me see some reason for his appalling actions. The fact that he'd had this planned only amplified the hate I felt for his manipulation.

"But he's getting impatient," Kathryn said. "If you lose your worth to him, he's going to get rid of you and take your kingdom by other means." She glared at the floor once more. "Just as he did with Roderich."

Well.

Fortunately, I still had cards to play in my game.

I felt our time running short, so I quickly asked what I'd been wanting to know since our breakfast. "Have you heard anything of Lecevonia? Or *anywhere* on the Peninsula, for that matter? Has Gryffin made any more moves?"

Kathryn shook her head. "I don't know enough to truly be informative. Like I said this morning, Gryffin is in his office for hours on end, and I know our army's general walks in and out at least twice a day." The corners of her mouth turned upward just slightly. "General Lamel visits me first."

It took me a moment to read her smile, and I almost laughed aloud at how cavalier she was. I undoubtedly admired her confidence. I had to remind myself again that she was seventeen. "And he hasn't said anything, just between the two of you?"

She shrugged and leaned back against the bench, arms crossed over her chest. "I haven't asked. We are normally preoccupied."

Well, that wasn't helpful.

"Once you agree to marry Gryffin, he may include you on some of those decisions," Kathryn said. "You'd be his queen, after all, right?"

I didn't answer, for I couldn't fathom that he'd ever trust me enough to tell me such things.

My self-preservation was torn in two. The more primitive, immediate response knew that this man was unsafe, that I needed to stay away from this self-serving murderer. The secondary response, however—the reasoning response—encouraged the notion that marrying him would be the *only* way I lived, just as Kathryn had said.

You won't have to marry him, Rose, I reminded myself harshly. I just needed to give Amos and Zeke more time. I needed to stay alive.

When I returned to my rooms, thank Haggard without running into Kreodin, I closed my door silently and locked it from within. It might raise questions as to why it wasn't locked from the outside, but I didn't care. All I cared about in that moment was the hot bath that had been drawn for me behind the screen in the corner of my bedroom. A little note lay beside it in Cassia's handwriting. *I couldn't let you go to bed without your bath. Welcome back. Your secret is safe.*

My chest tightened at the gesture. Maybe there were more people in this castle that I could trust after all.

Maybe.

~HILLSTONE~
ZEKE

I slammed my fist down with so much force that the massive table shook on its legs. "Then I will go unaccompanied!"

"I won't allow that," Isabele said tiredly. In the council room, as she sat there in Rose's seat, I could tell she felt small. I did feel sympathy for her—of course I did—for being thrust into this position of rule so suddenly.

But for Haggard's sake, I needed her to do *something*.

"We haven't heard from Rose in over a month, Isa!"

Her eyes flashed. "You think I don't realize that?"

"Sir Ezekiel, calm yourself," General Gambeson said gruffly. "Assailing the princess won't help the situation at hand."

I didn't care. I *wanted* to push Isabele into action. I wanted war. I wanted to march through Viridi with that boar of a man's head on a spike.

But instead, under the order of my superior, I collapsed into the nearest chair with a fuming huff.

The council was in outright shambles. No one could think straight.

The royal advisors were utterly hopeless, torn between either sitting there with confused gazes or shouting out speeches, the storm between the two churning in their eyes. For some outlandish reason that I didn't understand, they still had lingering moments when their eyes would glaze over, and they believed Gryffin wasn't an enemy. Crite, even the general and colonels still had their doubts at times before they would snap back into the present.

But after finding Rose missing, I decidedly did not trust the man. Never again. And Isabele seemed to be the only one unfalteringly on my side, but she was too scared to make a decision. Gryffin's betrayal was so sudden and unexpected that there was confusion on how to act.

Not for me, though. I would freckin' kill the crite.

Colonel Burnstead seemed to be in clearer sorts today at least. "Sending a scout could help us, Your Highness," he said. "If we could discover Prince Gryffin's plan—"

"I will *not* order any move against Tarasyn," Isabele said again. "He could kill her. And please, Colonel, remember that he is the *king* now. He has more power than ever."

That was always her main fear. That if she made any move to upset the monster, Rose would return to Lecevonia in pieces. Though I hated to admit it as angry as I was, the possibility was very real. Had I been standing in that moment, my knees might have given out beneath me at the thought.

If Isabele didn't want to move the army into action, fine. But if she'd just let me *go* to the wretched kingdom, place my eyes on Rosemary . . . My chest tightened as I pictured her so clearly, her brilliant green eyes shining through the bars of some dank Tarasynian prison cell.

With a deep breath, I began again. "No one in Tarasyn will know I am there. Especially if I go solo. I'm good at my job."

But Isabele stubbornly shook her head.

"Your Highness, please," Lord Castor said hotly. "They attacked our capitol, burned our homes, killed our people—we are already in a war with Tarasyn!"

"That was King Roderich," Lord Brock said. But his voice shook with uncertainty. "Prince—King—Gryffin *called off* the attack on Hillstone. Surely—"

I let out an angry roar that echoed through the room. How could they be so stupid? "You have to step out of that belief! *Think*, Lord Brock!"

General Gambeson checked me again. "Sir Ezekiel!"

I couldn't stand their insolence any longer. With a loud screech of my chair against the floor, I stood and gave a hurried bow to the general and Colonel Burnstead. Then I turned sharply on my heel and paced—almost ran—out of the council room.

As soon as the door closed behind me, I yelled so loudly I was sure the gardeners outside heard. I tried to channel all of my anger and frustration into that one drawn-out, incomprehensive outburst, and by the time my lungs heaved out their last trace of air, I was left only with my worry and heartache. I slumped to the ground against the wall, head in my hands.

My Rose. What was that crite of a monster doing to her in Tarasyn? What was he doing that would strip away her bravery, her will? Was he breaking her stubborn spirit? I tried to tell myself, *no, not my Rose—she'd never give in*. But my thoughts continued to take morbid twists and turns, until I was sinking into some dark corner of my mind, a corner that I visited too often lately.

I wasn't used to feeling this hopeless.

The rustle of fabric sliding down against the wall next to me might have surprised me had my ears not been scout's ears. Isabele's quiet sigh was the only noise that filled the space around us, and since I was too immersed in my own morose thoughts to care to speak, a long silence stretched between us.

"I don't know what to do," Isabele finally whispered.

Ah, Isa. She was strong in her own way, sure, but not queenly strong. Not like Rose. Isabele wasn't made for this, and she knew it.

"I'm worried about her, Zeke. *So* worried, like you. I know Gryffin's note said she was all right, but I won't trust anything he says. And—if I were to do something that caused her death, I . . . I couldn't live with myself."

I had no response to that. If Rose died, I knew that I would hate everyone. Myself included.

Gryffin's message had taken us all by surprise and had only divided the council more deeply. But Isabele was right—nothing that crite said could be trusted. I'd almost left for Tarasyn the day that note arrived, with no clearance whatsoever. I could've gotten discharged from the scouts, but I hadn't cared at the time. In the end, I stayed for Isa. I couldn't leave her to face the council on her own.

The next time she spoke, her voice was muffled. "I can't give to Lecevonia what she gives. I can't do this like she does."

I lifted my head from my hands and glanced at Isabele. She had buried her face into the skirts of her dress, hugging her knees.

"Isa," I said softly, "that's why we need to get her *out* of there as soon as possible. Before he can hurt her."

"And if he already has?" She lifted her head, horror shining in her eyes.

I didn't let myself think about that now. If I did, I'd probably do something stupid. "All the more reason to act quickly."

Isabele took a deep inhale, held it for a bit, and let it out slowly. "You might be right." Outside of the scrutiny of the council, her eyes looked a little clearer, like she could think straighter. "But we need to understand more of what happened. Amos will be able to tell us what happened that day. Once he's . . . well."

I scoffed. Amos hadn't come out of his drunken stupor since he'd found Thomas's body in the woods near the stream. I bet he had *very* useful information, but he wasn't in any shape to tell us anything that made sense. Though, if I'd found my comrade of twenty-plus years so disrespectfully bled out like a hog for slaughter, I knew I wouldn't be in much better shape.

No one knew what had happened that day in the woods.

I had my own theory.

So sure, Amos might have useful information. But I was done waiting.

CHAPTER FOUR

'I SPENT THE next week thinking over what Kathryn had said, and I paid closer attention to Gryffin.

I thought that it might have been my own imagination making his temper seem shorter and more irritable than normal, but by the third day, I knew that what I was seeing was no result of paranoia. He no longer smiled when he kissed my hand. He spoke to me over my little breakfast table very tersely, practically spitting his words. And he ate quickly, as if he'd had better things to do in that moment than eat breakfast with his prisoner.

As I felt my time here running shorter than I'd thought, I was immensely grateful for Kathryn. Had she not told me that his patience was wearing thin, I might have continued holding my cards too closely until it was too late. And, in a way, I was grateful for Gryffin—or, rather, for the patience he'd given to me thus far.

But now, I was ready to take back some control.

So, when Gryffin walked in through my door one morning, already appearing as if he was willing to turn around and walk out, I greeted him with a sweet smile. Ready to play my next hand. "Good morning."

He froze in his tracks, then carefully straightened the collar of his vest. "Good morning, Rosemary."

After my unnerving success with Kreodin I was emboldened to act my part more convincingly. Kreodin hadn't been able to meet my eyes since that night, but I'd heard from Cassia he'd been whispering that the queen was *helplessly* interested in him, and that his bruised rib was from a tavern brawl. I walked toward Gryffin, my eyes glowing with a seductive smile. "I've allowed myself time to think lately," I murmured, letting my hand reach for his fingers, "and I've decided." I turned my face upward as I stood toe-to-toe with him. His scent of smoke and honey was strong this close to him.

"Decided?" A guarded excitement gleamed in his red-flecked eyes.

I let my smile grow more eager. "I've decided that I will marry you."

The words tasted like acid. But as they left my mouth, I ensured they sounded like the sweetest, smoothest syrup imported from Somora.

I remembered vaguely that I'd said the same thing before, in the corridor outside my own Great Hall. But again, the memory was hazy, draped in fog.

However, through the fog, the same smile as he wore now burned through, shining in elation and triumph—a smile I now understood.

A smile that meant he'd gotten his way.

That was when I noticed the pressure of his Talent encompassing my mind, closing in, squeezing. Coaxing.

I immediately began constructing my castle until a stone wall stood between me and Gryffin.

His gaze faltered just a little as he felt my mind close him out, but that didn't stop him from letting out the most jovial laugh I'd heard in a very long time. He grabbed me by the waist and lifted me into the air, spinning me in a circle.

Every part of my mentality screamed, *Get away! Don't let him touch you!*

Those internal screams only got louder when he put my feet back on the ground, placed his hands on either side of my face, and kissed me.

This was the first time he's kissed me, truly *kissed* me, since he stole me out of Lecevonia.

It's all part of the game I need to play, I desperately tried to tell the voices. But they only screamed at me over my countering thoughts. I fought against them, for if I pulled away from my captor, he'd know my lie.

I wished, so sincerely, that Zeke was here.

I wanted my lips to be pressed against his instead, my arms around his waist. I began to remember, for my memories with Zeke were not clouded in confusion. They were sharp, every sensation easily recalled. The love with which he'd touched my face, my hair. The tenderness of his hand pressing into my back.

My longing became so earnest, then, that I began to re-imagine things.

I let Zeke in behind my castle walls.

Gryffin's lips were no longer his, but Zeke's. The warm hands on my face were Zeke's.

And, slowly, kissing Gryffin became easier. So much easier, in fact, that I was able to move my lips with his, and I found my hands gripping his arms, pulling him closer.

When Gryffin pulled away, I was almost disappointed. Almost.

"Rosemary," he murmured. He pressed his forehead to mine. "I knew that you would eventually see reason." His smile turned wicked, hungry, his eyes alight with victory. "With Lecevonia's strength, we'll have all Five Kingdoms at our feet."

He straightened and took a step backward, holding my hands tightly in his. "I'll have a gathering arranged. A banquet! You should be formally introduced to your people!"

With another kiss planted on my surprised lips, he turned on his heel and exited my rooms, his hasty footsteps sounding down the hallway.

My chambers returned to silence, the crackling fire in the hearth the only sound reverberating off the stone walls.

I heard quiet footsteps approach me, and a gentle hand touched my shoulder. "Congratulations, my queen," Cassia murmured.

"Thank you," I whispered. I did my best to smother the tears forming in my eyes.

Gryffin returned earlier that afternoon than normal. It was just after lunch when his bright smile dazzled its way into my chambers. The same cheerful air from this morning still radiated from him.

"Come with me," he said, eyes excited. He snaked his arm around my waist. "We'll have someone pack your things." He nodded to Cassia, who immediately scurried to a large chest at the foot of my bed and lifted the lid. I didn't see anything more as Gryffin whisked me into the hallway.

Shock had delayed my response. "Pack my things?" As if I had any of my own things here in Tarasyn.

He only smiled as we walked briskly through the Great Hall, which was still empty, and passed through the doorway leading to the newer section of the castle.

This was now the farthest I'd been into Snowmont, and the corridors spared no grandeur. Just as in the Great Hall, the high ceilings rose above our heads impressively, easily three floors high, with a type of ornate candelabra that I've never seen before hanging down from iron chains affixed above the rafters. The walls harbored more tapestries, scenes of every kind, and tall windows that let in the warm sunlight. These windows were glazed over in frosted panes, and long, gold-strewn shutters flanked the sides of each window. I could only imagine the manpower it took to actually close those things. Ruby carpets with winding gold embellishments ran along the length of the stone floor, so my slippers only padded softly as we walked.

Why was everything about Snowmont so *grand*? Surely, the expenses paid on these luxuries were a waste, if Gryffin cared so much about resourcefulness. This thought was only amplified when a droplet of molten wax landed on my shoulder from the strange light fixtures above.

My confused aggravation must have shown on my face, for Gryffin laughed. "Chandeliers. Very popular in the West Lands. Splendid, aren't they?"

"Splendid," I repeated quietly, though a bit peeved by the pomposity of it all. I made a mental note to walk only along the edges of the halls from now on.

He led me up five floors of a glorious spiral staircase to what appeared to be where the living quarters were located. The largest door in the corridor loomed to my right, and just past that, a slightly smaller door stood ajar.

"My queen," Gryffin said with a smirk, releasing me from his hold. "I hope you'll enjoy your new chambers." He gestured to the open door, urging me through the mahogany entryway.

My eyes didn't know what to absorb first. The entire room seemed bathed in snow.

The large wooden posts of the bed had been painted white, and a cream canopy draped overhead. The fireplace had been strewn out of white marble, and the granite walls sparkled in the sunbeams pouring through the open window. A brass *chandelier* hung from the ceiling.

But what truly stuck out to me was the *newness*. Everything was untouched, as though the snow had just fallen. I would be the first woman to sleep in here.

"Where does that door lead?" I asked, pointing to a wooden door nestled into the wall on the right. It seemed out of place. The doors to the bathing room and study were left open, and the small door in the corner of the room was clearly the maid's door. But this one was closed tightly, hiding its contents.

Gryffin chuckled as he stepped into the room. "Those lead to my rooms."

I cursed the involuntary blush that rose to my cheeks and turned away before he could see. Of course, it made sense. The queen's quarters naturally would connect to the king's. The thought of him sleeping one room over, however, deeply unsettled me.

"I do have one more thing for you. Then I'll leave you to get settled."

His smile became the warmest thing in the room, but it only sent chills of dread running down my back. He reached his hand into his vest and pulled out a small, metal-woven box.

"Go on," he said. "Open it. I've been holding onto it for a while now."

I unlatched the tiny lid, and suddenly, Gryffin's next words sounded very distant.

"I had it made to match your eyes."

Nestled inside the trinket box, on a pillow of velvet, was a ring. The same sunbeams that made the granite walls sparkle glistened off the pear-shaped emerald, and the collection of tiny diamonds around the gem had turned into faceted prisms inlaid in the thin gold band.

I snapped the lid shut and fought the hyperventilation that threatened to expose me. "Thank you, Gryffin," I managed to rasp out.

Gryffin looked at me, puzzled. "Don't you want to—"

"I'm just . . . absorbing it all," I said quietly. I peeked up quickly at him and offered a tiny smile. "Next time you see me, I assure you that I'll be wearing it."

My promise sounded forced to my ears, but Gryffin must not have picked up on it. His red-flecked eyes flashed with happiness as he bowed his head. He turned on his heel with a smile. "This evening then."

Before he could walk through the door, I wheeled around to face him. "May I keep my same chambermaids?"

He considered, just briefly, then nodded once. "Of course. I'll have them sent to you right away."

He closed the door softly behind him, and I was alone.

In this rare moment of solitude, before my chambermaids could arrive and before a guard could be posted outside my door, I let my tears fall.

My tears were that of grief, of fatigue, of anxiety. How much longer could I bear keeping up this act of loving a murderer and a liar? I belonged in Lecevonia at Hillstone. Certainly not here, in this gilded war zone.

I cried for my sisters. My sweet Isa—was she acting as queen-regent now? Poor girl. I hoped Lisette was helping her. But—had Isabele, or *anyone* for that matter, discovered that she was Talented? And Clara . . . Sterling had only been gone for a little over a month. How was

Clara coping?

I cried for my kingdom. I still had no idea what kind of state it was in now, what actions they were or weren't taking. Had they moved against Tarasyn? Or was Gryffin's effect still lingering in their minds? Perhaps my waiting for Amos, Zeke, or Isabele to realize something was moot. For Haggard's sake, I hoped they figured out that *everything* was wrong.

I wished wildly, probably idiotically, that I possessed a Talent to fight Gryffin's. That I was Sighted, like Isabele—whatever that meant—or a mind reader, or even just a Talented swordswoman that could slice him to shreds. Yes, that would be nice.

I was reminded by that train of thought of a long-ago conversation with Zeke. A conversation about the existence of Talents, which I now knew I'd been naive to think nothing of. But he'd asked, if Talents did exist, what mine would be. I'd thought mine would be mental strength, and in this moment I almost laughed aloud.

Indeed, mental strength.

Not enough strength to fight Gryffin's influence over me, yet plenty enough to hold onto that influence like a lifeline.

How stupid.

My tears had stopped, and now I found myself *angry*, though I didn't know exactly at what it was directed. It could have been toward myself for my mental weakness, or toward Gryffin for his deceptive nature. Or even toward the ridiculous chandelier above me that was dripping candle wax onto the rug at my feet. My anger boiled in my blood until, finally, I let out a yell that didn't sound loud enough to me.

I picked up the silver brush that sat on my vanity and hurled it at the shuttered window. Then I ripped the annoying pins out of my hair and threw those too. If I could have ripped the door that led to

Gryffin's chambers off its hinges, I would have, and I would have tried to claw his eyes out right there in his own study. I realized then that I was simply mad at *everything*.

And, despite the chambers being larger than any place I'd slept before, I'd never felt so trapped.

When Cassia and my three other chambermaids came through the maid's door in the corner nearly an hour later, they found me bundled by the open window, still smoldering as I looked out over the city. The view was undoubtedly the most redeeming quality of this room. We were so high, higher even than the chapel at Hillstone, and I was amazed once again by the vibrant rooftops of Viridi.

"Why is everything so colorful?" I asked no one in particular. My voice held much more acid than I'd meant it to, so I cleared my throat and tried to soften my tone. "I've never seen so much paint used in all my life."

It was my chambermaid Vasilie who replied. "It began after the late King Falk died." Her quiet voice faltered as she said Gryffin's father's name. "The late King Roderich was set on beautifying the city."

Well, that didn't fit my image of Roderich. "Did he also spearhead Snowmont's renovations?"

"Yes, Your Majesty."

It surprised me that the bloodthirsty monster would care about luxuries and appearances. And I didn't miss that Vasilie had called me "Your Majesty." So much had changed so quickly.

Cassia ran her hand along the marble mantle, eyes wide. "This is an improvement from the guest chambers, isn't it?"

Though her question was rhetorical, I chuckled dryly. "So much so that I almost miss that musty old tapestry."

While my handmaids explored the new chambers, there was a light knock on my door. Definitely not Gryffin's quick, solid knock. The door pushed open, and my look of shock matched Kathryn's as she stepped into my room.

Her grin lightened the entire space. "Well, the door actually opened for once! Guess who's your new neighbor?" She walked to me and extended her hand, palm facing me. The old Magian greeting for loved ones.

I smiled and met my hand with hers, fingertips aligning. She was just the person I'd wanted to see. "Can you tell me something?"

"Of course."

I grasped her hand and pulled her into my new study, quietly closing the fresh pine double doors behind us. The study was probably the room that most lacked any grandeur, with shelves of sparsely scattered books and scrolls lining the walls. It was suddenly my favorite room in Snowmont.

As soon as the doors sealed us away, I turned to Kathryn with wide eyes. "*Please*, what in Haggard's green earth is going on right now?"

Her forehead pinched. "What do you mean?"

"I've gone from being treated like a prisoner to *this* in a matter of hours."

Kathryn looked at me questioningly. "And? It's an improvement, no?"

"Of course it is. I . . ."

I what? Was not grateful for the sudden upgrade? Wanted to run down to Snowmont's dungeons and stay there for the rest of my days?

"I just don't understand how Gryffin thinks—how his mind functions." I collapsed onto a velveteen couch situated in the middle of the room. "He confuses the moon and stars out of me."

Kathryn heaved a deep sigh and sat down next to me. "This"—she gestured with her hands, alluding to the entirety of this room—"means you're playing your part right. Gryffin believes you. He has had these rooms prepared for you for weeks, you know. I'm assuming that all he needed was a solid 'yes' from you."

I smiled wryly. "Ah, so you've heard."

Kathryn rolled her eyes. "I imagine the entire castle has heard at this point."

"If these rooms have been ready for so long, why has he kept me hidden away?" Storing someone into a dark corner of the castle was not necessarily the way to convince her to marry.

Kathryn shifted in her seat and crossed her arms over her chest, sending her gaze to the floor. "I'm not sure. My only guess is that he didn't want too many people to . . . notice. If he needed to get rid of you."

Get rid of me. As I absorbed her words, I realized that they made complete sense. The empty Great Hall, all the meals in my rooms. No visitors. I'd been right, then. He *hadn't* wanted people to see me.

In the event that he'd needed to kill me.

"You told me that you became Gryffin's confidante," I said carefully. "What has he told you?"

Kathryn sighed again and leaned against the back of the couch. "What would you like to know?"

Everything, I wanted to say. But that wouldn't necessarily be helpful. So, I started at the beginning. "When did he start coming to you?"

Kathryn uncrossed her arms and thrummed her fingers against the armrest. "When Roderich left for Hiddon. Roderich chose to leave Gryffin behind, which suited him just fine—Gryffin thought Roderich was being foolish anyway. Then, after Roderich's success, when he wrote to us that he planned to do the same to Lecevonia, Gryffin almost lost it. I'd never seen him so angry." She then put on her best impression of Gryffin. "'He can't *waste* our army on the strongest kingdom on the Peninsula! We will be crushed! He needs to be smarter than that!'"

Her words caused a bloom of pride in my heart. Gryffin had known that I'd had a formidable army, even though our numbers may have been fewer.

"Was that when he concocted his plan to come to my kingdom?"

She nodded. "We'd heard that the Queen of Lecevonia was looking for a king-consort, and he saw it as a perfect opportunity. So, he told me of his plan to take you as his wife. I was too caught up in the thought of having another woman in this Haggard-forsaken castle to realize how far he was willing to go. But I should have seen it. If things didn't go his way . . ."

At first, I'd thought she'd meant his plan to use his Talent to get me here.

But then she said, "I can't believe he killed our *brother*." Her eyes stared unseeing toward the bookshelves. "Gryffin had been power-hungry as far back as I can remember, but I didn't think he'd be capable of *killing* anyone." She sneered in disgust. "That was Roderich's passion."

I felt my eyes narrow, and disgust rose in the back of my throat. What a pair of brothers. One bloodthirsty and maniacal, and another so cunning that he could *hide* his savagery. "Did his Talent keep you from seeing who he really was?" I asked.

Kathryn's responding laugh was so bitter it was almost comical. "Oh, no. I took my will back years ago. He doesn't trick me anymore—that's just how he is."

Her will. Gryffin had used the same word in the woods. My gaze darted to Kathryn, and the question I'd been dying to know all these weeks in isolation shot out from me as swift as an arrow.

"How does his Talent work?"

Her eyes widened at my intensity, but her answer came quick. "It's not as complex as it probably seems. He's got you under his influence as long as you're either oblivious to it or open to it. But who would want to be open to it, knowing they're being deceived?" Kathryn scoffed and crossed her arms over her chest. "Anyway, as you know, every Talent is different. We're just lucky that his has limitations."

I stifled a sarcastic laugh. "I don't know anything about Talents. I'd thought they were childish tales until I met Gryffin."

Kathryn's dumbfounded expression was beginning to make me feel a little self-conscious. She opened her mouth to say something, then closed it, then opened it again.

But before she could utter a word, the sudden squawk of a crow sent a chilling shock through my body.

The door to my study swung open slowly until it hit the wall behind it, and Gryffin's silhouette appeared in the doorway. Seeing him there with Roderich's crow perched on his shoulder brought a familiar wave of panic crashing over me. But I quickly worked to stifle it.

"Oh, for Haggard's sake!" Kathryn shouted, shooting to her feet. "That *thing* is obnoxious!"

Gryffin clucked his tongue as he stepped into the room. "That's no way to talk about Roderich's dear bird."

"What do you want?" Kathryn shot back. "Don't you ever leave this poor woman alone?"

He looked hard at his sister for a moment, his expression guarded.

I cleared my throat before she could say anything more. "What is it, Gryffin?"

When he turned toward me, his smile was triumphant. "I've sent messengers to every corner of the kingdom. The people of Tarasyn have been invited to Snowmont in ten days' time."

"Oh!" I painted on the mask of excitement that was expected of me. "That's wonderful!"

Gryffin's smile widened, and he took a large step toward me, grasping my hand in his. "We'll have a grand banquet celebrating our engagement, and anyone who wishes to meet you will have the opportunity."

"Perfect," I said, beaming. The more people that laid eyes on me, the harder it would be for him to kill me quietly. Perhaps the people of Tarasyn could act as my shield for a while.

CHAPTER FIVE

IN THOSE TEN days, I quickly learned that Gryffin had kept most of Snowmont hidden from me.

The Dining Hall was on the first floor, adjacent to the Great Hall and just as grand. The tapestries there centered entirely around hunting. Great white bears, wolves, rabbits and elk, geese, grouse, even these odd little weasel-like critters—just about any terrestrial being imaginable. These were the tapestries I'd expect out of Hiddon, not Tarasyn. When I asked Kathryn about them, she simply said that a love for hunting ran in the family—and gave her excellent skills in archery.

More apt for the kingdom were the vines climbing the pillars and stretching across the mantle of the large fireplace, adorning fresh grapes. Long banquet tables were perpetually set, always seeming ready to host a large crowd.

I also discovered that there were not one but *three* courtyards. The latter two were smaller and more private than the main courtyard, pretentiously called The Atrium of Viridi, that my window overlooked.

One of these courtyards was situated outside the library, which was a majestic collection of rooms but contained very little in the way of books or maps. And the other was actually an outdoor extension of the conservatory, putting even more rare plants on display.

Behind Snowmont, from the edge of the castle to the base of the nearest mountain slope, was a sprawling garden of fruits, vegetables, and herbs. I'd still had absolutely no idea how these plants grew out there in the frigid cold until Kathryn explained it to me.

"An employee of the castle, Dothymus, is a Talented who can manipulate the weather," Kathryn had said between bites of breakfast one morning. "He keeps the snow off to the mountains and forests, away from the city. The sun warms the city enough, and he only sends rain when needed."

I'd harrumphed at that. "Why doesn't he warm the entire city while he's at it?"

"He may control the weather," she'd said, taking a bite of fried egg, "but he can't do much about the *climate*. It's just cold here, no matter the amount of sun that shines."

As if to remind me, a gust of wind through the window had rippled and lifted the bottom of my skirts and climbed up my legs, leaving me shivering in its wake.

Kathryn became my most trusted friend in Tarasyn, as well as my teacher. When she learned that I hadn't any clue about anything related to Talents, she launched into history lessons.

"Of course, you know Haggard and the Five Talented, right?" she asked me now as she scanned the titles on the nearest bookshelf in the library. It was early afternoon, still seven days before the banquet. "I mean, anyone who doesn't know the legend did *not* have a very good childhood."

I rolled my eyes from my seat on the couch. "Yes, I know the legend. Haggard was the last of the magi on the Peninsula, and he gifted his magic to his five children. His children then went on to establish the Five Kingdoms."

Kathryn squinted her eyes at me. "That simple?"

"Y–yes?"

My hesitation garnered a hearty laugh from Kathryn. "Do *you* get along with your siblings that easily?" She slid a book from the shelf and studied the binding before placing it right back where it had been. "Equos was the oldest, Arbos the next oldest. Then Viridi, Vena, and Mareus."

The names of the Five Talented, and subsequently the names of each kingdom's capitol city. I knew this much.

"Believe it or not"—Kathryn glanced back at me over her shoulder— "Mareus was the first to stake his claim on any land. He simply wanted a home by the sea, and that was easily granted. It's easy for the youngest in the family—we know our place." She winked. "And his request went right along with his Talent, the ability to influence tides and currents, large or small.

"It was the rest of the family who squabbled. Equos believed he should have the land with the most prairie for his horses, but Viridi thought *she* should have the most fertile land for her gardens. And Arbos and Vena had their own separate argument over who should get the land with the most forests. Arbos was a Talented woodworker, you see. He could build *anything* out of the wood from his forest."

Her eyes glazed over for a moment, in awe, before focusing on the bookshelves once again. "As it turns out, harvesting trees is rather difficult in the Silver Mountains, so he set his eyes on the southwestern portion of the Peninsula. And Vena, with her huntswoman Talent, needed the wildlife habitat. The two siblings ended up working hand-in-hand, as forests and wildlife often do. They split the land in two,

Arbos taking the flatter land. Hiddon and Somora have always had good relations as a result."

Well, their argument resolved easily enough. "And Equos and Viridi?" I asked. I noticed my hands were pressed firmly against the velvet couch upon which I sat, and I worked to loosen my fingernails from digging into the fabric. I had to wonder why Papa hadn't told me any of this.

Kathryn sighed and looked back at me. "Both were . . . stubborn. After years and years of war, Equos eventually won with his endless army. Viridi was pushed into the mountainous north, a region that none of the other siblings coveted." Then she quickly shrugged and looked to the scattered books. "It worked out. Because of the hard, frosted soil, Viridi's Talent was invaluable. She kept her family and her people alive."

I contemplated her words with a frown. How unfortunate for Viridi, to be pushed out into no-man's land, driven as far into the Silver Mountains as feasibly possible. Tarasyn had always kept to itself, and now I wondered if it stemmed from this long-ago betrayal by Viridi's siblings.

Then, I remembered that had things gone any differently, life on the Peninsula would be very different today. Lecevonia would be here, shoved into the mountains, with no way to survive the unforgiving climate. Limitless horses can only provide so much. Tarasyn would most definitely be a complete powerhouse of a kingdom, controlling any and all produce trade throughout the Peninsula—especially with the Riparia River system in its clutches. The kingdom would be too strong for the rest of us.

Checks and balances, I supposed.

"And so," Kathryn said, taking another tattered book off the shelf, "the siblings established their borders and built their followings. The magic of the magi flowed through the blood of the Talented to some of their children." She sat down next to me and flipped open the book she'd removed from the shelf. "And they learned quickly that the magic was very unpredictable—no two Talents were the same." After turning the thin pages carefully to avoid ripping them, she slid the book into my lap. "See? All different."

My eyes scanned the page, first unable to make out any of the aged, faded ink. However, after my eyes adjusted and focused on the nearly invisible sprawls of writing, I saw a table running the length of the page, divided into numerous microscopic rows. On the left side, names. In a middle column, cities or villages. And on the right, descriptions of Talents, if any.

"This is a Tarasynian census from one hundred and eighty years ago," Kathryn explained. "Father rounded up as many as he could. This is the last one that we have that even *considers* Talents."

Squinting my eyes, I was able to decipher a few.

Thom Garrison, Viridi, brute strength.

Bess Lytehuse, Borea, dancing.

Clarice Whittenhill, Pruin, glowing skin.

That last one was a bit odd, but I supposed it could be helpful in the right situation. Lost in the woods at night. Stuck in a cave. Something like that.

Then, a set of sisters.

Alexandra Frigaste, Viridi, mind-reading. Then more writing beside that. *Limitation: only nearby minds.*

Anastasa Frigaste, Viridi, mind-reading. Limitation: only men. That one made me laugh under my breath. I wondered what thoughts she'd had the fortune—or misfortune—of hearing.

A familiar name caught my eye, and I glanced up at Kathryn. "Dothymus Riganar?"

She shrugged. "Family name, I suppose."

"Talents weren't as rare as I'd thought," I murmured. Though many of these names had *none* scribbled in their rows, a respectable number had some form of Talented ability.

Kathryn's laugh surprised me. "They still are not very rare! Look at Tarasyn! One in every twenty people now, can you believe? Even in other kingdoms, the magic of the magi still runs through many families. The present-day Talented are descendants of the Five Talented, one way or another, though their heritage may have been lost in the shuffle of time."

She closed the book in my hands and stood. "The problem is that, four hundred-odd years ago, people stopped *caring*. Some people thought their Talents pointless, as did their kings. So people stopped exploring their capabilities. Even those that have more of a mental Talent, they *have* that ability and are most likely aware that something makes them different. A thought heard here, an emotion sensed there. But they don't know what it is or care to find out!" She heaved a sigh that felt laden with disappointment. "Talented are out there throughout the Peninsula—their Talents just haven't been sharpened or even awakened."

I could see her point. I'd be the first to admit I hadn't really tried new skills until I'd asked Gryffin to teach me how to use a sword. I'd been too busy learning from my advisors how to run a kingdom that I never had time for anything else.

But her words did raise a question.

"My younger sister, Isabele," I began slowly, turning to Kathryn. "She's always been very . . . empathetic. She saw a haze around Gryffin—and only Gryffin. The longer he stayed at court, the thicker the haze grew. Gryffin said she has 'Sight.' What does that mean?"

"Your sister?" Kathryn's eyes went wide. "Gryffin hadn't told me about her. She's Sighted, you said?"

I nodded, and after a long sigh, she continued. "It means she can 'see' when someone is using their Talent. She saw Gryffin shrouded in a fog because he was using his Talent to hide his nature and to manipulate the way people perceived his words."

Slowly, I came to understand her explanation. Gryffin was probably the first person Isabele had met that was actively using a Talent. The haze thickened with time as Gryffin had increased in using his Talent, deceiving more people, hiding more lies.

His presence had awakened her Talent.

"Most Talents in the Five Kingdoms remain hidden, dormant, just as your sister's was. The same was true for Tarasyn." Kathryn cast her eyes to the floor of the library, and a darkness shrouded her features. "Of course, until my grandfather started his search seventy years ago. He'd wanted Talented to join his court so he could use their abilities. In the most horrid way possible, his actions caused several Talents to manifest, usually under the pressure of torture. But the majority of people who fell victim were not Talented. And Father only continued my grandfather's efforts."

Though Gryffin had already told me this, a rising anger still took hold, and a hatred for the men—all four of them—who'd hurt their own people for personal gain burned like an iron rod through my veins. *Berries plucked from the same bush*, I thought viciously, though I didn't dare say that aloud in the publicity of the library.

Roderich and Gryffin were just as monstrous, but in polar opposite aspects from their father and grandfather. All four were power-hungry, but while their grandfather and King Falk didn't seem to care what damage had been done to their people, the two brothers had only hurt the people of *other* kingdoms.

Tarasyn hadn't had a decent ruler in three generations, yet they were on the brink of complete supremacy. I almost scoffed. Talents trumped civilized living, it seemed.

I made a point to spend most of my time with Kathryn. We often ate meals together, or sat in the warmth of the conservatory, or walked through one of the many courtyards bundled in our furs. I trusted her words more than anyone else's, as well as her company, and with her endless knowledge, I began to further understand Tarasyn and the Danicio family.

For example, just as Vasilie had said, Roderich *had* been the one to start beautifying Viridi and the castle. In fact, this effort extended even to the small towns hidden away in the deep valleys of the Silver Mountains. It had been Roderich's way of defying his father, who had supported only the necessities of existence and had left the entire kingdom bare and desolate.

However, when I'd finally asked her over dinner one night the burning question of how the late King Falk met his demise, she'd shut her mouth tightly and refused to look anywhere but down at her own soup bowl.

I initially took that to mean that her father's death, as awful of a man as he sounded, had still left her wounded in some way. As the days passed, though, I noticed her slight glance toward Gryffin when any subject of their father arose, and I began to understand that it was not grief that always slammed her lips shut.

For Gryffin was *always* close. Having meals either with us or just a few seats down the long banquet table. Never no more than ten paces behind us as we walked through the corridors or the courtyards.

Always a couch or two away in the Great Hall.

His constant proximity drove Kathryn mad. It made my hair stand on its ends. And it did limit what we could talk about.

So, one day, in the rare privacy of my study, I asked her again about her family.

"Kathryn, I need to understand. Why is any mention of King Falk so . . . forbidden?"

Kathryn snorted and turned her blue gaze to the lit candle flickering on the little wooden side table. "Well, the people already hated Father, so people naturally don't want to talk about him. Even still, Roderich and Gryffin have instilled a stigma against his name into the citizens and the castle workers so thoroughly that I don't dare speak too much of him, either."

"But why would they forbid mention of him?"

Kathryn let silence stretch between us, eyes never leaving the flames, before speaking again. "I suppose, since you've shared your secret with me, I can share my family's secret with you. Or, more so, Roderich's secret." She glanced up at me then. "But there's more you need to know first."

I waited patiently for her next words, smoothing out my burgundy skirts and hoping my expression did not betray my eagerness.

"While Father was still alive, he was especially harsh on Roderich and Gryffin. I'm sure Gryffin has told you that. Father's attentions did not fall on the twins—he never saw them fit to rule anyhow. And Mother kept me away from him as much as she could once he started acting . . . well, you can imagine . . . after Grandfather passed. More unhinged, more unpredictable." Kathryn held her finger over the tiny flame. "But hiding away hadn't been necessary. He didn't pay me any mind, as I am the youngest. His only interest was his heir."

"Why didn't King Falk see the twins as fit to rule?" In fact, I realized with a start, I hadn't even *seen* her twin brothers in the nearly two months I'd been here. I'd all but forgotten that Kathryn and Gryffin had other siblings.

Kathryn shrugged, but her eyes gleamed in what seemed to be envy. "Both are actually perfectly fit to reign. But Father treated them as though they weren't his sons." Kathryn snatched her hand away from the flame in anger. "Michael has a stiff knee, and Laris is nonverbal. But kings have had stiff knees before—Michael has never let it stop him. And Laris is smarter than anyone I've ever met. He can write more clearly than *me*! Neither ever wanted the Crown anyhow, but even so. They didn't deserve Father's neglect. They've essentially dissociated themselves from the family on their own terms." A dry chuckle passed through Kathryn's lips. "I don't blame them. They and their families live in a small fortress near Borea."

My heart ached for Michael and Laris. My siblings and I may have been orphaned, but at least we'd all been loved. "Do you see them often?" I asked.

Kathryn shrugged. "Every now and then, we will visit back and forth. Things have gotten better between all of us since Father died. I don't think Gryffin or Roderich knew at the time how Father treated the twins, caught up in their own form of mistreatment, and I was too young to understand. I have to admit, I'm jealous of the freedom Michael and Laris have found."

We both sat lost in thought for a moment, the candle beside us flickering. Two prisoners in our own rights.

"Now, you've distracted me, talking of my brothers." She nudged me with her shoulder, a chagrined smile on her lips. "As I was saying, Mother was the only force between each of us and Father's obsession with Talents. But, as she was ill more often than not, she was not as strong a force as Roderich and Gryffin needed. Gryffin's Talent

manifested early on, so he was spared from Father's harsh treatment."
Her tone turned darker. "Roderich, though, never showed signs of
having a Talent. So Father took . . . certain measures."

As the horror of it registered in my mind, my voice was no louder
than a whisper. "The scars on his face?"

Kathryn nodded solemnly. "I was only a child at the time, but every
time I saw him, he had new cuts before the old ones had even healed."

In my shock, I felt a pang of pity for young Roderich. How awful
that a father would do such a thing to his own son. And why? Why
cause pain? Could such pain truly awaken some ability that the boy
might have had?

I reminded myself that this boy grew up to be a cold-blooded man—
a murderous monster who hurt people and burned down kingdoms
without a second thought. His father had undoubtedly played a role in
that outcome.

Then, another part of Kathryn's words struck me. "There are signs
of being a Talented?"

Kathryn nodded. "Surely you've seen the red flecks in Gryffin's
eyes. The more someone uses their Talent, the more flecks they have.
If the Talented don't use their ability, the flecks can fade. Gryffin
thinks it has something to do with exertion."

A bone-rattling chill ran through me as I recalled Gryffin's blue
eyes, shrouded with crimson once I saw through his deception. Those
eyes resurfaced another memory. "Roderich's eyes," I said suddenly.
"They had those same red flecks."

Kathryn dropped her gaze to the study's red rug, looking
uncomfortable with tight eyes and even tighter lips. "Yes, Roderich was
Talented. That was no secret. His eyes started bursting after Atroxis
hit the Peninsula, so there was no hiding it." She exhaled heavily and
squeezed her eyes shut. "What we did hide, though, was the nature of

his Talent."

She quieted then, and so much time passed that I thought maybe that was all the information I'd be given. But her eyes flashed open again and settled on me, her eyes flat as a glassy lake. "You know Corvus? That wretched bird Gryffin keeps?"

I almost snorted at the absurdity of her question. How could I forget Corvus? "Of course, Roderich's crow. I hear him squawking every night one room over."

"Oh, right—of course." She shook her head quickly as if to clear it. Her expression almost looked pained. "Well, Roderich *adored* Corvus. He'd always had an odd fascination with crows, but Corvus showed a particular interest in Roderich. So, Roderich kept him, cared for him. That crow must be twelve or thirteen years old now." Kathryn scoffed. "He's lived longer than any crow I've seen. But last year, Corvus became deathly ill. We still don't know what was wrong with him." Kathryn's voice lowered, and she averted her eyes. "So, Roderich tried to heal him."

Heal him? Was healing Roderich's Talent? I found that very hard to believe. When I looked at her, I found her eyes lifted to mine, awaiting my response. "I'm not sure I understand," I admitted. "Healing?"

Kathryn nodded slowly, still tiptoeing around the subject. "Roderich could heal . . . but he could also hurt. But not in the way you're thinking. Roderich tried to heal Corvus, but healing wasn't what he had perfected. He healed the bird, yes, but the extreme effort caused a sickness, a *disease*, to begin spreading through the crows on the Peninsula."

My voice was quiet. "The Corvid Incident."

Yes," Kathryn said. "Roderich—he *created* that sickness."

Her eyes begged me to make some connection.

- 71 -

I remembered the Corvid Incident well. Diseased crows had littered the streets, most fallen dead, and so many rumors had spread of horrible omens to come. Perhaps those rumors weren't very far off, seeing how far Tarasyn had gone for power.

So, Roderich was able to create diseases. That was his Talent, and that was how he hurt people. That power had surely been placed in the wrong hands, as evil as he was. He'd had the power to riddle anyone who'd hurt him—or anyone in his way—with some incurable sickness.

That notion began tying threads of thought into loose knots in my head. "He could hurt anyone, anyone he'd hated . . . with a disease?"

Kathryn's eyes never left mine.

"And he loathed King Falk. Absolutely loathed him."

Did he create something to rid himself of the king? Had he killed his own father with an illness? Was that the family's secret?

Then, the knots of thought tightened, unbreakable.

"Roderich created Atroxis."

I uttered the words and immediately knew they were true. Roderich had tried to kill his father with a disease, and that disease spread throughout the Magian Peninsula. To think a Talent was capable of such a thing was unthinkable, yet undeniably true. His power had touched everyone in some way with sickness and death. Rendered me and countless others parentless.

Roderich had killed Mama and Papa.

The rage I felt toward this monster had steeped to a new level.

"It didn't work." Kathryn's voice was so small, but I would have hardly heard her anyway through the rush of blood in my ears. "His Talent killed our mother instead, and I don't think he ever truly did forgive himself. I'm not sure if *any* of us have forgiven him. He killed Father a year later with a pillow to the face, but he and Gryffin made the announcement that he'd died in his sleep, made sick with sadness by Mother's death. And, with Gryffin's Talent, well, there was no ill will against the new king."

"Sounds familiar." Anger seethed inside me, but the one with whom I was angry was already dead, killed by his brother in the streets of my capitol. This rage, this loathing, almost overwhelmed the hatred I held for Gryffin.

"That's why Roderich and Gryffin had always so strongly discouraged any utterance of Father," Kathryn continued quietly, coming full circle to my earlier question. "People may start to wonder what actually happened. And if holes are poked in Gryffin's deception . . ." She trailed off with a halfhearted shrug.

"Then people will know Roderich's true Talent," I finished for her. "And the damage he's caused." For even Tarasyn had not been spared the destruction of Atroxis. Even their queen had fallen victim.

She nodded once more. "And once they learn that they'd been lied to, they'd suspect Gryffin's Talent as well." Kathryn's acidic sneer mirrored my own emotions. "Besides, dying of a broken heart for Mother is more easily accepted and forgotten than asphyxiation. The people may have hated Father, but no one wants a blatantly murderous king."

"Unless it's to save the love of his life of course," I said sarcastically.

Kathryn rolled her eyes. "All exalt King Gryffin."

"Why not expose them?" I suddenly asked. Kathryn knew *all* of this, these secrets revolving around her father and brothers. "The people of your kingdom have lived a hazy existence thanks to Gryffin's years of deception! If the Tarasynians *knew* . . . then perhaps Gryffin could be stopped!"

But she shook her head. "Who would believe me? No one sees his eyes as you and I do. I am not *beloved* by the people as he is."

"The general! You see him every day!"

Kathryn crossed her arms over her chest. "Lamel knows—of Gryffin's Talent anyway. He hated Roderich in the first place and is completely faithful to Gryffin. He protects him." She cursed under her breath. "I honestly don't know why I welcome him into my bedchamber."

I patted Kathryn's hand, but I didn't have the capacity to worry of Kathryn's dysfunctional intimacies at the moment. I was dumbfounded. If the general, the leader of Tarasyn's *entire* force, knew and didn't care, then what power did we have against Gryffin?

CHAPTER SIX

THE SMELL OF aged paper and ink welcomed me as I stepped into Snowmont's library. When I was not with Kathryn, it was where I spent most of my time. Though there was not a wide selection, I figured if Gryffin could learn so much from Hillstone's library, maybe I could play his game as well.

My fingers grazed the shelves, but my mind still clung to Kathryn's exposing secret last night.

For Roderich to have possessed such a Talent was simply . . . *wrong*. Of anyone on the Peninsula who could have a Talent of both healing and creating diseases, why did it have to be him? Even my hard-bargaining Uncle Merek would have used such a Talent more wisely.

I'd wager that anyone else would have perfected the healing nature of the Talent first, even if just for self-preservation. But no. Instead, Roderich had decimated the people of the Magian Peninsula. He should have focused on healing his own mother, rather than killing his father. That in itself spoke volumes of the kind of person Roderich had been.

I wondered suddenly, then—had Roderich focused more on healing, would he have been able to heal his own scars? Heal sword wounds and swipes from daggers?

Practically become invincible?

Before another panic attack could set in, I set my focus on the curve of the tall window frame. It didn't matter anymore. I knew Roderich's body had been set afire high upon the nearest mountain peak, right outside that window—as was Tarasyn's tradition for kings, according to Gryffin. I almost regretted not attending now, if only to smile as his ashes flew into the air. His people might have done the same had they known what he'd done.

Once I got back to Lecevonia, I would spread the word far and wide of the brothers' actions. Then *everyone* would know.

I had to.

I drew my eyes away from the window and back to the row of books in front of me. My mission now was, while I had the resources, to learn more about Isabele's Talent. Her *Sight.*

Though Snowmont's beautiful library was ill-stocked, there were still plenty of books on Talents. The past few days, while Kathryn was spending time with Lamel, I'd had luck in finding titles pertaining to Sight, while also grabbing anything else that caught my interest.

From a tightly bound book called *Talents: Origins and Guidelines,* I discovered that Talents were so diverse because the magic from which they were derived stemmed directly from Haggard, who as a mage had almost limitless ability. I also learned that every Talent *must* be mastered, though this was more important for some Talents than others. Generally, if left unchecked once manifested, a Talent could emerge in uncontrollable outbursts, deteriorate from disuse, or even drive a Talented mad over time.

So, Isabele needed training, and quickly.

In another book, *A Condensed List of Known Mental Talents*, there were so many abilities that I hadn't even considered possible, like mental conversation and the ability to move objects with the mind. I found Sight listed among others labeled "Informative" along with mind-reading and truth detection.

I'd had to close the book before I got too overwhelmed.

Gryffin accompanied me most days, and when he did, he read over my shoulder. It was excruciatingly difficult at first to concentrate on anything with his horrid eyes peering down over my head or having his sweet scent of smoke and honey clouding my brain. It was all I could do to keep myself from falling into a fit of hyperventilation.

I *hated* that he had this effect on me. He'd taken so much from me. But fighting against this panic he aroused was my own act of defiance. My own grasp at control.

Some days, though, it was helpful having him near. Though his arm draped over my shoulders and his hand on my knee disgusted me, he knew more of Talents than even Kathryn. If he saw something interesting, he'd pipe up and explain, for he was *very* supportive of my studies.

Yesterday, I'd just come across ancient words, *igneri* and *laperi*, in a tattered tome, when he'd spoken.

"Old language for some Talents," he'd said, probably catching my confused expression. "Elementalists, as they're called in more recent books, work with earthly components. Equos and Mareus were Elementalists by today's definition. Powerful, yet limited."

I'd squinted at him, shocked. "Limited? Is your weather-maker not an Elementalist? Would you call him 'limited'?"

"He's limited to the energy in the air, just as Mareus was limited to the energy in the ocean. Even Equos had to rely on some other being to bring his creations to life."

I'd just shaken my head in disagreement and sighed, curling my legs underneath me on the couch. "I think your definition of 'limited' is too strict."

His amused laugh had sent a chill running through my spine. "Or maybe your idea of 'limited' is too generous! When you set boundaries, you begin to see the true power you possess, or *don't* possess."

Hmm. Boundaries. I supposed he had a point. He'd set boundaries on *me*, hadn't he? My freedom, my privacy, my very life if I didn't do what he wanted. I saw the power I did not possess.

Still, with Gryffin's definition, the only being without limits was Haggard. And that seemed a little excessive to me.

Today, though, Gryffin had gotten caught up in straightening out the final details of our engagement banquet. He had instead assigned a guard to accompany me to the library. A female guard, which was quite a refreshing change. "Just for safety," he'd said innocently, planting a kiss on the top of my head. I knew better. But without his watchful eye, I could fearlessly delve into my research.

With a stack of books in hand, I made my way over to one of the many claw-footed velvet couches, choosing one close to the library's dangerously massive fireplace so that I could feel its radiating warmth, and sat down with my legs crossed under me. I put the stack of books on the floor and settled once again with *A Condensed List of Mental Talents* in my lap. I thumbed to the page I'd marked referring to Sight and began reading, running my fingers under the words as I went.

Those Talented with Sight have
the ability to perceive and distinguish
between Talents during the duration

*in which Talents are actively used.
These Sights are most commonly
perceived as a type of haze, or aura,
encompassing another Talented and
growing stronger as the Talented
more frequently uses his or her ability.
Less commonly, Sighted have also
described their vision as gritty and
particulate.*

Gritty? That must look especially odd when you meet someone for
the first time.

*The deciphering of Talents is
particularly dependent upon the
mental aspect of Sight. Through
guided and consistent practice, the
Sighted can come to feel and know
the type of Talent placed before them.
Thoroughly practiced Sighted may be
able to see one's Talent before it has
manifested, thus inducing the
common practice for mothers and
fathers to present their newborn
children to a Sighted for evaluation.
However, this aspect of the Talent
takes years to master, and there are
several cases reported in which
Sighted have mentally deteriorated if
their learning process was rushed.*

That was the extent covered in the book.

So Isabele needed to hone her Talent, or else she may be driven mad. But she could not try to master it too quickly, or else the same outcome may occur. And I still had absolutely no idea how the Talented train their abilities.

Frustrated, I let the book fall shut.

But as the pages flipped past me, a word scrawled onto one of the worn sheets in a dark, messy hand streamed past my view. Carefully, I thumbed through the pages once more, starting from the back until I caught sight of it again, scribbled into the margin.

A name I knew all too well.

Gryffin

It had been written next to a list of Talents labeled "Imperious." Several Talents in the list had been underlined, unsettling abilities like mind control and sense impairment. However, circled repeatedly in several different colors of ink was a Talent called Persuasion.

Huh.

After briefly glancing toward my assigned guard to ensure she was still lounging several couches away, I read on.

> *Those Talented with Persuasion have the ability to cause unsuspecting persons to think, feel, or act a certain way. This is done through an elevated sense of trust in the mentality of the subject. Advanced Persuasionists may even be able to affect the way in which*

they appear to others—such as altering
their appearances in the eyes of the
subjects so as to aid further
Persuasion.

The process of the Persuasion
Talent differs from that of Mind
Control in that Persuasionists rely on
already established trust, usually
influenced through words, rather than
blatant mental force. In this way, the
actions of the subject are still his or
her own, though the actions are
brought about through skewed or
influenced thoughts.

I slammed the book closed with a hiss of disgust.

Whoever wrote this book—I didn't care if it was Haggard himself—they were wrong. Actions that were unknowingly and uncontrollably influenced, or "persuaded" in the terms of this book, by another were *not* one's own. I stood abruptly from the couch and turned on my heel toward the exit, my deep green skirts billowing around me.

I should have left him in Hillstone's prison.

I hadn't asked Gryffin to stay at Hillstone.

I hadn't wanted to kiss him.

I hadn't been the one to put my kingdom in Gryffin's hands under Roderich's threat.

I hadn't felt love for him.

No, Gryffin made me do it. All of it.

Even still . . . Though none of it may have been real, the consequences were *very* real. Sterling's death. The attack on my kingdom. Thomas's death. So much death.

My conscience did somersaults as I walked through the large library doors, making my head throb and my stomach nauseous. I suddenly very much needed air.

I had in my mind to walk through the small courtyard just outside the library, thinking the crisp, cold air might cool my frustration. But I had no cloak with me, and though I was slowly growing used to the frigidity of Tarasyn, I was not going to subject myself to complete discomfort and possible frostbite. I liked all my fingers and toes, and I planned to keep them.

I began marching up the endless flights of stairs, and only then did I realize my guard hadn't followed me. It made me pause mid-step, just for a moment, before continuing my trek. For me to be alone in Snowmont's corridors was a rare occasion. It was almost unnerving.

As I conquered the final flight of stairs and stepped onto the landing, the echo of booming voices trickled down the corridor. I craned my neck down the hall and found the door to Gryffin's office left ajar, thrown open in a hurry. As I crept forward, the voices became clearer.

"We *cannot* lose the Hiddon border!" Gryffin's voice as I'd never heard it before, growling and furious, spilled into the hallway through the open door.

Then a calmer voice, trying to reason with him said, "Vena is still ours, Your Majesty—"

"Gambeson and the queen's sister have not even called upon their forces yet, Lieutenant! We are losing men and land to *countryside militia!*"

Countryside militia? My people were fighting back . . .

My people were fighting back!

"If we recruit more men, Your Majesty," the lieutenant said, "to replace the ones we've lost—"

"Bah!" Gryffin spat. "More men. No. More men won't fix my brother's mess."

"Then what, Your Majesty?" The lieutenant's voice taken on its own frustration. "What else is there to do? Pull back?"

There was a silence that carried the weight of a thousand horses.

Finally, Gryffin spoke, his voice quiet but deadly. "Find your colonel and General Lamel and send them to me."

"Yes, Your Majesty."

The lieutenant appeared through Gryffin's door, her hands clenched into fists and mouth set into a worried scowl. When she saw me standing there in the hallway, her eyes widened, then narrowed into a glare. I'd never felt such hostility from a stranger before. But she still bowed, and she muttered a quick "Your Majesty" before continuing down the hall, boots clicking sharply against the stone floor.

As she disappeared down the staircase, Gryffin emerged from his office, straightening his vest as he pivoted around his door.

My voice was ice when I spoke. "Trouble at the border?"

He looked up from his vest, eyes wide. "Rosemary," he said quickly. "I—good morning."

"Banquet plans done for the day then?" I asked, crossing my arms over my chest. "On to military plans against my kingdom now?" For the first time, I felt no fear at the sight of him.

Only anger.

The corners of his eyes hardened. "Only trying to protect what is ours."

I scoffed. *Ours.* Hiddon was not *ours.* Nor his. Not rightfully so.

He glared down at his boots and took a deep breath. "I'm sorry that you had to hear that. I hadn't wanted you to know that Lecevonia was at odds with Tarasyn. I knew it would be painful for you." When he looked up again, his eyes held a glint of remorse.

I didn't feel any pressure of his Talent on my mind, but I wasn't fool enough to believe in his apology at all.

"The only option I see is to pull Tarasynian troops off the border," he said carefully, gauging my reaction. "I don't want to lose any more troops, and once we're wed, Lecevonia's countryside won't be a problem anymore, yes?"

I didn't trust myself to say anything. I was too angry to tell a convincing lie.

He sighed and took a slow step forward. "Let me make it up to you," he said softly, taking hold of my hand. His lashes shaded his eyes as he looked down at me, almost obscuring the red flecks. He lifted our hands to my face, and his touch was feather-light as the back of his fingers stroked my jawline. Strangely, I found myself leaning into him.

What was happening?

But my stomach still roiled as he asked, "Have dinner in my rooms with me tonight?"

In my stunned silence, I nodded.

"Thank you." A gentle smile played at his lips, and he kissed my cheek so tenderly that my breathing hitched. His breath was warm against my flush.

What was happening?

"I'll see you tonight."

He backed away, and I was able to breathe again. I watched him as he walked down the corridor and disappeared around the corner of the staircase.

Alone again, I reeled myself in.

What was I thinking, letting him talk me into dinner? Distract me from the fact that he'd been fighting my *people* at the Lecevonia-Hiddon border? My people! *My* farmers and butchers, my blacksmiths and carpenters! Insufferable, Rose!

And I'd wanted to talk to Kathryn tonight about the book I'd found in the library, and the name scribbled inside. Not sit in Gryffin's chambers nibbling on bread and venison.

Gryffin's silver tongue was just as deadly as his Talent. I needed to guard myself with more than just my anger and hatred.

As I walked through the doors of my chambers to search for a cloak, I tried to work out what I'd heard from the lieutenant.

Lecevonia was fighting back, and that in itself made me swell with pride.

It was not uncommon for my people of the Lecevonian countryside to have family across the Hiddon border. Once news had reached them of Tarasyn's actions, they must have decided to band together and fight. And, without Gryffin's Talent to persuade them, Tarasyn would very much be the enemy to them.

I snatched my favorite deep burgundy cloak from the vanity chair.

But why were Isabele and General Gambeson holding back? Surely, Amos must have reported to them everything that had happened in the streets of Equos and what he'd found in the woods. They must have suspected foul play by now.

Then why has no action been taken?

I groaned as I slammed my chamber doors closed behind me. It seemed that I truly was wasting time in waiting for a rescue party.

I didn't have time to dwell on that, though, for the footsteps of my delayed guard finally found their way up the staircase.

CHAPTER SEVEN

TAKING A DEEP breath, I studied myself in the mirror. Cassia had found a twilight blue dress in my wardrobe with silver threading along the cuffs and collar, and she'd gathered a few sections of my hair into braids that ran down my back with the rest of my waves. I looked like a lady of the court.

But my fear had returned, and it stared back at me now through my green eyes. The emerald on my finger seemed like it was taunting me. I was scared of Gryffin's Talent, scared of his words. Scared of falling again into his Persuasion. I tried to keep in mind what Kathryn had said about me taking back my will—that his Talent couldn't touch me anymore. Even still, after my encounter with him this morning, I realized that my control was not as concrete as I'd thought.

Cassia touched my shoulder lightly. "Are nerves getting the better of you, Your Majesty?"

I closed my eyes tightly and clenched my fists. "Yes, only nerves," I answered, letting chagrin slip through my grimace. "Though I hoped it wouldn't be that obvious."

Calm down, Rose. It's only dinner.

By the time I opened my eyes again, I made sure that they would appear smooth, calm. Ready.

As Cassia put final touches of small golden leaves in my hair for a bit of extra detail, the lock of the door separating my rooms from Gryffin's clicked. A vaguely familiar voice called through the crack. "Is the queen ready, Miss Cassia?"

Cassia met my eyes through our reflection, waiting. I took a shallow breath, put on a small smile, and nodded.

She winked at me in the mirror, and she replied, "Yes, Lord Campton. You may come in."

I recognized Lord Campton, though it had been a couple of weeks since I'd seen him, as he opened the door wider and stepped into my chambers. The smell of food wafted in after him, and my mouth watered. Well, if nothing else came of tonight, at least I would have a good meal.

"Your Majesty," he said, bowing, and he gestured with his hand through the doorway.

Cassia gave my shoulder a reassuring squeeze, and I smiled at her in return. Sometimes, the only way forward was through. I stood taller and walked through the doorway, into the viper's nest.

Gryffin's chambers were in stark contrast to my own, yet still as opulent. Where my rooms were white and bright, his were black as midnight. All dark stone and black marble, deep walnut woodworks, smoky granite. The only color that accentuated the chambers through rugs and draping curtains was red, dark as wine. His scent of smoke and honey was stronger here, and it mingled too well with the aroma of food.

I walked farther into his rooms, and Lord Campton closed the door behind me, cutting off the light from my chambers like an eclipse. My eyes adjusted to the candlelight, and as I turned a corner, I found Gryffin standing near his great window. And beneath the sill, a candlelit table laden with food. It all would have been very romantic, had I still trusted the man not to kill me one day.

Gryffin's white teeth shown through the shadows as he smiled. "Hello, Rosemary."

"This is quite extravagant," I said, chuckling to hide the tremor in my voice.

"I've told you, I *can* be a gentleman."

He unhooked his hands from behind his back and met me where I stood. He took my hands in his and slowly kissed them one by one, and it was all I could do to keep my face composed with a small smile.

Gryffin then nodded toward his attendant. "Thank you, Campton."

Campton bowed, and he left out of Gryffin's main door and into the hallway, leaving us alone.

Alone. My heart pounded.

Gryffin gave a small smile and nodded toward the door, blue eyes shimmering beneath the flecks. "It's rare that you and I have moments when it's just the two of us."

Well, that hadn't been for lack of trying on my part.

He gently ran his hand up my arm. "You look beautiful. The leaves are a nice touch." He grabbed hold of one near my ear and rustled it between his fingers. Then his hand came to rest on my face, and, so slowly, he bent his head down toward me.

But I went rigid. No kisses. No Zeke. I couldn't let myself relax in these rooms.

He must have sensed it too. His lips hovered above mine for what felt like too long before he backed away. He studied my face, my eyes, and honestly, I had no idea what expression I was wearing in that moment. I just hoped it was one that didn't give away my secret.

He sighed, and disappointment colored his eyes. "You're still mad at me."

Oh, thank Haggard. He thought I was *mad at him.* Which I was, of course, but I was always angry with him. I was just relieved he didn't see my fear—or my lies. I could play off anger easily.

I extricated myself from him and walked over to his window, arms crossed tightly over my chest. The glass of the window kept out the cold, and the torchlight of Viridi gave the air above the city a warm glow.

"It's beautiful, isn't it?" Gryffin asked, quietly sidling up from behind me. "I love seeing the city at night from up here."

I nodded, a reluctant longing betraying my act. "It is beautiful. I'd like to see more of it."

I heard Gryffin shift on his feet, boots rustling on the carpet. "Perhaps after the banquet I can show you around."

Of course. After the banquet. By then everyone will have seen me, and he had nothing more to hide from them.

Gryffin lightly touched my elbow. "Come, eat. While it's still warm." I let him lead me to my chair. As we sat down, he said, "I've told the general to pull back our forces. It seemed the only sensible thing to do."

I kept my fist clenched around my chalice of wine. "Good. Thank you." Though I wondered if he actually did. He *seemed* to be telling the truth. But then again, didn't he always? I raised the wine to my lips, avoiding his eyes.

"But that's not enough of an apology." He said it as a statement rather than a question.

I answered him with only a smirk. Where was he leading us with this conversation?

He took a bite of his sliver of meat and chewed, slowly laying down his fork. "Do you understand why I'm doing what I am doing?"

"Why you are doing what? Conquering kingdoms?" I laughed dryly. "No, I don't understand." I probably shouldn't antagonize him, but it felt too fitting.

He nodded slowly, taking another thoughtful bite. He poured himself a glass of wine from the decanter and said, "Rosemary, I'm not some power-hungry brute looking for land or subjects. I'm not doing this for wealth or glory or pride. I'm not even doing this for Tarasyn!" He chuckled incredulously, shaking his head. "No. I'm doing what I'm doing for the Talented."

The Talented.

"You've said that," I said, nodding my head once. "But I don't understand it. Why would you want to lead the entire Peninsula on your own?"

He reached across the table and lightly stroked the back of my hand. "I won't be on my own."

Too close, Rose. Don't be foolish. I smiled at him and caught his fingers with mine. "No. Of course not. But . . . I'm just not sure if this is something I can support. Overthrowing rulers? Surely there is another way."

"No. There isn't." He retracted his hand. "Think about this, Rosemary. Would the other rulers know how to handle having Talented in their kingdoms once I awaken them? What if they do as my grandfather tried to do? And my father?" He crossed his arms over his chest with a sound of disgust. "They'd only use them in court. Abuse their abilities and reduce them to nothing more than a pawn."

I felt blood rushing to my ears. "As you said you would do with Isabele."

His eyes narrowed just slightly. "I merely said she would be helpful."

I turned my glare down to my plate. I distinctly remembered the word *exploit* passing through his lips. I had to take a drag of wine to calm myself.

Gryffin uncrossed his arms and took another bite of his meal, shaking his head. "I wish more than that for the Talented. I wish them a life of freedom as I have found. The freedom as all those Talented in Tarasyn have found under my and Roderich's rule."

"How altruistic." I hoped he didn't catch my sarcasm.

He smiled, which led me to believe he hadn't. "I simply want what is best for the entire Magian Peninsula."

Then I felt it. The smallest of pressures prodding against the edges of my mind. Nice try. I built up my castle wall, sturdy and impenetrable. "I can feel you, Gryffin," I blurted, my fork clanging against my plate as I slammed it on the table. "Did you know that?"

Gryffin sat a bit straighter in his seat. "What?"

"Your Talent. I can feel that you are trying to use it against me."

"Never against you," he murmured, looking down at his plate with a perplexed brow. "No one has ever told me that they can feel it."

"Well, I can. *Please*, for Haggard's sake, stop. If we are to be married, I can't have you constantly trying to influence my mind. It isn't right."

He looked at me as if I'd just spit fire. "Of course. I'm sorry."

I sat back in my seat and took a deep breath before picking up my fork again. "Thank you."

Gryffin studied me for a long moment, his lips pursed. I dropped my eyes to my plate and finished the last few bites of my meal in silence.

Finally, he said, "I'm not doing a great job with apologies tonight, am I?"

In that moment, with his contrite tone and worried gaze, I glimpsed the Gryffin I'd known back in Lecevonia. Before everything fell to madness. A kindhearted, genuine man. The red flecks in his eyes remained, but his sentiment made me laugh. "No, I suppose you're doing a boarish job of it."

He chuckled halfheartedly and looked down at his empty plate. "It's impressive that you can feel my Talent. That never occurred to me. I'm sorry. I won't do it again." When he raised his eyes to me, they held something different in them. I'd seen this look before, long ago, in the halls of Hillstone. Almost respect?

Hmm.

"And . . ." He paused, rubbing a hand over his jaw before continuing. "And I'm sorry that I took you out of Equos without your knowing. In hindsight, that was . . . wrong of me."

Well, that was an apology that I was not expecting.

"Certainly not a way to treat your bride-to-be," I responded wryly.

He groaned and covered his face with his hands. "I know. I'm sorry. At the time it seemed the only way." After a moment, he let his hands fall away from his face. "But I *am* glad that you're starting to see things the way I do."

Ah. Well, that apology was short-lived.

Still, his words brought me a sense of reassurance. I offered him a little smile and rolled my eyes. "Well, I'm *so* glad you were able to get that off your chest."

My response made him laugh, a great big belly laugh, and he waggled his eyebrows at me. "Maybe dessert will help me with my apology."

He reached behind him to a platter that had been lain aside and covered with a wooden dish, and as he removed the cover, I wanted to sing for joy. He'd remembered my favorite dessert—blueberry pastries. He slid three onto my plate and kept one for himself.

If this was his way of apologizing, I would gladly take it.

And what was more, I felt in control once more. Gryffin's Talent had no control over me, and now he knew it. Now *I* knew it, for certain. That little flicker of respect in his eyes told me that my position was a good one.

My secret was still safe, and I still had time.

"Hmm. Gryffin must have missed that book."

Kathryn and I wandered through the courtyard near the library the next morning, the marble stone floor almost metallic in the sun's bright beams. It was the day before the banquet, the morning following our dinner, and Gryffin was again busy with last-minute planning. Taking advantage of his absence, I'd finally gotten the chance to tell her about the handwritten additions to *A Condensed List of Mental Talents.*

"What do you mean he 'missed' that book?" I asked.

"Gryffin had made a pass through the library and removed any book that might relate back to Father." Her features darkened at the mention of King Falk. "And, of course, Roderich hadn't minded. From the sound of it, that handwriting was Father's."

"King Falk had been conducting his own research then?"

"Any day he wasn't terrorizing some village. He had Roderich and Gryffin help him."

"Research of what?"

Kathryn shrugged. "Haggard only knows."

"That's a shame," I muttered, a disappointed pout on my lips. "To simply throw out so many books that must have housed *endless* information."

"Oh, Gryffin did not throw them out." Kathryn chuckled. "You know Gryffin would not waste such resources. No, they're sectioned off in his personal study."

His personal study! I'd been so close to it last night. What was Gryffin hiding in the dusty shadows of those shelves?

"I wouldn't consider it," Kathryn murmured, her words threaded in caution.

I looked at her in surprise. She must have seen the wheels turning in my head.

"Corvus's perch is inside Gryffin's study," she said. "That dreadful bird would never keep quiet."

Indeed, the crow would be a problem. He hadn't been present last night—I was sure he'd been off intimidating whomever he felt was having too good of a day.

"Well, no matter," I finally responded. "Maybe I can sneak a peek next time I'm invited into his rooms."

Kathryn gasped. "Oh, yes! How was the dreaded dinner?"

I shot her a glance. "How did you know about it?"

"Lamel told me."

"Of course he did," I said, smirking. "It actually went . . . well, much better than I expected." The surprise in my own tone matched the look on Kathryn's face. "He said he would pull his troops off the Lecevonia-Hiddon border and leave my countrymen alone, but I don't know if I can trust him on that front."

Then, an idea came to me.

"Kathryn," I hedged. "You meet with the general often, yes?"

She smiled flirtatiously. "Quite often."

"Well . . . would you mind asking him about any military action taking place?"

"How on Haggard's green earth do you expect me to work that kind of conversation into our time together?"

"I have no doubt that you can be creative." I laughed under my breath.

After a thought, Kathryn's coy smile returned. "I'll see what I can do. But why?"

"Lecevonia's forces haven't made a move, yet," I said. "And I don't understand why."

Kathryn sighed, almost impatiently. "You are not under Gryffin's Talent anymore, Rosemary. But *they* might be. Even in Gryffin's absence, the effects of his Talent linger."

"It's been two months!"

But Kathryn only shrugged her shoulders. "I've seen Gryffin's Talent still affect people for much longer than that. He's never had any trouble influencing the Tarasynian people all these years, even those in remote villages that take weeks to access even in the snowmelt of summer."

I shook my head stubbornly. "No. I don't believe it." Surely not after what Amos must have seen in the woods. Surely they'd all taken their will back by now.

I needed to change the subject before I started to doubt myself. "I told Gryffin that I can feel when he is trying to use his Talent to influence me."

Kathryn's eyes widened as she turned to look at me, her blue eyes catching the sunlight. "You can?" After a moment, she pursed her lips and turned away thoughtfully. "You must be more strongminded than my brother believes you to be. How did he react?"

I almost laughed, though I ardently hoped there was truth to her words. "Humbled," I finally answered, and I couldn't help but feel smug.

Kathryn smiled and flipped her black hair over her shoulder.

"Well, good. It's about time someone knocks him a bit."

"He keeps mentioning an 'awakening,'" I said, looking toward the pillars at the edge of the courtyard. "Do you know anything about it?"

"Less than you, I'm sure," she said, scrunching her nose against the gust of cold air that wrapped around us. "That has been one thing that Gryffin and Roderich had always kept *tightly* under wraps amongst themselves." She tucked the hem of her furs around her body. "Much like myself in this cloak. This banquet is going to be frigid if this wind keeps up. It's nearing summer, for Haggard's sake!"

For once, I hadn't been bothered by the cold. What sent true chills down my spine was the banquet.

But I would be ready.

~HILLSTONE~
ZEKE

The folded parchment felt heavy in my vest pocket, as if the ink itself weighed a wagon's worth of cobblestones. I pounded down the steps to the stables as rain pelted my eyes like pins. The storm that had been looming over the Silver Mountains for days had finally arrived and made it a point now to soak me to the bone.

But I hardly noticed. I only focused on keeping that piece of parchment dry. If all went well, I wouldn't be thrown into a completely hopeless position, after all.

I heaved open the east-facing stable door and addressed the first person I saw, a young girl with pale hair. "Celeste. Have you seen her?"

"No, sir," she replied, eyes wide. "Not recently."

I turned away from her and walked up and down the hay-strewn aisles, searching for any familiar face. Had I really been away from the Royal Stables this long?

Finally, I caught sight of a woman that vaguely drew out some old memory. What was it? I remembered her blue eyes, her red curls bouncing with the haybale she was lugging around. Why—?

Ah.

A cringe prickled from my tailbone to my neck as I approached the woman—Loryna, I remembered her name suddenly—and raised my hand in greeting. This was going to be horrendous. "Hello."

From her scathing glare, she had no problem remembering me. "Zeke."

"Have you seen Celeste?"

She dropped her haybale roughly, frowned when it didn't land on my feet, and put her hands on her hips. "Why? Are you trying to sack with every woman in here now?"

I felt a low, frustrated grumble rise in my throat.

It had been five years ago. We'd been young, and Rose had refused to see me that evening after accusing me of spending too much time with other girls. Which was a fair accusation. So, I'd gone out and found Loryna.

But I hadn't sacked with her, though it had come close . . . And the night hadn't ended too prettily. I'd had to tell her no, that it didn't feel right. And I hadn't spoken to her since.

She apparently had taken it personally.

"No—I'm not here for that." I held up my hands in peace. "I just need to speak with her."

Loryna's hands left her hips as she crossed her arms over her chest. "I haven't seen her in over a month."

My mouth parched instantly. "Over a month? Where has she been?"

Loryna's eyes looked down to the ground, suddenly turning downcast. "I don't know. No one has seen her since—since the attack. I'd assumed she'd been . . . y'know . . . like so many." Her voice had lowered to a whisper. "Killed. In the battle."

Killed?

No. Not Celeste. I didn't believe that for one second.

Had I been a smarter man, I would have refrained from resting my hand gently on Loryna's shoulder. "You know that must not be true. Celeste is clever."

Loryna glared at my hand as if it had just done the most offensive thing, and I immediately dropped it to my side. There was a stretch of silence between us, and when she looked at me next, I expected a hateful gaze and a scolding remark.

But to my surprise, the corner of her lip turned upward into an odd little smile. "You're still a crite but thank you."

I didn't know what to say to that, and the folded parchment in my pocket felt as if it were burning through my tunic. "Are any others gone?"

"Just two more, Josef and Leo."

"Listen, I need a letter sent to Tarasyn. To Viridi."

Loryna's confusion was clear in her scrunched brow. "To the prince and Her Majesty?"

"Directly to Her Majesty," I said pointedly, lowering my voice below the squeaking wheels of the pushcarts and the snorting of the horses. "Does that little boy and his father still do that type of work?" I couldn't remember the names of the stablehands off the top of my head, but their side hustle of smuggling was sort of an infamous rumor throughout the city.

Her furrowed brow deepened. "Why do you need them? Isn't discretion *your* job?"

Time to be frank. "I'm not doing this on the job."

"Oh." Loryna's green eyes widened. After a moment, she nodded slowly. "Yes, I believe Xal and Brom are still in that business. Though Xal isn't so little anymore."

The relief that washed through me still did not stifle the urgency.

"Where can I find them?"

"Xal is normally tending to the northern section of stalls around this time."

I placed my hands on her shoulders again, and this time she didn't flinch. "Thank you, Loryna. Thank you so much." I turned on my heel and bounded toward the north-facing area of the stables.

"Zeke!" I heard her call.

I turned swiftly, walking backward.

"We've both grown in the past five years, you know." She winked, a sultry smile playing at her lips. "If you ever want to—"

"I'm sorry, Loryna!" was the only thing I could think to yell over my shoulder without blatantly shouting out a denial. A memory of that night popped into my head, and I shook it away before I could feel any more guilt. She was relentless, wasn't she?

I laid a hand over my pocket as I ran.

CHAPTER EIGHT

CASSIA HAD RECEIVED special instructions from Gryffin: dress me in a fine, dignified gown befitting of a queen and a wife, and style my hair in a way that would demand respect and admiration.

Gryffin apparently had high expectations for his wife.

I would have protested, but I still had a role to play. Tonight's banquet, and the days of court following thereafter, would be pivotal. If I could pull this off—if I could convincingly become the charming betrothed of the king—I would have a safety net in the people of Tarasyn.

Cassia had hidden the scar on my forehead with a bit of cosmetics, and she'd painted my lips as red as the holly bushes in the courtyard. She yanked my long waves, desperately trying as she might to be gentle, into an elaborate knot atop my head. Meanwhile, Vasilie laid a glittering golden gown onto my bed.

"There are already so many people here," she said, eyes wide. "I've never seen such a crowd in the halls!"

In the gilded mirror, I saw Cassia nod. "This is the first big event that's been held at Snowmont in seventy years. Certainly the first *I* ever remember! I imagine everyone is curious to see what the kings of Tarasyn have been up to." She nudged my shoulder and smiled. "Not to mention catching a glimpse of the new queen-to-be."

I rolled my eyes through the mirror at Cassia and turned to Vasilie. "What did you see?"

"Well," she said, taking a seat on the corner of my bed, "as I was collecting this dress from the dressmaker, I peeked my head through to the kitchens, and *for Haggard's sake*! King Gryffin has the castle's entire workforce running!"

Cassia grumbled. "Humph. King Gryffin must want to make an impression."

Their conversation kept me grounded as I sat quietly in my chemise, mentally preparing myself for the feat that lay ahead.

Gryffin hadn't told me how many people he'd invited, but I'd seen the preparations in the Great Hall. If the four long banquet tables dressed to perfection with red and cream table linens were any inkling, I had to guess there'd be at least two hundred or so guests. He did say that he'd arranged for several people to stay in the old guest chambers. He'd also told me that a couple of *distinguished* guests, whoever they may be, were going to be using the twins' chambers right down the hall, so I should expect more traffic through the corridors than usual. The rest who wished to visit Snowmont for a while would be staying in inns throughout Viridi.

And truly, the preparations for this banquet had been city-wide. From my window overlooking the brightly painted roofs of Viridi, I'd seen citizens hanging banners in the streets, trimming the blue spruces and red maples, unloading carts upon carts of supplies for their shops. It seemed *everybody* was trying to make an impression.

Perhaps, as Cassia had said, this truly was the largest celebration the kingdom has seen in seventy-odd years.

Celebration. I almost scoffed aloud. That was hardly the word I'd use. To Gryffin, surely. But to me, it was more of a sentencing.

Just until I got out of here.

How do I get out of here? As hard of a truth as it was, I had to accept that no one was coming to help me.

That comprehension caused such a sudden and overwhelming sadness that I instinctively shut off my thoughts and focused instead on Vasilie's fingers lacing up the back of my dress.

I hadn't realized that the interior of the gown was lined with fur until I felt the soft warmth of it against my skin. The white pelt folded over the collar of the dress, caressing my neck and collarbone in a snug luxuriousness. I stretched my arms out to either side and found that the golden gown had a deep red velvet incorporated into it, which traveled up the long sleeves and across the bodice of the dress, trailing down into the skirts. Hazel would have been *very* impressed with the dressmaker's craftsmanship.

"The velvet was another one of Gryffin's instructions," Cassia said absentmindedly as she watched my fingers graze the fabric of my bodice.

I remembered my red velvet gown that I'd worn long ago on a now very hazy picnic, and I unnervingly understood Gryffin's reasoning.

Then, as if he'd heard his name, the door between our chambers opened, and I kept my gaze straight ahead into the mirror as his pleased chuckle pierced my ears.

"Ah, Rosemary," he murmured, coming to stand behind me in our reflection. He lifted his hand and touched my cheek with his fingertips. "My queen."

His gold medals pinned to his white fur-lined vest caught the light of the flickering chandeliers above our heads, the same light that glistened threateningly in his blue, red-flecked eyes.

I held my ground as he bent his head and kissed me just below my jawline.

"You look absolutely breathtaking."

"Thank you, my king." The words felt like dirt and gravel on my tongue. *Breathtaking*. I held on to the memory of that very word leaving Zeke's lips once upon a time.

His fingers left a heavy trail down to my waist. "How do you like the dress?"

"It's lovely," I replied, red lips smiling into the mirror.

The wisps of hair at my ear tickled my neck as he laughed. "I think so too. See what the Talented can do?"

I didn't have a response to that, but I didn't need one. Gryffin's nose skirted my jaw, my temple, lips grazing my skin. "Mmm. Breathtaking," he said again.

I only thought of Zeke.

I closed my eyes and imagined him in Gryffin's place. I pictured Zeke's golden waves, his brown eyes, his warm hands hugging my hips as Gryffin's did now.

Zeke's lips found mine, and I leaned into him gently.

I almost laughed. My feelings for Zeke, those feelings I'd selfishly ignored for so many years, were now the only things holding me through any physical encounter with Gryffin. An unhealthy coping mechanism, surely.

As if something had awoken inside me, I was wanting more, gasping against his kiss. I turned my body to face him and wrapped my arms around his neck. Zeke held me tighter. As our lips moved together, I let out a soft moan.

Then his lips daringly traveled down my neck, toward my exposed collarbone. His hunger made me sigh, and as I opened my eyes in surprise, my vision was shattered.

This was not Zeke, and this was far enough.

Boundaries, I thought as I leaned away from Gryffin. I smoothly detangled myself and sidestepped out of his reach, flushed and breathless, keeping a convincing little smile painted on my face. But I couldn't bring myself to say a word. My mind was reeling.

Gryffin was breathing heavily too, the medals on his chest glittering in the candlelight with each inhale and exhale. He ran a hand through his dark curls with a chuckle and shook his head softly, eyes meeting mine in our reflection.

Then, he stepped forward and grabbed hold of my hand, just a little too tightly. "Are you ready to greet your people?"

I worked to steady my smile, but I knew my nerves showed through. That was okay, I told myself. I was supposed to be nervous.

"As ready as I can be."

Though it was quiet out in the corridor, the atmosphere of the castle had a lively thrum to it. It was different enough to distract me from the kiss that almost went a little too far with a man I didn't love.

That liveliness only increased as we descended the first few flights of stairs, until finally down on the second floor, we encountered our first guests. They bowed their heads and offered mumbles of "Your Majesty" as we passed.

As I gazed down the grand staircase to the first floor, with its vaulted ceilings and chandeliers, the one or two small gatherings of people soon turned into a crowd. They spilled down the stairs and out of rooms lining the hall through the door to the courtyard where more tables had been set. Everyone had dressed as exquisitely as they were able, glittering gowns and colorful vests, sashes and shawls and furs. The lively thrum had turned into a roar as conversations collided into one another, creating such a clamor that no individual words were distinguishable. It was the loudest I'd ever heard the halls of Snowmont.

Then, a loud bugle sounded directly behind me, almost making me jump out of my dress and complicated updo, back up to the quiet of my rooms. I needed to get my nerves under control.

The horn easily caught the crowd's attention, and a quick hush fell through the castle's main hall.

The statesman who had blown the bugle, looking smart in his red buttoned vest, cleared his throat, and his strong voice rang out through the corridor. "His Majesty King Gryffin Danicio, and your prospective queen, Her Majesty Rosemary Avelia of Lecevonia."

Gryffin led as we descended the final staircase through the packed crowd, who had haphazardly clung to the edges of the hall to form a sort of aisle. The endless curtsies and bows made me want to crawl into my skin and disappear. These strangers were not my people, nor were they meant to be.

Outwardly, however, I kept my head held high and a bright smile stretched across my lips, as if I were the master of Snowmont. For I was supposed to be.

This was my part to play.

I caught the eyes of several men who hadn't the decency to avert their stare as we passed. Cassia had done her job, then. Gryffin didn't seem to mind their wandering eyes. In fact, he only smiled more brilliantly each time he saw my cutting glare.

"Embrace it, Rosemary," he murmured as we walked. "This only means that these men will adore you faithfully."

"'Faithfully' is not the word I would use," I responded with a grumble. After all, several of these men had their wives' hands resting on their arms. "I don't need their adoration, Gryffin. Simply their respect."

"All in due time, my queen."

We continued among the crowd and through the doors to the dining hall, where the four long tables were already filled with people. As Gryffin led me to the front of the room, I saw the long head table set for twelve people. I was not to be seated next to Gryffin it seemed, for the large kingly seat was already flanked by Kathryn to its right, and a tall boy with black curls like Gryffin to its left. Laris, I presumed. Seated next to him was his wife, then another boy that looked very nearly exactly like him. Michael. And finally his wife, seated at the end.

Gryffin had followed my line of sight and chuckled. "There is a method to the seating, I assure you. Each position was handpicked."

As we approached the table, I saw my chair situated between a couple and a family, none of whom I recognized. Gryffin led me to my seat and, with a sudden smirk, introduced us.

"Rosemary, I'd like you to meet Lord and Lady DeGrey," he said, gesturing to the couple. "And Lord and Lady Urbin, and their daughter-in-law, Lady Jessa Urbin." He extended his hand to the family.

Lord and Lady DeGrey. My eyes widened.

"Lord DeGrey is the younger brother of the late king of Hiddon."

I stared at Lord DeGrey as Gryffin spoke. With the princes' deaths, this man would be next in line for the Hiddon throne. However, instead of seeming upset or angry about being invited to the same banquet table where his brother's murderer once sat, he looked dejected, sodden, hopeless. His wife, on the other hand, with her head high and her graying hair pulled tightly back, looked indignant enough for the both of them. She did not acknowledge Gryffin at all, not even a glance, even though he was their new king.

My mind was still working through why they were here when Gryffin turned toward the family seated to my left. "And Lord and

Lady Urbin are the parents of Sir Jerrim Urbin, a fallen Tarasynian soldier. And the charming Lady Jessa here is his wife. I'm sure you remember him, Rosemary." His expression turned serious as he looked pointedly at me. "He met his demise in the streets of Equos."

There was only one man Sir Jerrim Urbin could be. The memory of my sword piercing through his armor resurfaced, his bright blood now flooding my vision.

And from the unforgiving glares I was receiving from each of the Urbins, they knew exactly who I was and what I'd done.

"These families are our distinguished guests this evening, to honor their family members who have fallen for the sake of the Peninsula." Gryffin gave a deep nod to each of them. "Our sincerest condolences. Rosemary will gladly do whatever is needed to assure your losses are recompensed."

At his words, the Urbins visibly relaxed. Was Gryffin's Talent was at work? With a final smile, and a small smirk of amusement thrown in my direction, he retreated to take his seat.

I was fuming. What was Gryffin playing at, inviting Lord and Lady DeGrey to Tarasyn after what Roderich had done to King Theon and Queen Alys? Was he trying to remind them who Hiddon now belonged to? It was sick and cruel.

And placing me next to the family of the man I'd had to kill!

As if I hadn't been burning with enough guilt over taking a man's life, now I stared into the forlorn and angry faces of his mother and father. And there was his young wife, who may have children waiting for her at home.

Another sick and cruel punishment, for everyone involved. And Gryffin loved it. His smug look only grew as each of us was forced to deal with our turmoil of emotions.

Any respect I'd thought I'd gained from Gryffin during our dinner last night seemed to have evaporated into oblivion.

Across the Urbins, Kathryn caught my eye. I didn't know if she knew why this arrangement was so uncomfortable for me, but from her sympathetic grimace, she certainly knew I was drowning. She winked at me so subtly I would have missed it had I blinked, and she touched Sir Jerrim's wife on the hand. "Lady Jessa, how is the new tailor settling at your manor?"

So, with Kathryn's blessed help, the Urbins were occupied for the time-being.

As the first course was served, a warm potato soup with crumbled bread, I turned quietly to the DeGreys.

"I was so sorry to hear the horrible news of King Theon and Queen Alys, and their children," I said. "Their deaths were completely unwarranted."

Lady DeGrey's response was quick and sharp. "Watch what you say, girl."

Oh.

I sat there in silence, taken aback. I hadn't been spoken to in such a manner since I'd been a child. What had I said? I turned forward, focusing instead on the soup placed in front of me.

After we were all served, the Lady touched me on the shoulder.

"I apologize, Your Majesty," she said, her strained voice hardly above a whisper. "I just mean to warn you—King Gryffin has eyes and ears throughout this entire dining hall."

I nodded, understanding now. Anyone who had been laying down food could very well relate everything we say back to my captor. Even now, just behind us against the wall stood a kitchen worker. I corrected my words carefully. "Loss is never easy, especially a member of the family." I thought of Sterling's bright roses and peonies, and sadness gripped my heart. "My grandfather passed recently."

Lady DeGrey nodded solemnly and spoke again at a normal volume. "Loss is difficult. It can open new doors though. Can't it, Harrold?" She gently nudged her husband's shoulder, but Lord DeGrey didn't react. "Yes, the late King Roderich certainly opened new doors." Her tone was happy and civil, but her eyes, blocked from view of the kitchen staff, glistened in rage. "You must forgive my husband's absent behavior. He is still grieving."

"Of course." I bowed my head.

"We all must grieve," Lord Urbin murmured from my other side, his voice grim. It appeared he'd finished his soup, and the talk of tailors had not interested him.

I turned to face him, preparing myself for the hate and anger still storming in his eyes. I would hate me too, if I were him.

But when he met my gaze, I didn't see the storm. Instead, I saw his deep grief, etched in every hard line of his face.

A weighted silence sat between us. I felt as if I were standing on the edge of a parapet.

Finally, he spoke again, his deep voice careful. "You lost your grandfather, you say?"

Though rattled by his question, I nodded my head once.

He appraised my expression closely, his eyes exploring mine. "How?"

"He was murdered. Struck by an arrow." I dared to say no more, fighting the urge to glance toward the nearby kitchen worker.

"And of your parents?"

A little pierce through my heart. "Taken by Atroxis."

His gaze never left mine, unwavering as gears seemed to turn inside his head. I wanted to look away from this man, away from the guilt his grief caused me. I'd *had* to kill Jerrim to live, yes. But I'd still taken a son and a husband out of this world. Possibly even a father. So, I kept my eyes steady on his.

Then, I saw the tiny red sunburst.

The first of its kind, suddenly blooming in his left eye.

He blinked rapidly, surprised, and rubbed his eye with his fingers as if it stung. "Consider Jerrim recompensed," he said quickly, turning away from me with a final nod. He began whispering to his wife then, indecipherable conversation passing anxiously between them as Lady Urbin studied her husband's eye.

I looked away, shaken. So, the deaths of my family had equalized the death of his son by my hand? Whose call was that to make?

And what was more, this man was Talented. Something about our conversation had triggered his long-latent Talent to spring forth, right then and there. And it had shocked him as much as it'd shocked me. Did Talents always just manifest as simply as that? And, a thought that was more prying than anything, what *was* his Talent?

As our soup bowls were being cleared, I turned to Lord and Lady DeGrey once more. "How prevalent are Talents in Hiddon?"

Lady DeGrey looked at me as if I'd just asked something ridiculous, like how many liters of water flowed through the Riparia River each day. "Talents no longer exist. Didn't your father teach you these things?"

I bowed my head amicably but maintained eye contact, refusing to be belittled again by the woman. "That is exactly what I was taught."

"And you must remember, Hiddon is Tarasyn now," she said, pointedly eyeing the workers milling around, carrying large plates garnished with the main course of our meal.

I turned away, thankful for the excuse of the entree to stay silent for a good portion of the rest of the banquet. I sliced my knife into the roasted pheasant and remained deep in thought.

I felt relieved more than anything, in all honesty, that Hiddon also had no idea that Talents still existed. Lecevonia had not been the only kingdom in the dark. I wondered what Somora and Loche knew. Uncle Merek had never mentioned any Talented in his letters, and he surely would have. He would know if any Talented were in his kingdom, and he would undoubtedly put them into service at his court.

Kathryn's words returned to me, though, that Talents were still in each of the kingdoms—just not understood for what they were. I chewed absentmindedly, barely tasting the cooked vegetables served with the pheasant, as I thought of anyone else in Lecevonia that may be Talented.

I would have never initially guessed Isabele. But then, as empathetic as she was, perhaps she has always *seen* more in people than we knew. Lisette, surely not. She was so strong minded that she would have discovered it by now. If Clara were Talented, she would have the ability of spreading joy to anyone around her. And as much as I was learning about these abilities, maybe that *was* a Talent.

Zeke, no. Unless charming every girl he met could be considered a special ability. I was surprised by the sudden rush of jealousy I felt as I imagined his arms around another woman, holding her instead of me, his lips against another's—

Rose, I chided myself. It was not as if I could have him, anyway. I was his, and he claimed to be mine, but I could not hold him to that if I could not offer him marriage.

Before I could grow any more pitiful, I continued to distract myself as I took a large bite of buttery smashed potatoes.

Zeke could possibly be Talented with evasion. He was very good at his job as a scout, and he always bragged of never having been caught.

That thought is what I chose to believe as dessert began making its rounds. My blueberry pastries made a reappearance topped with some sort of deliciously sweet frozen cream I'd never had before, and I knew

I had Gryffin to thank for this. I was not sure why he gave me this kindness, but I did not let one bite go to waste. The Urbins actually chuckled at my enthusiasm, which I took as a good sign that Lord Urbin had meant his earlier words.

There was no opportune time to ask Lord and Lady DeGrey if they knew of the discontent between the Hiddon and Lecevonian border. I hoped that they were some of the couples staying here in the castle. I might find a time to talk to them if that were the case.

I was looking down at the table, utterly ready to return to my rooms, when the rough, slender hands that picked up my empty plate caught my attention.

I knew those hands. I'd grown up with those hands. Those hands that had worked tirelessly since their owner had been five years old.

But—no, that would be impossible. She couldn't be here.

Before the kitchen worker could leave with my plate, I turned my gaze upward. Straight into her face.

Though her pale blonde hair was hidden underneath her bonnet and her face was draped in shadow, Celeste's hazel eyes stared back at me.

CHAPTER NINE

CELESTE AND I stared at each other for a fraction of a second. Then, she whisked my plate away to the kitchens.

I cut my gaze to Gryffin and found him watching me, his face unreadable. But I made sure that I was *very* clear in my expression: I was angry. Very angry.

"Excuse me," I murmured, standing from my seat. Gryffin stood with me, which meant the entire dining hall followed suit, chairs scraping loudly against the stone floor. I walked to Gryffin and placed a hard hand on his arm, and a confused whisper traveled through the guests as we walked through the doors to the hallway.

As soon as we disappeared around the doorway, I turned to him sharply. "Why is Celeste here? Is she a prisoner? I *demand* that she's released!"

"For Haggard's sake, Rosemary, lower your voice," Gryffin muttered. "There are visitors nearby."

He motioned to me with a jerk of his head, and he led me to a room off the main hallway, a quiet sitting room I had no idea existed.

It was adorned with the same velvet couches as in the Great Hall. He quickly closed the door behind us and faced me, but his face was hard to see through the darkness. "A small group of Lecevonians were taken as captives by my soldiers after the attack, and yes, Celeste was among them."

"You took *my people* as prisoners." My voice was murder.

But Gryffin scoffed. "She serves the castle, yes, but she is hardly a prisoner. She is well provided for, I assure you. I assign any able-bodied person to work in the castle. Keeping them in the dungeon would be a waste of resources."

Waste of resources. Of course. "Why haven't I seen her before tonight?"

I saw the shadow of Gryffin's shoulders shrug. "I thought it best to keep her out of your sight. Less distressing for you."

Less distressing for me. As if I believed that.

Gryffin's red-flecked eyes caught the light of the lone candle near the back of the room. "She's fortunate that I don't have her punished for tonight's disobedience."

I stifled a sharp breath and glared toward his voice. "I would not let you, anyhow."

He studied me for a moment, gauging my response, the severity of my stance. But I made my position very clear. If he so much as let anyone lay a finger on my friend, he would not have a queen.

Finally, he sighed and smiled softly, as if he were doing some sort of good deed. He lifted his hand and stroked the fur of my collar. "I wouldn't, for your sake. I know she's your friend."

His proximity revolted me, and I could hardly keep up my pretense. Thankfully, my anger was a good excuse to step away from him.

I needed something else on which to focus, so I spit out another question. "Why did you put her in the kitchens? She works with horses, not bread dough."

"We did not need more stablehands."

"I want her assigned as one of my chambermaids."

My demand sent waves of shock and indignation across his face. "Rosemary—"

"Assign her."

He narrowed his eyes stubbornly, but eventually, he relented. "All right. I will arrange for her reassignment. If"—he looked at me pointedly—"you finish out this banquet as the dignified queen you are expected to be."

Though I was seething, I nodded. "Of course. That is no problem for a dignified queen."

I pushed past him and threw open the doors to the hallway.

I paced in my chambers, my fur cloak hugged tightly around me against the cold. I'd closed my window over an hour ago and had had a fire blazing ever since, but the frigid Tarasynian air managed to linger, clinging to the granite walls.

The banquet had ended on a high note, with a Talented musician playing his stringed instrument out in the Atrium well into the evening as couples waltzed across the smooth marble floor. I'd played my part well, laughing graciously with guests and dancing with Gryffin, allowing him to hold me around the waist most of the night. And when he'd kissed me good night, I hadn't cringed as his drunken lips lingered against my cheek, my jawline, my neck.

Now, I focused on only the floor beneath me, glancing with each pace toward the maid's door in the corner.

"Is there anything you need, Your Majesty?" Cassia asked from her chair near the fireplace.

"No, thank you." Unless she could make Celeste move any more quickly.

When the maid's door finally creaked open, I stopped my pacing and stared, hoping, until Celeste's slender form emerged.

"Oh, thank Haggard!" I rushed forward and wrapped my arms around my friend.

"Are you sure that's not just the wine talking?" she asked, smirking. "Because you absolutely reek of it."

Her familiar teasing sparked a surge of comfort within me, and suddenly, we were crying. Me more so than her, but still. Celeste *never* cried, so this felt monumental.

She led me to the edge of my bed and sat down with me, running her hand over my hair and shakily humming a tune I placed as the Lecevonian lullaby as I sobbed into her shoulder. Every moment I'd felt alone here in Tarasyn—every night I'd had to talk myself out of despair, longing for my kingdom—they all hit me now with the dark emotions I'd been fighting off, refusing to acknowledge for my own sanity.

"Why aren't you always this happy to see me down at the stables?" Celeste swiped away a tear from her cheek and pouted her lips teasingly. "Not even Midas gets this kind of reaction from you."

I finally calmed my breathing enough to slip a few words through my gasps. "I-I'm sorry, I'm just s-so . . . so *happy* to see you!"

That garnered a few more tears from Celeste, and she quickly shook them away. "I'm happy to see you too, Rosie."

With a few more deep breaths, I was able to form coherent sentences. "I'm sorry. It's just that—you're the first familiar face I've seen in two months. My first real reminder of Lecevonia. Of Hillstone." As I wiped my hands over my face, memories of home flooded back to me, emotions I hadn't realized I'd tucked away until now. All this time, I'd truly been solely focused on survival.

"Really?" She shook her head in confusion. "That's . . . odd. That is not what Prince Gryffin told us." She stood and took my hands in hers. "Well, what's holding us here then? Tell your prince you want to go home."

I stole a glance toward my handmaids in the corner. "It isn't that simple, Celeste."

She took a breath to speak, but I gave her a warning look. "Cassia," I said instead, turning to her. "Do you know how to make tiliarose? I think we'll be awake for a while longer."

Cassia shook her head but stood quickly from her seat, probably grateful for an escape from my tearful outburst. "I don't, but I'm sure someone down in the kitchens does." She nodded to my other chambermaids. "Come, girls. We'll gather up the ingredients."

As the maid's door closed behind them, I turned back to Celeste.

"I need to escape this place. Gryffin will not permit me to return home."

She frowned, eyebrows pinched together. "Prince Gryffin said—"

"You cannot listen to a word he says," I said firmly. "And he is *King* Gryffin now."

Celeste waved me off. "Yes, yes, king. But you aren't making sense. He said that we'll all be permitted to go home after the wedding. That *you* will take us home."

"He's lying, Celeste." Every ounce of my frustration made itself known in my tone. "Who else is here with you?"

"Two other stablehands, Leo and Josef. A couple of groundskeepers and gardeners. A handful of kitchen workers—"

"Lucinda?" I asked quickly. I hoped to Haggard she was not here.

"No, not Lucinda." Celeste watched me closely. "What do you mean, he's lying?"

I stood from the bed with a sigh and sauntered toward my fireplace. This confession never got easier. "He never cared about me or Lecevonia's wellbeing. He's only using me to gain power over my kingdom. He has this . . . plan . . . for the Peninsula." I shook my head. That was too much to get into right now, and I wasn't even sure if I knew the entirety of it. "He wants Lecevonia, and he knew he wouldn't be able to muscle his way to victory. By our marriage, he will rule *three* of the Five Kingdoms. I need to get back to Equos to put an end to this."

My friend crossed her arms over her chest, in very Celeste-like fashion. "If that was what he wanted, then why did you agree to marry him? Wasn't that the whole point of this banquet?" Then she gasped. "Wait—did you never agree?" Suddenly, her eyes narrowed, and she pushed herself up from the bed. "What is this man on, *making* you marry him!"

I had to take a deep breath to keep myself from screaming. "No, I did agree. I had to. It's the only thing keeping me alive, Celeste. If I don't marry him, I am only an obstacle in his way, and he won't hesitate to kill me."

Doubt shadowed her eyes in the silence that followed, but I didn't know if it was geared toward my words or Gryffin's.

I walked back over to the bed and took a seat with her once again, taking hold of her hands. "What happened back at Hillstone?" I asked. "How did you end up here?"

Celeste's forehead furrowed, and now, she seemed unsure. "I brought the two horses into the woods, as he'd asked. Then, everything went to disaster. Soldiers, fires—they were everywhere. A group of us was rounded up, stuffed into a wagon." She huffed and rolled her eyes. "After an awful week of jostling on the road with Tarasyn's army, we were brought to the dungeons of this place. We were all mad as hornets, and outright *confused*. Prince Gryffin had called off the attack, we knew that much. Then your prince came barging in, apologizing, saying he didn't mean for us to be here." She shrugged her shoulders as if it meant nothing, but her entire form had gone rigid. "He said that you would take us home."

Quite the deceiver, wasn't he? I could not fault her for believing his weak lies, for she had no power against his Persuasion. "Then what, Celeste?"

"Then he gave us all different jobs, said we weren't prisoners and didn't belong in shackles. I was assigned to the kitchens." At that, she laughed. "They found out mighty quickly that I am *not* meant to be cooking."

Her truthful joke cracked a smile on my face, but I refused to be thrown off-course. Gryffin's Talent was funny like that. "What did he tell you that stopped you from finding me?"

"He—well, he didn't *say* anything really. Just had the other Tarasynian workers keep me busy. Everything felt fine . . . until now, now that you're saying all of this." I saw the doubt in her eyes summit, her mind trying to tear itself into two. "Rose, what's going on?"

"Celeste, I'm going to tell you something, and it is going to make you angry."

Her doubt morphed into worry, a look so uncharacteristic of her that it looked out of place on her face. "What do you mean?"

I took a deep breath and let it out slowly. "Gryffin is Talented."

At first, she scoffed. "Talented? You mean like the nursery tales?" She rolled her eyes and tried to pull her hand away from mine. "Right."

But I tightened my grip. She *had* to understand. "He can say anything, do anything, and people will trust him unless they know otherwise."

She sat there for an endless moment in silence, squinted eyes appraising me. Then, finally, she lowered her gaze, staring at me squarely for the first time this evening.

"You are being serious."

"Yes."

"Prince Gryffin *made* me believe these things."

"Yes."

Her face slowly went slack, eyes staring ahead as she slowly accepted my words, a new, unabridged light entering her eyes. Realization. I watched in awe as her features lifted, almost as if Gryffin's Persuasion had been weighing them down until this moment. It was like a fog that had settled in after a rainy day had dissipated, burned away by truth.

So, this was what it looked like to beat Gryffin's Talent.

Then, an anger like no other flared into Celeste's eyes.

She stood abruptly from the bed and began charging through my rooms. "That lying son of a boar! That—that—" She grabbed my brush off my vanity and threw it at the wall. Poor brush, assaulted twice now.

"Celeste!" I jumped up and grabbed her arm. "Not so loudly! His quarters are next door!"

"I don't care! That deceitful crite can hear every word I need to say!"

"Then he'll kill us both, and that solves nothing! Please, hush!" I yanked her back toward my bed to sit with me again. "Cassia and the others are returning any moment."

Celeste hissed through her teeth, still seething, her hands wound into fists. She lowered her voice and asked, "Do they know?"

"No. But Cassia has been faithful to me since she's been my attendant."

"Good," Celeste said, folding her arms over her chest again. "Trust can't be thrown out farther than a sack of flour here."

My eyes fell to the floor as I hesitated before my next line of thought. But I wouldn't be able to hide it for very long. Might as well rip off all the wax at once. "Gryffin's sister knows everything. She can be trusted."

"Gryffin's *sister*?" She wheeled her head around and looked at me incredulously. "Was that the smartest thing?"

"I needed an ally here, Celeste. She'd been the one to tell me how quickly Gryffin would dispose of me if I did not do his bidding. And she's known of Gryffin's Talent for years now."

"And what if she's telling him everything you say?"

"Then I'd be dead already."

Celeste pursed her lips, but in her eyes, I could tell she knew I had a point.

Just then, the maid's door creaked on its hinges as it swung open, and there sealed the end of our discussion. Cassia appeared with rose petals and linden leaves overflowing from her hands, followed by Vasilie and my other two chambermaids, stacked high with glass cups and saucers.

"We brought enough for all," Cassia said cheerfully, heading over to the table near my fire.

As Celeste went over to help, fumbling with her hands a little as she'd never been a handmaid before either, she passed one more glance toward me of disgruntled trust. She'd play along with me for now.

And I'd find some way to get us both out of here.

The following days at court were much more bearable with Celeste by my side, especially in Kathryn's unexplained absence. Even with the guests from the banquet milling around Snowmont's grounds, I was able to keep a pleasant smile on my face because, for the first time in two months, my happiness was genuine.

The people of Tarasyn were quite open about their Talents, and Lord and Lady DeGrey were in just as much shock as I was. At every turn, someone was doing something that was nothing short of miraculous. Setting candles alight with a hand full of flames, lifting chalices to their lips without using a muscle, strumming a harp or handling a flute effortlessly. I saw one woman conversing with a white-furred squirrel as if it were an everyday occurrence, which for her, it might have been. Lady DeGrey had been nearby, and upon seeing this woman, she'd murmured, "It's as if I've been taken to another world."

The atmosphere of Snowmont completely shifted with the presence of so many people chattering and laughing, feasting and drinking. The chilly air itself felt joyful and light. Everyone seemed thrilled to finally see what lay behind the grand walls of Snowmont, and the simple invitation to celebrate the king's engagement morphed into something more like a festival. One night, a Talented alchemist who had a reputation for dabbling in pyrotechny let loose his inventions just outside Snowmont's front gate, and great explosions of crimson and gold shot high above the castle, interrupting the black solemnity of the night sky. Anyone in or near Viridi would have been able to see them, and not a soul, including my own, was left unamazed.

However, the glares of the non-Talented did not go unnoticed. There was definitely some jealousy rooted behind their animosity.

In the midst of the glimmering shoots of fire raining back down to the mountain peaks, I found the chance to speak to Lady DeGrey unaccompanied. I sat next to her on the cold stone bench and hugged my cloak tightly around me. "Tarasyn is certainly surprising if nothing else, yes?"

"That is a very kind way to put it," the older woman mumbled, her hooded eyes never leaving the fire in the sky.

I chuckled. "Kind, yes. There are certainly other ways to describe the kingdom. And its kings," I added, lowering my voice.

Suddenly, she gave a wide grin and nodded. "Keep it looking light, dear. People are watching."

I laughed more loudly this time and glanced around us. A man dressed in the crimson and gold of Tarasyn stood close by, certainly not close enough to hear our muted words, but definitely within sight. I patted Lady DeGrey's hand. "We haven't gotten a chance to speak since the banquet."

"That has been by design," she admitted, grasping my hand in both of hers. "The less attention we draw, the better. My husband and I are lucky to be alive, as are you." She quickly waved to someone passing by, and the partygoer waved back with a confused look before disappearing into the crowd.

"As am I," I repeated quietly.

"This is an interesting game you are playing with the king," the woman said with an approving nod. "Clever of you to play into your worth. It is certainly keeping you alive for now."

Well, it surely hadn't taken her very long to figure out my ploy. Clever woman, she was. My respect for her only grew. Still, my stomach plummeted to hear my secret so blatantly revealed in the middle of Snowmont's courtyard.

"Yes, well, staying alive is a good goal for both of us," I said, tapping my foot to the music of the minstrels.

"He must actually care, seeing as all of this is for you."

I shook my head, but I kept a smile as I let my gaze travel over the crowd. "It is all to show Tarasyn's prosperity."

"My husband's brother did not throw parties such as these. Atroxis turned Hiddon into a very private kingdom."

"Lecevonia, as well," I murmured. "I hadn't been in contact with any of the other rulers for the past five years. And look at where it has gotten me."

To my surprise, Lady DeGrey snorted a genuine laugh. "Better here than married off to my nephews. And that is saying something, considering we are on the brink of death at every turn. Now, my niece—she would have made a fine queen. You remind me of her." She passed a sideways glance at me before smiling into the throng of people once more. "It was unfortunate that she was born after the oldest."

Lady DeGrey's niece. I hadn't known that King Theon and Queen Alys had had a daughter. When Sir Terrin delivered the news of the family's murders, he'd only mentioned the princes. Now, by the slight quiver in the woman's voice, I thought it best not to inquire. "How is Hiddon, after everything that has happened?"

Lady DeGrey's aloof smile wavered. "Aside from the smoldering embers of Vena, it's—no, even then, it's horrible. This king's brother wreaked irrecoverable havoc." She patted my hand again and found it within herself to chuckle. I glanced again at the Tarasynian man, who had inched just a smidge closer.

I leaned in close to her ear. "Is the unrest at the border as bad as it sounds?"

The woman laughed as if I'd just whispered a joke. "Undoubtedly." She heaved a sigh. "From the news we gather anyway. My husband and I are lying low for the time being at our manor in Vespost.

Thanking Haggard for our fortune." She looked up at the sky, and there was a mocking glint in her eye. "So much good fortune."

I wasn't quite sure what she'd meant by that. Fortune as in wealth? Having the means to get by without much contact with the invaders? Or some other kind of fortune, like a stroke of good luck?

"Speaking of my husband, I believe I see his balding head bobbing this way." She pointed into the crowd, and sure enough Lord DeGrey was making his way back to his wife, his body jostled to and fro through the mass of laughing people. His eyes still held the dead static I'd seen at the banquet a few nights prior.

I touched Lady DeGrey's hand softly. "Will he be all right?"

"This is not his first tragedy," she said. "He always pulls himself through whatever darkness intrudes upon our doorstep."

Lord DeGrey finally stumbled out of the crowd and straightened his vest, emblazoned with the magenta and green leaves of Hiddon, though the DeGreys' coat of arms had been removed from its chest, leaving a ragged edge of thread and surrender. When he saw me, he bowed deeply. "Your Majesty."

I quickly stood and helped him straighten by the elbow. I wrapped my arms around him in an embrace and leaned into his ear.

"No need to do that here. You are a king."

I looked at him squarely before turning back to his wife with a light laugh. The Tarasynian man had inched even closer to our bench, most certainly within earshot now.

"It was wonderful talking with you." I bowed my head to her and gave a tiny curtsy. "I do hope you enjoy your stay here at Snowmont."

"We are, my dear. I assure you." She smiled at me warmly, and her eyes were fierce in the light of the bursts of fire above us. "Take care."

That was the last chance I had to speak with Lady DeGrey. The rest of the week was a bustle of dinners, teas, and dances. Snowmont's gates were left open at all hours as partygoers came and went.

The best part of having guests at Snowmont was that Gryffin left me alone. *Actually* alone. He was too busy entertaining, as was I, and we really only appeared together in formal settings. I continued to play my part, gazing at him as lovingly as I could manage across the banquet table and holding his hand gently while dancing. But behind closed doors, Celeste heard my every complaint about his eager eyes and too-strong grip.

I was looking forward to introducing Celeste to Kathryn, for I knew Kathryn's ruthless candor would instantly win over Celeste. However, I hadn't seen Kathryn since the banquet, and one day, I finally found out why.

Celeste and I had been walking through Viridi's Atrium one day when we saw figures moving in the shadows of Snowmont's great pillars. For a fraction of a moment, I saw Kathryn's shining black hair slip into the light of the sun. She was pinned against the shaded wall by a man I'd never seen before. At first, I'd panicked and rushed toward them to intervene, but as we approached, Kathryn's throaty laugh told us she was exactly where she wanted to be.

That same evening, after dinner, I caught up with Kathryn before she could disappear into her rooms. She'd been easy to spot leaving in her bright orange skirts.

"You've been busy, haven't you?" I teased, sidling up next to her in the hall. My dress of jade green was a stark contrast to hers, the color of a tangerine. "Lamel keeping you awake at all hours of the night?"

Kathryn rolled her crystal blue eyes and spoke quietly, though we were the only ones present in the hall. "You wanted me to get information, didn't you? Well, that's what I've been doing."

"Oh." My mouth hung open in surprise. "Thank you."

"Yes, well, it's been exhausting."

"Oh, Kathryn," I said softly, guilt staining my tone. "I'm so sorry." The fiery woman hadn't struck me as someone who would do something she didn't want to do, and I certainly hadn't meant to pressure her in any way.

She only waved away my apology with a lighthearted smirk. "Lamel and I have had good moments too, I suppose. Despite his occasional idiocy."

"Don't do it anymore. Please," I said, catching her hand. "I don't need information so badly so as to make you do something you don't want to do. Especially something like this."

Kathryn shrugged stubbornly. "We'll see."

Still, I wanted to give her some escape. "Visit with me in my study? I have someone I'd like you to meet."

She looked back once toward her door before sighing and following after me.

Celeste was haphazardly pulling back my bedsheets when we entered my chambers. She straightened her shoulders at the sound of my door, and when she looked up and spotted Kathryn, she froze. In fact, they both did.

They appraised each other for a silent second before Celeste spoke. "You could be his twin." Beneath her wariness, her voice held a strange fullness, like the hot dew left in the wake of a summer rainstorm.

"But I'm much better than him in every way, I assure you," Kathryn responded with a smile, in that same sweltering tone.

"Kathryn has been an unwavering friend," I said, putting a hand on her arm. "And Kathryn, this is one of my oldest and dearest friends, Celeste."

"From Lecevonia?" Kathryn asked incredulously. "How did she get *here*?"

Celeste's story gushed out of her, complete with curses and ill wishes toward Gryffin. She started from the moment of her unwitting capture from Hillstone and ended with her reassignment as my chambermaid.

"Which you don't have to *actually* do," I said to her for what felt like the thousandth time. My childhood friend should not be drawing my bath and emptying my chamber pots.

But Celeste shrugged her shoulders. "I told Cassia I'd at the very least have your bed turned by the time she returned from the laundry wing."

"So they aren't here?" Kathryn asked, heading toward my study. "Good. Come with me."

We filed into the study after her. Behind closed doors, she relayed what she'd learned from General Lamel.

"It was harder than I thought it'd be, getting him to speak of military matters," she grumbled. "He always really only had one thing on his mind."

For Haggard's sake. I could never be grateful enough for Kathryn. "What did he say?"

She lowered her eyes to the scarlet rug beneath our feet. "Still no sign of official military action from Lecevonia. Lamel thinks your sister is scared to act. But, like you heard, things at the Hiddon border are rocky." Her gaze lifted to meet mine. "Gryffin did call off Tarasyn, but there have been a lot of casualties. Mostly Lecevonians, it sounded like, but some Tarasynians too."

A heavy boulder of anguish fell onto my chest and sent me sinking to the couch, stealing my breath from my lungs. My countryside—my *people*—cut down by Gryffin's forces. The people of the countryside had probably not heard a word spoken through Gryffin's Talent. They were clear-minded, fighting because they were able to realize who the enemy was. Anger toward my captor swelled, quickly replacing my distress. "Anything else?"

"Gryffin's been delivering messages to your sister, saying that you're all right and will return home after the wedding. I doubt his Talent works through letters, but I'm sure he is experimenting."

"Truly? To Isa?" Why would he even bother? Unless—he thought he no longer had Persuasion over her. "Has she written any reply?"

Kathryn shook her head silently.

I leaned back onto the couch cushion.

I'd of course hoped that Isa *had* written back, if only for me to hear her words again. But what was more, Isabele needed to take action—and soon. She could not sit there stressing, knowing what was happening at the border, without *doing* something about it. Those were our people being pillaged and killed out there. Surely, they knew what was happening. I wondered what my advisors thought—if they were trying to sway her pensiveness at all. Or if they were still trapped under Gryffin's Talent.

"Another thing," Kathryn said softly.

I looked up from the floor and met her steely gaze in the candlelight.

"Gryffin intends to have your wedding in six weeks' time."

My breathing hitched as the weight of those two words sent icy panic through my veins.

Six weeks.

That was so little time.

After that, I would be tethered to this man until he killed me.

Celeste placed a hand on my shoulder. "Rosie?"

"I'm all right," I said, waving her hand away.

But she shook her head and smiled wryly. "I know your lies when I see them."

She was right, of course. I'd just been given huge pieces of information, and I had no idea where to begin processing them. Gryffin did call off his troops at the border — good. He'd written Isabele, and despite the attacks at the border, she hadn't taken any action — bad. And my wedding to a man I both feared and hated was in just under two months — horrible.

I stubbornly fought against the panic, refused to let myself feel hopeless. There was nothing I could do about Isabele. Lecevonia was in her hands, and she would just have to find her place.

As for the wedding, well, I would just have to be away from here before then. No more waiting. I would figure out some way to get out of Snowmont, out of Tarasyn, with Celeste by my side. Maybe Kathryn too, if I could manage it. What to do once I was past the castle walls and deep in the frozen Tarasynian wilderness was another matter, but I would figure that out when I had to.

But there was one thing in this moment of which I was certain. I turned to Kathryn and grasped her hand once more. "Don't go to Lamel again. You deserve better."

A small smile tugged at the corners of her lips, and she nodded softly.

There was a quiet knock on the study door then, surprising all three of us. Only when Cassia poked her head through was I able to relax back into the couch.

Her cinnamon eyes burned with an urgent glow. "I have a letter for you, Your Majesty."

CHAPTER TEN

WHEN WE WERE children, Zeke and I had this game we'd play.

We would both pretend to be scouts for the castle, and we'd always have some perilous quest at hand. Save my sister from an erupting volcano. Meet with a witch who had turned Zeke's father into a lizard. Find a flying horse that could take us to a mythical fortress in the clouds.

One day, when we'd been tasked to sneak past angry Somoran villagers who wanted to fry us whole, we had come up with a way to write secret notes to one another, a method of writing that only we would know how to decipher.

Our first initial went in the top-left corner, always. I'd given Zeke a hard time as he'd always used a Z despite his true name being Ezekiel, but he said it'd be sneakier that way.

Our short messages would then make an upside-down V, starting in the bottom-left corner, traveling to the top row of letters, and back down to the lower-right corner. We'd then filled in every other blank space with a random letter, sometimes trying to make other words to throw off any wandering eye.

So, what I found on the weathered, tightly folded parchment made my soul dance in little circles, as if I were that young girl playing in Hillstone's pastures once again. To anyone else, it would have looked like just a mess of letters.

But I knew exactly what it hid in its nonsensical array.

Zeke's simple "are you alive" almost made me laugh aloud. I could feel his irritated sarcasm through his letters. Still, I couldn't possibly overlook the deep worry inlaid in this short message, either.

I didn't know how he'd gotten this note here, nor did I care.

He knew something was wrong.

"Quick, please, find parchment and a quill."

Cassia's hands shot into my line of vision, a plush goose's quill quivering with the swift movement over a tattered piece of parchment. As there was no proper desk in my study here, I leaned against the small end table beside the couch, dipped the quill into the well of red ink Kathryn had somehow found, and began scratching letters onto the parchment. By the time I finished, there was only a block of mismatched letters in my handwriting. However, I could see my message forming that upside-down V, with my R in the upper-left corner.

I folded it tightly and held it to my lips, silently and fervently willing it to return to Lecevonia as if the parchment could read my thoughts, let alone adhere to them. Then, I handed it back to Cassia. "Deliver this the same way by which it came."

The excitement of Zeke's letter quickly reduced to agony as the cold days stretched on. One by one, the banquet guests began to filter out of Snowmont and on their journeys home. As a finale of sorts, Gryffin announced our wedding date—six weeks from now, just as Kathryn had said—and invited everyone to return for an even grander party. When Lord and Lady DeGrey took their leave, Lady DeGrey had pulled me in for an embrace and echoed her last words to me in my ear, more fervently than last time. "Take care."

So, yes, agony was the right word.

Gryffin, however, was overflowing with excitement every time he burst into my chambers. And today, just a day after the final guests had left Snowmont, his eyes shone with a special type of thrill.

"My Rosemary," he crooned, taking my hands in his. "I have something very special for you."

I lowered my eyes in a way I hoped to be demure. I certainly did not want anything *special* from him. I wanted to spit on the carpet at his feet, to hit him as hard as I could. But instead, I softened my voice. "Do you?"

He gently pulled on my hands, coaxing me away from the book I'd been reading and out of my study. I glanced bewilderedly at Celeste, who had jumped into action of stoking the fireplace at the sound of Gryffin's entrance, before the door to my chambers shut between our gazes.

As we descended the stairs, floor after floor, an apprehension began to take hold of me. I narrowed my eyes as the grand door to the Dining Hall passed by, then the library, then the Atrium. My curiosity finally outbid my stubbornness. "Where are we going?"

Gryffin smiled as he turned the knob to a door I hadn't noticed before, discreetly tucked between the courtyard and the conservatory with the same colorful pattern of the wall painted across it. "A surprise," was all he had to say.

Behind the door, a stone passageway forged ahead into darkness.

My alarm immediately halted me in my tracks, but Gryffin coaxed me forward with a tug on my hand.

When he closed the door behind us, the light of the Great Hall disappeared, and the corridor was so dimly lit that I only had his hand to follow. I actually found myself inching closer to him as we walked, and he chuckled.

And it was *cold.* So cold. As though the rough stone walls radiated ice. I figured that this must be part of the older Snowmont, dug out long ago by miners. As the temperature continued to drop and the air grew stagnant, a realization sprang to the forefront of my mind.

We were inside a mountain.

And back home, only one thing was stowed away inside Hillstone's slope.

I tried to pull my hand free, but his grip tightened.

"Gryffin—" My voice caught in my throat.

The fear in my voice made him stop and face me. His eyes glinted in the flickering flame of the nearest torch as confusion knit his brow together. "Where do you think I am taking you?" he asked slowly.

The dungeons. I thought he was leading me to the dungeons, to the iron chains I'd evaded for the past nine weeks. He'd discovered my game, my own ploy, and decided he had no more use for me.

Even here in the dark, my wide eyes told him more than I'd ever meant to. Gryffin cocked his head to the side, and laughter shook his curls. "I see . . ." he said slowly. His hand slowly shifted, closing around my wrist like a shackle. He pulled me to him, his hand tight, and his arm encircled my waist, holding me to his chest. His breath whispered against my neck as he exhaled. "What did you do that would put you in my prison?" His teeth grazed my earlobe as the question raked its nails across any sense of security I'd had before now.

My fear seized my thoughts, froze my features, only sending goosebumps along my neck where his breath had warmed my skin against the chill. I silently cursed myself and wondered where I'd been careless, what had given away my true intentions—

Until Gryffin's lips pressed against my skin, just below my ear. Then along my jaw. Under my chin. The corner of my mouth.

As his lips found mine in the dark, I was able to relax. My secret was safe. This was just *his* game right now.

I fell back into imagining Zeke's arm wrapped around me, Zeke's hand holding my wrist. Zeke's lips moving against my own. *His* sigh of contentment, rather than my captor's.

His hand fell from my wrist and came to rest on the side of my neck. Our feet shuffled as he guided us over to the wall, his arm around me protecting me from the cold stone, and Gryffin—no, Zeke—leaned into me.

The lines of his body melted against mine, and I simply let it happen. His lips never left mine as his free hand stroked my neck, my collarbone, down the side of my dress to my waist, and he held his grip firm there.

The fervor radiating from him stole the breath out of my lungs, and I found myself pushing back into him, enjoying the warmth of his hands that contrasted with the iciness of the dark corridor. My lips parted, and his breath mingled with mine for a long, aching heartbeat. Then he ventured toward my neck, and the touch of his lips at my jaw made me shiver.

"Ah, Rose," he whispered.

Rose.

But spoken through the wrong voice.

Heated tears pricked my eyes as my illusion of Zeke slowly fell away. Fighting to stifle a sob, I turned my face away from him and bit my lip.

Gryffin mistook that as a struggle for self-control, and his deep chuckle rumbled his chest, pressed so tightly against mine.

"You're right," he said, and he kissed my cheek tenderly. "We shouldn't get carried away—not here."

Though my voice came as a whisper, it was as hard as the stone wall against my back. "Please don't call me 'Rose.'"

At that, he stiffened. His hands loosened his grip as he backed away from me, just enough to look at my face.

With his hands off my body, I was able to think a bit straighter, lie more evenly. "I prefer Rosemary."

Silence filled our little space as his eyes appraised me, and finally, he broke a smile. "All right," he said, nodding his head once. "Rosemary it shall be then."

He leaned against the wall next to me—I didn't understand *how* he didn't jump out of his skin at the cold—and remained quiet, thoughtful, arms crossed over his chest. The heat in the dark corridor had begun to dissipate, a chill seeping in once more in the space between us.

Then his deep voice broke the silence. "Why did you think I was taking you to Snowmont's dungeons?"

What could I say that was safe?

Nothing. Absolutely nothing.

So instead, I put on my best sultry smile and slowly ran a finger along his jaw. "If I told you, you might actually lock me away." I might've laid on the rasp in my voice a bit too thickly, but he certainly didn't seem upset by that. He laughed and caught my fingers with his, but before he could say anything I turned and looked around the corridor. "Where are we?"

He nodded, brought back once again to the subject of my "surprise," and pushed himself from the wall. "This corridor does *not* lead to the dungeons, though I can see how you'd think so. No, instead it connects the castle to the Snowmont's craftsmen. And craftswomen." He winked. "Dug through the mountain centuries ago for easier travel."

Gryffin led me forward by the hand. Soon, the air became fresher, and natural light began to infiltrate the passageway. "And which workshop are we visiting today?" I asked.

"You will see," he responded, grinning.

Hillstone's blacksmith, Jacobin, crossed my mind, and a sliver of hope gleamed at the possibility. Could Gryffin be having a sword made for me?

I could now see the end of the corridor. Shoots of brilliant sunlight found their way through the cracks of the aged wooden door and lightened the passageway brighter than I'd ever seen it. When I looked up at Gryffin, his eyes were burning with excitement.

Gryffin pushed open the door, and I had to shield my eyes from the sun's rays bouncing off every facet of the snow. Once I could see beyond the stars dotting my vision, I noticed that we had stepped into a world of little shops.

The buildings were all splashed with bright colors to match the rest of the city. Carts and barrows pushed past us through the snow, the hammer falls and chatters of workmanship falling between the squeals of wooden wheels. Though bustling, the shops lacked the urgency of Hillstone's craftsman's village the last time I'd been there. Though to be fair, the threat of war wasn't plaguing the atmosphere here.

As Gryffin and I stepped through the snow, several Tarasynians stuttered to a stop in their tracks and offered a quick bow before scurrying back to their tasks. Their glances often lingered, though I was unsure if it was my presence or Gryffin's that caused their interest.

The clashing of mallets and anvils found us through the buzz of activity, and I looked to Gryffin, hopeful. But too soon, the hammering faded as Gryffin led me farther into the village.

Instead, he approached a nondescript powder-blue storefront just as a boy ran through the yellow door, arms full of silks and cottons.

I shot my eyes to Gryffin again. "A seamstress?"

Gryffin smiled and opened the door for me, and as I stomped my boots free of snow, he called, "Mister Hilderic, she is here."

The name peaked my attention. A seamster, rather!

A man dressed in a smart golden-threaded vest appeared around the corner as Gryffin closed the door behind us. He bowed deeply, his graying hair falling in front of his face. "Your Majesty," he said with gusto, taking my hand in his.

"My Rosemary," Gryffin said, "this is Mister Hilderic, our Master Seamster. He is the one who has been making your fine gowns since you've been here."

The man straightened, and as he moved his hair from his face, the red flecks in his hazel eyes gleamed brightly back at me. "It is such a

pleasure to meet you, my queen, rather than just your measurements."
He offered me a kind, broad grin.

This man was the first Talented I'd spoken to directly aside from
Gryffin, and I'd have been lying if I said his eyes didn't unsettle me.
But the sincerity in his voice sent a wave of guilt through me, and I
struggled to push away the disquiet in my stomach. I tried to recover
with a polite smile. "And you, Mister Hilderic."

Gryffin took my hand and started toward the rear of the shop.
"Your surprise is just back here. I wanted to wait until after all our
guests left. I thought it'd be less overwhelming for you."

The seamster followed us through his shop, and when we reached
a wall of draping fabrics, he pulled aside the cloth and gestured us
through.

My heart dropped as hard as a lead brick sinks to the bottom of the
sea.

The gossamer and lace of three wedding gowns taunted me from
the bodices of their wicker models. Gryffin pulled at my hand, and
though my feet carried me after him to the nearest dress, I could only
think about how little time I had left.

"Mister Hilderic has been working tirelessly to ensure you had the
best selection," Gryffin murmured, smiling against my ear.

The dresses were indeed more beautifully made than any piece of
clothing I'd ever seen, and each one was vastly different from the next.
The high-necked satin of one could hardly be compared to the
intricate entwining of pearls and lace of the next, or the sheer, billowing
chiffon of the other. What they did all have in common, however, was
that they'd been embroidered with shimmering gold and crimson
thread throughout the cream fabrics, from the cuffs of the long sleeves
to the tails of the fur-lined capes. Each had been made for a cold,
Tarasynian wedding.

I hoped my distress passed for awe as I stared wide-eyed at the gowns. Trying my best to ignore Gryffin's excited grin beaming beside me, I turned to the seamster. "Your work is exquisite, Mister Hilderic."

"It is an honor, my queen," the man said, bowing deeply. "I feel that my Talent's purpose is to help people feel their best, and I assure you—in any of *these* gowns, you will own the room." He winked.

His answer made me laugh, and it calmed some of the unease his eyes had initially caused. Perhaps not all Talented were selfish like my captor.

Gryffin laid a chilling kiss in my hair. "I'll have them delivered to your room, that your ladies may help you try them on."

"Mmm, thank you," I said, cursing the tremor in my voice. I hoped to Haggard he couldn't hear it.

"I do have one more surprise for you." He turned away from me and walked back through the fabrics into the shop.

I wasn't sure how many more surprises I could take.

He returned with a black box in his hands. Its shape was a perfect square, giving no hint as to what lay inside it, but I—quite unfortunately—had my suspicions.

"I stopped by the goldsmith earlier this morning," he said, returning to my side. "The moment I received word that she'd completed it, I had to see it." With a smile, he slowly unlatched the box, and the top popped open with a foreboding click.

An almost ethereal glow greeted me as I lifted the lid. The crown inside glittered and flashed as its emeralds and diamonds caught the light of the lanterns.

"The gold is from my mother's crown, melted down and made anew for Tarasyn's new queen. I had it designed in reminiscence of your ring." He lifted my hand, the engagement ring suddenly so heavy, and pressed his lips to my fingers. "An emerald-laden crown for my emerald-laden bride," he said quietly, eyes searching mine.

I looked away before Gryffin could see the panic-stricken fever in my eyes and started to close the lid, cutting off the very unwelcome glow. "Thank you, Gryffin—"

But his hands caught the lid. "Don't you want to try it on?"

I swallowed painfully. "I . . ." How could I tell him no, that this was not my crown? That the overwhelming betrayal of wearing another kingdom's symbol of authority scorched my insides?

But I couldn't tell him any of that. I simply had to try to smile and say, "Of course I do."

He reached his hand inside the box and took hold of the crown. He placed it onto my head gingerly, though I thought he did that more for the sake of the crown than my skull.

"There," he said. He turned me toward the long mirror in the corner of the room.

My wide eyes stared back at me, shining underneath the emeralds, the expression in them thankfully unreadable. The delicate golden strands of the crown wrapped around the sides of my head like a carefully constructed bird's nest, vines of golden leaves woven precisely into place, the emeralds and diamonds like trinkets that had caught the bird's eye.

This crown belonged on a true Tarasynian queen's head.

And that would not be me.

If anything, the dresses, the crown, the fineries of the queen's quarters—it all flared only stronger the need to return to my kingdom. If getting home would be the one thing I could control—so be it. *No. More. Waiting.*

With a deep inhale, I gathered my wits. I turned my head from side to side with a painted smile and started gushing praises. "It's absolutely beautiful, Gryffin. Thank you. And these dresses?" I waved my arm around the room happily, sighing as I did so. "Who knew Tarasyn held such talent?" I almost winced at the irony of that phrase. "Everything is truly so breathtaking." I stood on my toes and touched my lips to his cheek.

Gryffin's ecstatic laugh filled the small room as he held me to him in a tight embrace, and out of the corner of my eye, Mister Hilderic's cheeks lifted with a proud grin.

Gryffin pressed his lips to my ear. "My queen."

Not quite.

By the time I returned to my rooms that evening, Gryffin had kept true to his word. My three dresses had been delivered to my chambers, and Celeste had wrapped herself in the satin train of the one closest to the open window.

Kathryn sat on the edge of my bed with her arms crossed, studying the dresses through narrowed eyes. "My brother has gone fully into this, hasn't he?"

I closed the door behind me and secured the lock. "You can have every one of those gowns, Kathryn. I'm not wearing them."

Celeste looked at me incredulously. "You won't even try them on? Rosie, even *you* must be dying to see how these look. These fabrics are the finest I've ever touched in my life."

But I shook my head. "I've had enough of playing Tarasynian Queen." I crossed over to the window and glanced down at the courtyard. "Where are Cassia and the others?"

"In the kitchens," Celeste answered slowly. "What's going on?"

For a moment I couldn't answer, afraid of my own words. Down at the seamster's, the idea of running had seemed easy. But beyond the courtyard below me, beyond the city, a tight and foreboding evergreen forest stood like a wall between me and my kingdom.

"I'm losing time," I finally said. "If I don't get out of here, I'm going to find myself chained to that man's side, and Lecevonia will be left to his whim. I need to escape."

Kathryn looked away from the gowns and set her squinted gaze on me. "Do you have a plan?"

I bit my lip. "Yes, albeit vague. I'll need help. Celeste"—I turned toward my friend—"you're coming with me. And you too," I said, meeting Kathryn's gaze again. "If you'd like."

But Kathryn hesitated. "I . . ."

Then, to my surprise, Celeste knelt down beside the bed and took hold of Kathryn's hand. "Please. Come with us."

Kathryn looked between me and Celeste, uncertainty stirring in her blue eyes. Finally, she settled her gaze on Celeste, and she slowly shook her head. "I can't."

A moment of surprised silence gripped the room as they stared at each other.

Kathryn tore her eyes away and looked down toward the rug. "I'd love to, but—my place is here."

Celeste scoffed. "With your crite of a brother? Really."

"Not with my brother," Kathryn responded tightly. "With my people."

Celeste's eyes narrowed in anger. "With the general, then."

"With my *people*." Kathryn glared at her and pulled her hand free, holding it back into her lap.

The unexpected tension in the room stretched on as I glanced back and forth between the two of them. Something had grown between them while I'd been off entertaining guests or placating Gryffin—something strong enough to cause this sudden rift.

"Well, if you decide otherwise, we'll be ready," I said quietly to Kathryn. "In the meantime, we'll need supplies. And maps."

Celeste stood and turned to me—or, rather, from Kathryn—roughly. "What exactly is your plan?"

I walked over to the bed and sat next to Kathryn. "Gryffin showed me a passageway today, to the craftsmen's village. We can escape through there. It'll be easy to slip away unnoticed."

"Unnoticed?" Kathryn asked. "You are soon to be the *queen*. What makes you think anything you do will go unnoticed?"

Celeste waved her away. "And then?"

"Well, then we make our way back to Lecevonia."

"Through the forest?" Kathryn looked at me with wide, disbelieving eyes. "How? On foot?"

I met her gaze in my periphery. "Is there any other option?"

"You'll freeze!"

"I'd rather contend with frostbite than hand over Lecevonia to Gryffin on a gilded platter!"

"That is ridiculous! He'll only lie if you *die!*"

"We'll be prepared," Celeste said, cutting in. "I surely don't want to freeze to death either."

Kathryn pursed her lips, seething, and threw her hands in the air. "Well, I can at least be sure you have a pair of horses." She stood and marched over to my window, mumbling as she went. "*On foot*, how ridiculous."

Celeste rolled her eyes, but she otherwise ignored Kathryn. "I think this can work. We'll bring clothes, maps, and a fire striker, and—"

"Food?"

The new voice startled us, and dread ripped its way through my

- 145 -

chest as my inhale caught painfully in my throat. We all turned toward the maid's door, and Cassia and Vasilie stood there in the entrance, wide eyed and as still as statues.

My plan was done for before it'd even begun. They'd turn on their heels and go to their king immediately. What was the point of me ever trying to be secretive?

But they didn't move.

I reached my hand out to them slowly. "Cassia. Vasilie."

"You're leaving us?" Vasilie's quiet question sat so heavily in the air.

"Please," I whispered. My eyes traveled between my two ladies. "Help me return home."

Silence laid between us, their stares so startled and their stillness so profound that I began to lose hope. Vasilie's eyes even flickered to the door separating Gryffin's chambers from my own.

I was done for.

Finally, Cassia spoke, filling the void with her voice, her words clipped and rushed.

"I suppose I always thought that there was something off with the two of you. Between His Majesty keeping your door locked and you looking so dour when you agreed to marry him—"

"Cassia," I said urgently. "Will you help me?"

She walked up to me and straightened her shoulders. "I serve *you*, my queen. Of course I will help."

"And I as well," Vasilie added bravely. She took my hand, still outstretched, and bowed. "Whatever you need."

I breathed out the relief I'd been stubbornly holding onto, and I let a smile cross my lips. "Thank you. Thank you both, so much."

"When are we leaving?" Celeste asked.

"The sooner the better. As soon as we can figure out what we need and gather it all together."

Kathryn had looked away from me and toward the courtyard window, but she said softly, "Three weeks should be enough time. I'll be sure that Gryffin doesn't suspect a thing."

The sadness in her voice triggered a heartache of my own. I didn't want to leave Kathryn. She has been a blessing to me here in Tarasyn. She was quite possibly the only reason I was still alive today. And even though she was younger than me, she has taught me more than I'd ever dreamed. Of confidence, of loyalty, of the Talented.

But not only that. She was my friend, and I'd found a confidante in her. A person I could trust entirely.

A sister.

I joined her by the window. "I understand why you feel that you can't leave. Everything I do—everything I've *ever* done—is for my people."

Kathryn chuckled halfheartedly. "I know. Frostbite and all."

I nodded. "Frostbite and all. But it won't come to that."

She only shrugged.

With a new idea in mind, I nudged her shoulder. "Food might be scarce. I'll need to learn how to hunt."

Kathryn snorted. "You? Get your hands bloody?"

"You shouldn't underestimate me," I countered. After all, I'd felt the hot sting of blood on my hands before. I quickly shook the memory away. "But I imagine hunting with a sword isn't very easy."

She turned to me in horror. "Oh no, you can't do that. You would never be able to get close enough to use it, and if you did, you'd massacre any viable meat. You need"—her eyes brightened then—"a bow and arrow."

~HILLSTONE~
ZEKE

"Sir Ezekiel?"

Boars, *finally*.

That voice was the one I've been waiting for the past two weeks, though I'd never heard it before in my life. I turned around, my heels sliding in the hay covering the stable's floor, and found Xal standing behind me.

Loryna had been right—the boy wasn't so small anymore. With his broad shoulders and thick arms from years of carting around sacks of horse feed, he certainly wasn't inconspicuous. I didn't know how he smuggled letters from place to place without getting caught.

But it didn't matter how he did it. I was grateful nonetheless as he passed a tightly folded note to me.

As soon as my hand grabbed the parchment, it felt as if a taut chord had been struck, like a string, a connection, tethering Rose to me.

"Did you see her?"

He shook his head. "Only her handmaid."

I swore under my breath. But I should've known even a glimpse was too much to ask for.

I glanced at Xal. "Thank you, truly," I said as I backed away through the aisle. "I'll have another for you this evening. I'll compensate you fivefold if you wait for me before your next trip!"

Without waiting for his response, I hurried through the stable doors and out into the late spring heat.

As I jogged through the courtyard, I unfolded the parchment and almost tripped over my own feet at the sight of Rose's rolling letters, her little R scrawled in the upper-left spot.

Alive and not alone.

Alive. Rose was alive, and free enough to have parchment and ink close by. That was a good sign.

Not alone. What did that mean?

I ran through the double doors of Hillstone and didn't slow until I found Isabele in the library, sorting through the charred books that hadn't been entirely reduced to ashes in the fire.

As I approached, she sighed and held out a ruined book to me. "This one was one of my favorites, and it's practically blackened through."

"I've got something that'll make you forget about any burned book, Isa." I thrust the letter toward her. "From your sister."

"From my—?" Isabele looked at me in shock and, tucking the book under her arm, frantically grabbed at the piece of parchment. "How?"

"Don't worry about that."

She quickly unfolded the letter, but after a single glance she rolled her eyes. "Oh, for Haggard's sake, I can't read this. You two never taught me. But it's her handwriting!" She hugged the letter to herself. "What does it say?"

"'Alive and not alone,'" I said. "Someone is with her in Tarasyn."

"With her in Tarasyn?" Isabele looked toward the floor before turning her baffled eyes back to me. "Who—who would be there with her?"

"Send me there," I pleaded, "and I can find out."

Isabele's lips pursed as she looked at me. She put the book tucked under her arm on top of a stone perch, where a now-shattered vase had once stood, and said grimly, "I will. But I'm not sending you alone. Amos finally came to."

"He did?" I raised my eyebrows. "How is he?"

Her voice grew quiet. "Furious. He's making me nervous."

"Where is he, Isa?"

Isabele worried at her bottom lip before answering. "Follow me."

We left sooty footsteps in our wake as I followed Isabele back down the main staircase to the first floor. Instead of turning left toward the kitchens, we turned right, down the path to the healer's wing. Amos's voice boomed through the corridor, carrying the weight of his anger along with it.

"Get me on a horse *now*, or in the name of the freckin' Solstice, I'm going to—"

"Sir Amos," a healer's softer voice chided, "please, calm down—"

"Like Haggard I will!"

"Amos, please," Lord Brock's more refined voice said as we rounded the doorway. "We will work everything out. I promise you."

Everyone in the room jumped to their feet as we entered. Lord Brock and the healer bowed their heads to Isabele in greeting. "Your Highness."

"Princess," Amos immediately started, his monstrous voice rounding on us. "I didn't come forward to be written off as mad and sanctioned off to a sick bed!"

Isabele froze at the confrontation.

So I deftly positioned myself between his anger and Isabele's distress. "Easy, Sir Amos." I lifted my hand peaceably. "What's going on?"

"We've all been fooled." Amos spit on the floor. "I don't know what type of sorcery that crite from Tarasyn has done, but he tricked us all. Everyone! Not a single word of his can be trusted. I'm going to kill him."

I had to fight a smug smile off my face. I glanced toward Lord Brock, who had probably heard this story from Amos already, expecting an eye roll or a shake of his head. But instead, his lips turned downward into a tight frown, his eyes grave.

"All right," I said. "How do you know?"

"I'm going to kill him," Amos repeated between his teeth. His eyebrows came together, his eyes enveloped in their shadows. "He deserves the worst possible death—worse than any man he's surely killed. When I found . . . when I . . ." He faltered, then, and fell backward onto the mattress.

His breathing slowed, painfully so, and his voice shook as he finally looked at me and went on with his story. "I tried to rejoin with the queen and Thomas the moment I could. Prince Gryffin"—he sneered through the name—"had already left the streets. Left King Roderich lying dead. He'd said there were horses in the forest, knew where they were. I didn't, but I had to try to go after them. I *had* to be sure they'd made it out of the capitol. I found the trail of broken branches, left by Thomas and the queen surely, and followed it." Amos swallowed loudly and trudged on through his story. "When I found Thomas in the woods, throat cut like an animal, with the queen and the prince nowhere in sight, I immediately suspected the prince had something to do with it."

He took a deep breath. "Then, I felt something happen. As if my brain could *think* again, though I hadn't realized anything was wrong before." He looked away from me toward the floor again.

"What do you mean?" I asked slowly.

His eyes darted around the room. "I'm telling you, Prince Gryffin did *something* to us. All of us. I'm *not* deranged!"

"I believe you," Lord Brock murmured. His grim voice cut through the tension of the healer's room.

"At first I thought it was your anger and drunken madness talking," Lord Brock continued, brow pinched. "But—I realized that I felt it too. Slowly, as the weeks have passed, my mind has been returning to me, almost like a fog thinning. I couldn't shake my thought that Gryffin had taken Queen Rosemary to safety, but something about it felt wrong. Off. As if I were *convincing* myself of that story. Then, when Sir Amos had his say, my fog lifted, and my mind jolted back into place."

What they were saying made no sense. A fog?

Then, Rose's words from months prior came back to me. *Isabele has been seeing a haze.*

I turned to her. "You said there was a haze around Gryffin."

Isabele nodded and looked down to the floor. "I've thought something was wrong from the moment I saw him at Clara's birthday. I just . . . didn't know what it meant. I *still* don't know what it means."

"Have you told the other advisors?" I asked Amos, my impatience sharpening my question like a blade. "The colonels and general?" I rounded on my heel to face Isabele once more. "We need to go to Tarasyn. Now. I'm going."

"As am I," Amos said, pounding his fist onto the stone wall beside him.

"You are going," Isabele said, pointing to me sharply. "But, Amos, I don't—"

"I can handle it."

Isabele, normally so meek, straightened her shoulders and hardened her expression. "No, I don't think you can."

Amos stood abruptly from his cot, fists clinched. "I can handle it! That man killed my comrade of thirteen years!"

I moved in front of Isabele once again and gave Amos a warning glance. If it came to a fight, I would probably lose, but I didn't care.

"Sir Amos." Lord Brock's bark was threatening. "You are a respectable man, but please, know your place here."

Amos looked between us and blinked. Reeling back, he sat back down onto his cot and bowed his head. "Of course. Your Highness, I apologize. I lost myself."

I felt a heavy tinge of pity for Amos. This was not the man who had laughed and cracked jokes, had the bravery to both tease Rose and take her up in her swords training. This man was darker, plagued with anger and guilt, his resolve loosened by grief. Yes, Amos had lost himself. And I understood why. I would have too.

After another second's silence, Isabele sighed. "Zeke, prepare to leave. Take Sir Roger with you. And Sir Terrin." She looked at me with steely eyes. "Bring my sister home."

CHAPTER ELEVEN

CASSIA PASSED THE folded note to me, parchment still warm from her pocket.

Zeke's words jumped from the parchment, clear in his heavy hand. *We are coming.* He hadn't bothered with encryption this time—he'd been in a hurry.

I let myself fall into my cushioned seat near the window. I was going to see Zeke soon, and I was going home. I turned to Celeste excitedly before remembering she was down in the laundry wing.

I tried to figure out a timeline. It'd taken Gryffin and me almost a week just to get to Pruin, and another to reach Viridi. But we hadn't taken the main road. My first message from Zeke had arrived two weeks ago, so I could assume it took about a week for our letters to reach their destinations. If the letter took a week to reach me here in Viridi, that probably meant Zeke, and whomever else "we" included, were already on their way. On horseback and following the main road, it should only take them a little over a week to arrive in Viridi.

But were they taking the main road?

If they were trying to stay discreet, probably not.

I could assume, then, that it would take them about two weeks to get here. If they'd left right after sending this note—however these notes getting here so quickly—then they were only a week away now!

What was their plan once they got here? I imagined Zeke slipping his way into the capitol undetected, somehow finding his way past the guards and into Snowmont—

The image horrified me.

I tried to remind myself that he was good at his job. And wasn't this what I'd been hoping would happen? A rescue attempt?

Gryffin had stayed true to the timeline he'd set thus far—in four weeks, I was to be standing at his side in front of the entirety of the kingdom as his queen. And the marriage vow was to be my prison and Lecevonia's downfall.

But that didn't matter, because I was to be leaving on my own with Celeste two weeks before.

So I would wait for Zeke. I had no idea what his plan was, but I trusted him to have it figured out. If he didn't show in time, I would stick with my original plan, and perhaps he could meet Celeste and me in Pruin. But no matter what, I was leaving. This was something I could control.

I scribbled this out on a piece of parchment and sealed it tightly. If our messenger rode fast, they could catch Zeke and his party before they arrived in Viridi. I felt an exciting little ache in my chest as I thought about wrapping my arms around Zeke again, and a tiny smile pulled at my lips.

Just as Cassia left through the maid's door with my note, Kathryn barged into my chambers, arms loaded down with wicker baskets. A loud squawk sounded from Gryffin's office as my door ricocheted off the back wall, and I gave Kathryn a warning glance.

"Oh, don't worry about him," she said, dismissing my concern with a shake of her head. She plopped all of the baskets down onto my bed and began unpacking one of them. "Look at this gorgeous coat I bought today." She held up a garment of white fur.

This had been our routine for the past week. She'd go to the markets in town, buy an outrageous amount of *stuff,* and deliver her findings to my room—supplies for Celeste and me. Coats, shoes, and hats, and leather bags in which to store them all. A length of rope. A small knife. Today, along with the fur coat, she'd found two more pairs of stockings and a fire striker.

I hugged the coat to me before stuffing it into my armoire with our other spoils. "Thank you so much, Kathryn."

"And . . ." she said in a singsong voice, "I've gotten the archery field ready."

Excitement carried my feet as I found my cloak and followed her out into the hall and down the stairs. She took me outside and into the courtyard, and through a wrought-iron gate that opened to a slim passageway between two outer walls of the castle. Finally, past the castle walls, I saw an open field that edged the forest just beyond the city's boundary. Snow was falling over the forest, leaving the trees' needles hanging low on their branches. But over the field, not a flake had touched the grass. That still took some getting used to for me.

Kathryn marched across the field and approached the wooden stand of bows, and strumming the bowstrings thoughtfully, she looked me up and down. "Let's see, you are just a bit shorter than me, so a smaller bow might do you well." I was reminded of Gryffin finding a sword in the armory that "fit" me.

She picked up a bow that met her expectations and handed it to me. "Here, try this."

I gingerly clutched it by the grip in the center of the limbs and felt its weight in my hands. To my surprise, it felt . . . *right*. Comfortable. Almost familiar.

I shook my head at the notion and looked at Kathryn. "I think this one will do."

Kathryn smiled. "Perfect. Here." She swung a quiver of feather-fletched arrows toward me, and I slung it over my shoulder.

"All right. Now, take a planted stance, shoulder facing the target." She nocked my first arrow for me, then she backed away and nocked her own. "Watch me, and follow my lead."

She planted her feet into the frozen grass, a direct right angle from the distant targets painted onto hay bales, and hoisted her bow in front of her. She drew back on the string, her elbow perfectly aligned, the bow creaking as its limbs bent to her will.

Then, silence. I heard her take a drawn breath, and her soft exhale released a cloud of warm breath swirling through the icy air.

Then she released her arrow, the zing of the bowstring snapping back into place ringing loud through the silent field. The thud of her arrow finding its mark quickly followed as it embedded itself deeply into the straw.

She turned to me, smiling brightly, and with wide eyes and pursed lips, I gave her a little bow.

"After you shoot a few times, you'll get a feel of the bow. How much you need to pull back, at what angle you should release . . ."

Her voice trailed as I held the bow steadfast in front of me. It was a beautiful weapon, with its sweeping wooden limbs engraved with intricate twisting designs, similar to the swirls of the dark metal in the hilt of Gryffin's sword. It felt welcome in my grasp.

The sun did little to warm my gloved hands as I pulled back on the bowstring. It was much more taut than I expected, and I almost lost my grip on my arrow. My breath warmed my fingers at my chin, the feathers of the arrow tickling my lips in the cold breeze. The target in front of me seemed so far away as it taunted me from across the field. But I kept my eyes locked on its center, and with a shallow exhale, I let my arrow fly.

An image of an archery lesson with Papa blitzed across my memory: my feet planted in dry fallen leaves, a chill reddening my nose, and my arrow never finding its target that day. *We will keep practicing,* he'd said. But we never did return to the archery range. The next week, he'd started coughing.

In six years since, my arrow had never found its mark.

Here in Tarasyn, however, the thud of my arrow's impact registered in my brain before its location in the center of the target did.

Kathryn reeled back beside me. "I thought you didn't know how to shoot."

I shook my head, my mind clouding in bewilderment. "I . . . I don't. Didn't." I looked down at the glistening bow. "I haven't touched a bow since I was thirteen." Still, this felt much more natural than holding a sword in my hand.

Curious now, and feeling more at ease with each second, I nocked a second arrow. Carefully taking my stance, I fired toward the target once more.

It landed directly next to my first shot.

Kathryn's gaze turned to me again sharply. "You've lied to me." Her accusation held such an indignance that I almost believed her.

"No! I . . ." The wobbling shaft of my second hit stole any explanation I tried to conjure, even to myself.

"Then how?"

Then, a distinct, brusque voice rose from behind me. "Look at me, Rosemary. Now."

The command made my skin slither. If I had hackles like a dog, they would have been bristled. Boars, I was already holding back a growl. And Kathryn's quiet curse told me she hadn't heard Gryffin approach, either.

I turned on my heel, the cold wind only growing colder.

Gryffin was already there. He grabbed my chin in his hand, and on reflex, I slapped at his hand and tried to turn my face away.

But his hand stayed strong against my chin, and he forced me to look directly at him. "Calm down, Rosemary," he said with a sigh. His pupils jumped back and forth as he took in every inch of my surprised gaze. The red flecks burned through his blue irises, and I couldn't read his expression. Intensity, certainly. But also—hope? Or anger?

Finally, I narrowed my eyes. "I will *not* be treated this way. Let go of me."

He chuckled once and slowly relaxed his fingers until I could yank my chin from his hand. He held his hands up, taking a step back.

"That was uncalled for," I snapped. "And if I am to be your queen you will never grab me like that again."

Gryffin shrugged his shoulders. "No worries. I only needed to see."

"See *what?*"

But he ignored my question. "Cassia told me I could find you out here. You are a natural, it seems." He smiled gently, as if the encounter a few seconds ago meant nothing.

"See what?" I asked again.

Kathryn's whisper from behind me gave my answer. "Your eyes."

Then I understood.

A Talent hadn't crossed my mind. Talents had seemed very "other," ambiguous, even after all that I had learned and the Talented I had met. Aside from Zeke's question so many weeks ago that seemed like nonsense at the time, I never had a reason to seriously consider if I had a Talent until now. But their reactions gave me my answer, and an unexpected disappointment rippled through me. I tried to erase any emotion from my face.

"Why were you looking for me?" I asked.

"I have something I'd like to show you." He nodded toward the stand of bows. "Why are you learning archery?"

My lie passed like butter through my lips. "The same reason I wanted to learn how to use a sword." That was not completely false anyhow. Survival included many scenarios.

Gryffin studied me with pursed lips, and he glanced past me to Kathryn before speaking again. "All right then. Afterwards, come to my office in my chambers."

I hadn't seen Gryffin's office when I'd been in his rooms before, but it carried the same dark aesthetic as the rest of his chambers. Black marble, dark wood, smoke and honey. His office seemed to hold more books than the entirety of Snowmont's library. Shelves upon shelves lined the walls behind his desk, which was topped with neatly stacked papers. Corvus's perch stood in the corner. The wretched bird wasn't here, but his caw through the open window did not sound too far away.

Gryffin took my hand and led me to his desk. "Since we will be married in just a few short weeks, I want to explain something to you. So that you may understand what I—why *we*—are doing what we are doing for the Talented across the Peninsula."

On his desk lay three objects. One was a thick golden bangle, etched with grapevines. Next to it was what appeared to be a wooden bow without its string. And finally, a familiar dagger—with a leather-bound hilt and a bright emerald at its pommel. The dagger I'd found loose in my castle's armory. I'd wondered what had come of it after I'd stabbed Gryffin in the shoulder with it. I'd assumed it had been abandoned upon the forest floor.

I ran my fingers across the objects. "What are these?"

"These," Gryffin said, "are relics from the Five Talented."

This news rocked me onto my heels. Relics of the Five Talented? That meant each of these objects was at least six *centuries* old. "How do you know that?" I asked, my tone weighed down by skepticism.

"Research," he answered simply. "This is what my father had us studying for him." He flipped open a book from the stack on his desk to a marked page and pushed the book toward me. "This book is from King Malus's reign, four rulers after Viridi. He noticed the beginnings of a decline in Talent-born, and he proposed a theory."

On the page were hand-drawn sketches of five items. Three of them lay before me on Gryffin's desk. In the book, they were labeled with the names of Five Talented: the bangle, Viridi; the bow, though in the book it still had its string, Vena; and the dagger, Equos. And two objects I had yet to see—a carpenter's chisel, a relic from Arbos, and a brooch of pearls and shells, worn by Mareus.

I looked down at the three objects on Gryffin's desk with a new reverence. "How haven't they deteriorated?"

"We believe that Haggard's magic strengthens them, even to this day. The Five Talented had these items on their person when Haggard gave them his power."

Well, that wasn't the craziest thing I'd heard. "What was King Malus's theory?"

Gryffin's eyes grew excited. "He had the idea that if the objects were brought together, Haggard's combined magic could set the stage for an Awakening."

An Awakening.

So this was his plan all along.

"I found this in Hillstone's armory," I said, pointing to the dagger. It'd been so carelessly thrown into the armory that I hadn't imagined it could be special.

"I was amazed when you pulled this out on me in the woods!" His animated laugh was almost charming. "The dagger of Equos—I could hardly believe my luck!"

When he fixed his red-flecked eyes on me, I cringed at their intensity. "Rosemary, if we gather each of these relics, you and I will rule the Talented together, across the Peninsula. There won't be any need for the division of kingdoms. The Rebels of the Red Sun have pledged to help."

I glanced at him quickly. "The Rebels of the Red Sun?"

"They've built their own force, independent from the kingdoms. They want the Talented reawakened, too, and Tarasyn has the means to do it." He smiled at me then. "Especially now, with Lecevonia's army under our wing."

I lowered my voice, careful. "Why do the Rebels want the Talented awakened?"

"You know of their connection to the Peninsula's origins in magic, Rosemary."

No, I didn't. Still, I refused to meet Gryffin's eyes and pretended as if I knew exactly what he was talking about. "That doesn't explain anything."

"Their belief in the magi is the entire base of their existence. It's only natural that they would want the Talented reawakened, the magic running through the very ground of the Magian Peninsula once again."

I stayed silent, absorbing. *That* was the purpose for which they burned down houses and ransacked marketplaces? Their actions never seemed organized, their motives unclear. But I supposed, if they were looking for something, like these relics in front of me . . .

"Why not simply *ask* the rulers for their relics?" I asked. "Why conquer? Surely with your Talent, you could convince them to hand over the relics." The words stung as they left my lips. Even if his power of Persuasion could save lives, it was not a fair advantage. Why was I *asking* him to use it?

"I've told you—the other rulers would only abuse the power of the Talented. They can't be trusted.

"Besides, my Talent doesn't work that way." He almost sounded sad about it. "It only heightens emotions that are already there. I need to gain trust first before I can elevate it. And, now that news of Roderich's barbaric actions in Hiddon has spread, gaining their trust won't be so simple. Would you have handed over this dagger to me, had I asked for it?"

"Not without suspicion, I suppose." I kept my response light, but really, I hadn't even known the dagger existed.

I lightly touched Vena's bow, the wood smooth beneath my fingers, and my thoughts darkened as they returned to Roderich. "How did your brother get this?"

Gryffin looked down to the stone floor. "It was displayed in the king's bedchambers."

Tarasyn had surprised Hiddon in the dead of night, while King Theon and Queen Alys were sleeping. This bow might have been one of the first things Roderich acquired, and he *still* tortured and killed them. My hate for the man only grew.

"When you gather the relics," I asked, "what then?"

Gryffin looked down at the papers on his desk. "My studies hadn't gotten that far. Hopefully, just having them in one place will conjure enough power to set off a manifestation. But if it doesn't, King Malus theorized that bringing them together on Solstice Day will give what is needed."

Solstice Day. That made sense, I supposed. Solstice Day was the day Haggard gave his gifts to his children, six hundred years ago. It was still a celebrated holiday to this day.

I began to understand Gryffin's desire to awaken the Talented. After seeing Mister Hilderic's work, realizing what Talented people could be capable of, I found myself wanting to know who in Lecevonia aside from Isabele may have these abilities bottled up inside them. Abilities that were itching to manifest with the tiniest nudge. To have such ability in each of the Kingdoms, the entire Peninsula would become a coveted trade partner, a prized destination.

Then I remembered—there were also Talented like Gryffin, people who would use their gifts for deceit and manipulation. And Roderich, who killed a quarter of the population with a disease simply out of hatred, however accidental.

Did the good outweigh the bad? Were there more Hilderics and Isabeles than Gryffins and Roderiches?

"Rosemary." Gryffin's voice interrupted my thoughts, and I felt his hand take mine. "I know this is a lot to understand. But you and I? We can do this."

I had no doubt about that. He'd been right, I saw now, so many weeks ago in the forest. With his Talent and my kingdom's strength, we *could* awaken the Talented.

"And I want to start focusing our forces on Loche."

His words returned me to myself. Reminded me of why this could not happen.

"We could use your lineage as a claim to the throne," he continued, his grip on my hand tightening excitedly. "A pure Loche bloodline may be more powerful than a royal one."

"We don't even know for certain that Sterling is—was—my grandfather." And what was more, I refused to use Sterling against his own people in Somora. "Besides, if those rumors spread, I could lose Lecevonia to my uncle."

"Then we'll focus on Somora instead. Use your perceived lineage."

I couldn't stop myself from growling in frustration. "These are our *neighbors*, Gryffin!"

Gryffin only shrugged. "They will all be grateful in the end, when their families prosper with the Talented."

I stared at the dagger on his desk. This man has already taken so much from me. How much of his plan could I go along with until I escaped these walls?

With a sigh, Gryffin brought my hand to his lips. "You will see," he whispered against my skin. As he released my hand, his fingers trailed around my wrist and slowly, deftly, left a path of ice up my arm to my shoulder. "Mmm."

I stood my ground, eyes closed, and waited for this moment to pass while fighting down the bile in my throat.

"Have you decided on a dress yet?" His breath at my neck raised my hair on its end.

My own voice was croaky as I evaded his question. "They are all too beautiful to choose just one."

He chuckled quietly in my ear and backed away. "You only have four more weeks, Rosemary."

For the first time, his reminder didn't trigger dread or panic. Instead, I felt a wave of anticipation. For in only one week's time, I would find my freedom once again.

That night, Cassia didn't return to my rooms. I asked Vasilie if she'd seen her, but she only shook her head, her own confusion at Cassia's disappearance muddling her features.

Celeste chimed in from beside my fireplace. "Maybe she is visiting her daughter."

I wheeled around to face her. "Cassia has a daughter?"

Celeste rolled her eyes and laid down her hand broom. "Your mind is slipping, Ro."

"She keeps news of her daughter quiet," Vasilie said softly. "Her daughter stays with Cassia's mother-in-law so she can continue to work. Yes, that must be where she is." Vasilie gave one sharp nod, convincing herself.

"How old is her daughter?"

"Just two years old, Your Majesty."

I frowned through my dark window. "I wish I had known." I decided then that before I left, my last action would be to ensure Gryffin relieved Cassia of her duty as long as she wished, with her wages delivered throughout her leave.

CHAPTER TWELVE

THE NEXT MORNING, Cassia was still absent. I took her absence as an opportunity to knock on Gryffin's door and make good on my word from the night before. But when his door opened slowly, his attendant Campton stood before me.

"Good morning, Your Majesty."

"Good morning," I answered, a bit reserved now. "I'd like to speak with King Gryffin."

Campton looked over my head as he spoke. "He is not in at the moment."

"Let her in," Gryffin's voice called from within his chambers.

Their exchange gave me an odd feeling of unease. Why wasn't Gryffin seeing anyone?

I stepped past Campton as he retreated back into the room, and I rounded the corner to face Gryffin in his office.

He was seated at his desk, head down, dark curls falling toward the paper beneath him. He didn't lift his head as he scribbled on the paper, and for a second only the sound of his quill scratching ink into words filled the space between us. Finally, he lifted the paper and waved it through the air to dry the ink. Only then did he look at me with a smile.

"Good morning, my queen."

"Good morning." I walked behind him and laid my hands on his shoulders. "What are you writing?"

"An order," he answered, waving my question away as if it were merely an inconvenient gnat. He folded the paper tightly and handed it to Campton. "See it done."

Campton nodded once and scurried out of the room, his dark cloak billowing behind him.

"An order so early?" I asked, carefully keeping my voice light.

Gryffin pursed his lips, his brow pinched together as he let out a heavy sigh. "It has been a long night."

"What happened last night?"

"Treason." His eyes flashed as he touched my hand. "I'm glad you've come by, actually. I have news."

"I have a request first," I responded quickly. "If you don't mind my asking. I'd like to temporarily relieve my chambermaid Cassia of her duties." He didn't immediately protest, so I continued. "She has a young daughter, and I'm sure she would like to be home with her rather than scrubbing my chamber pots and folding my sheets." I chuckled lightly, but Gryffin only stared ahead.

I squeezed his shoulders and laid my chin on top of his head. "Please, Gryffin. Relieve her with her wages."

Finally, Gryffin's smile returned. "Of course. Consider it already done."

"Thank you," I said, and I leaned down and kissed his curls. "What news did you have?"

"I'm supposed to meet the general," he said, eyeing the shrinking shadows on the ground. "I'll have to share my news later."

He stood from his seat, and I let my hands fall from his shoulders. He kissed my cheek hurriedly, and then quick as a gust, he ushered me out the door.

I tried to fight off the building dread inside my chest as I made my way back down to the archery range. Kathryn had beaten me there, and as I collected my bow from the stand, she hugged her cloak tighter around her. There was a new sort of pressure in the air, and a cold deeper than usual. It brought to my mind the heaviness before a thunderstorm. I wasn't sure if it was the heavy clouds encroaching overhead or the wariness that rode on the wind whistling through the pines, but we both shot our arrows with a new fervor.

My arrows still landed with uncanny accuracy, much to Kathryn's dismay—even the one aimed for the small whorl in the pine that stood over the corner of the range. Every shot, embedded exactly where I'd meant for them to be.

Kathryn huffed beside me. "Your target won't be so easy to find when it's darting through the snow."

She had a point there. Though I was making every shot now, none of them were moving, camouflaged targets.

Still, a beating hope ensnared me. My wary question was almost lost in the wind. "Is it possible to be Talented without your eyes showing?"

Kathryn gazed across the field to her target as she aimed her next arrow, and I thought she hadn't heard me. But after her bowstring resounded and settled back into place, she answered, "Rarely. I only know one person who is Talented but whose eyes do not show it. Of course, there are also people like Gryffin who can hide their eyes."

Though my face never left its neutral state, I could not fight the sting of a dangerous confidence. In all of this, after everything that had come to pass during my confinement to Tarasyn, could I be Talented?

What other explanation could there be for the natural feel of the bow in my hands, the fit of my palm and fingers clasped around the leather grip? Perhaps my Talent simply hadn't been ready to manifest when I was younger, practicing with my father.

Yet here I was in a strange, cold kingdom, with a new ability I hadn't even known I'd possessed.

Then, another part of her answer piqued my thoughts. "Kathryn, who is the one person?"

She opened her mouth, but the loud blare of a horn met us from atop the castle walls. A short, four-note phrase. Forlorn and menacing.

Kathryn's eyes grew wide. The color drained from her face, making it as white as the snow clinging to the pine needles behind her.

Small gusts of snow flurries began to whirl through the air, and I lifted my head to the sky as the flakes touched my cheeks. It never snowed inside the city. What was happening?

Kathryn still hadn't moved, not even when the trumpet blared its four notes once more.

I slowly reached a hand out to her. "Kathryn?"

Her grip loosened on her bow, and it fell to the frostbitten grass at her feet. "Why now?" she whispered into the cold air. Her eyes only grew wider as she stared at the small silhouette of the trumpeter standing high upon Snowmont's outer parapet. "We haven't had a public execution since Father passed."

"A public execution?" The words froze through me to my core. "Who?"

"I don't know," she answered grimly.

Consider it already done.

I picked up my bow and Kathryn's and haphazardly hung them on the stand before gathering my skirts in my hands. Snow was starting to collect on the ground. "Where are they held?"

"Just outside the Atrium," she responded airily.

Kathryn's "I refuse to go" followed me on the white-strewn wind as I bolted through the field, through the castle gates, through the somber crowds gathering. My feet dragged, heavy as lead, and my old ankle injury from two months prior began to resurface. But I pushed myself forward until I passed through the wrought-iron gates of the Atrium.

There, a larger mass of people trod before me, a wall of bodies between my horror and the raised platform in the street.

I fought my way into gaps and crevices through the crowd, and as I made it closer to the platform, the energy buzzing around me shifted from woe to a cautious excitement. Looking above countless heads, I made out two figures standing upon the platform, surrounded by the glinting armor of soldiers.

Just as I was leaning to surge forward once more, I was dragged backward by a boot on the hem of my cloak, and I tumbled to the ground, muddied by the new snow and trampling feet. I threw out an arm to catch myself, but I landed on the cobblestones, hard, onto my left shoulder.

Someone repeatedly mumbled his apologies as he held his hand out to me to help me to my feet, and when he saw my face, his eyes went wide.

"Your Majesty!"

The man fell to his knees, and his sudden prostration spurred a movement through the crowd as people realized the soon-to-be Queen of Tarasyn was in their midst.

"No, no—please." I held my dirty hands out in front of me, and only then did I feel the stinging pain in my shoulder. "Please, it's all right. I just need to get to—"

A horse shrilled, and the gasping and confused crowd parted even further as a white mare pounded toward me. Gryffin, dressed immaculately with his thick crown of gold upon his head, brought his horse to a stop a few paces from me and dismounted.

"Rosemary," he said curtly. His eyes traveled from my muddy face to the tattered hem of my cloak. "What happened?"

Before the man at my feet could lift his hand with an apology, I quickly stepped forward, doing my best to brush off my skirts. "I fell."

Gryffin looked at the man on the ground and back up at me. "I'm in an unforgiving mood today."

I set my chin high. "There is nothing to forgive."

Passing a final glance around him, he sighed and held his hand out to me. "Come. I'd hoped you would attend. See the souls who have done wrong by you."

Wrong by me?

From a glance at his face, I knew these words were not for me, but for the crowd around us. His subjects immediately wore faces of anger and malice and began spitting vicious remarks toward the platform.

Gryffin led me to his mare, but I held my footing at the stirrup. "I'd rather walk. But thank you, my king."

With an impatient grunt, he put his hands on my hips and lifted me into the air, and I had no choice but to clamber into the saddle. His eyes held their own hatred as they affixed themselves to me. He nodded toward the platform and spoke in a low growl, only for me to hear. "Those people are dying because of you."

He led his horse forward on foot, and I forced myself to keep my horror-stricken gaze hidden under the hood of my cloak as it all became clear.

Despite the effort I'd spent in controlling what I could up to this moment, I hadn't held the reins with enough care. I hadn't been as meticulously deceptive as I'd thought, and I hadn't considered outcomes such as this, of people dying for aiding me in my charade. I'd felt triumph too early, and an all-too-familiar guilt threatened to break me.

So, when Cassia's bloodied face came into focus, I did break.

A wail escaped my lips before I knew it was rising through my throat, and Gryffin quickly whispered to those around us, "She is distraught by the memories these two bring to her." He laid a hand on my knee that wore the mask of comfort, but through the pressure I felt his control. Indeed, he had the control, now.

"Rosemary," he murmured only to me, thick with warning. "If you don't calm down, it will be you up there before long."

But I didn't care. I had no game to play anymore. I could not— *would* not—silence my sobbing as we approached the platform. Vasilie, Celeste, and my two other maids stood nearby. Vasilie's sobs rivaled my own, and Celeste had trails of tears running down her cheeks as she gazed not at Cassia, but at the brawny boy who was tethered beside Cassia.

His face was broken and beaten worse than Cassia's, but as Gryffin and I came closer, he summoned the strength to lift his head and meet my eyes. A bloody smile stretched his cracked lips, and relief poured from his fractured expression. I could not hear his voice over the increasing roar of anger roiling through the crowd, but I saw his mouth move into familiar words.

My queen.

Gryffin gave a nod, and the soldiers knocked Cassia and the boy to their knees. Strain clear on the soldiers' faces, they pushed large flat-headed boulders in front of each of the battered prisoners.

"Please, Gryffin." I laid a hand on his shoulder. My plea sat heavily between us. "Don't do this. Please."

His angry eyes met mine for half a second, but it was long enough for me to see my words held nothing over him anymore.

"Cassia Amygera," Gryffin's clear, angry voice rang, "you are charged with treason against Tarasyn. You have conspired against the kingdom, defiled the name of the prospective Queen, and spread horrendous lies of betrayal. Your sentence is death."

The crowd cheered. It did not matter that they had never heard the lies or rumors Gryffin was talking about. All that mattered was that they felt hate, and their king could use that.

He raised his chin. "Say your last words."

The crowd went silent. A string of anticipation held taut.

Cassia did not cry. Her voice was level, unshakable as it traveled over the heads of the crowd. "Please," she said, eyes locked on me. "Take care of my daughter."

I nodded feverishly through my tears. "Of course, Cassia." Then, I raised my voice for the mass of people to hear. "I swear it!"

Gryffin growled beside me and shot me with a look of frustration before facing the crowd. "See how kindhearted your queen is, even in the face of crimes against her!"

The crowd murmured at his words, and several people around us nodded fervently as his Talent took hold yet again. Keeping up his own charade.

"Xalander Defirelde," Gryffin continued, "you are charged with treason against Lecevonia. By aiding Miss Amygera in spreading these lies, you have dishonored the name of Her Majesty the Queen. *Your* queen. Seeing that the ruler of Lecevonia is present, it is fitting that your sentence is drawn out here, in Tarasyn."

At that, I turned in the saddle and glared at Gryffin. "He should be tried in Lecevonia. I do not consent!"

Gryffin snarled. "Your consent does not matter."

He turned back to the platform and addressed Xalander once

again. "Say your last words."

Again, the crowd hushed in greedy, disgusting enthusiasm.

Xal's eyes shifted to mine.

I did not know Xal very well, aside from the services he and his father provided. I recalled his name as Gryffin called it out, and I placed it with a little stableboy with curly black hair and a cheeky smile, a boy swift as a falcon and sneaky as a fox. And even now, in this stocky teenager with a bloodied face and mud-crusted clothes, it was easy to see the little stableboy.

The little stableboy, now grown, opened his mouth, and his shout cut through the thick air. "For Lecevonia!"

For a moment, everyone was still.

Then, a quiet voice from somewhere close by resounded. "For Lecevonia!"

And another.

And another. Then five, six. "For Lecevonia!"

My people who Gryffin had captured and put into service here raised their voices, cutting off the crowd's malicious slurs. I silently raised my clenched fist in the air, and Celeste, after meeting my eyes, shouted from beside me. "For Lecevonia!"

Gryffin cursed loudly and grabbed the back of my cloak. "Your people will be silenced." He looked back to the platform, nodded once, and the soldiers shoved Cassia's and Xal's heads down to the stones. Cassia's lips began to quiver.

I'd never seen a public execution before. My father hadn't needed any in his time, not in the years I'd been old enough to remember. I'd sentenced one man to death, but that had been in the privacy of the prison. Here, in the cold, open air, amidst the once-quaint storefronts of Viridi's square, the energy was repulsive. A churning mixture of hatred, excitement, and horror rumbled through the crowd of hundreds. A crowd that perhaps, underneath the fear instilled upon them by their rulers, recalled the inert exhilaration of bloodshed. Bloodshed often meant victory.

The injustice of it all cracked something inside me, and I joined the angry shouts of my people.

"For Lecevonia!" Then, louder: "For Xal!"

With the simultaneous, definitive downfalls of an ax, Cassia's breaths and Xal's shouts were put to an end forever.

And with Xal's execution, the shouts of my Lecevonians were indeed silenced.

CHAPTER THIRTEEN

THREE DAYS.

That was how long Gryffin told me I had until the wedding ceremony.

After the execution, Gryffin had jumped onto his horse behind me, yanked the reins out of my hands, and bolted toward the courtyard.

"You thought you were being clever," he'd said into my ear through a snarl. His eyes had flashed with a red anger. "You're lucky I don't kill the rest of your people here."

It was hard to sound intimidating through chattering teeth. "Then you will have to kill me too."

He'd scoffed at that. "You would rather *die* than just surrender quietly?"

"Over and over again." My voice had held no waver.

By the time we'd reached Snowmont's main gates, I'd been drenched through with snow. He'd lowered his mouth to my ear and murmured, "We'll be waiting for your precious scout to show his face here in Viridi."

I hadn't had time to respond before Gryffin pulled me out of the saddle and shoved me toward a guard standing at the entrance. "Take the queen up to her chambers and lock her doors. Go with caution and allow no visitors until I say otherwise." His eyes had darkened, hardly any blue to be seen no longer. "She is ill."

Though I'd kicked, struggled, and screamed up the four flights of stairs, no one had turned an eye toward me.

Now I sat in front of my courtyard window, door locked, guards posted outside once more. I'd still been kept in the queen's chambers, but I was more like a prisoner than ever.

Celeste had been taken from me. She'd banged on my door, then Gryffin's down the hall, until there was some scuffle outside and she'd been pulled away.

Gryffin's harsh *three days* reverberated painfully through my skull.

Just over the Atrium's wall, I saw that the execution platform was still in place, still bloody, still silenced by death. Eventually, castle workers did appear to move the platform away, back to wherever it had been stored for the past six years, and once they were gone, the falling snow hid the blood that had dripped onto the street.

Aside from the Viridian citizens avoiding the square, there was no indication that two people had died there today.

Though I felt a surging sadness, the guilt that tugged at my heart was not the same as I had felt over Sterling. Sterling's death could have been avoided, had I not acted so stupidly.

Cassia's and Xal's, though, were a martyrdom. They had chosen to help me do what I needed to do, and somehow, they'd been caught. I could not control their deaths.

The maid's door opened quietly, and Vasilie came into my room with a cloth over her nose. Gryffin's word of my "sickness" had spread, apparently.

"Vasilie," I said quietly. "I'm not ill."

She looked from me to the clean linen in her hand. "Best not to take chances, Your Majesty. Atroxis took my parents."

If only she knew that Atroxis had originated in her kingdom, from the actions of an unhinged prince.

As she shuffled through my chambers, I was grateful that my grieving had company. We did not speak, but the sadness of losing Cassia was thick in the air, so thick that I opened my window a bit wider to let in a chill. The snow was falling harder now, heavy flakes whirling in the wind.

"Have you ever seen anything like this?"

"Not in the city," Vasilie said from behind me. "I wonder if maybe Dothymus is sick as well."

I realized the truth, then, and I glowered down at Snowmont's gates. No, Dothymus wasn't sick. He was acting under Gryffin's command.

Well, snowstorm or not, I had to get out of here.

"I'm leaving tonight, Vasilie."

It was quiet behind me, and for a moment I was shocked to hear myself say those words aloud. My plan needed to change, and perhaps keeping Vasilie out of them would be best. Plans seemed useless, anyhow.

But there was something I needed to do, and I couldn't do it myself.

"Vasilie?" I turned to her now, and she was a statue by my fireplace.

Her eyes stayed glued to the ground. I would understand her refusal, if I were in her position too. We'd just watched two people die because of helping me.

But perhaps.

"Vasilie, will you do something for me?"

"It's just through here." Vasilie pointed to a door from inside the maid's corridor. "But Your Majesty, I don't know if he's in there or not."

"Well," I said quietly, "we're about to find out."

I pushed open the door, pausing when it creaked on its hinges. When no sound came from the other side of the door, I pushed it open just enough for me to slip through.

Gryffin's office was almost pitch black. The only light was the glow of dusk dimmed by the heavy snow clouds through his window. I couldn't see well enough to look at any books I could take with me, though I was sure any one of them would tell me more than I already knew about the Talented.

But I wasn't after any books. I was after the few things he would *not* be successful without.

However, the relics were no longer on his desk.

Boars.

If I were Gryffin, where would I stow them?

Gingerly, I walked farther into his chambers. His bed sat situated at one end, adjacent to his fireplace. But there was something odd about the foot of his bed. His black sheets and white fur blankets jutted out past the end of the mattress, draped over something.

I lifted the blankets and found a chest, which was, thank Haggard, unlocked. The lid was heavy, extraordinarily so, but with a heave I was able to open it and look inside.

There, nestled in an old tapestry, were the three relics. I slipped the dagger into my boot and the bangle on my wrist, grabbed the bow, and scurried back through the dark toward the maid's door.

A whoosh of wings made me freeze.

I peeked around the dividing wall, and there, sitting on his perch in Gryffin's office, was Corvus.

His beady eyes found me in the dying light of day, and he *stared*. Hard. I was too nervous to move a muscle. One call from this blasted bird, and I would be done for.

After what felt like an eternity, I couldn't wait any longer. I took a step, then another, slinking along Gryffin's bookcases.

Corvus only sat on his perch, watching me.

Until I took a step too close to him.

He launched himself into the air, and his jagged caw jolted my bones. I shielded my face with the bow as I sprinted the fast few feet toward the maid's door, and his talon clipped the bangle on my wrist just as Vasilie closed the door behind me.

We hurried back into my rooms, and I unloaded my spoils into a bundle of scarves in my armoire. Vasilie quickly positioned herself next to my fireplace, pretending to stoke the fire.

But no one came to check on us. The door handles to my chambers rattled a couple of times over the next hour, but their locked state seemed satisfactory enough for whomever was on the other side.

And so, now, I waited.

In the meantime, I packed what we'd been able to collect in the past week. Without Celeste, I could only carry two bags with me, so I picked the two largest leather duffels and began stuffing in anything I could. Clothes, boots, undergarments, blankets. Food, a fire striker, and flint to start a fire.

The sounds of the castle quieted as the evening dragged into night. My two other chambermaids never showed, so I assumed they'd been given instructions not to come to me with my "illness." Vasilie left after she'd drawn my bath, which I made sure to relish, knowing it would be my last warm bath for a while.

But before she left, I extended my hand out to her, and she touched her fingertips to mine. The old Magian Peninsula greeting and, especially in this case, farewell.

"Thank you so much, Vasilie. For everything you have done for me."

She nodded her head once. "It's what Cassia would have done. Thank you for showing me the kind of ruler Tarasyn so desperately needs." Her quiet voice left an impression on my heart, and I drew her in for an embrace.

"I'll take care of Cassia's daughter," she whispered. "Don't forget about us."

Sweet Vasilie. I hugged her tighter. "I swear to you, I *will* help the Tarasynian people." It was a bold promise, but it was one I intended to keep, when I could.

Now, late in the night, I gathered together my final bag. Nestled in it were the last of the dried fruits and nuts I'd stowed away, my second fire striker, an extra quilt, and, bundled in scarves, the dagger and the bangle. The bow stuck out of the top of the bag after buckling it closed, but it would have to do. I was not sure what I would do with them. All I knew was that by taking these objects, I bought the rest of the Peninsula a bit more time.

I kept my room dark, my window open, as I threw on my last cloak. Sweat was already starting to trickle down my back from the many layers of pants, dresses, and cloaks I'd piled on, but the snow collecting on my windowsill reminded me that sweating would be the least of my concerns for the next upcoming days.

As I picked up my two bags from the bed, a knock—so quick and quiet, just a tap more than anything—sounded upon my door. I dropped the bags to the floor and cursed, and I waited for a lock to turn, my doorhandle to creak.

Instead, something slid into my room like a whisper beneath my door, and a shadow cut through the crack of light.

I strode forward and picked up the small folded paper from the ground, and Kathryn's script scrawled across the page.

I will protect Celeste. Be safe.

Her words sent the sting of tears to the backs of my eyes. I had no idea what had happened to Celeste after she'd been taken from me, and I'd put all my hope into Gryffin seeing Celeste as too able-bodied to be disposed of until I could return for her. With an army, hopefully. If anyone could take care of Celeste and spare her from Gryffin, it would be Kathryn.

I went over to my hearth and stoked the embers, just enough to restart a whisper of a flame, and dropped the note into the fire.

With bags in hand again, I stole one last glance at the luxurious wedding dresses near the window, the emerald ring I'd left on the breakfast table. *Make someone else Tarasyn's queen,* I thought savagely. Then I lumbered over to the maid's door and slowly, so very slowly, slid the door open.

Another one of Vasilie's acts of kindness.

With a final glance through my room, I lifted my hood over my head, covered my mouth and nose with a scarf, and stepped into the blackness of the maid's corridor.

I shuffled through the dark, lit only intermittently by torches. The maid's corridor here reminded me of the corridor back in Hillstone. Though, as large as Snowmont was, I imagined the system of mazes was much more intricate here.

I had no idea where I was going, until I came to a spiraling staircase. *Down* seemed like a good idea. My bags knocked against each other as I clambered on the stairs as quickly as I could, and by the time I reached the bottom step, my head had gone misty, and I felt drenched in my clothes. Surely I was down on the first floor of the castle now. Voices sounded too near, though, so I dared not stop.

I looked left, then right.

Light shined from the left, so I decided to stay in the safer darkness of the right. Less light, however, also meant colder. My sweat turned icy, and my teeth began to chatter.

Finally, I began to try doors. The first handle I lifted was locked, and the second opened into a dark storage space, full of flour and yeast from the smell of it. The third was the Dining Hall, which I quickly closed, though no one was in there at this hour. I did have one door in mind, though I had no idea if this particular door existed. Still, I kept going.

I continued down the path, which seemed to only get colder.

Then, as I passed another door, a strong gust of frigid air blew through the seams. Hopeful, I tried the handle and gave the door a push with my bags.

It opened to darkness. But a familiar darkness.

The corridor to the craftsmen's village. And just the door I'd hoped to find.

I hurried down the passage with no torchlight to guide me this time, praying that I was going the right way. Did Gryffin really care about resources *so* much that he would order these torches to be extinguished at night? Ridiculous.

The darkness in this corridor was unparalleled. Thick as pitch. It felt like I was walking through a stagnant void, with no end and no beginning. But, finally, the void *did* have an end. The dark outline of a door. The white snow almost seemed to glow in the stark contrast of darkness as it poured in through the bottom of the weathered wood. I pulled the handle.

Locked.

"Boars," I muttered angrily, and my voice echoed and carried farther than I liked. I froze, listening for any sound hiding in the darkness.

Once I felt safe, I turned around and sauntered back up the corridor. I pressed my hands along the wall to feel for the maid's door, only to realize that I could not feel anything through my double-gloved hands.

"Boars!" I said again, more mournfully now. Setting my bags on the ground, I slowly took off the gloves one finger at a time.

As the last of the warm wool left my skin, the cold air hit my hand like a vicious slap. I considered just taking my chances, hoping to simply happen upon the maid's door again, but I knew that was foolish. So, I took a steadying breath, and I pressed my hand against the stone.

Ice immediately found its way into my veins. But I picked up my bags with my other hand, though my injured shoulder screamed, and I ran. I didn't care to be quiet anymore.

It took all my strength to keep my hand on the wall, traveling rapidly over the crags and bumps in the cold stone. I was lucky that I could still feel them. My boots sounded loud to my ears as they clopped and reverberated through the darkness.

Finally, my palm felt the merciless stone relent to splintered wood. I fumbled for the metal handle, which was just as icy as the stone, and I yanked the door open. I let myself pour back into the warmer shadows of the maid's corridor.

With the door shut securely behind me, I dropped my bags, sank to the floor, and hugged my frigid hand to my chest. I fought back tears as my red fingertips throbbed against the hollow of my throat.

I laid my head against the wall and opened and closed my hand a few times. When I could feel the blood returning to my fingers, I gingerly put one glove after the other back on and tried to ignore the sting of the fabric. I let myself take a moment to reset.

The craftsman's village was out of the question now. And I could not retrace my steps back the way I came. The castle was the last place I needed to be.

My only other option now was to follow the maid's corridor until one of its doors opened to outside.

With a deep exhale, I heaved to my feet once again, gathered my bags, and started forward.

I cherished the warmth of the maid's corridor now that I knew what kind of cold awaited me outside these walls. My running had irritated my old ankle injury, and I almost laughed. Hurt ankle, busted shoulder, frozen hand—I'd be an easy target for even a child to capture. Still, I kept moving forward.

Eventually, a faint whistling of wind reached my ears, and it grew louder as I approached an old, weather-beaten oak door. The corridor kept on going, and I had to wonder where it led past this, but I had no intention of finding out. Bracing myself for the cold, I tucked the hood of my outermost cloak around me, tugged my fallen scarf back into position over my mouth and nose, and pushed open the door, hard, against the accumulated snow.

Gusts of snow whipped around me as I stepped out into the white expanse. There were only faint outlines of houses and shops nearby, but nothing really telling as to where I was. I trudged through the snow and thanked Kathryn endlessly for my boots and clothes. As I looked behind me, though, I saw two trenches in my wake. I cursed again, feeling stupid that I hadn't considered this factor. There would be no hiding my trail in this weather.

As I continued deeper into the heavy flurries, more houses began to loom on either side of me. I was on a street, perhaps? Light poured through the cracks of one doorway, and as I approached, I made out a sign swinging above the door in the gusts.

A tavern.

And my stomach immediately growled. I hadn't eaten since this morning, before the execution. Anything offered to me since then had sent my insides roiling.

No, Rose. I could not stop.

But . . .

Perhaps I could. When was the next time I would get a full meal? And if I didn't take off my cloak, perhaps no one would recognize me. My layers of clothes already made me look bulkier. I could even pass for a man.

My stomach won out. I trudged my way toward the tavern's door.

~HILLSTONE~
ZEKE

Where the Haggard were they?

I checked my saddlebags for the fourth time. Yes, I had everything. Food, bedroll, bow. Check, check, freckin' check. I adjusted Hugo's bridle, walked him around the aisle. He trotted in place and pawed the straw at his feet. Anxious to get a move on.

"I know, big guy." I scratched between his ears. "Me too."

Where *were* they?

We were leaving so much later than I'd wanted. Almost an entire week. Isabele wanted careful planning, but I could've told her that these trips usually don't go as planned.

Then, refugees from the Lecevonia-Hiddon border began trickling into the city. Haggard's sake, we hadn't even known they'd been locked in battle for the past two months. So that took a few days of helping Isabele figure out where to even start in dealing with that. Housing them, providing food, giving them medical care and burying their dead. Finally, when her advisors took the reins, I was free to leave.

I groaned and rapped my fingers across Hugo's saddle. Free to leave, my arse. *Where were they?*

Finally, I heard hooves approaching from the east-facing aisle, and I turned to see Terrin and Roger leading their horses toward Hugo and me. Terrin had his roan gelding, named Zephyr if I remembered correctly, and Roger had a colossal bay I'd never seen before bobbing its head next to him. Seeing them, eagerness took over all my frustration. *I'm coming, Rose.*

"Terrin," I said, shaking his hand.

"You're a sight for sorry eyes," he responded, smirking. "When's the last time you slept?"

I laughed and elbowed him in the ribs. "And I still look better than you. And Roger!" Memories of standing together, guarding Rose and keeping her safe, came flooding back to me. Boars, I should've never let her out of my sight.

The man stood tall over me like a tree, his big smile lighting up his face. We clasped each other's forearms. "Ezekiel!" he boomed. "Good to see you."

"Likewise. Have you seen Amos yet?"

His smile lessened. "Yeah. Poor bloke. But he'd thought I'd been dead, so I think seeing me surprised him a bit." He chuckled.

I felt my eyes widen. "Dead?"

"Yeah. Last they saw of me I was up against four Tarasynian soldiers." He smiled smugly.

I nodded, impressed. "That sounds like a story worth hearing. On the road." I said pointedly, putting my foot into my stirrup and hoisting myself up.

The two men nodded and followed suit. "On the road."

I steered Hugo through the stable doors and kicked him straight into a gallop. We entered the dark woods, and finally, *finally*, we were on our way.

Each stride through the dark woods brought me closer to that Haggard forsaken kingdom. To that sorry excuse of a king. And to my Rose.

I'm coming, Rose.

CHAPTER FOURTEEN

THE TAVERN WAS, thankfully, entirely empty.

I beat the snow off my boots at the door and bustled my way through the doorway. Looking around, the place was actually very quaint with thick oaken tables and chairs, a glowing hearth, and a long bar at the back of the room. Snow had collected on the windowsills outside, but its chill stayed outside.

The dry warmth felt so beautiful. I took a few deep, thawing breaths, eyes closed. I'd never been inside a tavern until today. I'd heard stories of raucous and tumbling, drunkards and fistfights, but this tavern didn't fit that idea. Rather, it was arm and welcoming.

"Hi, there."

My eyes shot open, and a girl about my age stood before me with a steaming cup of what I assumed to be mead.

I nodded in greeting.

"Real storm out there, isn't it?" she said with a shake of her head toward the window. "I haven't seen it snow like this in the city in, what, nine or ten years?"

Her pause was long enough that I realized she was waiting for an answer, so I opened my throat as much as I could and spoke from the depths of my stomach. "It's a bad one."

To be frank, my impression of a male voice was . . . unconvincing. But it was muffled enough by my scarves that the girl didn't seem to notice. She sighed heavily and pointed her chin toward the fireplace. "Well, make yourself at home. What can I get you?"

"One of those," I said gruffly, nodding to the mug in her hand. A growl of my stomach told me to venture farther. "And soup?"

She placed the mug on a table near the fire, pulled out a chair for me, and walked back toward the bar, wiping her hands on her apron. "Chicken and carrot stew is what we have today. That all right?" She was already grabbing a wooden bowl from a cabinet overhead.

"Perfect." My stomach certainly was not about to be picky. She could have said watered porridge and I would have been grateful.

I sat with my back toward the bar and lowered my scarf just as low as I dared. It was actually cider in the mug, mulberry, and it ran like warm honey down my throat. A quiet moan of gratitude escaped my lips.

A bowl of stew landed in front of me with a thud. I wrapped my gloved hands around the warm bowl and kept my head down. *Stay discreet, Rose.*

But then, the girl sat down at the table with me. "What has you out here in this weather? You're the first customer I've had since the snow started sticking." I peeked over to her around the hem of my hood, and I saw she was eyeing my bags. "Must be important," she murmured, and I caught the feeling she hadn't meant to say that aloud.

Why *was* I here? What would drive a man into a pelting, unprecedented snowstorm with two bags full to their seams?

I tucked my chin into my cloak to muffle my voice. "Just trying to get home." And that was not even the slightest lie.

The girl leaned back in her chair, crossing her arms over her chest, and she studied me with inquisitive brown eyes. Her demeanor reminded me of Zeke.

The stew in front of me swathed warmth into my face, and I couldn't help myself any longer. I leaned over my bowl heavily—a bit theatrically, really—and picked up the spoon in my gloved hand. I lifted my chin just enough to bring the spoonful of hot carrots and broth to my mouth.

The taste admittedly left something to be desired after eating the food made in Snowmont's kitchens, but I didn't care. In this moment, it was the most perfect bowl of stew I could have dreamed of. I shoveled bite after bite into my mouth, and I welcomed the warmth of it as it settled into my stomach. Between the stew and the cider, my top layer of clothes were begging to be removed, if I were brave enough.

But I wasn't. So I accepted the fact that I'd just have to swelter for a little while.

The girl leaned forward and rapped her fingernails on the table. "Where is home for you?"

I swallowed my spoonful of stew loudly and kept my face bent over my bowl. "Far."

"Far, huh?" The girl laid her head on her hands, an intrigued glow in her eyes. "How far?"

I took a sip of my cider and used it to answer gutturally. "I have a couple weeks of travel ahead of me."

"Surely you aren't traveling in *that*?" She nodded her head toward the storm raging behind the door.

Just then, the door swung open, and my heart thudded so loudly I felt that it could be heard through my three layers of coats.

Boots knocking against the doorframe.

Disgruntled murmurs.

Multiple sets of footsteps.

A man's voice. "Cherise, you gorgeous woman! Thank Haggard you're open. Three rounds, will you?"

The girl, Cherise, rolled her eyes and winked at me. "Don't you go anywhere." Then she stood and walked out of my line of sight. "Take a seat at the bar, Redd. Three rounds coming up. The king has you men working late?"

The thud of mugs hitting the wooden bar.

"Yeah," one answered with a grumble. "Can you believe it? In this thing blowing outside?"

"Redding and I have been trooping through the castle for almost two hours," another man said. "Have you heard yet?"

"Well, I've been here behind this bar all day and no one's come in except you three and that fellow."

Chairs creaking. Stares piercing my back.

I didn't breathe.

An annoyed sigh from Cherise. "No, I haven't heard anything. What happened?"

Chairs creaking again, the weight of eyes disappearing. I could breathe again.

The first man, Redd, spoke low. "The queen is missing."

My head spun at his words. My breathing became hitched, like trying to breathe through too-cold air.

Gryffin knew. So soon.

The entire city would know soon enough.

Cherise snorted. "What, as if she ran away?"

A dragging sip from a mug. "That's what the king says. 'Cold feet.' 'Troubled.' Those are his reasons."

A new voice, a bit younger than the others—the third man. "Did you hear he moved their wedding date to three days from now?" He gave a surprised laugh. "No wonder she ran off, that's what I think."

"But king's orders," the second man said gruffly. There was a loud, yawning stretch. "He's sending us to spread the word through the city and tell everyone to start searching."

Cherise whistled through her teeth. "What a day. An execution, snow in the city, and now the queen's gone mad."

I frowned. Mad wasn't the term I'd use.

But in a hurry now, definitely. I needed to get out before the citizens' eyes were keenly looking for a lone traveler.

Finishing the last of my cider, I lifted my scarf back over my nose and mouth and pushed my chair away from the table.

"Wait!" Cherise called from behind the bar.

Boars. I froze standing with my hands on the table, back to the bar.

I heard the girl's quick footsteps behind me, and a tied bundle appeared in my line of vision.

"For the road," she said quietly. "No charge."

I shook my head and pulled out my coin sack from my pocket, but she pressed my hands into my chest.

"Really, no charge." She lifted a corner of her mouth into a smirk. "Just promise me you'll be a returning patron on your next visit to the city."

I thought I might have heard a displeased grunt from Redd at her words.

I took out a few coins and left them on the table. "For the stew and the cider."

She frowned a bit, but eventually she picked the coins off the table one by one. "All right. Be safe out there, stranger."

With a nod, I picked up my bags and plodded toward the door.

The man named Redd called out from behind me. "Excuse me."

I froze again. Sweat beaded on the small on my back. I shouldn't have stopped. I should have continued out the door. I should have—

"You'll keep an eye out for the queen, yes?"

I turned my head slightly in their direction, just enough that they could see my curt, single nod. Then, I pulled at the door handle and stepped out into the snow.

I almost cried with relief as I left the light of the tavern and the pressure of the soldiers' presence. With a murky idea of which direction I was headed, I began pushing through the snow once more. I just needed a tree line to fall into.

Soon, the entire city would know that I was on the run. It would be nearly impossible to get out once people were actively looking for me. I wondered what motivation Gryffin had promised to anyone who could find me.

The relics probably had a higher prize.

I trudged on through the snow, silently cursing myself for not asking Kathryn to find snowshoes in the market. Lecevonia did not ever see this type of weather, not even the past particularly frigid winter. I had to remind myself that this was supposed to be *spring*.

Images of wildflowers, green grass, and warm sunlight kept me going as I passed rows of shops, obscured in white blankets of snow.

Then, a noise carried on the wind as it whistled around me. A door opening, a man's voice. I heard no more before the gust of sound blew past me.

But I heard enough to make out Redd's voice.

I looked behind me and saw the light of the tavern disappearing as its door shut, and just barely through the flurries, the dark shape of a man hopping off the steps.

I took the first turn off the main road I could and sidled between two buildings. Not a street, exactly, but an alley wide enough for a horse to pass through. I hardly registered that snow was dripping from the roof and onto my hood as I hugged the nearest wall, my bags tight at my sides. My pulse hammered through my veins, and I kept my head turned toward the main road, watching.

I reached the end of the wall before the man passed by my alley, so I slinked around the corner, still hugging the building as much as I could.

But large hands grabbed my shoulders and whipped me around on my feet. My ankle protested.

Redd's angry voice rose in my ear. "Why are you hiding?"

He threw me to the ground, my bags flying, and his boot connected with my ribs. The air in my lungs burst forth in a rugged spasm of coughs.

In my confusion, I tried to find him with a frantic lift of my head, but I found his fist instead.

Pain blossomed from my jaw, radiating into my head, my neck. My confusion only deepened, along with the new pounding headache. I found it hard to believe that beating me to a pulp was part of Gryffin's order.

His breath felt hot on my face as he leaned in. "You crite. You think you can just take Cherise's interest like that?"

I realized then what he meant, and I almost laughed at the irony—at the hope I'd had that my charade as a man was good enough to fool everyone in that tavern. As it turned out, it was *too* good.

He stood, shadow looming over me, and his boot found my abdomen this time. My ragged gasp raked against the sides of my throat, and I instinctively crunched into a ball.

At my feet, the bag with the relics had opened, and the hilt of Equos's dagger glinted dimly through the flurries.

His rough hand was at my chin, and he yanked my face upward to meet his furious glare. When he saw my eyes, his vehemence flickered with a doubt, but it was fleeting. He grabbed my face in his palm and smacked the back of my head into the ground, which thankfully was covered in a cushioning layer of snow.

Then, voices reached us through the flurry murk. "Redding!" "Redd!"

What else did I have to lose? He was going to beat me to death right here anyway, and his friends were going to help. I spit in his face with all the strength I could, and I did nothing to disguise my voice. I didn't think I needed to, as raspy as it was now. "She deserves more than a jealous boar of a man like you."

The doubt returned to his eyes, then, stronger than before, and he yanked my scarf down my chin.

I'd never seen a man's face change from such severe anger to regret so rapidly. He backed away from me quickly and fell to the ground, eyes wide. "Your—Your Majesty."

This time, I really did laugh, as painfully breathless as I was. I supposed my charade couldn't last forever.

But the man quickly came to himself. "Your Majesty," he said again, and he looked toward the calling voices. "My men and I are meant to take you back to the castle immediately." His eyes widened even farther. "Boars. The king is going to have my head." He packed snow against my bruising cheek.

The voices were too close. I needed to move.

"Redding," I said, and his name from my lips made him jump. I tried to straighten my legs and sit up, but my abdomen screamed. "Let me go. Please."

The man looked at my bags and back at me. He started to pack everything back as best he could. "King's orders, Your Majesty. You aren't well."

I mustered my strength to sit up, and the man hissed between his teeth. He murmured profanities repeatedly, along with apologies. "I'm—I'm so sorry, Your Majesty."

I reached for my bags, but he grabbed my wrist, a gentle but unyielding grip. He seemed to be at war with himself, and I couldn't blame him. He was expected to return me to Gryffin, but I doubted Gryffin would accept any explanation for bloodying me the way Redding had.

The voices were still approaching, just around the corner of the building.

I had no more time for negotiations. With a shout of determination, I thrust my other hand into the bag that had been at my feet and fumbled around for the dagger's hilt. Finally finding purchase, I whipped the dagger in front of me. "Release me."

The new threat shocked the man enough to loosen his grip with wide eyes. "Your Majesty—"

A man's figure appeared around the building.

With a look of regret and apology, I screamed and forced myself to run the blade against the outside of Redding's thigh.

Redding shouted in pain and released his hold as a bloom of blood appeared through his trousers.

Adrenaline pumping through me now, I fumbled for my bags in the snow and struggled to stand.

"Redd!"

"Don't let her escape!"

I was only able to wrap my hand around the bag with the relics securely. *This was the important bag anyway,* I thought in a quick note of relief. So I left the other in the snow, and I did not take the time to look behind me before I bolted between the next set of buildings.

Boots pounding, too close behind me. Or was it my head

pounding? Perhaps both.

I didn't stop running as I hit the main road once more. I couldn't even if I wanted to. My body had taken on a state of reflex—no thought, only survival.

The pounding had grown louder. A grunt of strain too close for comfort.

I couldn't outrun my pursuer. That much was starting to be clear.

But perhaps I could outmaneuver him.

I saw another alley between buildings on my left, and I drifted around the corner of the shop without slowing. I was again so grateful for the boots Kathryn had found for me. My pursuer slid to the ground behind me with a curse, and it gave me enough time to round the opposite corner of the shop and squat behind a double stack of crates. I held my bag closely to my chest, dagger still in hand, and took cover with bated breath.

Boots crunched in the snow again, approaching.

Then stopped.

So close that I could hear his heavy breath, right on the other side of my crates. My own breath clouded in the cold space around me. I imagined his eyes searching the snow around him, looking for boot prints. I dearly hoped it was just too dark to see mine.

Finally, my pursuer cursed under his breath, and the crunch of boots began again, growing farther away with each step.

I waited until I could no longer hear his pursuit before I let out my sigh. My entire body hurt now, and a wave of nausea convulsed through my abdomen. Painfully, and so depressingly, Cherise's stew made a reappearance on the snow at my feet.

With a groan, I lifted my head and looked around me. Just the wooden wall of a shop behind me, its windows covered in snow, and in front of me, another wall.

But beyond that wall, through the gap between the buildings, I saw the needled branches of trees, beckoning to me with the help of the wind. Or teasing me. One of the two.

I waited just a bit longer for my stomach to settle, and I listened for any sound of nearby soldiers.

Confidence built after hearing no voices, no shouting, and no crunching footsteps, I emerged from behind my crates and slipped toward the evergreen safety of the tree line.

CHAPTER FIFTEEN

A̧S THE TREE needles swallowed me into their dense cover, the strongest sense of safety I'd had since entering this kingdom washed over me. The men wouldn't venture into the forest, not here where the snow was knee-deep and the cold impossibly even more bone-piercing. I hugged my hood tighter around my face and trudged farther into the dark.

No, dark was an understatement. There were no stars and no moon. No glowing lanterns on porches or hearth light through windows. Soon though, my eyes adjusted, and I found myself able to distinguish one black tree trunk from the next.

And beneath the shadows, between the branches, there was the feeling again that Zeke had mentioned. The live energy that seemed to coat the forests of Tarasyn, like thousands of taut strings linked from one organism to the next, vibrating with every movement and every wind gust, sending a force of vitality through the air, through the very ground. It was like the conservatory but *wild*, uncontainable, as if the pines and spruces were bracing to uproot themselves and walk through the snow at their feet.

Despite the cold sting of the air around my eyes, my body felt warm underneath my layers. Still, I wasn't brave enough to shed any cloak or coat, nor remove a glove from my hands.

Only when I felt I'd gone deep enough into the forest to avoid being seen did I consider starting to look for shelter. The snow had stopped falling in the forest for now, but the fresh powder beneath me did little to support my weight as I trudged forward. My boots were still mercifully dry, but that wouldn't be the case if I didn't find reprieve from the snow soon.

I studied the dark, slumping shapes around me, boulders settled along the side of the mountain. But none were big enough or clustered together in such a way that would provide much protection. Finally, I came across the remnants of a once-towering fir that had fallen over a large stone, its trunk cracked and roots splayed around its base like a spider. A portion of its trunk leaned heavily against the boulder, the tree's branches sweeping the ground behind it. It was at least a structure, I supposed, more so than anything I could have made myself.

I ambled my way over to the tree and huddled between its trunk and the boulder. It was tight, with only enough room to sit and lean back against the rock, but it blocked the wind, and underneath the trunk was bare earth.

I stripped the needles off the low-hanging branch of a nearby pine, as I'd seen Gryffin do just months before, and laid the needles in my new little crevice to make a makeshift bed. I sat, finally, and my legs sang praise.

The chill on my face sent me to my bag for my fire striker. I slid the bag from my shoulder and unclasped the buckle, then paused as my hand wrapped around the striker's cold steel.

In my hurry to leave, I hadn't thought about the fact that I had no idea how to start a fire. Celeste did, and so I'd counted on her being here. Foolish.

Still, I figured I knew the basics. I gathered a few dry limbs from the fallen tree and set them in a small pile on the bare ground out of the wind. I rifled through my bag, looking for the drawstring bag of flint I'd packed. After a few moments of looking, I started hurriedly taking things out of the bag. I definitely remembered packing it—

In the bag I'd dropped in the city.

I abandoned the bag and frantically searched the ground for flint, or something similar like chert or quartz—anything with a sharp edge. Finding nothing in my shelter, I peeked my head out from behind the boulder, but I was met with such a furious wind that I quickly tucked myself back against the stone.

Frustrated, I groaned and kicked the heel of my boot into the frozen ground.

I could stay warm without a fire, surely. It was just one night, and the night was already half over. Soon, the sun would rise, and I could look for flint in the daylight.

Yes, that was what I would have to do.

Stay warm. Without fire.

I nestled into the quilt I'd unpacked from my bag and was again grateful for the wool beneath my leather pants and vest, and the fur that lined my two cloaks and my boots and gloves. I hugged my legs to my chest, draped my hood over my knees, and breathed. Thank Haggard my sweat had dried before now, or I would truly be freezing to death.

I tried to remember what else was in the bag I'd had to leave behind. Another fire striker. An extra set of boots, and a woolen undergarment. A compass. And most of my food. My dried fruits and nuts had spilled out of this bag as well when I'd been tackled to the ground in the city.

And no bow for hunting. Kathryn had said she'd get that last to avoid suspicion, but we'd run out of time. And Vena's bow had no string.

Well, at least I had a seemingly endless supply of water with the snow. Nothing to collect it in though.

I tried to stop my grim thoughts, but it was hard to ignore the fact that, though I'd done the best I could with what I'd had, I was dangerously unprepared.

How was I going to get back to my kingdom when the cold was already creeping into my fingers? Already working its way between my joints?

I almost laughed. So much work into keeping myself alive for weeks in Tarasyn, pretending I'd marry Gryffin for the sake of living another day, only to die in the forest just outside Viridi. Who knew if they would even find my body if it snowed again tonight?

Then, a howl as bone-chilling as the temperature carried lightly on the wind.

Wolves.

This time, I really did burst out into laughter. So, if the cold didn't kill me, a pack of wolves would!

No. I wasn't going to die. I'd put in too much work to get this far. To get this much closer to home.

I could not control the freezing air around me, and I could not control a wild animal's appetite. But I *could* control what I let grab my focus. And now, I let the warmth of my breath hold my attention. The heat of my chest. The steady rhythm of my inhales and exhales.

Inhale.

Exhale.

Inhale.

Exhale.

Breathe in the calm of warmth.

Release the unnerving anxiety with the exhale.

Draw in the will to live.

Breathe out thoughts of cold and hunger.

Inhale strength.

Exhale despair.

Inhale.

Exhale.

Then, it was morning.

Somewhere between my breathing and my battle for my will, birds had begun fluttering through the first songs of the day. I lifted my head from my knees, and the early gray of morning shone through the flat white of the sky above.

I made it through a blistering Tarasynian night without a fire.

And I was freezing.

I struggled to straighten my legs from my curled position, and the moment the cold air hit my abdomen, I began to shiver. It suddenly didn't matter that I was wearing three layers of clothing.

I also felt parched, and somewhere deep within, my survival brain told me I needed to stay hydrated. My teeth chattered as I gathered snow in my gloved hands and let it melt in my mouth, which made me chatter even more, like the white-furred squirrels beginning to stir around me.

My body hurt so *badly* to move, to straighten my arms and gather my feet under me. It probably had as much to do with the cold as it did with being beaten to a pulp the previous night.

But I had to move. I had to get home, back to my kingdom. I had to get back to Zeke, and Isabele and Lisette, and Hazel.

I had to warn Somora and Loche of Gryffin's plans and that the Rebels were somehow involved.

I had to—

"That's my hunting spot."

With a frenzied shot of adrenaline, I grabbed the hilt of Equos's dagger and swung toward the voice. But that took all my energy, and now I stood there in the snow, frozen, teeth chattering.

The face staring at me from the shadows of the hood was white and wrinkled, but the eyes, as gray as rolling thunder, were timeless. Ancient, yet brimming with life. Life begging to be told, and life begging still to be experienced. It seemed as if the sky, the stars, the sea, and everything within them were appraising me from their two points buried beneath the woman's heavy eyelids.

The woman nodded toward my right hand holding the dagger. "What do you plan to do with that, child? And what *happened* to you? All bruised and bloodied?"

She was right—I must have looked as awful as I felt. The blood from my nose felt crusted on my lips, and my jaw felt thick and swollen. Even just moving it left it feeling tender. A similar ache screamed from the side of my ribcage.

She let out a little puff of air and held a hand out to me. "Come. We'll get you cleaned up. I can tell you're just about frozen solid."

I lowered my dagger just slightly. "Wh-who are you?"

The woman's cackle filled the trees. "Just an old lady living with her husband in the woods. Might I ask who else would be out here?" When I still didn't lower my dagger, she lowered her hand to her side and sighed. "Well, if you aren't going to come with me, I'm going to sit right there in that little camp of yours and see if there are any game you haven't scared off."

As I shivered in my spot, I studied the woman, her leather cloak and her bow and bag full of trappings. She certainly seemed like she lived out here. That much was true. But was she Viridian? Loyal to Gryffin? Did she know who I was?

"Your questions are very loud," the woman said, settling onto my bed of pine needles.

Her words made me take a step back. Loud? What—

"You can hear my thoughts." There was no question on my lips.

The woman's gaze slipped to me with a smirk. "Among other things. Yes."

"You're Talented."

"Is that a problem?"

"No," I answered quickly. "But—" Her eyes. Why didn't they have red flecks?

Then, Kathryn's words on the archery field returned to me. "Do you know the princess?" I asked carefully. "Kathryn?"

The corners of the woman's mouth pulled downward into a shallow frown. "Only as she was when she was a child." Her voice was tinged with some emotion. Sadness?

Kathryn had known this woman, known her well enough to know she possessed a Talent. Even with clear eyes. But she hadn't had a chance to say very much else.

I could not find it in me to relax my suspicions. This woman living in the cold—a mind-reader, no less, with eyes that seem to have witnessed the birth of the sun—felt too surreal to be trusted.

"You don't trust me because you're smart." The old woman pulled her quiver of arrows off her back with a grunt. "You're right—who am I? You don't know me. Other than the fact that I can give you food and a warm place to thaw, why should you trust me?" She shrugged her leather-cloaked shoulders, and her timeless eyes flashed. "I know you, however."

I lifted my chin at her jarring claim. "Oh?"

"I've seen your face in the minds of travelers. Though you have never appeared as ragged as you do now." She smiled, her lips pulling back to expose surprisingly white teeth, before she set her eyes downcast toward the bow in her hands. "But the same look of desperation is there. No one has recognized it, no one that has passed through these woods at least. But it has been plain on your face, under your tiara and nicely done hair, and I recognized it. I've felt it before myself." She glanced up at me. "You wear that look now."

I tried to smooth my expression. She knew far more than what I was comfortable with. "And now you've seen me, and you've rifled through my thoughts. You must also know why I need to leave this place."

The old woman nocked an arrow and settled the bow in her lap. "It's true that your home kingdom wouldn't fair well with a dead queen." The infinity of her eyes met mine. "Lecevonia is only as strong as its leader, yes?"

Suddenly, standing here was more than I could handle, and I itched to turn my back on the woman. My father's words through her lips were too unnerving. I hadn't even realized I'd thought them . . .

Yes, she knew too much. Strangers with too much mental power had betrayed me before, and I would not make the same mistake twice. I began constructing the same castle I managed to use against Gryffin, stones mortared around me, and I let my hand clinging to Equos's dagger fall to my side. But my grip stayed tight. "I must move on, now."

The woman's eyes squinted just vaguely. "Interesting." Her voice lightened in a new sense of bemusement. "And that's not a word I use lightly anymore."

I reiterated my words firmly. "I must go."

She eyed my single bag next to her. "With this? You won't get very far."

Well, I did almost freeze to death overnight. But I refused to be shaken further. "I have what I need."

"Bah! You don't even know how to make a fire!" The woman threw her head back and flung a single, loud laugh into the cold air. "That's right—I caught that much before you conjured up your stonework. If you're so sure, fine. Go on. I won't be able to hunt anything with you standing there."

She gathered my things off the snowy ground and stuffed them into my bag, then tossed the bag toward me. I haphazardly caught it by the leather strap.

"If you change your mind," the woman said, situating herself more comfortably on my pine needle mat, "find the cabin on the east bank of the river. There's a bridge. And take care not to set off any of my traps!"

My blood flowed more warmly through my veins now, and I found the strength in my limbs to turn away from the woman and take my first heavy steps toward the south.

I continued downhill, sliding more than walking through the snow, out of the woman's sight. As I walked, I let my castle fall. The sunlight was slicing through the thin gaps in the trees now from the east, any trace of cloud overhead gone, pulled back toward the city where the sky churned with a tumultuous gray. I leaned against a sturdy tree trunk and took a steadying breath. How fast did I need to travel before the woman reported me to Gryffin's guards? How far could I get?

With these boots sinking in the snow, not far enough.

I'd only ever seen snowshoes in books, but I was able to recall enough to see the potential in the sheets of tree bark lying on the ground around me. I found two pieces of roughly the same size, almost twice the size of my foot, and used Equos's dagger to cut away several young, limber branches of a sprouting fir. I secured the bark to the bottom of my boots with the branches tied tightly around my foot, and I felt a surge of relief as I took my first few cumbersome steps without sinking to my knees. My ankle was grateful as well.

Able to move a bit faster now, I picked my way farther down the mountainside using trees and rocks for support. I felt the cold air especially in my injured shoulder, but I kept moving, listening for a babble of water. I still needed flint for fire, and I prayed to Haggard I would find some if I could track down the river the woman had mentioned.

The trees hovering above me allowed pockets of sunlight to warm the ground, and there, the snow was hard from melting and refreezing. I took advantage of these little spots when I could, and before long, I was warm enough to remove my top cloak and stuff it into my bag. As the sun crept higher into the sky, my steps grew lighter.

The sound of trickling water danced its way to me through the pine needles, and I breathed a sigh of relief. Soon, I would be able to build a fire. And I could cook, and warm myself, and dry my clothes—

Then I heard the shouting.

Men and women both, their voices carrying on the still air. Through the trees, I saw a flash of crimson and gold.

I cursed aloud as panic ripped through the precarious hope I'd begun to feel, and I turned around swiftly, eyes scanning the forest for a place to hide.

I hadn't expected Gryffin's soldiers to search the forest so soon, or perhaps I'd thought I'd be farther along on my way. Either way, I found myself scrambling for my wits as I crouched behind the nearest boulder.

I could not stay here long, however. I knew I needed to keep moving. They would find me eventually, or I'd freeze—whichever came first.

I held Equos's dagger steady in my hand, and with a deep inhale, I slowly stood from my crouch, scanning the forest.

A burst of gold to my right, so I went left.

A woman's shout behind me, so I hurried my footsteps.

I could see the river now through the trees, with drifts of snow floating on its current, and soldiers in Tarasynian uniforms searching its banks. There was no sign of Gryffin, but I doubted he would miss out on this particular search party. He had to keep up a front, after all. Concerned fiancé. Compassionate king.

I could have spit on his boots.

The snap of a twig behind me made me flinch and sink behind a nearby tree, my heart pounding against my ribs. A few moments later, the rhythm of hooves crunching through the snow had me running.

One of my snowshoes cracked under my step, sending a loud snap echoing through the trees. In the moment, it was deafening. No longer able to run without my snowshoes, I darted for a group of thick spruces, concealing myself in their needles.

There was the snort of a horse. In the tight spaces between branches, I saw dark hooves high-stepping through the snow.

A man clicked his tongue, and the horse stopped in its steps.

"Rosemary."

His voice made me want to shout and cry simultaneously.

"You don't have to die out here," he continued softly. "You can still come home."

My heart pounded in my ears, and my neck felt sticky with a cold sweat.

"I know you're here somewhere. I will find you." There was no smile in his voice. "And I will let you return to Lecevonia." He said something else then under his breath, unintelligible.

I heard his feet land in the snow. "I only need your vow."

I did not believe for one moment that he would let me return home. For the first time in two weeks, I felt the pressure of his Talent shove against the sturdy walls of my castle.

He was so close to my cluster of spruces. His black cloak blocked any view I'd had through the branches, and I could just faintly smell his familiar scent of smoke and honey.

Snow fell from the tree branches above me. A sudden rustling over my head conjured a sharp gasp out of my throat, and my gaze shot upward into the towering pine.

A red hawk burst from the tree and flapped its great wings, screeching loudly as it flew to the next tree over.

I was so tightly wound that I almost screamed, but I clamped my lips shut and clapped my gloved hand over my mouth.

Gryffin cursed loudly, more in disappointment than in shock, and spun on his heels, clearing my limited line of sight. "Come out then, Yetta."

Then, to my surprise more than the hawk had been, the old woman emerged from a thicket to my right, her hood lowered. She had a thick silver braid that brushed her waist thrown over her shoulder.

"Hello, Gryffin." Her voice carried the drone of indifference. "Has becoming king been as grand as you hoped?"

"You know who I'm looking for," he said curtly, ignoring the woman's question. "Have you seen her? Or heard her?" He rapped the side of his head with a finger.

I heard Yetta scoff. "If your young queen was in this forest, I'd know." Then her voice changed pitch, an amused lift. "So she ran from you, did she? She wasn't very keen on your big plan?"

Gryffin was quiet for a moment before responding in a low voice.

"I thought she'd begun to see. But her opinion doesn't matter anymore." He almost sounded . . . hurt. Disappointed.

Yetta clucked her tongue. "You're as narrow-minded as your grandfather."

Gryffin spoke through gritted teeth, and I saw his fists clench at his side. "I am more than twice the man my grandfather had been."

A stroke of pity crossed Yetta's face. "You certainly have the potential to be."

Silence filled the forest, until finally Gryffin asked, "You truly haven't seen her?"

"No. But I doubt she'll make it very long on her own, if she's still alive."

Gryffin's chuckle was strangely proud. "I wouldn't underestimate her."

"And you would do your heart wrong to overestimate her," Yetta said, which stung a bit. "These woods are dangerous when you are alone." Her words then felt pointed at me more than Gryffin.

Yetta continued speaking to Gryffin, speaking so matter-of-fact. "She loves another man, yet you pine for her. That's unlike you."

"You would not know," Gryffin said through a sneer. "You left us."

Yetta held up her hands amicably. "I see I crossed our line. Your queen is not here in this part of the forest, that much I can tell you. Focus your efforts elsewhere. Or better yet, count her dead."

Gryffin shook his head. "She is not dead. Somehow, I know that. But even if she were, she took something I need."

"Ah, yes. The relics." Yetta shrugged her shoulders. "Perhaps those are gone too. A shame."

"I refuse to count Rosemary as gone. Not yet." Gryffin stuck his foot in his stirrup and swung his leg over the back of his horse. "I'll be back soon. Hold her for me if you find her."

"Of course, Your Majesty," Yetta said, bending dramatically at her waist in a mocking bow.

Gryffin grunted once and turned his mare around in the snow. Without another glance toward each other, he kicked his horse into a canter and rode off, and Yetta turned toward the firs in which I'd been hiding.

But I dared not move, not until I was sure Gryffin was gone.

The old woman hummed lightly to herself, picking up broken twigs and loose needles and stuffing them into the bag on her back. Finally, she looked behind her once, then turned her stormy gaze directly to me. "He is out of earshot."

I let out a long, releasing breath and disengaged myself from the spruces, shaking needles out of my cloak. "Thank you," I said as I turned to her. "Really."

She shrugged, and her gaze drifted to the trees above us, perhaps spotting the red hawk. "I see your reasoning more than his. His mind is . . . changed. Darker. So different than when he was a boy." She shook her head, and I glimpsed for the first time a look of confusion on the woman's face. "And he killed that poor girl, and that Lecevonian boy! Now, *that* surprised me." She hiked her bag higher onto her shoulder. "Perhaps his mother's blood has been lost in his veins. Are you coming?" She turned then to look at me again. "You'll need new snowshoes, it seems."

And I followed her this time. Perhaps her knowing too much was a very good thing.

"How do you know Gryffin?" I asked, picking my way through the snow alongside her. The river had grown louder, and I spotted it again through the trees. The soldiers hadn't made it down this far yet, and a thin, wooden bridge peeked out from underneath the snow and glistening icicles. I didn't know how it was still standing, let alone supporting the weight of anyone. And along the riverbank, so close to where I'd stayed shivering last night, lay innumerable pieces of flint nestled together.

Yetta laughed and took a creaky step onto the worn bridge.

"Oh, child," she said, heaving herself up on the bridge with the help of the railing. "I'm his grandmother."

CHAPTER SIXTEEN

YETTA'S COTTAGE WAS what I imagined an old witch's hovel to look like. A simple stone-laid home with red shutters and a wooden door, with herbs hanging out on a line to dry and its humble chimney puffing billows of smoke into the cold air.

What was most peculiar though was the large juniper tree growing right in the middle of the house, with swooping branches draped lazily across the snowy ground, as if its innumerable years had taken a toll on the creature. However, despite its aged demeanor, the tree looked green and spritely as ever. It reminded me of Yetta in that way. The stones of the house had been laid and mortared around the branches, simply accepting the tree's existence in its midst.

Outside, there was a greenhouse that would have loomed over the tiny house had it not been dwarfed by the massive juniper, and it sheltered a plethora of herbs and vegetables from the harsh perpetual winter. It even housed five carefully pruned fruit trees.

"I was given this place at my request, when I'd been queen," Yetta explained as I followed her back out through the greenhouse door.

"My husband permitted a place outside of Snowmont for me to stay. I had threatened to leave if he didn't agree. His antics drove me mad." She gave a disgusted snort as she waved me forward into her home.

Inside the cottage, the fact that the house had been built around the juniper was even more prominent. The tree's massive trunk wound its way from the floor to the roof near the kitchen table, and the tree's draping branches doubly served as the back wall of the kitchen. Little sprigs had managed to offshoot from the trunk inside the home, adorned with the familiar periwinkle clusters of berry-like cones.

"Did the king know?" I asked as I slipped off my cloak, relishing in the warmth of the cottage. "That you were Talented?"

She nodded slowly as she set her bag of trappings on the floor and took a seat at her wooden table. "I told him upon our betrothal. I thought it only fair. But I also thought that I could trust him, my soon-to-be-husband." Her tone had turned dark, and she glared past me through her open window.

"But as soon as he knew, he began devising. He wanted more like me. He used me in his court, but I didn't know it until much later." She shook her head and frowned. "I'd had the silly notion he'd simply wanted me to be an active part of his rule, a prominent queen. I gladly took the role—I wasn't one to enjoy living in the shadows of another." She eyed me with a little smirk on her face. "I was thrilled for a while, thrilled to be seen as special. I'd joined him in his meetings, on his journeys, glued to his side and telling him anything and everything I could learn using my ability.

"One day, though, he took me with him on an excursion to Borea. A normal outing, I thought, to show our faces to the town. We stopped at an inn, and the innkeeper's daughter had the most curious eyes. Green, though not quite like yours—they were darker, earthy. With the subtlest hint of red."

"The red flecks," I said quietly.

Yetta nodded. "I hadn't known anyone Talented aside from myself, as rare as we were, and I thought the legends of red-flecked eyes were meaningless. Much like you did. My eyes never had red in them, after all—why would I believe such a trivial thing? You've heard the old saying, haven't you? 'The greedy will bleed while the righteous will heed'? I thought it was all nonsense.

"But I could see her mind, and I knew what she could do. She couldn't hide it from me, though now I wish she could have." Yetta folded her hands in front of her and sighed. "Then very nonchalantly over a mug of cider, the king asked her family if anyone was Talented. And the question surprised me. Why would he care?

"And what surprised me even more was that they lied! The girl's father went as far to deny ever having known a Talented. And when my husband turned to look at me, those blue eyes fierce, I did what I always did. I served his will. I shook my head. And that was the death sentence for the innkeeper and his family. Left to freeze in the stocks."

A chill ran through my spine at the image. Brittle skin, wind-torn eyes. "And the girl?"

"Taken back to Snowmont. I couldn't look her in the eyes, knowing what I'd done. I don't know what happened to her after that." Her gray eyes settled on the table, her fingers tracing a well-worn ring around a whorl in the wood. A habit, it seemed.

She lifted her head and smiled at me. "You're an observant one."

"It certainly does not feel that way," I said, letting out a dry chuckle. "Gryffin's Talent should have been so obvious, yet I gave my mind to him blindly."

"You cannot blame yourself for not knowing, child. That's all simply a part of my grandson's nature. Cunning, smart, resourceful. And determined. That is who he is. And you broke his Persuasion on your own!" She looked at me wide-eyed, impressed. "I haven't seen anyone do such a thing aside from little Kathryn."

"Kathryn isn't a little girl anymore, you know."

"Yes. I see her in your mind," Yetta said, almost wistful. "She is beautiful. But I haven't seen her since she was a child, so a child she will remain in my mind."

I feared my next question would be too personal, but then, without my castle in my mind, she knew what I wanted to ask anyway. "Why haven't you been back?"

Yetta sighed and dropped her gaze to the table. "I couldn't stand to see my son follow in his father's footsteps. I loathed my husband, but it was impossible to loathe my son. So I left, spent most of my time here."

"And you didn't return for Roderich." I stated more than asked.

Yetta met my eyes again and shook her head firmly. "Oh, no. I visited every once in a while, for Gryffin and Kathryn, and the twins. But Roderich always had a frightening mind. Unstable. And as he grew, his thoughts turned violent. Vengeful. I left for good when he was thirteen. It was too much, and I saw that he would choose destruction. By the time he took the throne, I had made my home out here and was perfectly content."

I nodded thoughtfully, imagining a small curly-haired boy already so prone to anger.

He did not have to be that way, however. He could have learned to cope differently than setting off a riddling disease across the Peninsula.

Yetta smirked. "Ah, so you know. Kathryn told you the family's dark secret."

I nodded. "It seems like Roderich was impulsive from the beginning."

"Many people are impulsive," Yetta responded as she stood from her chair to look out her window, her long braid swinging behind her. "Controlling those impulses is largely a part of what makes a person."

Just then, there was a loud commotion outside, and I stood from my chair and rushed to her side at the window.

The red hawk that had flown overhead earlier landed on the windowsill with a deafening screech that filled the little kitchen. Its talons dug into the wood, and upon closer inspection, it seemed that this was not the first time talons had left their deep marks on the windowsill. The hawk beat its great wings one final time before folding them into its sides, and it stared at me with large, intelligent eyes that reminded me of Corvus.

"Oh, don't think about that dreadful bird," Yetta said with a huff. "August is nothing like that heathen."

"August?"

Yetta smiled. "My husband."

Before I could fathom how odd a bird must be for a husband, the hawk took off from the sill and glided around a corner and into a room. What emerged just a few moments later was a man, tall and lean like Zeke, but older, in his sixties or so. He had light, thinning tufts of hair above his ears, and his jawline sported a few days of stubble. But he had a kind face with a relaxed grin. He wore a pair of leather pants, held up by a braided cord of rope, and nothing more.

I averted my gaze, but the rush of embarrassment I'd expected to feel at seeing a man's bare chest—a married man, no less—for the first time never came. Perhaps it was because he held himself so naturally, as if this were every day. And, well, this very well might be an everyday occurrence here. I nodded my head to him. "Hello."

"Hi there," he answered with a light smile. Then he turned to his wife. "They're gone, Yetta. Out of the forest."

"Thank Haggard," the old woman replied with a roll of her eyes.

As the man pulled on a tunic and walked back outside, Yetta dropped a wooden plate with brown bread rolls at the center of the table.

"Eat."

I gratefully picked up a roll. It was cold and hit my stomach like a rock, but I was famished. The last meal I'd eaten had been retched up on the back doorstep of some poor soul's shop.

"Don't expect to find court-level food here," Yetta said. "I'm not much for cooking."

"I'm thankful for anything, I assure you," I replied. "Had you not found me, I'd either be back at Snowmont or wandering the woods alone." I realized again how vastly unprepared I'd been for any trek through the forest.

"Very unprepared, indeed. What gave you the idea that you would be able to survive a trip back to your kingdom, let alone find your way?"

I felt a bit of indignance rising in me. "I would have managed." I had had a plan, after all.

"Without a map, or a compass? Or flint?" Yetta laughed unapologetically, just as she had in the forest. "Ah, you would have gotten by, I suppose. You're smart, and resourceful enough it seems. You made snowshoes, didn't you? Well, no worries, child. We will help you on your way."

I folded my hands together in thanks. "I truly appreciate your kindness. Kathryn had been gathering me supplies, and my friend Celeste was supposed to come with me . . ." I trailed off as my mind returned to her. I'd abandoned her.

"You had no choice," Yetta said, surprising me again with her Talent. "You were hardly escaping with your life. In a few days, you would have never seen the light of day again."

Her words then only confirmed what I'd assumed from the day I'd been taken from my kingdom—that Gryffin had every intention of killing me as soon as he had a claim over my kingdom with our vows, if I made things difficult for him. If anyone could possibly know the truth in Gryffin's mind, it would be this woman.

My voice was low. "How would he have done it?"

Yetta paused before answering, untying a dried herb from the line and crumbling the leaves into a small jar. She repeated this a few more times, until the jar was full. "He was still sorting out the details," she finally said. "Poison, most likely."

Poison. That would have been the most convenient, surely. Slipping too much of a sleeping draught into my wedding wine, or perhaps lacing my breakfast tea the morning after with wolfsbane or hemlock. The thoughts were horrid, and I shivered.

"It would have hurt him," Yetta added, still turned away from me. "I do hope you know that."

I scoffed. "No. He would have enjoyed seeing me out of his way."

"Do you think he enjoyed killing his brother?"

"Did he not?" I felt my cheeks redden with anger. "He certainly did not seem remorseful."

"I did not say he was remorseful," Yetta said dryly. "But just because he does not regret it, does that mean he wanted to do it?"

To be honest, I did not care whether his intentions were good or not. What mattered was his decision in the end.

"Gryffin's mind is more complicated than that." The old woman turned toward me now. "He thinks and acts as if he has no other choice. That does not mean he wants to do what he does."

"As if he has some destiny to fulfill?" I shook my head incredulously. "Well, if that destiny involves killing me and anyone else who may not do his bidding, I believe it is delusional."

At that, Yetta let out a loud cackle. "That is fair!" Then, her voice quieted again. "Still, he cared for you. Perhaps even loved you. Still may."

"He loved the fact that I could give him a kingdom," I said, crossing my arms over my chest.

But Yetta shook her head. "It was more than that."

I thought I'd loved him once too. I remembered our kiss in the stable, our last moment of certainty before he rode off to meet his brother on his march to Equos. The security I'd felt in his arms, the strength I felt in our bond—although it was all shrouded in a haze now. Yes, I thought I loved him.

But I knew now that it had all been coerced.

Now, I hated him. His feelings had no right to sway me anymore. He'd lost that when he knocked me unconscious and stole me from my kingdom. Even more, he'd lost that when he killed Thomas, and Cassia, and Xal.

I felt my anger rising still, like heat gathering in my chest, so I found a different matter to worry about.

"I dropped my other bag in the city." I looked down at the bundle of leather at my feet. "It'd had my compass, and my food. I don't have a working bow, or any arrows, but I do have this." I took out Vena's stringless bow. "I was hoping to somehow restring it along the way." With what, I had no idea, but the intent was there.

Yetta's eyes widened for just a second, all talk of Gryffin forgotten, and her fingers reached toward the curved wooden arms almost reverently. I hadn't heard the door open, but August was there suddenly as well, arms loaded down with firewood, gazing down at the relic.

"So much magic runs through this one object," Yetta murmured. Her gray eyes were bright, energized. Consuming.

"I have others," I said cautiously. "Two other relics."

Her eyes jumped up to meet mine, seemingly eager for the excuse to look away from the bow, and she pulled her hand back. "Good. Keep them close. We should be able to restring this one with little problem."

August sat next to me at the table and grabbed a roll. "Two queens in this house. This is almost unheard of!"

"You're Talented too, yes?" I asked. "You were the bird."

"Reduced to but a bird," he said with a sad sigh, his voice heightening in hurt. From his smile, though, I figured he was teasing. "Yes, I am the hawk, and the hawk is me."

I returned his smile with a small grin. "Thank you. For pulling Gryffin's attention away from me."

"Of course. Yetta said you were worth saving." He winked at me, red-flecked hazel eyes sparkling.

"Well," I joked, "I'm glad I met her criteria." To which Yetta, who had returned to plucking her herbs, only shrugged without turning around. "How did you two meet? If she was the queen . . ."

"It was after King Romus had died," he said, taking the last bite of his roll. "Her son, King Falk, hired me as a caretaker and teacher for Roderich when the prince was just two years old. He'd made it very clear that he believed my Talent would make some ability in Roderich manifest." He glanced up at Yetta. "I left when she did."

"Good riddance too," Yetta chimed in, putting her gloves back on and planting a light kiss on August's cheek before disappearing into another room toward the back of the cottage.

"How was Roderich growing up?" I asked him.

August sat back in his wooden chair, thoughts deep. "He was always a determined boy. Not as driven as Gryffin, but indeed a contender. The difference between the two was that Gryffin was canny, like a fox.

Roderich was more like a rogue bear. Ferocious at every turn. Stephen certainly had it easier than me." He let out a small chuckle.

That name. My brain struggled to remember anything through the haze, but still, I returned to the breakfast I'd had with Gryffin in Snowmont, so many mornings ago.

"His caretaker," I managed to recall. "Gryffin had spoken fondly of him. But didn't . . . didn't something happen to him?"

August shook his head, and his face fell into a sad grimace. "I couldn't know. He was still assigned when I chose to leave."

Yetta came back into the kitchen and took her seat once more. In her hand now was a coil of hemp. "Let's see about that bow."

In just a short span of minutes, Yetta had Vena's bow restrung and was testing the tautness.

"That should work well enough." She held the bow in her gloved hands with a stare so intense that I felt as if I were intruding on something. There was an inexplicable tension in the room.

Then, she slowly began taking the glove off one hand, finger by finger.

"Yetta."

August's voice cut through the tension like a carving knife, and the old woman blinked hard several times. She slipped her glove back onto her hand and handed the bow to me.

"Keep it close," she said again.

The couple gave me a place to sleep—a cozy room toward the back of their cottage that was packed to the brim with odd objects and supplies rather than bedroom furniture. A mace that seemed too large for either of them to wield sat in the corner next to a potted plant with strange burgundy marks on the leaves, which seemed to be quite healthy in the utter darkness of the room. There was a wicker basket full of rolled parchment, and a crate of trinkets both metal and wooden, springs and blocks and spare parts. I thought I caught a glimpse of a few spools of hemp in there too. An impressive deer's head that had been mounted on the wall flickered in my lantern's light.

"My father," August had said somberly when he and Yetta led me to the room. When I'd looked at him in silent horror, he'd laughed so hard that he'd had to lay his hand on my shoulder for support. "I'm only teasing, girl. Don't be so serious."

I tucked myself into the woolen blankets of the small cot and so gratefully closed my eyes.

Then, in hardly a blink, it was morning.

When I awoke, the lantern's wick glowed with the last traces of oil in its basin, and there was a fresh set of clothes at the foot of my cot. I quickly put on the fur-lined leather pants and tunic—which fit me surprisingly well, so they must have been Yetta's—and went to the kitchen.

The light was still early, just before dawn, but Yetta and August were already bustling around the little cottage.

But the juniper tree stopped me in my tracks. Tiny lights danced around the trunk and branches. They weaved in and out of the green needles, disappearing and reappearing like magical orbs. It seemed like hundreds of them, flying from the floor to the ceiling. They added a warm glow to the room still otherwise shrouded in darkness. They reminded me of the fireflies I would see in the hot Lecevonian forests of late summer, but this climate was much too cold for them, surely.

"It is," said Yetta from the head of the table. "We don't know why or how fireflies are here. But they've picked our home as their home."

She shrugged her shoulders, a move that I was recognizing as one of her characteristics. "So we share."

Then Yetta hiked her leather bag over her shoulder and grabbed her bow by the door. "Put on your cloak, child, and bring that bow of yours. I am going to teach you how to hunt."

She said it so authoritatively that I didn't think twice about rushing back to my little room and grabbing my things. Soon, we were out the door, hoods pulled low against the falling snow. A red hawk flew overhead, and Yetta rolled her eyes.

"You should thank Haggard you didn't have to endure his 'early bird' jokes this morning." Still, though her voice was gruff, her eyes held an undeniable smile.

The first rays of sun glimpsed through the tree trunks and hit my face, warming my cheeks. "He hunts as well? As a hawk?"

"Indeed. He has more success than these traps do," she said, jingling the bag on her shoulder. "But they are still worth setting up, and I can lend you a few for your journey."

As we walked, she pointed out the tracks of animals in the snow. Today, we were after a deer, though she said I wouldn't be after deer on my own. They'd apparently been tracking this one for a week now. She also showed me ideal places to set up this trap or that, and she taught me how to tie and set up a couple of snares. I took to the snares all right, since knot-tying had been one of Zeke's favorite things to practice as children. A pang jolted my heart at the thought of him, and I realized then that he had never gotten my message. He would continue on to Viridi looking for me. He might have even been in the city now.

But I could not go back.

Yetta broke the silence, confirming my thoughts with a shake of her head. "No, you cannot. My grandson has his soldiers and citizens scouring the city and the edges of the forest as we speak. It's more likely you'd get caught than find your young lover."

The word "lover" made me falter in my steps, and heat immediately rose to my face.

"Child," Yetta said with a chuckle. "I can see what he is to you, clear as day!"

I sighed. "Well, it certainly took me a while to realize it. I'd never truly entertained the thought. Still cannot, not really."

Yetta stayed silent, thoughtful as we continued crunching through the snow. Finally, she said, "A queen's duty is to her kingdom, that is true. I know that as well as you, and that is why I stayed with Romus for so many years. Hiddon needed the produce from Tarasyn's greenhouses, and Tarasyn needed a queen for an heir." She stopped walking and turned to face me. "Your position is a bit different than mine, however. You have power that I did not have, and your decisions change things. If we get you home alive."

She nodded me forward with a little smile on her lips, and I realized we'd stopped at the base of a tree, where a nearby boulder had been half-buried in the ground by years of stagnation.

But I was still stuck on her words. What did she mean, change things?

Yetta dropped her leather bag on the ground and set her bow in the crook of the rock and the tree. She then snapped her fingers and motioned for me to look over her shoulder. "Focus. Here you can see downhill for safety, and the rock and trees will block you—and hopefully your scent—from the wind. A place like this makes for a good shelter as well, with a bit sprucing up. A fire pit there, a branch of pine needles there . . ."

"Hiddon," I said, smiling. "That's why you're so good at this. Trapping and hunting. Outdoor living."

She shrugged. "Even we princesses are taught to hunt."

"And that's why Kathryn is so skilled in archery!"

Yetta grinned. "Who do you think handed her first bow to her?"

Kathryn's words of her family's interest in hunting made more sense than ever. It had come from Yetta. I equated Hiddon's hunting to Lecevonia's horse riding. It would be hard to find a better horseman or horsewoman anywhere else on the Peninsula. Too bad I didn't have a horse now to cut my travel in half. That was another part of the plan that had fallen through.

"You can buy a horse when you arrive in Pruin," Yetta said, waving her hand nonchalantly.

"Will I ever get used to you answering my thoughts?"

"I can keep quiet if you'd rather."

"No," I responded quickly. "It's nice, actually."

Yetta chuckled. "Good. Because I'm not sure if I could actually keep quiet."

However, as Yetta's hunting persona set in, our conversation faded into silence. She stared intently into the trees, while I listened for leaves crunching, branches cracking, trees rustling. We stayed like this for an hour or so, and I was beginning to wonder if Yetta was going to have to go home empty-handed.

Then, about thirty meters away uphill, a thicket of young spruces rustled together. Slowly, a deer as white as the snow at its feet emerged from the thicket. Its deep black eyes glimmered as it turned its head left, then right, before huffing a cloud of warm air into the chill. After a silent and still moment, it faced away from us and began nibbling at the branches of the young trees.

Yetta pulled back her arrow slowly, took her time taking aim, and let it fly. The arrow embedded itself into the deer's shoulder, and the deer took off into the trees.

I turned sharply to Yetta. "It's gotten away?" The poor thing was hurt!

But she shook her head. "It was a clean shot, so he won't get far. He might be already down. It will have been quick."

I followed her from our spot and through the thicket of spruces where the deer had disappeared. She pointed out droplets of red blood on the needles and on the snow. Sure enough, only a few paces further, the deer lay in the snow, already dead.

Yetta nodded, standing a few feet back from the fallen deer. "It's a good habit to approach carefully, just in case they have a last reflex ready for you. But yes, this one is dead. Its essence is gone."

I looked at her, my brow pinched together. "Essence?"

She tapped the side of her head. "Animals don't have thoughts exactly, but they have a presence—an essence—that I recognize." She approached the deer now and laid a hand on its head. "I've been watching this one for a while. He had been rejected from his herd. Bad bloodline, I suppose. He never grew his antlers." She strapped a rope around each of its hind legs and handed them to me with an impish grin. "And you get to drag him back. Build up those muscles you'll need to survive out here."

I stared at her for a moment, and seeing as she was not joking, I took the ropes from her hands.

It was slow going, but I eventually dragged the deer back toward the cottage. My injured shoulder complained, but I gritted my teeth and kept on. On our way, Yetta checked the traps and snares, which gave me a chance to rest every now and then. We'd gotten one rabbit in a snare, but the others had been empty, so Yetta left them in place.

When we finally got to the foot of the old bridge, I was sweating and sore. August came loping over with a smile, took the ropes from me, and dragged the deer the rest of the way. Oh, I could have kissed his boots, I was so grateful.

Back at the cottage, August had his quarry laid out on a wooden table outside: two rabbits, one squirrel, and a long-bodied animal with small ears and a long snout. Ermine, he called it.

My eyes traveled incredulously from one pristine pelt to the next. "Does every animal here have white coats?"

Yetta only shrugged. "There's no reason for them to be any other color. There is always snow on the ground."

I watched the two work together in skinning and cleaning the animals while Yetta taught me what to do, and eventually I took over a rabbit Yetta had started while she began working on the deer.

We cooked a rabbit for lunch over a fire, which Yetta let me light with my flint and fire striker for practice. Then we salted and stored the rest of the small game for a later day. "Food keeps easily here, in the cold," Yetta explained.

That afternoon, Yetta finished with the deer and coated the animal skins with some foul-smelling concoction to begin the tanning process. Some of the bones from the deer she boiled with herbs and berries from the juniper tree and made a broth so deliciously unlike anything I'd ever smelled before, while other bones she cast away for later to make tools. Nothing was wasted.

While I helped her divide the deer meat into what was to be smoked now and stored for later, my mind drifted back to Zeke and his companions. What would he do once he found out I was no longer being held inside the walls of Snowmont? Would he venture into the snowy woods like I did?

He would be more prepared than me, for one. He had the knowledge I lacked when it came to this sort of thing. Settling disputes, delegating funds, and overseeing a kingdom's trade strategy—that was where my expertise lay. But survival, well, I had the stubbornness to do so at least.

I needed a way to let Zeke know I would continue down to Pruin. Maybe he could meet me there.

"It's a shame what my grandson did to that girl and young boy," Yetta suddenly said, upon hearing my thought.

I looked at her, eyes wide as the memory of Cassia's steady gaze and Xal's broken-toothed grin resurfaced. The axes fall, and their lives ended. It was more than a shame. "It sickens me that he has the whole city believing they were executed in my name."

"His power is strong," she said. "He has the entire *kingdom* under his Persuasion in one way or another." She glanced up at me then. "Yet you build a barrier. How?"

The now-fallen wall I'd maintained so carefully against my feelings for Zeke nudged just a hair. "I had a good bit of practice."

Yetta lifted her chin. "Your barrier stood against me. Your castle. That was . . . quite new to me."

I huffed a single laugh. "Well, I didn't trust you at the time."

"You have a skill, child." The old woman looked at me squarely. "Be sure you don't take it for granted."

I averted my gaze to the diced deer meat on the table in front of me. A stupid hope returned. "Is it—?"

"I don't think it's a Talent," Yetta answered with a shake of her head. "Not everything is about Talents. But it is interesting."

Then, her posture lifted, and she returned to her usual air of nonchalance. She rubbed a generous handful of salt onto the slab of deer cut for roasting in her gloved hands. "If your young man finds himself looking for you in these woods, I will tell him you've gone on to Pruin."

The relief I felt at her words made me work a little faster, cut the meat with a bit more gusto.

Now I just had to hope I could actually get there.

The next morning, Yetta took me hunting again, though this time was more so to teach me how to shoot. August joined us in human form, but he seemed to be itching to be flying above our heads.

Kathryn had been right. Moving targets, camouflaged no less, were more difficult. Still, after only two missed shots and too much time searching for those arrows, I found my mark on a rabbit, which Yetta said I could keep for my journey. She'd suggested I get on my way soon. The more distance I was able to put between me and Gryffin, the better.

On the way back to the cottage, she showed me certain plants and mushrooms that were edible, and others to avoid at all costs. She even pointed out a few berries that persisted in the cold climate. "Leave most of these for the wildlife though," she said. "They need it more than you do. Only forage when you cannot hunt. Which might be more often than you think." She glanced around the forest, her gray eyes flashing. "The animals are smart here."

"Well, let's hope Vena will bring me luck with her bow." I held up the bow with a wry smile. I could certainly use as many blessings as possible.

Yetta's eyes landed on the bow and lingered.

Then, August clasped a hand onto Yetta's shoulders lightly. "Maybe we can try to teach her to fish," he said. But his eyes were narrowed, speckled with worry.

His suggestion made Yetta blink and turn away from the bow, and my confusion only thickened.

They did try to teach me to fish once we reached the river. At first, I was intrigued. I hadn't eaten fish in years, not since a visit to Port Della with my parents. I could hardly remember what it tasted like. But soon, I found my bow much more cooperative than my fishing line, so I let my desire for fish wane. I doubted that I would have much resting time to sit on the river's bank anyhow.

After a while, Yetta left the river to begin gathering things for my travels, but August insisted I stay back and try to cast one more time. So he and I stood along the bank, my flashy lure rippling in the current. Still, the shimmering bodies of fish simply darted past my hook, continuing on their way downstream.

I felt I'd have more success aiming my bow toward the water.

"August," I said, "what was going on with Yetta in the woods? With this bow? It's happened before."

August sighed, pulling in his line. "Yetta's Talent is intense. Yes, *intense* is a good word." He chuckled to himself. "She can hear thoughts, yes, but she can also see."

"See?" I recalled when I'd seen her clear, gray eyes for the first time—like they had so much to tell, and so much still to learn. "What do you mean?"

"She always wears gloves, as you've noticed surely, but it isn't just for the cold." He cast his line again into the water. "When Yetta touches something, anything that has happened with that object, she sees. It's the item's past in a way, if that is possible. With something as ancient as that bow—something so full of *history*—naturally it calls to her to be touched. To be known." He nodded his head slowly and touched a finger to his temple. "My Yetta always has a lot going on up there, every minute of the day."

Just the thought overwhelmed me. Still, to see everything an object has *seen*. So much could be learned.

- 235 -

"Then why not let her touch the bow?"

"Because too much is deadly." His expression went dark. "It takes a toll on her. Scrambles things."

"Oh." Words from a book in Snowmont's library came back to me. About going mad if one's Talent was left unchecked.

"We all go mad eventually," Yetta's voice called lightly from up the bank. Her silhouette appeared. "Come. We should get you on your way."

I sighed heavily, reluctant, but I pulled in my empty hook and scrambled to my feet.

Along with my one bag, Yetta had packed me another loaded down with maps of Tarasyn and Lecevonia, a compass, a bag of flint, a spool of hemp twine, an extra set of boots, some dried fruit, a leather canteen for water, and my rabbit skinned, cooked, and wrapped tightly in leather. As I shuffled through the bag, I found an old book, titled, *Of the Sighted.* I looked up at Yetta, and she gave a simple nod.

"For your sister."

My heart swelled with the woman's kindness. "Thank you."

And, to my surprise, she'd found a sword and leather scabbard. Stained and unpolished, but sharp.

"Since you know how to use it," she said, cinching the scabbard's belt around my waist. She took a step back and smiled. "There."

Then, her gaze faltered. "I'd offer for you to stay here a while, but my grandson will return any day now. You have a better chance of hiding in the woods than here."

"I cannot even begin to express how thankful I am for your help," I said. "I truly would not have made it very far without you two."

August stepped forward with a smile and wrapped my cloak around my shoulders, securing it at my neck. "You will do just fine."

Yetta pressed my bags into my hand, then unlatched the one that contained the relics. Eyeing them carefully, she said, "Keep these close. These are what Gryffin is after, more so than you."

"I will."

"What do you plan to do with them, child?"

I paused for a moment before answering. "I'll most likely return them to their kingdoms." I had no use for them, after all.

Yetta nodded thoughtfully and latched the bag shut once more. After a weighted sigh, she said, "You know, my grandson's motive really isn't so evil. His methods aren't agreeable," she added as she caught my wide stare, "but awakening the Talented could very well be a good thing."

Hmm.

I knew she had a point. I'd thought the same, when Gryffin had been explaining the relics to me. Still, these were wrongly taken from their kingdoms. People had been killed—by Roderich and Gryffin both, the horrid murderers—over a scant possibility that these objects could stage something as large as an Awakening. It was as barbaric as King Romus's and King Falk's actions against their own people in Tarasyn.

"It is no *scant* possibility." Yetta put her hands on her hips. "These objects hold more power in them than the entire Peninsula on Solstice Day. If all five are brought together, an Awakening *will* happen, one way or another." But her gray eyes narrowed then, and they flashed a glint of caution. "And an Awakening is but a gateway to a new future for the Peninsula. But something in Gryffin's mind . . ." She trailed off, her gaze traveling beyond her cottage, beyond the woods, beyond Tarasyn. "Something familiar, something that I couldn't quite see."

Her murmuring made me glance toward August, who was staring hard at his wife.

Whatever it was that Gryffin had obscured from Yetta, it was enough to reinforce my will to ensure an Awakening did not happen.

Yetta's eyes found their way back to my face, squinted and curious. "As you wish, child. Now"—she patted my bag—"you best get on your way. Stay off the main road. Follow the river, and you'll get to Pruin."

August gave me a reassuring pat on my shoulder. "I'll fly with you until nightfall."

So, with his promise and Yetta's stern instruction, I latched my snowshoes over my boots and turned away from the cottage. August disappeared around the side of the greenhouse, and a moment later, a red hawk swooped in and perched on the corner of the greenhouse's glass roof.

I shared one last look of gratitude with Yetta, threw the hood of my cloak over my head, and headed toward the river, with August swooping through the trees above me.

~*PRUIN*~
ZEKE

The snow-clad roofs of the small Tarasynian village finally came into our view. I'd been here before, only once, and only for a quick supply run.

"A warm mug of mead is calling to me," said Roger.

I chuckled. "Me too. We'll stop, but let's keep it discreet." Telling a hulking man like Roger to be discreet was like telling someone to cross the entire Peninsula in a day on foot.

On the road, he told us how he'd been able to survive being trapped in a corridor freckin' teeming with Tarasynian soldiers. It turned out the soldiers were no match for his battleax and brute strength, and he'd barely been scathed aside from a sword swipe to his forearm. After he'd cleared the armory corridor, he'd joined the battle in Hillstone's courtyard until the Tarasynian soldiers were unceremoniously called back.

"It was too sudden," he'd said, his deep voice low in the trees. "I'd assumed Her Majesty had been victorious. Until Lord Brock told me the queen had left with Prince Gryffin. I had my suspicions then." He glowered at the ground. "I'd had plenty of chances to kill the man."

I cursed myself for that too. I should have skewered him during our first swording practice.

Boars, I should've strangled him in the hall outside Rose's door!

I should have—

"Zeke." Terrin's voice brought me back to myself. "We're close to the gate."

Just inside the tree line, we slowed our horses and threw our hoods over our heads. I nodded to my comrades, and we led our horses onward, plodding through the snow to the wooden doors.

A torch lit from above the gate, and a man's face peered at us through a small sliding hole at our eye level. "State your business here."

I let my lips turn upward into a languid smile. "Good evening, sir. Since when is Pruin shut up so tightly?"

The man stroked his beard. "We can't be too careful these days, what with the unrest in the new Tarasynian lands." He shook his head somberly. "You've been here before then? What's your name?"

"I've just traveled through once or twice." I offered a little smirk of chagrin. "You probably wouldn't remember me. I am Gooderich Fally, and these are my companions, Bernstein and Tobiah." The lies came easy, the names grabbed off a rotating list in my head.

"Gooderich?" the man repeated. "Hmm, that's my brother's name."

I silently cursed. Too memorable already. "It's a good, strong name, sir."

Then the man looked behind me, took in Roger, and whistled. "What did you say your business was here again?"

"Merchants," I answered, "headed to Pax Pass."

"Pax Pass? That's quite a way north."

My easy smile returned, touched with just enough fatigue. "Indeed, sir. We'd like to stop and rest for a moment."

Finally, the man grunted and closed the sliding door. With a loud clang of the doors' latches, they slogged open before us.

Outside the town's tiny tavern, we dismounted and shook our hoods and boots free of snow. As we stepped through the sturdy door, a warmth I hadn't felt in days welcomed us and prompted us to collapse into the nearest seats we could. The tavern owner's son approached our table in a busy flourish, and I waved for a round for the three of us.

"How much longer to Viridi?" Roger's voice was as dark as the wood beneath our hands.

Terrin leaned back in his seat. "Another week or so, I'd wager. Maybe less."

Too long, I thought to myself.

But Roger's and Terrin's conversation had become background noise to me. Instead, I had my ears tuned toward a trio of travelers two tables away.

"I bet those sorry souls wish they hadn't spoken against the queen," one with a graying, scraggly beard said.

His cloaked companion shrugged. "I still don't understand why the Lecevonian would have done so." She picked up her mug and took a drink. "Or why he was in the city in the first place."

I glanced over to Roger and Terrin and saw they too had started listening.

"My theory's that he got angry when she agreed to marry the king," the man said, crossing his arms over his chest. "Did you hear that he started a shouting match along with the other Lecevonians just before he lost his head?" A sharp scoff. "He probably didn't want Lecevonia and Tarasyn to join forces. Selfish brute."

The tavern owner's son returned with our steaming mugs of mead, and Roger thanked him quietly.

"It still seems odd to me," the woman in the party answered. "If he had so much pride, it seems like he'd never spread ill rumors of his queen."

"Every kingdom has their radicals."

"Did you know there were so many Lecevonians in the city?"

"All assigned to work in the castle, I've heard."

Our table kept a relaxed composure, but when Terrin spoke in hushed tones, his voice was tense. "Her Majesty *agreed* to marry the king?"

My eyes locked with his. Argh, Rose . . . What had Gryffin done to break her down into an agreement? A sharp blade of anguish plunged through my chest as flashes of torture raced into my mind, each one worse than the last. Or maybe he'd done it with a deadly threat, either to her or to the Lecevonians trapped in Tarasyn.

But I didn't voice these things to my comrades. Instead, I kept a stone face as I murmured, "The crite is probably using his sorcery on them as we speak. All the more reason to get her out of there."

"And he has other Lecevonians too?" Roger growled. "He *murdered* one of us in Tarasyn!" He almost banged his fist onto the table, but he caught himself at the last second. A child nearby eyed him fearfully and pulled on his mother's skirts.

Terrin and I both gave Roger a warning glance. Discretion may not have been Roger's strong suit, but here, surrounded by the leaning ears of Tarasynians, any slip up was deadly. He could yell all day tomorrow in the woods if he desired—I didn't care. Just not here.

Instead, Roger settled for a grunt and an angry scowl. "We need to get the rest of our people out."

I remembered, then, Rose's message. *Alive and not alone.* Maybe she'd been referring to the other Lecevonians.

None of them were safe in Viridi.

Terrin mentioned something about furs at a normal volume, and I chuckled through another sip of mead. Finally, as heads nonchalantly turned away from our table, I spoke once more in a low voice. "Our mission is to bring the queen home. Once Her Majesty is back in Lecevonia"—where I would never let my eyes off her again—"we will figure out a rescue plan for the captured Lecevonians. The sooner we move, the better."

Both men nodded, and one by one, we downed our mugs of mead and stood from our seats. My legs protested, and I figured this was how the horses must have felt. But a force of will drove me from the comfort of the wooden table, leaving behind a few silver coins for payment.

As we turned toward the door, however, a man in the far corner caught my attention. His head was buried in his arms and shoulders shook violently, though he remained silent.

His grieving felt too familiar.

So I approached the tavern owner at the bar and ordered a round for the man in the corner. As I dropped a couple more coins on the dark wood, the tavern owner's son brought a piping hot mug to the man, who lifted his head and found me through the crowded mess of tables. I offered a silent nod and turned away, but as I followed Roger and Terrin again into the cold evening air, I could not shake the idea that the man in the corner had reminded me of an older, less brawny Xal.

CHAPTER SEVENTEEN

I TRAVELED SOUTH, following the river as closely as I could. The snowshoes from Yetta helped immensely and were so much sturdier than my makeshift shoes of bark and branches. My bags were surprisingly light, and now that Vena's bow had a string, I could hike it over my shoulder with ease. August flew with me, his screech resounding from high in the trees any time I looked up to the bright gray sky.

But the afternoon went by too quickly. Before I even made it to the first big curve in the river, the sky turned to the dark violet of evening.

Still, the feeling of progress kept my head held high.

August landed on a nearby rock, his talons holding on to the uneven surface, and stared at me with human-like eyes.

I gave him a nod and a smile. "Thank you, August. I'll be okay." And I believed it.

I made camp that night in a hollowed tree, and before long my fire was blazing, lighting the forest around me. Alone, I began to feel once again the thrum of energy floating through the branches, the shrubs—

the very ground beneath my feet. It left goosebumps on my arms, this constant energy.

I ate half of my rabbit in silence, filled my canteen with snow, and curled up with my blankets in the hollow of my tree. I slept warmer than I'd ever thought I possibly could in these snow-laden woods.

That warmth was short-lived, however, for the next morning, I woke up to a dead fire, a cold tree, and a growling stomach. I cursed myself for not thinking to keep the fire going throughout the night. Shivering, I wrapped my cloak and blankets tightly around me and huddled in the tree until the sun had risen enough to cast a few warming rays. Still, I kept my hopes up as I packed up camp. I'd made it through a night on my own, and *not* fighting for survival this time.

And onward I went.

I munched on a bit more of my rabbit as I walked, and I ate a handful of the dried fruit Yetta had packed for me. Following the river wasn't so bad, and it gave me something on which to focus, to pass the time. Fish jumped in and out of the current, and after an hour or two of watching them, I realized the shimmering bodies were not silver as I'd thought—everything else here was devoid of color, after all—but rather green with red stripes, and some with yellow spots above their gills.

Along the bank, fast flying insects whizzed above the water's surface, diving and resurfacing faster than I could fathom. Smaller fish would sometimes catch them, and bigger fish would eat the smaller fish.

I was so busy watching the river that I walked straight into a mud pit.

"Agh!"

Cold mud squelched into my boots and up the legs of my trousers. It was all I could do to keep my bags from falling into the mud with me.

Thankful for the snowshoes yet again, I only sank to my knees. But Haggard, the mud was *so cold.* Cracked bits of ice floated around me on the mud's surface. It looked like the mud pit was actually a little inlet of the river, a small marsh created by the ebb and flow of water, maybe whenever the river rose.

I threw my bags onto the snow, and by gripping a nearby pine's branches, I was able to pull myself free one leg at a time.

I considered just trudging on. But the cold clung to my legs, and it didn't take me long to realize walking with caked snowshoes and leather pants wouldn't do. So, I was forced to stop for the night while my boots, pants, and snowshoes dried out after dousing them clean in the river.

But my fire was warm, and Yetta's guidance in finding a shelter helped immensely. The snowy, rocky landscape no longer looked desolate and foreboding, but full of boulders and fallen trees for my use.

After changing into one of my spare sets of clothes, I draped my wet pants and boots over pine needles, laid out to dry by the fire. I ate the last of my rabbit, suddenly aware that I'd need to find more food tomorrow.

I was moving much slower than I'd intended. More than once, I'd had to glance quickly behind me, sure that I'd heard something—or someone—in the woods, only to remember I was utterly on my own. It must have just been the energy of this place.

Looking for anything to take my mind off that fact, I thought about taking out the book Yetta had given me for Isabele. But something about reading it did not feel right. Isabele should be the one to know about herself first, not me. I already had so much knowledge about her Talent that she didn't have.

So, I had no choice but to sit and listen to the forest as night fell, and sleep found me more fitfully than the night before.

The next morning, my clothes had dried but were rigid as boards, frozen to the touch. I did my best to bundle them up, and I stuffed them into my bag with the dagger and bangle. After snuffing out the embers of my fire and strapping on my snowshoes, I continued on my way.

The rushing of the river guided me, and I kept an arrow nocked in Vena's bow just in case some critter decided to unwittingly run by.

As I walked on, rocks and boulders began to dominate my surroundings. I didn't think anything of it at first, only starting to question it when the shade of the trees overhead became sparser.

Then, when the sun beamed through a break in the clouds about midmorning, I came face-to-face with a wall of rock.

"No . . ."

The cliff towered above me at least five times my height, gray stone striated with orange and blue. It would have been very pretty had it not felt so foreboding. And the river ran right through it, cutting deep and fast through the rock, continuing out the other side as far as I could tell.

Forced to leave my guiding sound of the river, I walked along the base of the cliff, hoping to get around it some way. Going over it was simply not an option for me. The rush of water grew quieter and quieter until I could no longer hear the river, and I tried to combat the tendrils of nervousness that had begun to wrap themselves around my sanity. To distract myself, I built up my familiar castle, and I stood at the balcony of its turret, sword in hand.

My stomach growled, reminding me that I should be looking for food. I grabbed another handful of the dried fruit and ate slowly as I walked, taking sips of melted snow from my canteen.

As evening began to creep over the trees, the forest—which had thickened again—became livelier. A rustling in some nearby bushes, a twig snapping, a lump of snow falling from pine branches above my head. Eventually, a rabbit poked its head out of its brushy cover at the most inopportune time, and I was able to land a clean shot.

I decided to stop there for the night, then, the cliff face still rising beside me. In the last bit of sunlight, I took a quick glance at my map and compass to make sure I would head in the correct direction in the morning, and finally, I let my bags slide down from my shoulders.

I felt the fatigue of walking all day slowly taking its toll, especially with my injured ankle and shoulder. But I tried to focus instead on building up my fire. Once my fire was blazing, I skinned the rabbit— not doing as clean of a job as Yetta or August, but well enough I supposed—and set it up on a little spit of twigs for cooking.

I had just begun gathering my pine needles for my bed when I heard the first howl of wolves.

My heart hammered in my chest, reminding me of my terror the first night I'd spent out in the forest, huddled with no fire and listening to wolves howl in the distance.

They didn't sound so distant now.

But as I gazed out into the darkening forest, I saw no movement, no gleaming eyes, no snarling teeth.

Now on high alert, I continued roasting my rabbit, my back pressed against the cliff. Once the rabbit was done cooking, I ate my fill quickly though it burned my tongue and tucked the rest of it away safely in my bag. I ventured as far as I dared from my camp, a few meters, and threw the rabbit skin into the woods.

That night was a rough one for sleep, even though I really needed it. My eyelids had refused to stay closed for longer than ten minutes at a time, for fear of finding glowing eyes pacing my camp, and I'd been adamant to keep my fire bright all night. Only when the gray of dawn inched its way into the black forest did I sleep, and only for an hour or so, for once the sun rose, the need to get moving outweighed any exhaustion.

I slogged along the cliff face again for most of the morning, stopping only to rest and drink a bit of water. When my shoulder stopped throbbing, I hoisted my bags up once more and kept moving.

What had I been thinking, wandering out here on my own? I felt more lost with every step, more isolated, as far away from my destination as I'd ever been. To recenter myself I took out my map, but in all honesty, without the river, I had no idea where I was.

Was the cliffside getting any shorter? I thought maybe it was. Or maybe it was just wishful thinking.

To pass the time, I began counting the trees around me, dividing them into pines and spruces and firs and junipers. Anything to keep me from unraveling.

Forty-two pines.

I was alone in the middle of the Tarasynian woods.

Thirteen spruces.

Twenty-nine firs.

Was that a footfall behind me?

Sixteen junipers.

Somewhere in my counting, a familiar and most comforting sound reached my ears.

The roar of rushing water.

I picked up my pace, despite my rolling ankle, and kept one hand on the cliffside to keep myself from getting too caught up in my excitement. A cold mist began clouding the air around me as the roaring grew louder.

I could have cried tears of joy as I found myself along the bank of the river once more. It flowed more violently here, cutting around the jagged edge of the cliff in a harsh, pinpoint curve, but I ran to it all the same like a long-lost friend, taking my gloves off and dipping my hands into its freezing current, splashing its water on my gritty face. When I couldn't take the cold anymore, I quickly wiped my hands and face on my cloak and shoved my fingers back into my gloves.

Good mood restored, I continued my trek along the river and even snagged a squirrel with my bow on the way. My steps were lighter, quicker.

This small victory of finding the river again had more of an effect on me than I would have ever expected. Anything felt possible now. I still had some of my rabbit and now a squirrel for food. I had a canteen full of water. I had the river to follow. I'd get to Pruin in a matter of days, no problem!

I could only pray that no one would recognize me.

Then, I remembered the grime I'd removed from my face in the river. As disheveled as I'd be by the time I got to the village, surely I'd be unrecognizable even by the keenest eye.

Feeling like I'd made more progress today than any day before, I decided to stop a bit early for the night. There was still some late afternoon light to illuminate my campsite. Once I'd made my shelter between two boulders and gathered enough pine needles for my bed, I ate a bit more of my rabbit—though I was getting tired of the taste at this point. Then I reclined back onto my needles, listening to the woods come alive with the sounds of insects. I'd forgotten how much livelier the forest was near the bank of the river.

It was my fourth day traveling alone in the woods. But I had to count back a little more. Two nights with Yetta and August. One night before that, alone. I'd escaped Snowmont seven days ago.

One week since I'd slept in a real bed or wore something other than leather and wool.

One week since Cassia's and Xal's executions.

I'd thought that I would be in Pruin by now. I wondered if Zeke had made it to Viridi yet. Maybe, depending on how fast he and his companions were traveling. Certainly faster than me, and the thought sent a bitter laugh through my lips.

Laughing to myself, alone in these frostbitten woods. Perhaps I *was* losing my sanity, after all. All of this to save myself from Gryffin, and I was only going crazy. And that made me laugh even harder, guffawing into the last of the evening light, until I felt the sting of tears behind my eyes. And even then, I still laughed. I really was losing it.

Until I heard a huff in the brush, not far from where I sat.

That brought me back to myself and cut off my laughter with a choking gasp. My head swiveled from left to right, sight blurred by tears. Through the distortion of water, I scurried over the wood and tinder I'd gathered and struck a flame with my flint.

There was a scuffling in the brush as something—big—hurried away from the new flare of light. I shot to my feet, hand on the hilt of my sword.

To my left, a pair of tawny eyes shone through the shadows of the forest. Then two. Then five. All glinting in my fire's light before disappearing into darkness.

I stole a glance over toward my bags, and the snow had been disturbed by claws, padded toes, as big as my hand—if not larger.

Wolves.

Were they *following* me?

My blood pulsed loudly in my ears, cold and piercing. My bones felt frozen as the presence of the pack stifled the air around me. And night had barely fallen.

More scuffling. A scraping in the snow. A short, throaty howl.

The entire forest, with its constant thrum of energy, felt like it was hanging on a decision.

I unsheathed my sword. I'd gotten this far. I had the reign of a kingdom to live for, and I wasn't going to lose that to a pack of wolves.

In a rush of either courage or stupidity, I struck my sword against the boulders of my shelter. And again, and again. The metal grated against the stone in sharp, splitting peals that echoed through the dense forest. Over my grating I heard a whimper, and I shouted with all the air I held in my lungs. Sure, I knew I couldn't take an entire pack on my own. But I could take one, scare them off—

Then there was a deep huff, and a moment later, the thundering of feet followed each other one by one, claws scratching into the frozen earth. A wolf's sharp howl pierced the night, shattering my ears and filling my brain with nothing but the sound.

Then, finally, all fell quiet.

I inhaled a shaking torrent of air and collapsed to my knees, sword falling with a thud into the snow. Any energy I'd had a moment earlier evaporated from my body. Besides, had I had anything left, I would have been hyperventilating.

But as my bones warmed again, I focused on what I could—stoking my fire and keeping it bright, nibbling at the last of my rabbit. I couldn't find the urge to skin my squirrel, so I tucked it away in my bags with the relics and buried it in the snow. As I curled up on my bed of pine needles between the frozen boulders, I tried to slow my hammering heart. My chest ached and felt so tight.

That night, my exhaustion finally dragged me into the deepest sleep

I'd had since Yetta's cottage. I didn't even dream.

I awoke stiff and groggy to a dead fire and a bright day, the sun already high into the tree canopy.

And deep wolf prints surrounding my camp.

My bag I'd buried in the snow had been dug up, flung around, the latch shredded. Equos's dagger glinted in the sun as it lay next to the base of a nearby tree, and the hemp string on Vena's bow had snapped and unraveled, now useless.

I rushed over to gather them up, and I frantically looked around for Viridi's bangle. Shuffling snow back and forth, searching the limbs of the surrounding bushes, I turned in a circle, panicked. Of course I'd lose a centuries-old magical relic in the middle of the woods.

Then, I caught a glimmer of gold in the very edge of my periphery.

The bangle had caught on the needles of a pine, hanging in the low branch just above my head. Relieved, I reached up and plucked it out of the tree.

They'd taken my squirrel. That must have been why they'd been following me. They hadn't wanted me—yet. They'd wanted my food.

Yetta's words rang clear in my head. *The animals are smart here.*

They were probably what I'd thought I'd been hearing traveling behind me this entire journey, and the thought sent a chill down my back.

It was almost a relief, as I realized I'd been imagining Gryffin lurking through the woods in my wake. His red-flecked eyes gleaming through the shadows of a fir . . . A new shiver ran down my spine. Which pursuer was worse?

Still, I wasn't foolish. The wolves were too terrifying to be real relief.

The wolves hadn't taken any care rummaging through my things. My bag was still usable, but just barely. The leather latch had been shredded by claws and teeth, the buckle lost to the trees and brush. They really were smart. Though I bet they were disappointed to find only one small squirrel. One of them probably ate it in one bite.

The fire striker and extra quilt lay close to each other in the snow, the quilt thankfully intact, but my scarves had been ripped to ribbons. I ended up tying the pieces together into a long rope, and I used it to wrap around my bag and tie it closed.

As I packed up my camp, I was forced to face my glaring situation.

I needed to hunt. And my only tool to hunt with had been incapacitated.

I considered setting up a snare as I'd learned from Yetta, but that would mean sticking around the area for the day. The sun was already so high in the sky, so a successful day of travel already seemed impossible.

Still, even a few hours of walking would get me closer to Pruin, and the thought of staying where wolves had been was far from tempting. So, a snare was out.

And that meant learning to restring a bow.

~*VIRIDI*~
ZEKE

Roger's boot slipped on the ice, and a loud curse escaped his mouth. I tried to ignore the eyes that turned in our direction and gripped his elbow as he steadied himself. From what I could tell, a colossal snow had fallen, melted in the sun, and refrozen with the nightfall, leaving a sheet of glass for all of us to flounder through.

And while I understood Roger's frustration, I *really* needed him to stay quiet, duck his head, something. His size alone drew too much attention to our party. We didn't need him swearing loud enough for all of Tarasyn to hear.

Haggard, I wished I was on this assignment solo.

But we made it to this forsaken gaudy city. That much was a success.

Terrin nudged my shoulder. When I cut my eyes toward him, he ducked his head low, wearing a smirk. "You look murderous."

I forced myself to take a deep breath. A stranger looking to kill would draw unwelcome attention just as much as a cursing giant.

Still, I had pretty a good reason to feel homicidal. After months of fighting to get here, fighting for Rose, now I was so *close*. If I saw Gryffin right now, I didn't think I would be able to stop myself from putting my hands around his neck.

"Let's just keep moving," I muttered.

Roger and Terrin were on edge too. It rolled off them like smoke. Here we were in the heart of the enemy, among red roofs and green storefronts, blue spruces and golden spires. Though we were a couple of hours into nightfall, there were still hordes of people meandering the streets, lanterns in hand, laughing and conversing loudly. After almost a week of travel between here and Pruin through silent snowy forests, the crowds were freckin' off-putting.

As I watched the crowd, a certain exchange caught my attention.

First, it was the cloak. A bright purple fabric, lined with white fur. Clearly an expensive piece of clothing, and out of place on the muddy streets.

The cloaked figure, a woman by the looks of it, approached a bearded man outside a shop, who promptly bowed his head low. The woman quickly shook her head and motioned with her gloved hands, urgent. The man answered whatever her question had been, shrugged his shoulders, and pointed across the street to a tavern, where the buzz of conservation spilled through the door.

As the woman nodded her head and turned away, I tried to keep my gaze even as I turned my head to Terrin. "I've got a lead."

Terrin nodded and motioned to Roger, and they both slipped off into a jostling mess of people in the street.

I kept eyes on the woman as she crossed the street and shuffled her way into the bustling tavern. I doubted that I would be able to get in without getting noticed, looking like a lone traveler on a busy night, so I stayed outside and leaned against the stair railing, facing away from the open door.

Voices still traveled.

"Can you believe what the king is offering?" A man near the window gave a haughty laugh. "That'll make every Viridian keep an eye out!"

And another. "What does he even want with them?"

"That woman's got it coming, for sure!"

All of these snippets of conversation were total nonsense. I could not care less about some bounty that boar of a king had on some stolen objects. I just had pity on the poor servant who took them.

The loud slam of a door echoed through the alleyway to my right, and a woman's frustrated voice carried. I casually dusted off my cloak and disappeared silently into the space between the tavern and the next building over. There was a flash of purple around the side of the tavern for just a second before disappearing again.

I slinked along the wall, stepping light on the strip of ground that had been sheltered from the snowfall.

A woman groaned loudly. "Look, I just need to know if you've seen her. I was told she'd been here."

"Over a week ago!" another woman, young by the lift in her tired voice, answered. "I didn't know it was her when she came in. I thought she was a man, a traveler on his way home. He—she—drank a cup of cider, ate some stew, and left."

"Did you see which way she went?"

"No, I didn't know to look. You should ask Redd. He's the one who chased her down. Beat her bloody too." The second woman clucked her tongue. "I didn't know he could be such a jealous crite. Taught me a good lesson though. I haven't let him back into my tavern since, no matter how many rounds of mead he promises to buy."

"Beat her bloody?" I pictured the cloaked woman with a hand over her mouth, hanging open in shock. She sounded young too, maybe younger than the other woman. "I . . . I didn't know."

"I'll bet the king didn't take too kindly to that." The tavern owner's dry chuckle echoed softly through the alley. "Redd didn't know in the moment that he was pulverizing the queen's pretty face. But I heard he'd gotten dismissed from service."

The queen's pretty face.

A flash of red-hot anger jumped across my vision.

"You know more than I do," the cloaked woman said through what I imagined was a sorry grimace.

"Like I said, find Redd. He might be able to tell you more. I've got customers in there." A door creaked on its hinges and slammed back into place, leaving me and the cloaked woman in seething silence.

I heard the boots of the woman outside crunching through the snow, and as I peeked my head around the corner, I saw the hem of her cloak disappear down the next alleyway, back toward the main street. I followed, keeping my head down as I entered the crowd of people outside the tavern once more.

Then she turned sharply down a narrow side street to her left.

Matching her pace, I took the next street over. When I reached the end of the street, the back of her cloak was billowing away along the backs of the shops. I stayed behind for a moment, not willing to risk being seen by the woman or whoever Redd may be. But I did follow, slowly, until the woman turned down yet another corridor to her right, one street closer to the tree line of the snowy forest.

I bolted up the next available alley on my right, stopped at the concealed corner, and waited.

This time, her footsteps were headed in my direction.

As the crunching got louder, I bided my time. Then, just as the tip of her hood peeked around the corner of the building, I stepped into the open, blocking her path. "Hello."

The woman's wide blue eyes shocked me. They looked *so much* like—

Then she opened her mouth to scream.

I wrapped my arms around her tightly and clamped a hand over her mouth before she could let out a most unwelcome wail. "Hear me out. Please. I'm not here to hurt you."

She shot me a glare so murderous and stomped on my foot with her boot, and though a sharp pain shot up from my toes—was that a crack I heard?—I painfully held my ground. "Please. I'm a friend of Rose's."

At that, her struggling lessened, and her eyes turned from anger to a careful curiosity.

"From the way you're slinking through the streets alone, it seems you don't want a lot of attention," I murmured. "I won't draw attention to us if you don't."

She studied my face, blue eyes penetrating, before nodding once.

I relaxed my arms, and she weaved out of them before I could say another word.

"Stalking women isn't really something 'good guys' do," she said with a glare, brushing off her cloak with curt movements. "You should work on your approach."

"Stalking is my job. And I normally don't approach people on my assignments. But thank you for your input—I'll report it to my higher-ups."

The woman narrowed her eyes and stayed silent for a moment. Then, she crossed her arms over her chest. "Fine. I can appreciate sarcasm. A friend of Rose's, you say?"

I nodded. "You and the tavern owner, you were discussing something about the queen."

"You've been following me for that long?" The woman's eyes fell to the ground, displeased. "I'm normally more aware."

"I'm good at my job," I said curtly. "Now, the queen?"

She looked up at me, eyes bright but guarded. "And you don't work for my brother?"

Her brother. I hadn't been a fool, then. Those eyes had looked so familiar for a reason. The nice cloak, the entitled lift of her chin. "You're the princess."

"No, you must not work for him," she murmured, mostly to herself. "Well, you know who I am now. Who are you?"

I ground my teeth together. Could she be trusted? "A good friend."

"The one who sent the letters?"

Well. If Rose had told this woman about our exchanges . . . "Yes."

"Well, it's high time you've arrived. Too late though."

Too late. "Please. Tell me what happened."

The woman looked down to the muddied snow. "My brother discovered a message Rose had tried to send back to you. To tell you if you didn't show, she would meet you in Pruin."

"But I told *her*—argh!" I turned away from the princess and kicked the ground. I wanted to pull my hair right out of my freckin' skull. Meet me in Pruin? Ridiculous. How was she going to get to Pruin? "What was her rush? Why didn't she wait for me?"

"You were taking too long," she answered simply. "Rosemary couldn't wait for you. And . . . things had escalated here, forced her to leave earlier than expected."

I struggled to keep my face neutral. "Escalated. How?"

The princess looked down, her voice hushed. "Rosemary's lady-in-waiting and a Lecevonian boy were executed. Your messenger."

"Xal." My whisper was carried off with the chilled wind. The older man in Pruin, alone and weeping . . . I should have recognized him as Xal's father, Brom.

The princess nodded, somber eyes meeting mine. "Once my brother discovered Rosemary had been hiding her true intentions, he moved up the wedding. It was supposed to be held four days ago."

Four days ago. "The tavern owner had said it'd been a week."

The princess scoffed, her nose crinkling in distaste. "Rosemary wasn't going to wait around like a pig for slaughter. Tonight, she will have been gone for eight days now."

Eight days.

Rose has been in the woods for eight days.

She didn't know how to survive in the woods, let alone the cold. A wave of agony coursed its way through my mind, invading even my most hopeful thoughts. Rose was smart, resourceful—but a queen who had lived in a castle her entire life. We'd spent one night in the stables together and she'd gotten so sick she'd been sequestered to her room for nearly a month—much to her dismay, claiming she "felt fine."

"You don't think she made it," the princess said. "I can see your sadness."

I turned my gaze away from her, toward the line of pines just a few more streets down. "I don't know how she *could* have made it."

Her sudden chuckle surprised me. "Are you and I talking of the same Rosemary?" she asked incredulously. "I've never met someone so determined to live. You don't know what she'd had to endure to keep my brother off her trail. Not that Celeste and I didn't help," she added almost proudly.

"Celeste." My eyes grew wide at her words. "Rose's friend Celeste?"

"Yes, Rosemary's friend. She was in the group that had been taken from Lecevonia." The princess spoke slowly, and her gaze turned to one of skepticism. "Surely you all have noticed some people missing."

"We'd heard, yes," I murmured. Still, shame assaulted me. I hadn't seen Celeste at the stables recently, but we'd rarely run into each other before Rose's disappearance. Even so, we should have noticed. Rose would have noticed, and she would have collected the names of each and every missing Lecevonian.

I shook the tangent out of my head. Rose was my priority right now. "So, you think she could have made it to Pruin?" I asked her.

"I think her very capable, in the least," she said with a strong nod. "And we'd gathered her a good bit of supplies. Not as much as we'd planned, but enough to get by."

"You helped her escape."

"Of course. She is like a sister to me. And my brother is *far* from his right mind."

So, Rose had made friends here. Loyal ones, at that. My amazing, determined Rose.

I held out my hand to the princess, and after a moment of hesitation, she took it gingerly. "Thank you," I said. "Sincerely."

She pursed her lips. "Hmm. That look in your eyes." She tilted her head to one side with a small smile. "That love. I haven't seen it or felt it before, until very recently."

"I've got to find her," I said, as certain as the clear star-spackled sky above our heads.

The princess nodded quickly. "Are you alone?"

"I have two companions."

"My brother has eyes all over the city searching for you, so be careful. And move as quickly as you can. I'm not sure how long Rosemary will be able to stay undetected in Pruin."

I nodded, already thinking two steps ahead. "I'll get to her."

The princess began backing away, hugging the hood of her cloak close. "When you do find her, send her love from Celeste and Kathryn."

We parted in opposite directions, and I didn't see her purple cloak again as I weaved through the busy streets, searching for Roger and Terrin.

I left the city the next morning. We decided I'd travel faster alone, so Roger and Terrin agreed to stay for a few days to gather information about the captured Lecevonians while I went after Rose.

"We'll see you in Pruin then," Terrin said, shaking my hand. We were standing outside the stable where we'd boarded our horses, and I'd just walked out with Hugo saddled and ready.

"One week at the latest," I replied. "I wish you both luck. The queen would want to know her people are safe."

"And we want to know the queen is safe," Roger responded. He'd been most upset to find out Rose had already left Viridi. "Find her. Please."

"I will." My promise was more to myself than anyone else.

Then, I followed the road out of the city.

I had been on my way for only about half an hour when I heard distant hoofbeats approaching from behind. Though I was certain no one aside from the princess knew I'd been in Viridi, I led Hugo off the road and into the dense brush, just in case. The snow was so deep that Hugo sank to his knees in it, and he protested with a horrendously loud whinny.

"I know, I'm sorry," I murmured to him as I dismounted. I cursed quietly when the snow topped over my boots, but I continued to lead Hugo farther into the dense forest until I felt we were safe enough. Thankfully, his dappled gray coat blended in well. With the shadow of my hood low over my face, I chanced a peek through the brush.

My blood began to writhe.

His mare was a flash of white as she galloped past us, but I stared hard at his face. I thought I remembered his eyes being blue—I was *sure* they were blue, in fact—but now they seemed to be more like the color of rust. Odd. His face was lined in stress, which made me happy, but I still wanted to knock that golden crown off his head. Among other things.

Hoping for the chance to do just that, I followed him.

I struggled to keep up with him as I stayed to the trees with Hugo, but soon Gryffin took an overgrown path off the main road and continued at a trot. I followed him for what felt like a terribly long time, and I was beginning to wonder if he had any destination in mind at all.

Then, the woods opened, and a cottage that looked like it was out of an old storybook sat in the clearing. I heard the rush of water, but any river or stream was still obscured from my point of view. I lost sight of Gryffin just for a moment, then he reappeared without his horse near the cottage's greenhouse and went inside.

I waited, keeping my hood low, cloak closed tightly against the cold. Haggard forsake this frozen place.

Finally, I dared to inch closer to the tree line. Hugo followed behind me, his snorting and grunting too loud for my liking. But I understood his frustration.

I caught sight of the river, a swift current of water flowing between snowbanks, and a small wooden bridge spanning its banks. Gryffin's horse stood tethered to a pine branch near the bridge. I considered running over and letting her loose, just to inconvenience the crite of a man, but then he reappeared through the greenhouse door and began making his way through the snow. Across the bridge. Back to his mare. Just a few meters from me.

He was so close.

I put my hand on my bow, nocked an arrow.

Crimson began to take over my vision. This man betrayed Rose, my trust, Lecevonia. I lifted my bow in front of me.

I'd told Rose she should *marry* him. My stomach rolled at the thought. I drew back on my bowstring, the feathers of my bow resting against my chin.

This man killed good people.

I had a clear shot, just through the trees. His back was turned to me.

I took a deep inhale of frigid Tarasynian air.

Then Gryffin laid his forehead against his saddlebag and let out a sob that echoed through the trees. He buried his face into the leather.

I kept my arrow at the ready.

When he lifted his head, he shouted indecipherable words into the forest canopy above him, sending small birds propelling off the branches. He took the glinting crown off his head and flung it into the snow. Still shouting, he spun in a tight circle, punched the trunk of the tree nearest him. Punched it again. When he drew back his fist, his knuckles were bright with blood.

Finally, he collapsed to his knees in the snow, head in his hands, shoulders shaking.

I could shoot him. Kill him, even. He had no armor, no weapon, nothing but the sword buckled to his saddlebag. He didn't even know I was here. I had every upper hand.

I wanted to release my arrow. I tried to tell my fingers to let loose. My aim was strong, and my anger was stronger. I could kill him.

Why did I hesitate? I'd killed a man before. And this man was just as guilty, if not guiltier. Yes, he was guiltier.

I should kill him. Just release the arrow.

But something felt wrong about killing a crying man.

Then, Gryffin lowered his hands, stared at his palms. Stood up. Brushed the snow off his knees.

With an inaudible curse, I lowered my bow as he wiped his cloak across his face and took a few breaths, hands on his horse's saddle.

He turned and picked up his crown from the snow, but he didn't place it on his head. Instead, he tucked it inside his saddlebag, and he took one final deep breath before pulling himself up into his saddle. He kicked his horse into a gallop straight away, and he disappeared from the bank and from my line of sight.

I glanced over my shoulder at Hugo. "I should have just killed him."

In response, he twitched his ears and shook his withers.

Shaking my head, I grabbed his reins and turned toward the way we came. "All right, big guy. Let's get back to the road." I'd already wasted enough time throwing away my shot.

But the greenhouse door opened again, and I ducked into the trees.

A woman emerged. Spry, but older, with a long gray braid running down her back. She followed the same path as Gryffin had, to the river and over the bridge. But then she continued toward the forest, and suddenly, she seemed to be in a beeline for my hiding spot.

I dipped farther into the trees, leading Hugo behind me into dense cover. Sure, I couldn't hide his deep tracks in the snow, but I sure didn't need to be sighted by anyone.

I picked my way through the brush as quietly as I could, already dreading the amount of snow I'd have to pick out of Hugo's hooves, when a voice spoke from the spruces to my right.

"Hello, child."

CHAPTER EIGHTEEN

———

"*BOARS!*" I STARED at the popped string dangling in two from Vena's bow, fuming. That was the fifth string I'd tried, and the third arrow I'd had to track down.

The sun had traveled across the sky and now gave off its late afternoon rays, and I still had no way to hunt. Animals were starting to stir with the warmth, and I knew it would be the best chance I'd have at finding any food. But the animals stirring also meant glancing over my shoulder repeatedly, certain I'd see a wolf in my wake. I just hoped I scared them off enough last night that they'd leave me alone from now on.

I'd at least made some progress on my journey along the riverbank, and I tried to keep that in mind as I took out my spool of hemp twine again. I cut more strands than ever with Equos's dagger and twisted them all together, hoping to Haggard it would be enough.

For the umpteenth time, I recreated what I thought I'd seen Yetta do. I looped one end at the notch in the bow's arm, and I tied off the strands at the other. This time, the string was strong enough that it held as I tightened it, the bow bending to its will, and I held my breath as I pulled back on the string gently.

It held.

Relieved, I gave off a practice shot, and the arrow embedded itself neatly into the trunk of a tree. I couldn't stop my giddy laugh as I yanked the arrow out of the bark.

My eyes were bigger than my stomach, and I took down two rabbits, sure that I would eat them both tonight cozied up at my campfire. Not sure how much longer my bowstring would last, I found a squirrel just before the sun sank below the horizon. Finally satisfied with my quarry—I might even be set until I made it to Pruin—I refilled my canteen with snow and set off to make my camp.

Shelter was not quite as easy to come by, for the boulders and crevices were becoming smaller in size as I continued south down the mountains. Then, thank Haggard, when I ventured away from the river as far as I dared, I found a stone overhang protruding from a snowy rockface. I could just barely stand beneath it; Zeke surely would have knocked his head had he stood here with me.

I dropped my bags, unclasped my scabbard from my waist, and immediately began working on my fire. Collecting anything that would burn into a pile as quickly as I could, I struck my iron against flint and sent sparks flying onto my pile. The dry pine needles took, and I fanned the flame until it grew and caught to the wood. Before the forest dropped into darkness, I had my fire sending rolling tendrils of flame into the air. I kept feeding it, growing it, tending it until it was so tall, so bright, so angry that it seemed I was trying to be spotted from the tallest peak in the Silver Mountains.

There. I dared any wolf to come near this place tonight.

Safe in the glow of my own personal sun, I took out one of my rabbits and began skinning and cleaning it. Then, I decided to just go ahead and do the same to all my wares tonight. Might as well. They wouldn't go bad in this type of winter. Since my fire was so tall, I had to situate the three spits around the outskirts of the fire.

While they cooked, I collected a few fallen branches with needles still attached and piled them against one side of the overhang in the direction of the wind. But midway through, the wind changed on me, sending a gusty chill through my cloak. So with an irritated groan, I dragged my branches to the opposing side and repeated the process.

I went back to my fire and began making my rounds around the flame, rotating my rabbits one by one.

But when I walked around the fire to my squirrel, it was no longer there.

Its spit lay collapsed on the ground, the flimsy branches helpless as my fire's hungry flames reached out to them and took hold.

I spun around, eyes scanning the ground and the low growth of the forest. Looking for any trace of my squirrel, or for the culprit. My heart fell to my feet when I saw the deep cuts of claws in the snow.

Initially, I was angrier than anything. And overwhelmingly hungry.

These wolves were going to kill me just by making me starve! I was doing their hunting *for* them!

But then the fear set in, and everything but that fear melted away.

Especially when the familiar tawny eyes stared at me through the brush.

Without turning my back to the eyes, I took achingly slow footsteps backward, toward my bags. My sword lay draped over the bag containing the relics, with Vena's bow next to it.

But as I retreated, the eyes followed me out of the woods. First a black nose gleamed in my fire's light, followed by a white muzzle.

Then a head more massive than I would have thought possible.

My heel kicked the tip of my scabbard.

The wolf bared its teeth.

It lunged with a snarl just as I leaned forward to grab my sword.

My hand closed around the hilt, and I whipped the sword out of its scabbard and held it in front of me.

But the wolf hadn't lunged at me. It had lunged at my other rabbit, and it tore off a bit of the rabbit's roasted flesh as another wolf bounded forward out of the brush. The second wolf tore the rabbit away from the first and ran off with it toward the edge of the fire. The first wolf followed after it, and a third wolf stepped into the light of my fire, sniffing at my last rabbit.

I dropped my sword into the snow and lunged for Vena's bow instead. As quickly as it took for the third wolf to look in my direction, I had an arrow nocked and the string pulled back.

This one was a female—I could tell by the leanness of her face. Her eyes were not tawny but a deep brown, black in the shadow of my fire. She didn't snarl at me as the others had. She just stared, daring me to make a move.

I did not want to shoot her. But I wanted her to leave, and her sheer size and the curl of her claws made the prey in me quiver.

"Take it!" I shouted hoarsely. "Take the rabbit, for Haggard's sake!" I almost laughed at myself again. I was talking to a wild animal. But if they were as smart as Yetta said they were, perhaps it was worth a shot.

My voice made the other two wolves look up from their spoils, the rabbit already torn apart, and suddenly three stares of killers were fixed on me.

I let loose my arrow, aiming for the female in front of me.

I shouldn't have missed. I'd made harder shots, and she was so close. Yet my arrow whizzed past her head and into the fire behind her, sending sparks flying into the night air around us.

Now was a *very* bad time to fully realize that archery was not my Talent, after all.

The sparks sent the other two wolves darting into the brush, and a howl in the not-so-distant woods told me more were out there.

The large female stood her ground, but now her teeth were bared, a snarl building in the back of her throat. I shot another arrow, not taking any time to carefully aim this time, and grabbed the quiver of arrows by the strap. While my arrow made her turn her head, I shot to my feet and bolted around my fire. She looked back at me showing all her teeth, ears flat against her head, but then I lost sight of her as I put the flames between us.

I walked carefully around the fire, keeping sight on the tip of her white tail as she followed me. The heat burned my face, singed my hair. I was sweating beneath my cloak, so I unclasped it from around my neck and let it fall to the ground. But I never once stopped circling.

Until the tip of the wolf's tail did.

I froze in my tracks.

She'd stopped to sniff my cloak. That was my guess. But when I heard the scratching of claws into the snow over the fire's loud crackle, I looked up too late to see her long body soaring through the very top of my fire, sending embers falling over me and burning the skin on my face.

The smell of singed fur filled the air, but she showed no sign of pain as she landed only an arm's width away from me with a sharp, barking growl. She was so large, a mass of muscle, fury, and hunger. She lunged at me with teeth snapping, but I dove to the ground to my right, away from the fire, and her claws grazed the leather at my hip.

I gathered myself just enough to send an arrow in her direction, as two other wolves slouched their way into my fire's light.

But this time, my arrow found a mark.

Not a deadly or solid mark, but a mark all the same. The wolf's high yelp pierced my ears as my arrow cut into the skin at her hindquarters and landed near the fire behind her. It shocked her enough to turn and run toward the cover of the forest. The other two that had stepped out briefly followed in her wake, one of them grabbing my last rabbit off the ground before sauntering off into the trees.

The female turned her great head to face me, and her deep blazing eyes appraised me for one final moment before she disappeared, limping every few steps, through the brush.

The snowy bushes shook as large bodies bolted between them, huffs and growls tearing through the wind. A deafening howl filled every centimeter of my camp, my veins, my bones. The power and command in its finality felt familiar, and I felt that, somehow, maybe the female and I were not so different. Two queens—providing for their own, choosing their battles.

The animals here were smart.

Then, slowly, the howl tapered into silence, and the nightly hum of insects took its place once more.

I stayed where I was, kneeling in the scuffed snow as I let the cold night wash over me and calm my sharp inhales. My limbs felt heavy as lead, but eventually I found the strength to push myself off the ground. I walked around my fire and collected my cloak from the snow, only to find a horrendously large tear through the middle that continued up to the hood. I didn't even have the energy to be disappointed.

The pinprick burns on my face from my fire's embers throbbed, and not knowing what else to do, I took a handful of snow and nuzzled my face into it. The cold bit, but it provided such a relief to my tiny burns that I let out a sigh. I touched my hip where the wolf's claws grazed me and winced at the pressure. Nothing too bad—it had barely reached my skin through the leather. Blood puckered at the scratch, but it could have been much worse. I fully expected it to be tender for the next few days. Luckily, it was the same leg as my injured ankle, so I at least still had one fully functioning leg at my disposal. The dismal thought made me chuckle and roll my eyes.

I scrounged up what pine needles I could and made a bed under the overhang, close to my makeshift wall of evergreen branches. Curling up with my bags, the heat from the fire reaching into my little space, I closed my eyes. I ignored any other cracks and snaps in the night, holding on to the hope that if I didn't acknowledge any other intruders, the possibility would simply pass by.

But I didn't sleep. How could I? The fading of my adrenaline left my muscles tired and my mind muddled, but my brain was still wired to think about anything and everything. No clear point between my thoughts, just jumping around from one topic to another. A survival instinct, I supposed, to keep me awake.

How many hours until sunrise?

What did wolf taste like? Probably very lean.

I didn't realize how valuable flint was.

I should have cherished that last full meal I'd had at Snowmont.

How was Isabele?

How much longer to Pruin? Hopefully only a day or two more. For Haggard's sake, I prayed only a day or two more.

Eventually, the gray dawn infiltrated my little space and my rambling thoughts, and my stomach growled.

~THE TARASYNIAN WOODS~
ZEKE

Follow the river. That was what the old woman had said.

She was strange, that one, with her too-knowing eyes and her answering my thoughts before I spoke them. She'd seemed to be expecting me when she'd approached me in the woods, and that was unnerving.

But she'd known Rose, and somehow, she'd known I would be looking for her. I'd admit, she had a point in that Rose couldn't follow the road without being seen.

So I rode along the riverbank, taking no rest. Hugo wasn't very keen on the snow and mud, but I still traveled faster with him than I would have done on foot. Thank Haggard for that—this forest still gave me the freckin' creeps. It constantly felt like the branches wanted to reach out and grab my cloak.

I was glad to see the deep mud pit when I did before Hugo could end up chest-deep in freezing muck. There were frozen splotches of mud on the opposite side of it, a few days old. Some poor animal must had fallen in. Traces of wildlife were *everywhere*. Tracks lined the river, large rabbit feet and tiptoeing squirrel prints. Even the deep grooves of deer approached the water. I urged Hugo on as the sun began to dip into the tree canopy.

To anyone else, the dark scratch in the bare earth not far from the mud pit probably would not have looked like much. But to a scout, it meant a campfire, and to me, it instilled a bit of hope. It was the second one I'd seen so far. I didn't think Rose knew how to make a fire, but how many other people would be out here? Even to this day, she continued to surprise me.

But soon, I saw the wolf tracks.

Reining Hugo to a stop, I jumped off and landed calf-deep in the snow. The deep claw marks were maybe three or four days old, and from the snow's unsettled appearance, there were at least four sets. Maybe five.

Then, as I moved farther down the riverbank, even more sets of prints. This pack was larger than I'd care to contend with. Had Rose run into them? Boars, I hoped not.

The wolf tracks veered farther into the forest after a while, and a timid sense of relief filled my chest. Maybe they'd left her alone, then.

Aside from the old fires, I had a hard time finding any trace of Rose. I'd thought it would be easy—broken branches, footprints, snags on tree trunks. But she'd surprisingly left little mark. I spotted a print that could have been from a snowshoe, but where would Rose have gotten snowshoes? I prayed the old lady had led me correctly. Otherwise, I was only wasting time.

As evening crept on, the river cut into the mountainside, leaving only a jagged cliff edge. With Hugo, I had no choice but to continue on the ground and hope I ran into the river again later on. And hope that Rose had done the same.

As I walked along the base of the cliff, I cursed this forest, this kingdom, and its king. If that crite hadn't done whatever he'd done to make Rose leave, she wouldn't be wandering out here in the snow. Boars, if he hadn't betrayed us all, she would never have left Hillstone! She would be safe inside the castle walls, under my careful eye, and she never would have had to make—

A camp. Or rather, the remnants of it. Rose hadn't taken the same precautions here when she'd left.

I dismounted again and led Hugo to the makeshift fire pit, the charred logs broken down to a mess of soot. I stirred the black snowy mound with a nearby twig, and the shells of the logs fell into dust. I took my glove off and touched the remnants, only to find them cold and icy, the fire long extinguished.

Then, more wolf tracks surrounded the camp, and my heart ached. They were newer than the campfire though—these were maybe two days old. They arrived after Rose. There seemed to be no sign of struggle either.

I considered stopping here for the night. It was well past sunset now, and I was satisfied with this first day of travel. I didn't think I could get any more tired, and Hugo would probably appreciate the rest.

But as I eyed the wolf tracks again, I couldn't shake this dark foreboding that had overtaken my mind.

I wouldn't rest. I *couldn't* rest.

I turned back to Hugo with a rueful smile. "Sorry, my friend. On we go."

He snorted as I hiked my leg over his back and settled into the saddle, and we continued on through the frozen dark.

CHAPTER NINETEEN

MY HUNGER STRETCHED on into the next day, and my stomach felt as if it wanted to turn in on itself. I tried to remind myself to drink water, but I didn't want water. I wanted *food*. The pain in my abdomen made it hard to walk, hard to focus, hard to lift my bow nocked with one of my last two arrows.

As I walked along the riverbank, I did my best to keep my ears open to any twig snaps or leaf rustles, anything that might have meant food. But the rushing of the river was so loud. Too loud. Too maddeningly loud. Just like this entire forest, constantly thrumming with energy.

I groaned and, turning to the nearest pine, ripped some bark off the tree and nibbled on the harsh edges. The sap tasted sharp and bitter—but even the sensation of eating was satisfying.

For a little while.

As night approached through the trees, I finally caught the sound of scurrying across a branch above me, raining snow down onto my head and shoulders. A loud chittering cut through the air, and I looked up in time to see a furry tail disappearing behind the trunk of the tree.

I gathered what strength I could, mostly fueled by hungry anger now, and pointed my bow up into the tree. I waited. And when the squirrel popped its head from the other side, I let my arrow fly.

There was a loud, angry chatter, and a tremendous shuddering of pine needles. But no fall to the earth. No squirrel at the end of my arrow. No food.

And another arrow lost to the forest.

My disappointment just fed my frustration, and I felt hot tears prickle behind my eyes. But I held them back. I refused to give up my hope just yet.

But *boars*, it was difficult.

I decided then to stop for the night, and I prayed I'd find my arrow in the morning. I made a small fire, and I forced myself to remember to appreciate the flames. My fires were still strong and warm. That was more than I'd had that first night, over a week ago.

At the memory, I tethered myself to the determination I'd had to survive that first night. The sheer, unrelenting willpower. Yes, that willpower was still there, buried beneath the crippling cramps of hunger. I would live. I *had* to live, for my people. I served my people, and this was the way in which I could serve them now, in this moment. By staying alive.

So yes, I appreciated the flames. Though I had nothing for them to cook, at least they would not let me freeze.

No wolves visited my campsite, so I also allowed myself to feel pride in the fact that I'd scared them enough to leave me alone. And eventually, I found sleep.

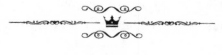

I awoke to a low sun and a warm face, just as my lips touched Zeke's.

I'd thought.

I glanced around groggily and pushed myself up onto my elbow. Where had he gone? I touched my lips, expecting them to be warm from his, but no—they were as cold as the snow under my bed of pine needles.

It'd only been a dream. A wonderful dream. A dream I desperately wanted to return to. My face flushed as I recalled how Zeke's fingers had trailed along my arm, how his lips had whispered against my bare shoulder. We'd never been so close, but lucky for me, I had an active imagination. But as I continued to rise from the edge of sleep, the touch of his fingers slipped away with my subconsciousness.

I couldn't control the small whine that escaped through my lips as I sat up straighter and stretched my spine. The burns on my face didn't hurt as badly as yesterday, so they must not have been too serious. Only when I stared at the sun hanging low between the tree trunks did I realize how late it was. Evening was inching its way through the forest, the shadows of the trees long and dark.

I'd slept the entire day.

I fought off the last few fingers of sleep that still tried to drag me under and pushed myself to my feet. Immediately, my head spun. My stomach felt tight, as if it'd been dried in the summer heat and shrunken like a raisin.

Still disoriented, I looked down at Vena's bow, and my last arrow. I told myself that I should pick them up and search for food. No one else was going to feed me.

But that last arrow was daunting.

What if I missed, like yesterday? I no longer had hope of finding the arrow I'd shot yesterday. What if I lost this one? Could I make more?

I scoffed aloud. As if I knew how to make arrows. I could figure it out, sure, but not before I starved to death. No, I couldn't chance it. Not until I could eat again.

As I eyed the sun again, I decided that I wouldn't travel today. It was close to time for me to make camp anyhow—might as well stay where I was.

My hunger drove me to grab the twine from my bags and set out to lay a few snares. I trudged along the river back the way I'd come, looking for any of the telltale signs of animals passing that Yetta had taught me. Trails in the snow, a clearing in the thick of the brush. I set up one or two well enough, I thought, and started on my way again. I kept my eyes open for any of the berries and mushrooms Yetta had pointed out to me, but luck didn't seem to be on my side in that regard.

But the *fish.* They were what kept catching my eye. They were jumping in and out of the water, arcs of red and green coated in silver.

I looked back toward my camp, my thoughts on Vena's bow, and the rope in my hand. I pursed my lips, tired gears turning through the muddled mess of my brain.

I could catch a fish.

Surely, I could catch a fish.

Finally, without really deciding, I turned on my heel and ambled back to my camp. I picked up the bow and the last arrow.

I wouldn't lose it though. I couldn't. With the twine in my hand, I tied a knot around the feathers of the arrow. Double knotted. Triple knotted.

My eyes swung back to the river. It would only take one shot.

I walked over to the riverbank and stopped just before the toe of my boots touched the water, following the leaping fish with my gaze. I didn't really know where to tie off my arrow, so I tied the other end of the rope to my wrist. I aimed toward one of the glittering bodies streaming through the water, and I shot.

I missed. But the pressure tugging at my wrist was not hard to fight as I pulled the arrow out of the current. I ran down the bank, following the fish down the river, and I aimed again, my stomach rumbling as if it were cheering me on. This time, I tried to estimate where the fish would be by the time my arrow reached it in the water. And I let my arrow fly.

The jerk at my wrist told me it hit. I yelped as I was yanked toward the water, and I stumbled before I could hold my footing once more. I grabbed the rope with my other hand and began wrangling in the fighting fish.

Though I didn't remember what fish tasted like, the corners of my mouth moistened as I kept the shimmer in my sight, just below the water's surface. I dared to smile as I walked a few steps down the bank with the fish before bracing myself more sturdily against a boulder. I began pulling on my line again.

Yes, I'd build my fire again, fierce and roaring, and I'd roast my fish until it was lovely and flame-licked—

The snap of my line sent me toppling backward, slamming into the boulder and down into the packed snow.

"No . . ."

I slowly pulled at my line again, and there was no resistance. Despair already creeping in, I kept pulling in my twine, until the wet, frayed end of the rope left my hands cold and empty.

"No, no, no . . ."

I rolled to my knees, and my head fell into my hands. My tears were hot against my frozen cheeks, but there weren't very many to be shed. I mostly just felt tired, and truly for the first time since being here in Tarasyn, I was smothered in a shroud of hopelessness.

What good was control? I built my fire high—the wolves still came. I secured my knot three times—I still lost my arrow. I'd played my part for *months,* the elated and infatuated queen-to-be—my secret had still been discovered, and people had been killed. I'd escaped Snowmont and Gryffin's murderous hand—I was still going to die out here in the cold.

I would never see the rolling hills of my kingdom again, or hug Isabele or tease Lisette or laugh with Clara. Or feel my heart soften at Zeke's half-smile.

I lowered myself down onto the ground, ignoring the biting frost of the snow on my cheek. My stomach rolled against my abdomen, but any energy I had left had been spent on a wasted arrow. Who knew three days of no food could be so brutally debilitating?

The water rippling and surging over boulders lulled me into a state of rest. I wasn't dying—I knew people who had gone longer without food. But it felt as if I were. I couldn't bring myself to move, even as my cheek went numb. I only stared ahead at the beams of the evening sun as they shone through the prismatic droplets of water jetting over the bank.

Splashes of color glinted in the mist hanging above the rocks in the river, and I was reminded of the colorful rooftops of Viridi. In those early days, I'd thought it was ostentatious, untasteful. But now as I recalled them, I had to appreciate the efforts of moving forward from a dark past. An era of blood ended, and a new one of hope—for the Tarasynian people, at least—began. So many of them Talented, their abilities manifested because of the threat placed on their heads, now no longer forced to live in fear.

But it had plunged the rest of the Peninsula into its own era of blood, flaring into existence with the slaughter in Hiddon. All due to the skewed ideologies of two Talented Tarasynian princes turned kings. And hardly anyone knew.

But Kathryn knew, and Celeste. And Yetta.

I knew.

And I was the only one on her way out of Tarasyn.

I kept my eyes glued to the colors in the river's mist as I lifted my head off the snow. I forced my mind to work and bend, wake up, by associating the colors with something I'd seen before. The muted red of one of Sterling's flowers, the dim yellow of the dogs in the hunting tapestry. A hint of green that echoed the Beryl Foothills, the powder blue of Sir Hilderic's storefront. And a sharper blue that didn't seem to fit with the rest of the colors.

A *striking* blue. On the opposite bank of the river.

I lifted my head a bit more and squinted through the mist.

It couldn't be.

I pushed myself carefully to my feet and inched toward the water, snowshoes sloshing through the frozen sheets of mud. My vision swayed as blood rushed from my head, but I kept my eyes firmly on the opposite bank, looking above the misty rainbows.

It was! Even in the disappearing light, the patch of bright blue petals and red pistils stood out starkly against the frozen world surrounding it. I found myself back in Hillstone's chapel, looking at the stained-glass image of the nerys lily.

But that was impossible . . . They didn't grow here.

From here I couldn't see how many there were, but if the old Lecevonian legends held any truth, I only needed one petal to feel full again.

I looked at the water rushing at my feet. I had no way of knowing how deep the river was here, and the current looked so swift. Besides, I would freeze if I tried to cross on foot.

A sudden burst of indecision rushed from deep inside my chest.

Was it even worth it? Many of the legends I'd thought foolish had been correct so far—but what if this one wasn't? What if this one had stemmed from just a traveler's exaggeration, as Hazel had said?

But the stained glass of my beloved chapel aided in my decision. I had to see this flower for myself.

I looked down the river and eyed the boulders that lay across its breadth. I could possibly jump from one to the next. Or I could slip and fall. There was no fallen tree as far as I could see that spanned the river, and I figured my hopes of finding one of those would require an immense stroke of luck. My luck had been spent on simply spotting the nerys lilies.

Even as I unlaced my snowshoes, my nerves were firing. If I fell into the river, I had no idea if I'd be able to get out. Papa had taught me to swim in Port Della, but it was not as if I was a very strong swimmer. Those visits were normally packed with hearings and committee meetings, not beach outings. Those had been for Mama, Isabele, and Lisette.

But I didn't really feel like I had a choice either. My shriveled stomach ached with something deeper than hunger. I had to try.

I stepped onto the nearest rock. My boot held its place, gripping the stone well enough for me to catch my balance and drag my other foot up to meet the first. I stepped down onto the next rock, and water licked the side of my boot. My heart pounded, the blood rushing in my ears almost drowning out the river.

Up onto the next boulder, farther of a stretch than the first two, and I found myself halfway across the river, surrounded by water rushing around the rock. I focused only on my balance, arms stretched out to either side, as I lifted my eyes to the next stone. A tiny thing, only large enough for one of my boots, and slick with water rushing over the top of it. Mist clung to the hood of my cloak and my eyelashes.

With a deep breath, I jumped.

The toe of my boot landed on the stone, and my other immediately traveled to the next rock jutting out of the water. A little laugh of triumph bubbled through my lips as I stood tall, gloved hands hugging the tip of the rock. I was more than halfway across. In the fading light, I found the patch of nerys lilies, just a bit more upstream than when I'd started. I set my mind firm on reaching them.

"Rose!"

My head whipped around, back to the bank of the river.

Then, a branch that was caught in the current, such a small thing, something that I would have seen had I kept my eyes on the river, clipped my boot still propped on the submerged rock.

My foot slipped off the stone, and I was left dangling by my grip on the big rock.

Had I not been so physically weakened by hunger, had I not injured my shoulder, perhaps I could have pulled myself up. Perhaps I could have clung to the tip of the rock, could have found my footing once more.

But those were not my circumstances.

I fell into the river. The unforgiving sting of the icy water hit my back almost immediately through my cloak, and my feet just barely scraped the riverbed before the current whipped around them and dragged them upward.

A figure on the edge of the bank grabbed my focus for a fraction of a second before I was pulled underneath the river's surface.

~ALONG THE RIVER~
ZEKE

As the sun broke the horizon, I found the river again as it careened around the side of the cliff it had carved into the mountains. I imagined the joy Rose had probably felt when she saw the river again, her green eyes round and excited, and the thought made me smile. Excellently done, my Rose.

I continued along the river into the evening, until Hugo grunted and refused to walk another step without a rest.

"All right, all right," I muttered, hopping down from his back. I took off my saddle and saddlebags, and the big oaf immediately rolled in the snow, legs kicking in the air as his satisfied nicker filled the still air. Then he stood and shook his coat out vigorously, and he pranced his way to the river's edge for a drink.

I, on the other hand, had to force myself to settle against a great pine trunk, even though my body was itching to keep moving. With a sigh and a quick shake of my head, I rummaged through one of my bags and fished out a piece of dried meat I'd bought while in town. I nibbled on it as I let my mind wander to Rose.

She'd really done this. A surge of pride for her warmed my veins. I'd thought it stupid at first, to leave Viridi on her own, but now I saw that she'd had no choice. Something in the way the old woman had talked of Rose—the sudden softness in her voice, the certainty in her eyes—something told me Rose had done the right thing. Now, I just wished I'd gotten there sooner, so she wouldn't have been alone. I should have left when I'd wanted to, no matter Isabele's disapproval. Queen-regent or not, I should have just *left*.

I had to reel myself in. Here I was, convincing myself that treason would have been the correct freckin' answer.

With a deep breath, I rested my head against the tree trunk and closed my eyes.

I awoke hours later, just before dawn. *Boars!* I hadn't expected to fall asleep. Hugo had helped himself to the bag of oats bundled next to me, leaving little bits of grain all over my cloak and scattered across the ground. I shook them out of my hair, trying to ignore the guilt I felt for falling asleep before I had thought to open the bag for him.

I jumped to my feet and stretched out long before making my way down to the river. I knelt on the bank and splashed some cold water on my face, washing away the last bit of sleep. Then, I patted Hugo on his neck. "Time to go, friend."

He didn't protest as I cinched him up and latched my bags to the saddle. I gave him a last handful of oats before tying the bag up with the rest, and then, we were off again.

Not much farther down the river, as the sun climbed through the trees, I found the remnants of another camp. And more wolf tracks. A sense of foreboding as heavy as rocks settled in my stomach as we pressed on.

Soon, there were so many wolf tracks set into the snow that it was hard to see anything else. They were fairly new too, only a day or so old. Just long enough to have been frozen in place, yet still fragile enough to be broken by my boot. They veered just a bit away from the river. I hated the feeling that they were following Rose, but it was impossible to shake. So, I left the river's bank and led Hugo after them.

The wolf tracks led us to an overhang, where a large fire pit had been set and fallen branches stacked against one side of the overhang to create a wall. A swift smile crossed my face as I imagined Rose hauling these branches here and building this massive fire. Why had she needed such a large fire?

Then I focused again on the wolf tracks, and I felt my brow furrow.

Was that why her fire had been so large? Had she encountered them?

I dismounted from Hugo and walked about the campsite, and I realized the wolf tracks here were not simple prints, but deep grooves of claws digging and grinding into the earth. Disorder. Rushing maneuvers. A fight.

I paced around the site, looking for any clue that Rose may have been at the brunt of it. Circling back to the overhang, I ducked inside, and spotless snow and a bed of pine needles garnered a bit of relief from me. At least Rose hadn't been ambushed in her sleep.

I backed out of the space and let my eyes scour the camp again. Then, as I approached the fire pit once more, I saw a spattering of blood in the snow, darkened to a dark brown with exposure.

I almost crumbled to my knees, my heart now racing. Was it Rose's blood? Or a wolf's? Could Rose injure a wolf like that? I found an arrowhead in the soot of the fire pit, so she had at least put up a fight. Wait—did Rose know *how* to use a bow and arrow?

Had they dragged her off? Surely there would be more blood if that were the case.

My mind spun. The wolf tracks seemed to double back the way they had come, and I almost made the decision to follow them. If they'd taken Rose . . .

No. If they'd taken Rose, she wouldn't be alive.

And if she *had* survived this attack, she would have continued on down the river.

I had to hope that she was still alive.

I threw myself into my saddle and kicked Hugo forward, back to the churning river.

The sun hung low now, golden beams slicing through the trees. I cursed the sun for falling so quickly. I wasn't sure if I'd ever ridden so fast in all my life. I kept telling myself that it was for Lecevonia. That the kingdom needed its queen returned safely. Even that Isabele, Lisette, and Clara needed their sister.

But truly, I knew this was for me. I needed Rose to be okay. I needed her warm in my arms, safe with me. Not gallivanting through the Tarasynian woods getting chased by wolves.

Focus, Zeke. I ran a hand through my hair and let out a frustrated sigh.

Then I saw it. The print of a snowshoe. Then another. I jumped off Hugo and bent down above the prints. Clear, new, the snow still soft in its impression. They led a bit into the brush, where I found a snare with a rabbit.

A snare? Did Rose know how to set snares?

A tinge of doubt colored my mind, suddenly unsure. But no one else would be out here, surely, so far off the road.

A few more steps down, there was another snare—this one still set. Then the prints doubled back to the river.

I continued more carefully now, leading Hugo by the reins. I kept my other hand on the hilt of the dagger at my belt.

As the sun began dipping below the horizon, I found a small campfire smoldering, and two leather bags sitting in the snow. One was torn through, wrapped up in ribbons of cloth to keep it together. A dagger's hilt protruded from the bag, the emerald in its hilt glinting in the fading light.

I looked back to the river, my eyes following the prints. I dropped Hugo's reins and crunched through the snow to a bow that had been left near the bank, with a length of rope lying next to it, one end wet and frayed.

Then, farther down, a pair of snowshoes. "What in the—"

I froze. A figure moved downstream.

CHAPTER TWENTY

~THE RIVER~
ROSEMARY

I WAS TUMBLING.

Rolling, completely uncontrollable. The water took me as it wished, forward and back, side to side. My entire body felt heavy, dead weight shrouded in waterlogged leather.

As my head broke the water's surface, a fleeting glimpse of a person swimming after me instilled a complicated mix of fear and relief. Relief, because I was not alone in this river. Fear, because *I was not alone in this river.* Only one person could have followed me this far, no matter how careful I'd been. The footfalls behind me, the presence I'd felt this entire time—they'd been real. Gryffin had found me.

Then the river whipped me around away from the figure, and I was left to its mercy yet again.

I'd fought this feeling of helplessness before, but I had no energy now. Any thoughts of survival felt too heavy. I didn't *want* to die, no— but I couldn't conjure enough strength to change anything either.

It was an odd feeling. Letting go. It was almost *easy*. My mental stays loosened, and I could breathe again—even if I was breathing water. I could look around me, at the trees rushing past me and the river's boulders just narrowly missing my limbs, sense the fish grazing my legs, and feel awe instead of fear. *This* was what power was like— this river had more power in it than anyone on the Peninsula. And to think it only got *stronger* as it rushed south to Port Della! Maybe that was where I would wash up, in Port Della. Would my lungs be full of water by then, as it dribbled past my lips now? I supposed I didn't care either way.

The river continued to take me, its current snaking around my ankles and wrists like writhing shackles. I didn't mind this prison.

Until fingers grabbed my wrist. Then, I very much cared.

I was brought back to that armored hand grabbing my cloak. But instead of my vision going black with panic, the red of anger began creeping in. I would rather die at the hands of an irrevocable force of nature than allow myself to die at the hands of the man who had already tried to take everything from me.

I reeled my elbow back to strike him in his face, but his arms closed in around me.

And instantly, they felt familiar. Like a protection I'd felt as a little girl. Maybe Gryffin's Talent had worked its way into my mind after all. I could hardly think straight as it was. My body and mind screamed in two separate directions, and having strength only to focus on resurrecting my castle, I allowed him to push us out of the river's current and toward the bank.

~THE RIVER~
ZEKE

A figure rose from behind a boulder in the middle of the river. Cloaked in leather, arms extended for balance. I squinted my eyes, searching for any detail that might tell me who was determined—or crazy—enough to be crossing this river. I eyed the current incredulously as mangled branches and snow drifts traveled downstream almost in a blur. That water would be ice.

Then the figure jumped.

And a brief memory of Rose and I jumping rocks across the stream behind Hillstone flew across my vision. I'd told her that she wouldn't be able to do it, and of course, she'd had to prove me wrong. She'd worn that look of determination she still possessed to this day, and her arms had flailed as she'd hopped from rock to rock, right across the water without a pause. I'd been too embarrassed to tell her that I was terrified to cross after her.

As I watched the figure leap, their arms outstretched, and land so proudly with one foot on one rock and one foot on the next, I knew.

I cupped my hands around my mouth and yelled as loudly as I

could above the roar of the water. "Rose!"

She turned, beautiful green eyes wide with surprise. A relief so strong washed over me that I almost clambered onto the rocks after her.

Then, somehow, she lost her footing.

And I felt all warmth leave my face.

She tried to pull herself up—I could see even from here how hard she was trying. But she couldn't get enough leverage.

I jumped into the river before her hands slipped from the rocks. I felt suspended in the air as I watched her fall backward into the water, her head disappearing below the water's surface.

When I landed in the water, my entire freckin' body stiffened with the cold. But the adrenaline pumping through my veins kept my arms moving, my legs kicking, until I was swept into the same current carrying Rose away from me. Fish bumped past me as they too let themselves be swept downstream. My eyes scanned the surface, looking from one bank to the other so quickly that I almost gave myself whiplash.

Finally, her head emerged from the water just a few arm strokes ahead of me, mouth wide and gasping. I lunged toward her, so close to closing the distance.

Then, the current whipped her around and dragged her farther out of my reach, and I shouted angrily into the thick mist rising from the river. Branches rushed past me on either side, and one narrowly missed Rose's head.

With a grunt of sheer will, I pushed my body through the water, arms grabbing the current in fistfuls and launching myself forward with every ounce of force I could manage. I stretched forward as far as I could, and my fingers grazed a boot. I heard her coughing over the rush of the water as I fumbled through the water.

"I've almost got you, Rose," I managed to utter through my own gasps, but I seriously doubted that she could hear me. My fingers kept searching through the water, desperately hoping to find purchase on a bootstrap, a belt, anything—until, mercifully, they found her wrist.

I pulled her into my chest and wrapped my arms around her in a vise. I couldn't even appreciate how good she felt there. First things first—don't die.

I kicked toward the nearest bank, praying it was the one that led to dry clothes as I reached forward with one hand, stroke after stroke. I felt the river's current relinquishing its hold on us little by little. Finally, I grabbed hold of a tree branch extended low over the river and pulled us into a watery alcove behind a boulder.

Rose climbed up the bank first, spewing water from her lungs loudly. As soon as I lifted myself out of the water, the cold immediately hit straight through my drenched clothing to my flesh. *Boars.* It was more than a bite or a sting—it was an outright assault. The sun had set, taking all chance of warmth with it.

With a hitched breath hissing between my teeth, I shuffled on my hands and knees over to Rose and patted her back as she continued to cough. Crite, she'd retch out a lung if she kept this up. Between my smile and my own gasping breaths, I managed to say, "You're always one for the dramatic, Rose." But she was here. She was alive.

And she'd heard me. Her eyes shot toward me through her periphery, and her coughing turned into a weak fit of laughter.

Oh good. She was crazy now too.

Then, she let herself fall into me, and I gathered her into my arms. I could never fathom letting this woman go again.

~THE RIVERBANK~
ROSEMARY

I had plans to push Gryffin back into the river the second I clambered up onto the snow, but my lungs had other ideas. I hadn't realized how close I'd been to drowning. They left me no choice but to pull myself up onto my hands and knees and cough out all the water I could. My throat burned and my chest ached, lungs tired and cramped. I felt Gryffin's hand on my back suddenly, trying to aid me, which took me by surprise. Then, I heard a voice that I was sure my mind had fabricated.

"You're always one for the dramatic, Rose."

Amidst my coughing fit, a jolt of disbelief gave me the willpower to steal a glance through the corner of my eye, and Zeke's sopping mess of golden hair and intense brown eyes stole my breath. He'd grown something of a beard too, as if he'd been on an assignment for weeks and hadn't had a chance to clean himself up, and the look sent a quiet little thrill through me. I inhaled sharply, and my next exhale was a relieved laugh. I sounded as on the verge of death as I felt.

I leaned into him—more like collapsed—and rested in his arms. I should have recognized these arms in the river.

He crushed his lips to my wet hair, and my sheer joy and relief attempted to heat the blood sluggishly pumping through my veins.

"*Rose*," his whisper filled my ear. "*My Rose.*"

Then, a little louder, he asked, "What were you thinking? If you wanted to die, you could've just let the wolves do it for you!"

I could hardly hear my own voice, feel my own smirk. "Believe it or not, dying was not my intent."

A violent chill ricocheted through both of us as a gust of wind plummeted down the mountain, and I curled into him more tightly. I realized then that all light of the sun had disappeared, twilight blanketing the forest in indigo.

Zeke nudged my head with his scraggly chin. "Can you stand?"

"Honestly?" I responded. "I don't think so." The weakness of hunger still gripped my bones, and the river had washed out all feeling. Besides, I wouldn't mind having him carry me anyway.

I felt him sigh as he gathered me into his chest and rocked himself to his feet with a groan.

As we began making our way back upstream, I asked, "Did you see them?"

Zeke glanced down at me, teeth chattering. "See what?"

"The nerys lilies."

His scoff answered my question. "I wasn't looking for flowers. I was too busy fishing you out of a river."

With what strength I could, I struck his chest with my fist.

"What happened to your face?" he asked.

But between the rocking of his stride, the darkened sky, and my entire essence weakened by hunger, my world faded.

CHAPTER TWENTY-ONE

WHEN MY EYELIDS fluttered open, they found a ceiling of leather.

Firelight flickered against the back wall through a small slit in the tent flaps, which lit the space just enough for me to make out the outlines of bags—more than just my own—and a quilt-laden pallet on the ground against the opposite wall.

My body felt as if it were still rolling in the current of the water even as I laid here stiff as a beam, and my head was heavy with sleep. As I stretched and curled my fingers, my fist grabbed a handful of warm woolen blankets, and a slow smile spread across my lips. I hadn't felt this comfortable since my chambers in Snowmont, and here, the fear of death didn't loom over my head. I buried my face into the layers of blankets, thankful for warmth and dry clothes.

Dry clothes?

I felt my face heat. I remembered, then, who had set up this tent, who had tucked me into this luxuriously warm pallet. And who must have been sitting outside near the fire now.

I pushed myself up to a seat and gave my head a chance to stop spinning. My withered stomach felt past the point of empty. When I looked down at my clothes—one of my woolen undergarments and an oversized tunic—I had to fight back a snicker. Zeke's style apparently lacked finesse.

Still buying time, I stood rockily and looked around the tent, eyes now adjusted.

The bags were not as neatly lined up as I'd originally thought. One that was not mine, with its buckle flipped open, spilled its contents across the leather floor—wooden cups and metal flasks, a burlap sack of oats, a drawstring bag of flint.

My bags were not much tidier. My maps had been laid out flat, my compass weighing down one of the corners. My extra quilt and a dark muslin skirt I didn't realize I'd had with me spilled haphazardly from my bag, and the book Yetta had given me for Isabele lay face-down at the head of the other pallet. The relics had been arranged out in the open next to my bag, poised almost as a question. The bow returned to the collection, and it had been unstrung, relieved from the poor job I'd done.

I slipped on dry boots and spent a few steadying moments putting things back in their places, taking my time. Rolling the maps up slowly, inspecting each wooden mug. I slipped into the skirt, tucking the tunic into its waistband and securing the laces at my hip, and I arranged my damp hair into a loose braid draped over my shoulder. I folded my quilt and laid it on top of the pallet opposite mine.

Soon, though, the fire outside beckoned to me. Not to mention the smell of something roasting on a spit, which my stomach joyfully woke up for.

I fished out my spare leather cloak from my bag, and taking one more strengthening inhale, I stepped out of the tent and into the firelight.

Zeke was crouched next to the fire, his back to me. His silhouette gleamed at its edges. He was my silver lining, my light. The fire he'd built was small but strong, for I could feel the heat radiating out to where I stood. He didn't turn to look at me, and I wasn't sure if he'd heard me until he nodded his head and sighed.

"Ah, so she awakens." There was a smile in his voice.

I grinned but said nothing as I strode forward slowly and stopped beside him.

He held up a jagged slice of dried meat to me. "Hungry?"

I felt my eyes widen, and I snatched the food from him as quick as a viper. "You haven't the slightest clue," I mumbled through my first bite. The salty, savory meat excited the entire surface of my parched tongue, and moans of satisfaction rumbled in my throat.

My tone made him glance up at me. "Hey, hey, hey," he said quickly, shooting to his feet. His fingers closed around my wrist just as I was going for my third bite. "Not so fast. You'll be sick."

Just as he said so, the food hit my aching stomach, which almost immediately protested at the intrusion. It was so intense that I had to close my eyes and sink down to the log situated at the base of the fire.

Zeke followed, sitting next to me as I let the wave of nausea pass. His concerned eyes locked with mine for the first time tonight, briefly, before dropping back to the fire. He let go of my wrist quickly.

"That was your snare out there, right?" He nodded toward the rabbit cooking over the fire.

The curtness in his voice surprised me, but I nodded. "I hadn't known anything was in it."

He squinted his eyes, eyebrows lifted. "So you *have* been eating?"

"I have," I said indignantly, not sure why his tone sounded so accusing.

This certainly wasn't how I'd been picturing our reunion.

"I was doing rather well for myself, actually. Until the wolves," I added, almost as an after-thought.

"The wolves," he repeated dryly. "You've been out here traipsing along with wolves, and frostbite, and freezing rivers!" He stood abruptly and paced around the fire, checked on the rabbit's progress, paced again. Looked out to the woods, up into the trees. Anywhere but me.

His mood really seemed uncalled for. It was my job to overreact, not his.

"Zeke"—his name, spoken directly to *him*, felt so good on my lips— "I had to leave. But I'm fine. Especially now, thanks to you."

He barely turned his head in my direction and scoffed. "Yes, well, we don't all give drowning a try like you."

I stood and crossed my arms over my chest. "I fell. I would have made it had someone not distracted me."

That made him turn on his heel. "Oh, so this was *my* doing?"

Before, back in Hillstone, I probably would have been baited by his words. Said some snarky retort that I would have regretted later. But I wouldn't do that this time. I owed him too much. "No," I said instead. "All of this is on me. But you're being rude."

"Oh, *Your Majesty*, excuse me." He bowed to me in an exaggerated manner. "I shouldn't dare be *rude* to you, not after you run into these Haggard-forsaken woods and invite a pack of wolves over for dinner. Not after you get yourself mixed up in the throes of a river and emerge in sopping wet clothes." At that, he scowled into the fire, his cheeks as bright as the flames.

I hadn't seen him blush in years. It was adorable, really. I let my arms fall to my sides. "Is that what this is about? You having to change my clothes?" An incredulous laugh threatened to break through. But, thinking there were less fragile situations in which to laugh, I held it back.

His eyes never left the flames, but they were no longer hardened in anger, at least. "I—had to," he muttered. He sounded like he was confessing to murder. "You would have frozen."

I took a step toward him and placed a hand on his rigid forearm. "I know," I said softly. "*Thank you.* Really."

He looked down at my hand, and I felt his arm relax. "You aren't angry with me then."

"No." How could I be?

I would have been lying if I'd said the notion of him seeing me unclothed didn't thrill me a bit, even if it had been a matter of life-or-death. I just wished I had been awake for it. I was disappointed more than anything.

Finally, he huffed out a sigh and turned toward me, head still down. When I placed my hand on his cheek, he lifted his gaze, forehead furrowed and eyes churning with some emotion as they searched mine.

I looked at him as transparently as I could, hiding nothing. Lifting onto my toes, I kissed him on his forehead, and I tried to overlook the way my heartbeat stuttered. "No worrisome creases are warranted here."

Zeke chuckled, and his face relaxed just a tad. As if he could no longer help himself, he wrapped one arm around my waist and pulled me into him. His other hand cradled my cheek. He pressed his forehead against mine, and my lips felt a pull toward his.

I closed my eyes, breathing deeply, my fluttering heart surely loud enough for him to hear. I painted on a teasing smirk. "Surely I'm not the only woman whose clothes you've unlaced."

His breathy chuckle felt like feathers across my skin. "But none of them were you."

My sigh merged with his as he kissed me.

And again, I was welcomed home. Right where I was supposed to be, all this time. His hand was so gentle on my face, as reverent as the wind rippling through the grass of Lecevonia's hills. But in this moment with Zeke, after so many days of imagining him, *him*, I didn't want wind.

I wanted a storm.

So, when I leaned farther into him and parted my lips, Zeke's little noise of surprise set loose a monsoon of everything I'd kept veiled, protected inside me since arriving in this frozen kingdom. My hope, my resolve, my devotion—all of it poured from me to him, because Zeke I could trust. I no longer needed control of anything, not with him. For now at least.

His hand shifted to the back of my head, fingers combing into my hair. I bowed against his body as his tongue slipped between my teeth. And his arms around me tightened as he lifted me off my feet, which was a good thing because my legs had gone weak. He sat on the broken log near the fire and gathered me into his chest, and I twisted in his arms so that I sat in his lap, facing him, my arms locked around his neck. I crushed myself to him, the lines of our bodies blurring, and I shivered when I felt his hand slip between my tunic—*his* tunic—and my bare shoulder. His touch drove a hunger I'd never felt before, a hunger to somehow find a way to be closer to him.

His lips traveled down my neck, gentle kisses, to the crook of my collarbone. His warm breath made my skin rise with goosebumps, and I entwined my fingers in his hair, burying my face in his rugged blonde waves. He smelled of leather and firewood. When he pushed my tunic aside and kissed my shoulder, I sighed into his hair, my grip on him tightening.

The tip of his nose grazed my skin as his lips found their way back to mine again. His hunger matched my own as he kissed me, breaking only for our ragged breaths.

Too soon, our lips parted. I grazed my teeth against his lower lip, coaxing a low groan from him, and I planted a small kiss on his cheek with a smile.

He rested his head in the nook of my neck, and I laid my head against his, my fingers twirling a lock of his hair at the base of his neck. The winter cold crept in again, but nothing could stifle the warmth flowing through my veins.

"My Rose," he murmured against my skin. "Boars, how I've missed you."

"I've missed you too," I responded, drawing circles on his shoulder. "More than you could know."

He hugged me to himself and chuckled. "I doubt that." He lifted his head then and looked at me squarely. "Why were you on those rocks, Rose?" But his accusatory tone, widened eyes, and hands roaming across my back said something more along the lines of, *Why were you going to leave me in this world without you?*

I pressed my lips to his softly, assuring him that the feeling was mutual. "I was starving, Zeke—I'd never been so *hungry* . . . And . . . I saw nerys lilies on the opposite bank." I looked toward the patch now, but darkness had swallowed even the river.

His brown eyes narrowed. "Here. In the Silver Mountains."

I nodded, already aware that it sounded ridiculous. But I knew what I saw.

Zeke scoffed. "Why would you risk your life for legends you don't believe in?"

"I'd thought I didn't believe them," I said quietly. I climbed out of his lap and sat next to him on the log. "Until I was brought here. Zeke, there is so much we did not know. Everything about Talents, and the Five Talented—it's all true."

He looked at me wide-eyed for a moment. "Not just nursery tales."

"No," I replied. "It's all *so* much more."

"Wait," Zeke said, holding up a hand. "Slow down. Start over, from the beginning."

I laughed dryly. "How far back do you want me to go?"

"The moment I last laid my eyes on you in the stables."

So, I told him. I wasn't sure how long we'd sat there for, firelight flickering on our faces. While I talked, we ate the rabbit, and my stomach had no objection this time. I recounted Roderich, the woods with Gryffin, the journey back to Viridi. The musty guest chambers with the hunting tapestry, and later the Queen's chambers with its granite walls and gilded bedposts. The dresses, the banquets, the chandeliers. Celeste, and the other Lecevonians trapped inside Snowmont's walls, servants to their captor.

I told him of Kathryn, and Yetta—everything I'd learned about the Talented, or at least a quick version of it all. Of how I'd learned that there was magic inlaid in the very earth of the Peninsula.

He sat quietly through it all, absorbing. But when I spoke of Gryffin's Talent, his gaze darkened to something murderous as he stared into the flames of the fire.

And of course, I told him of the deceit—my game. And how my game had ended in the deaths of Cassia and Xal. My voice hitched into silence as I looked away from their faces in the firelight.

"You aren't the only one to feel responsible for Xal's death," Zeke said quietly. "My message to you was the reason why he was in Viridi in the first place. And for what?" He kicked loose snow and dirt into the fire, and the flames engulfed them with a sizzle.

But I shook my head. "Your letters gave me hope. I had no other way of knowing if anyone in Lecevonia suspected anything. I'd thought, maybe, Gryffin still had all of you under his influence."

Zeke grimaced. "It's been a challenge." He stood from his seat and glared into the dark forest. "Amos had been right."

My ears perked at the name of my guard. "Amos?"

He nodded and let out a long sigh. "When he finally came to, he was certain Gryffin had some sort of . . . sorcery . . . at his disposal. It had sounded crazy—but everything Amos said *felt* true."

I wrapped myself tighter in my cloak against the memory of Gryffin's hold. "That is only the beginning of Gryffin's Talent. With the right words, he can convince anyone to do his bidding."

"Except you." Zeke turned back toward me with a grin.

"What?"

"The old woman in the woods—Yetta, you called her—said you have a mental defense of some kind. Gryffin can't fool you anymore."

"Nor whoever else sees through his lies," I said. "But yes, I do something a bit . . . different."

His eyes lightened. "Is it a Talent?"

"No." As much as I wished it was. "But I know that Gryffin wants to Awaken the Talented across the entire Peninsula. And supposedly he can, with the relics of the Five Talented in that tent." I pointed behind us.

"Aah, that's what those are." Then, he took a rickety step back. "Excuse me—the relics of *the Five Talented*? What the boars does that mean?"

"It means those objects contain more magic in them than we know."

"Those *objects* are over six hundred years old!"

I nodded.

After the shock of it wore off, Zeke spit into the fire. "Why don't we throw them in the river? Be done with them?"

Gryffin's words, echoed by Yetta's, circled in my head. "Not all

Talented are like Gryffin," I said quietly.

"If *any* are like that crite, no Awakening can happen." He marched to the tent and disappeared inside. I hurried after him, only to slam into his chest as he emerged with the bangle and dagger in his hands, bow slung over his shoulder.

"Zeke, wait—"

He maneuvered around me easily and tossed the dagger into the air, catching it by the hilt as it descended. He reeled his arm back, ready to throw it into the darkness.

I planted myself in front of him. "Isabele is Talented."

That garnered a staggering look. "What?"

"A powerful one, from what I've gathered." I plucked the dagger and bangle out of his hand, and I rubbed the dagger's emerald with my thumb. "Like I said, not all Talented are like Gryffin. Besides, who are we to rid the kingdoms of their founders' relics? We'll return them to their rulers, once things are settled."

"And until then?"

"Well . . . I'll have to warn them of Gryffin's advances, so they'll be on their guard."

"And how do you think that conversation is going to go? 'Good afternoon, King Merek! Talents exist, and the King of Tarasyn wants to steal from you to perform some sort of ritual!'" Zeke rolled his eyes. "Brilliant idea."

I slapped him in the shoulder. "I'll figure it out."

After a tense moment of silence passed between us, Zeke sighed and shrugged the bow off his shoulder. "All right. As you wish."

Taking the bow from him with a huff, I flipped through the tent flaps and stuffed the relics back into my bag.

Truly, I didn't know what I was going to do with them. Perhaps Yetta had a point, that having more Talented wouldn't necessarily be a bad thing. I even saw Gryffin's reason—more Talented meant better supplies, more secure trade agreements. And to think—all those people with Talents they didn't know they possessed! To have that part of yourself locked away, and not even realize it . . .

But was an Awakening my call to make? I hadn't thought it was Gryffin's.

I heard Zeke enter the tent behind me, and I flipped the bag's cover closed, though it didn't latch anymore.

"I suppose we should try to get some sleep," he said, rubbing his hand along the back of his neck. "We should be able to make it to Pruin by tomorrow evening. We'll meet my men there."

We were so close to being rid of this forest. I could already feel a warm bath soothing my cold-bitten skin. "Then home," I whispered aloud.

Zeke chuckled as he leaned over and unbuckled his boots. "Yes. Then home. But for now, sleep."

Sleep did seem nice. Even though I'd already been out for who knows how long, I found my entire body fatigued.

But I was also hyper aware of Zeke removing his cloak, and his leather shirt, and his vest.

When he looked up at me and caught me staring at him in his thin cotton tunic, he smirked. "If you think you'll be able to sleep."

I tore my eyes away and straightened my shoulders. "Sleep. Yes, I agree. And—and Hugo? He's okay out there?"

Zeke crawled underneath his blankets. "He's fine. Happy as a meadowlark."

"Are you sure?" I hugged my cloak around me, and I felt my eyes darting for the tent flap. "Perhaps I should go check on him—"

"He's fine, Rose. I promise." He propped himself up onto his elbow, and I couldn't help but notice the way his tunic's laces had come undone. "What's wrong?"

I stood in the middle of the tent, half of me being pulled to my bed while the other half was drawn by the fresh air of the woods. Air that was not suddenly stifling hot.

"Nothing," I finally answered, and I knelt down by my pallet and unclasped my cloak from my neck, pulled my feet free from my boots. Before I could change my mind, I quickly unlaced my skirt and let it drop to pool around my feet. My woolen undergarment still covered most of my legs, but a sense of vulnerability dominated my insides until I could crawl into my blankets and hug them to me.

Without looking behind me, I buried my face in the wool and cotton and took a deep breath, inhaling all the scents on which I could focus. Horsehair. Leather. Sage. Woodchips.

Zeke. All of them smelled like Zeke.

I huffed and turned around in my blankets, facing back toward the interior of the tent.

To find Zeke's widened eyes looking at me through the darkness.

"Ah," he said quietly. "I see."

I laughed once, humorlessly, and squeezed my eyes closed, trying to ignore this new warmth in the pit of my stomach.

I lay like that for what seemed an eternity, my fists clutched to my chest, my teeth gritted together. I was tired—my aching muscles told me that much, but despite lying in the most comfortable bed I'd had in a week, my brain refused to release itself to sleep.

No, instead I had to listen to the insects humming outside the tent wall, the firewood cracking and splintering.

Zeke's smooth breaths.

A twig snapping under a rabbit's foot, the constant rush of the river's current.

Zeke rustling in his blankets.

Finally, I groaned and pushed my blankets away from me. "This won't work."

Though he faced away from me now, I heard him chuckle. "Tell me about it. Not like when we were kids, is it?" He sat up and kicked his blankets off, and he began buckling his boots back on.

I shot up into a seat. "Where are you going?"

"Hugo is a better sleeping partner than you," he said, teasing. But his eyes were tight. He shrugged through his leather shirt and grabbed a quilt from his pallet.

"Wait." I grabbed his hand as he tried to pass by. He looked back at me, my favorite half-smile on his face. Steeling myself, I said, "Stay. Please."

An expression between hopeful and hopeless danced on his face. I imagined my face looked similar. "Are you sure?"

"As your queen, I demand it." It wasn't a real order, of course, but it still felt nice to say.

"Well, my queen will also have to contend with a tired and irritable man tomorrow, then." But he retreated back into the tent and sat back onto his pallet, unbuckling his boots once more. He threw off his leather shirt and disappeared under his blankets, grumbling something indecipherable.

I sat there on my bed, worrying at my bottom lip, my insides at war.

I had one night. Tomorrow, we would be in Pruin. Then on to Lecevonia, where I'd have to wear my crown once again. The thought didn't intimidate me—not like it used to. In fact, I very much looked forward to returning to my throne.

But the throne meant responsibilities. It meant no more Zeke.

But tonight, this last night, I had no responsibilities. I had no maid in my chambers, no guard posted by the door. I did not have to be Queen Rosemary Avelia, Reigning Sovereign of Lecevonia tonight.

Setting my jaw firm, I stood from my bed and sidled my way over to Zeke's. He didn't turn around as I slipped underneath his blankets, pressed my feet against his legs. His body was rigid, and it seemed as though he'd stopped breathing.

Zeke's voice sounded forced when he finally spoke. "Your Majesty—"

"Not tonight," I murmured. "Just Rose."

He shifted and turned to face me then, his brown eyes content in the dim firelight. His arms wrapped around me and held me to him tightly, and the kiss he gave me was so tender, so gentle, so adoring that afterwards, I found myself gasping, breathlessly in awe. I nestled into his chest, feeling safer than I ever had in my nineteen years.

"I still love you."

His chuckle sifted through my hair. "I know, perhaps better than you do."

His familiar words made me smile, and that smile never left my face as I felt myself drifting into a perfect sleep.

CHAPTER TWENTY-TWO

WHEN I AWOKE the next morning, I was the warmest I'd been in months. I almost forgot that I was in a frost-covered forest, wrapped in the same blankets as the man I loved.

"Good morning," his voice whispered, tickling my ear.

I smiled up at him, and the blush on my cheeks made me feel even warmer. "Good morning."

"Queens sleep very late."

I glanced around and noticed the ambient light floating around the tent, the white hue of midmorning. I groaned loudly and nuzzled into his tunic. "Not always. Can we still make it to Pruin by nightfall?"

"If we hurry. But . . ." He rubbed a finger gently along my jaw. "What's the rush?"

I sighed, tempted. What harm would a few more stolen minutes do? But I let myself enjoy last night—now I needed to jump back to reality. "The rush is I have a kingdom to return to."

Zeke nodded slowly, and he planted the lightest kiss on my forehead. "All right, my queen." He threw the blankets off us, and I yelped as the cold air rushed underneath my wool underskirt. "Up we go!"

He threw on his vest, leather shirt, and cloak, buckled his boots, and was out of the tent before I even had the chance to sit up.

While he bustled around outside, I slowly worked my way around the tent, collecting my things together and packing them in my bags. I dressed in my own tunic and leather vest but opted to keep the skirt, and I tried my best to arrange my knotted hair into a bun. As I was folding our plethora of blankets the tent disappeared above my head, leaving only the leather floor.

I glared at him, steaming with indignation. "You're lucky I was finished dressing."

"You're in a hurry, aren't you?" He hardly looked in my direction as he rolled up the tent and stuffed it into one of his bags. "We'd best get moving then. Hugo won't like us riding double for very long."

My eyes followed him as he buckled his bags onto his saddle. How did he just . . . turn it off like that?

Well, if he could, I could too.

After kicking snow over the remnants of our fire, I fastened my cloak around my neck and pulled my gloves on. I rolled up the tent's leather floor and handed it off to Zeke, who attached it to the very back of the saddle, and then I hoisted my bags up onto my shoulders like a backpack.

"Off we go then," I said, extra chipper as I stuck my foot into the stirrup and swung a leg over Hugo's back.

Zeke rolled his eyes but followed suit, and soon, we were high-stepping through the snow. I looked behind us one more time, toward the patch of nerys lilies, but the river's mist was thicker today, completely obscuring the opposite bank.

We didn't need to follow the river anymore, for Zeke knew exactly where we were after a second of studying the maps. As we walked, he asked me any and all questions pertaining to the Talented. How did one know they were Talented? What was the oldest age one could be to have a Talent manifest? What types of Talents were there? Were they as diverse as the legends said?

Red flecks in their eyes.

I didn't know, but I witnessed one man in his fifties manifest a Talent at the banquet.

Any type of ability you could think of.

That diverse and more. Laughably more.

"So you and I could be Talented, and just not know it," Zeke said, voice full of curiosity. "I could be Talented with—I don't know—stealth. Or tracking."

"I suppose you could be," I said with a shrug. I glanced back quickly, studying his eyes. No red flecks.

"How many are like Gryffin?" He said my captor's name as if it was poison.

"I don't know. Truly." Something Kathryn had said—how no two Talents were precisely the same—well, perhaps *no one* was like Gryffin. "I didn't know very many people with a mental Talent," I said. "There's Gryffin and Yetta. And Isabele. But most people I came across were Talented with physical skills, or tactile things." I should have slipped that book of mental Talents from the library when I'd had a chance.

His questions continued—most of my answers a resounding 'I don't know'—until, around sunset, he slowed Hugo to a walk alongside a tall wooden gate. His disposition changed immediately, serious and dark.

"Pruin?"

He nodded. "Keep your hood low. And don't say a word."

Though an instinctual indignation rose within me, I knew better

- 314 -

than to challenge his brusque command. I bowed my head and let the shadows cover my eyes. I was grateful that I had decided to double up on my clothes underneath my cloak, to give me a bit more bulk to my frame.

I'd been so *close.* Pruin had been just a day's travel more. Maybe two, at my speed.

Hugo's feet left the snow and clopped through gravel. I heard Zeke mumble, "Oh thank Haggard, it's a different man."

"Good evening," a voice called, and Zeke gradually pulled Hugo to a halt.

The smile in Zeke's voice could have warmed anyone's mood. "Good evening, sir. How are you faring?"

"Well enough, well enough. What's your business here?"

"Just hoping for a night of lodging." Hugo's feet shifted in the gravel. "Have any recommendations?"

"What brings you and your lady out on the road?"

Well, he was curious, wasn't he? I felt my hair bristle.

But Zeke didn't falter. "We're traveling, you see. To see family who very recently built a home in Vespost."

The man grumbled. "Vespost. Travelers from the Hiddon territory have been bombarding us for the past three months."

Refugees? Or captives?

"Yes, well, given the new land acquisition, that is to be expected." Zeke chuckled, but I heard the underlying darkness in his tone. "Do you have any recommendations for lodging?" he asked again.

"Down the road a ways, to your left. The Singing Spruce, run by a respectable woman. My wife!" He laughed so robustly that I imagine tears sprung to his eyes, and his laughter brought a smile to my face.

"Thank you, good sir," Zeke responded, sounding so sincere. The gates began to creak open.

But the man chimed in one more time. "Might I ask the lady to remove her hood?" Apologies tinged his voice. "King's orders."

"Oh, come now," Zeke protested. "It's much too cold—"

"It's all right," I said quietly, lowering the hood of my cloak. "We've nothing to hide."

My heart fluttered like a bird in my chest as the gatekeeper studied me, his large blue eyes squinting, trying to see my face underneath the grime and scrapes. When his eyes zeroed in on my forehead, his bearded mouth turned downward into a scowl.

"King's orders?" I asked as I lifted my hood once more.

"Aye," the man said. "We're to be watching for the queen, in the case that she's made it this far south. Poor woman. You look like her a bit, you know, from what I've gathered. It's been nearly two weeks now. People of her status don't survive in the snow for two weeks. The king is devastated, as is the princess. I'd heard they'd gotten close." His scowl deepened.

This man certainly heard a lot. Probably by keeping people hostage at the gate as he was doing to us—which wasn't a fair thought, because he seemed nice enough. Genuinely concerned, surely. I almost giggled, imagining the gossip passing from so many travelers to this man.

"Well, thank you so much for the conversation," I said, "but we really—"

"Should get going," Zeke finished for me. "I know my horse here is ready to have us off his back." He laughed and patted Hugo on his neck. To lay it on a bit thicker, Hugo stomped his feet and snorted.

"Fine beast you have there," the man commented with a nod. "The Singing Spruce has a small stable out back."

"Thank you, sir." Zeke nudged Hugo forward through the gates.

We walked just a bit farther into town after the gates had groaned shut behind us.

Finally, when it felt safe, Zeke dismounted. And when he rounded to face me, he wore a mask of anger. "I told you to keep your hood down and stay silent." Though his voice was hushed, every syllable burned with frustration.

"And I had every intent to listen to you," I said amicably, hopping down to the ground. "But it would have been more suspicious if we didn't oblige."

He narrowed his eyes, but his silence told me that he knew I was right.

We did not stop at the Singing Spruce after all, although the doors were thrown open and the melodies of a lute poured through the windows. It looked like it belonged in Viridi, with its chartreuse walls and yellow roof peeking from underneath the heavy quilt of snow.

Zeke apparently had arrangements with his men to meet at another inn in town. Or a tavern, really. As we approached, this place was much quieter, no bustling of patrons or brightly burning fires. Its walls matched the rest of Pruin, wooden and weathered, with a beaten door barely hanging onto its hinges. They didn't even have a sign hanging above their door.

"How did you know he would not recognize you?" Zeke finally asked, tying Hugo's reins to a post outside the tavern.

I sent my gaze to the ground. Any snow that had fallen recently had been trampled into mud and gravel. "Queens do not typically have scars on their faces. The only time anyone has ever seen me, I was done up all nice and pretty. Scar hidden. I'm sure I don't look very queenly at this moment." I gestured to my leather-clad form.

He smirked, and after a quick contemplation, he placed a hand on my cheek. The heat in my face rose up to meet his touch. "If only it were easy to forget," Zeke grumbled, mostly to himself. Then, with an abrupt sigh, he dropped his hand and turned toward the tavern's steps. I scurried after him through the rickety door.

"Look," Zeke said, raising his chin toward a table near the fireplace. Two men sat quietly with steins in their hands. While one was near Zeke's size, though not as tall, the other man was a hulking giant. Sturdy as a tree. He lifted his head as we entered, and I saw the familiar face of a ghost smiling at me from underneath his hood.

While Zeke went to speak with the barman, I stumbled my way as calmly as I could toward the table, tears pricking my eyes, and my guard met me with open arms.

"It's good to see you alive and well, Your Majesty," Roger whispered, his deep voice filling my ear through his big smile.

"We were getting worried you two wouldn't show," the other man said, whom I now recognized as Sir Terrin. "Your Majesty," he added in a hushed voice. He bowed his head to me, disguising it as taking a sip from his stein.

I took a seat in one of the empty chairs around the table. "Thank you, both of you. I can't even begin to describe how good it feels to be in the presence of familiar faces."

Sir Terrin shared a small smile while Roger chuckled.

"How—how are you here?" I shook my head incredulously at my guard. "You were one against *four* . . ."

"Five is my record," Roger replied, his deep laugh filling the tavern. Sir Terrin eyed him in caution, and Roger cleared his throat.

My smile was bittersweet. Thomas would have been thrilled to know his comrade was alive.

Zeke returned with two steins of mead and two keys. "For you, Lady Feyrna," he said, placing one of each in front of me on the table. He winked at me as he declared my alias, loud enough for the rest of the tavern to hear.

All right, then, Feyrna it was for tonight.

I nodded in thanks as he sat in the empty chair next to me.

"Tomorrow we'll head out at daybreak," Zeke said quietly. "Before the rest of the town can see who's coming and going."

Sir Terrin shook his head slowly and took a sip of his mead, foam dusting his beard. "I still cannot believe you found her. It's remarkable."

"Your queen is the one that's remarkable," Zeke replied. "She kept herself alive for over a week!"

I sipped my mead quietly as Zeke recounted the story in hushed tones, of wolves and rivers and cliffs. But it was all from his point of view. He did not mention the way my bones chilled at the sound of wolf howls, or my clawing hunger, or how the sight of the nerys lilies gave me one last push of hope for survival. But I didn't care to add those details to his tale. I would keep those struggles to myself for now, perhaps forever. It was *my* battle—a battle I'd won.

I sat there throughout the evening listening to the men banter back and forth as more patrons of the tavern began to file in. After a while, when it became too noisy for my tired brain to think straight, I bid the men a good night and took my leave.

I made my way up the stairs, through the dim hallway of rooms. I found my room, and as I put my hand on the handle, a man stepped out of a room just a couple doors down. He fumbled with his keys, then dropped them and cursed.

I couldn't tear my eyes away as his dark curls fell forward as he bent down to pick them up. When the man righted himself, blue eyes with red flecks gleamed at me in the dark.

My scream caught painfully in my throat.

He'd found me. He'd beaten me here.

How did he know where I would be staying?

"Miss?" The man reached out his hand to me, calloused and wrinkled.

I took a deep breath, shrinking out of his reach. *Breathe, Rose.* Those weren't his hands. When I lifted my eyes to his again, the red-flecked eyes were gone, instead replaced by a dark brown.

"I-I'm sorry," I murmured, cheeks flaming. "Forgive me."

I twisted my doorknob and let myself in, leaving the man standing confused in the hallway.

When I closed my door behind me and shoved the lock in its place, I sank to the floor and squeezed my eyes tightly shut.

Despite being safer now than I ever had been in Snowmont, Gryffin still haunted me. His eyes, his voice—I wasn't free of him.

A volley of panic pierced me like an arrow, and I had to remind myself that I *was* free now. No need to pretend here. No need to fear what might have been behind any of these doors. No need to flinch at every creak and snap.

Then why did Gryffin's eyes plague me even now?

With a deep, bolstering inhale, I buried the red flecks down deep into a corner of my mind. A corner I had no intention of revisiting. Then, I opened my eyes and pushed myself off the floor.

The room had been prepared with a crackling fire in the small fireplace, and women's clothes had been draped over the footboard of the bed: a chemise for tonight, and a cotton tunic, adorned with black beading at the bodice, coupled with a mauve skirt for tomorrow.

What was more, situated behind a screen was a tub filled with water, steam rolling over its surface. My chest tightened at Zeke's thoughtfulness, knowing he had made these requests of the tavern owner for me. I shimmied out of my clothing and peeled off my woolen undergarment, which had a more horrid smell than I'd realized. As I passed a mirror, I caught a glimpse of a wild woman staring back at me. Unkempt hair, grimy body, face and neck speckled with red dots from flying embers. A grim line for a mouth set in a hard, tired expression. The only thing familiar about the woman was the pair of green eyes staring back at me.

I stepped into the bathtub and submerged my entire body into the water's depths, hair and all.

I didn't know how long I soaked, but only did I move again once the water had become more cool than hot. I scrubbed the soap that had been left next to the tub all over my body, into my hair, my face, every crevice. By the time I stepped out of the water and into the cotton towel hanging over the screen for me, I'd left the tub brown and gritty.

But I felt cleaner than I had in weeks—and smelled better too—when I pulled the chemise over my wet hair. When I looked into the mirror again, I recognized myself again. Changed surely, hardier than before, but Rose.

Satisfied, I crawled underneath the blankets of the bed. Oh, *wow*. A bed. As I began to doze off to the snapping of the firewood, there was a knock on my door.

"You may come in," I managed to say through my grogginess.

The door jiggled as it was unlocked with a second set of keys. It cracked open, and Zeke's golden head popped in through the light. "Did you enjoy your bath?"

"Mhmm," I murmured. "Thank you, Zeke."

His quiet chuckle filled the room like velvet. "My pleasure, Rose." There was a brief hesitation in his stance, then he began to back out of the doorway. "Good night."

I wasn't conscious enough to grapple with whatever feeling had crept up inside me at his departure, but it stung, and I shied away from it. Instead, I remembered the contentment of last night. I wanted that again. "Stay."

The door hinges squeaked. "Rose . . ."

"Stay."

I barely registered the weighted air of the room as Zeke shifted on his feet. Finally, he groaned and muttered, "I'll be right back."

With his promise, I rolled over with a smile and nestled into my pillows as my door closed behind him.

"Right back" turned out to be an exaggeration, for when my door next opened, I was jolted out of sleep. Out of the snowy woods, out of the line of sight of the white wolf in my dream. The light from the doorway appeared behind my eyelids and disappeared just as quickly.

"Rose?"

"Hmm," I murmured, holding onto the tendrils of sleep as tightly as I could.

Zeke's voice sounded closer next time he spoke. "Truly?"

Through a cranky yawn, I said, "Get in this bed before I change my mind." But I wouldn't have changed my mind. I was too tired to make any decision, really.

The sheets behind me rustled, and I felt Zeke's warm body line up with mine. He'd changed clothes and freshened up, but he still smelled perfectly of leather, sage, and fire.

He mumbled something, but my ears didn't try to catch his words. I sighed as his arm draped over my waist and held me to him, and my relief was the last thing I comprehended before I sank back into sleep.

We left the next morning just as early as planned, exiting through the gates of Pruin just as the sun stretched its first rays over the horizon.

If Roger and Sir Terrin thought anything of Zeke staying in my room last night, they did not say so as we rode down the gravel road, heading south. They'd purchased a horse for me, a small bay with the spirit of a chestnut, and I spent most of my time wrangling with her rather than listening in on the men's conversation. But once the filly had tired out, Roger asked me to recount again what had happened in Tarasyn.

So, I did, for what I was sure would not be the last time. When I mentioned the Talented, both Roger and Sir Terrin scoffed, until they realized I was speaking in all seriousness. They remained quiet for the rest of my story, trying to absorb as much as they could, just as Zeke had by the fire the night before last.

There were burning questions, of course, that still needed answering. What more did Hiddon know, that Lady DeGrey did not tell me? What would an Awakening mean for the Peninsula if it happened? How did the Rebels of the Red Sun factor into all of this?

And the question that burned in my mind brighter than any others: how were we going to get my Lecevonians out of Snowmont? Sir Terrin had said they'd discovered twenty-six were in the servitude of Gryffin. That was twenty-six too many. And Celeste—

A sob built in my throat, but I took a shaking breath and held it down. Instead, I smiled, as Celeste would have wanted me to.

At the first sight of green plains, my heart ceased to beat, and when it started pounding again, it raced like a drum in my chest. My apprehension, anxiety, uncertainty—it was all whisked away on the wind that rippled the blades of the grass of the Beryl Foothills. I did not need Zeke or Roger and Sir Terrin to tell me when we'd stepped over the border into my kingdom.

My kingdom welcomed me home.

And it was no longer spring. The summer sun burned brightly

overhead, shimmering over the tides of verdant grass.

What awaited me in Lecevonia was its own list of unknowns. The state of Hillstone, the state of my advisors and my sisters. The state of my *people*.

However, fear of my capability had no hold on me. Not anymore. Whether he knew it or not, Gryffin had made in me a queen more powerful than ever. A queen forged of fury and fire. I was more certain than ever that I would do what I could—what I *must*—to keep Gryffin's war out of Lecevonia. I would control what I could, and I knew now that my control only lay in using what was dealt to me. This was the reason I'd fought so hard to stay alive the past three months. I was returning home as the ruler Lecevonia deserved, Talented or not.

The city of Flecte lay on a hill ridge, providing a stark juxtaposition between the jagged Silver Mountains to the north and the gentle roll of the Beryl Foothills to the south. We crossed a wide, sturdy bridge over the Riparia River and approached the city as the sun disappeared behind the peaks of the mountains. It was odd, how dark the sky had already gotten even though it was still early evening.

Sir Terrin continued to ride on ahead, to let those in Hillstone know that I was safe, and that I would be in Equos in just over a week's time. After we bid him goodbye, Zeke steered Hugo around to walk beside me. His excited brown eyes danced as torches began lighting our way, illuminating the broad wooden and silver gates of Flecte. "Are you ready to greet your people, Your Majesty?"

My answering smile had never felt so confident. "Of course I am."

As the gatekeeper called out from his post, I heard the creaking of the heavy gates, the excited shouts of the crowd within. The triumph of my kingdom, at least for this one victory.

But then my smile faltered.

Over the crowd, over the victory, a whisper so faint I was almost certain I'd imagined it as it tickled my ear as delicate as a grain of wheat.

Find them.

As quickly as I'd heard it, it was carried away on the next gust of wind, tinged with the brine of the sea cliffs.

My horse's ears perked, then laid flat against her head.

I tried to shake off the chill down my spine as I waved to the gatekeeper, but it was impossible to ignore the low hum emanating from the relics in my bag.

EPILOGUE

~Yetta's Cottage, Two Weeks Later~
Gryffin

"YOU *HELPED* HER." I pinched the bridge of my nose with my fingers, my elbows on the wooden table the only thing keeping me upright in my seat. "You let me think she was dead!"

Yetta shrugged her shoulders as she sat across from me. "It was better that way."

The turmoil of relief and anger flustered my mind, making my thoughts whirl from one extreme to the next.

She was alive, thank Haggard for that.

But she should have died in the woods.

The relics may yet be easy to reclaim.

Or she may have destroyed them.

When my scouts had returned with the news of Rosemary's return to Lecevonia, with Sir Ezekiel at her side no less, I'd punched the stone wall until the pain in my knuckles was all I registered. Above the disappointment, the heartbreak, the jealousy—

The jealousy. Bah. It wasn't smart to waste any of my energy on jealousy. Such a useless emotion. I rubbed my bruised knuckles.

I wouldn't be entirely truthful if I said I hadn't thought of offing Yetta. And the gleam in her eyes now told me she knew it. She couldn't be trusted. That much was certain.

But I would regret wasting such a Talent as hers. So much knowledge, centuries of it, lost to an ax fall. It did not feel right.

"She had the relics with her when you saw her?"

Yetta crossed her arms over her chest. "I don't recall."

My glare did nothing to faze her. No flinch, no shrinking into her chair. She could not be trusted.

Without Lecevonia on our side, things would be exceedingly difficult going forward. To be honest, I doubted my army could withstand another battle with Lecevonian forces. The last thing I'd wanted to do was to create an enemy of the largest kingdom on the Peninsula. And that was exactly what had happened. Boars.

If only Rosemary had *seen* what we were capable of together, what the Talented were capable of beneath our rule . . .

Without Lecevonia, the Rebels would have to pull more weight than I'd promised. If anyone instilled fear in me, it was Amicka. Her ruthless leadership made Roderich look tame. The difference was that she was smart. Careful.

Perhaps we could split our efforts. Send Tarasyn to retrieve the relics from Somora and Loche while the Rebels went after the relics Rosemary had taken.

No—I would go after Rosemary. Who knew what the Rebels would do when they found her?

"I see your motives for going after Rosemary yourself," Yetta said suddenly. "And after seeing her mind, your advances will not work.

She wants nothing to do with you."

I scoffed. Advances. This woman did not know me at all. A marriage wasn't my goal anymore—as much as I had wanted it, admittedly. Of course I'd pictured her next to me in one of those dresses from Hilderic, her strong smile beaming under the Queen's crown on her head.

But no matter. I shouldn't think of impossible things.

"I only hope to make her see *sense* before she finds herself at the end of Amicka's spear."

"Hmm." Yetta huffed, smiling. "You do have a special place in your heart for her. I don't even have to read your thoughts to know that." She looked pointedly at my hand at my chest.

I hadn't noticed I'd been clutching the emerald ring hanging from the leather cord around my neck. Bah. I quickly dropped my hand.

"She would have been a beautiful bride," Yetta said. "And a fine ruler to have beside you."

I stood from my seat, chair groaning loudly against the old floorboards, and marched toward the door. I didn't need to be reminded of what I'd lost to that roguish scout of hers. I failed to see the appeal, with his snarky remarks and bad temper. They could not marry anyhow. It was foolish.

"Consider yourself fortunate that I don't have you executed for treason," I said, yanking on the door handle. The wind whipped into the room, rustling the old juniper branches.

"Has Amicka been truthful with you?"

Yetta's question made me halt in my steps. Why would she say that? I hadn't been given any reason to doubt. The Rebels had been cooperative thus far.

What would this old woman know? She'd never met Amicka. I took a step into the snow.

"You truly believe your grandfather hadn't dabbled with the Rebels?" Yetta chuckled darkly. "They all wanted the same thing."

My grandfather had been a murderer. My father had been a torturer. Amicka had only emphasized she and the Rebels wanted the Talented to rise again, as they had on Solstice Day when Haggard gave his magic to his children. The Rebels had always been a magic-minded people, if a bit extreme. But they did not murder blindly.

They did not want the same thing.

The old woman clucked her tongue. "Truth is hard to find these days."

I exhaled into the cold air of the forest, hands on my hood. I stood there long enough for one of my guards to speak up. "Your Majesty?"

With an irritated groan, I turned on my heel and stepped back into the cottage.

"Tell me what you know."

OF DECEIT AND SNOW

A MAGIAN PENINSULA NOVEL

ACKNOWLEDGEMENTS

Writing this second book proved to be as much of a learning experience as writing *Of Legends and Roses*, if not more. This time, I was not only trying to produce a book ready for your eyes and heart, lovely reader, but also marketing *Of Legends and Roses* and building up the confidence as an author to really put myself out there (no matter how much I would love to stay perpetually in my little writer's hovel). I've learned to relish in the productive days and accept the not-so-productive ones and to go easy on myself. Writing and publishing is tough work! But it is oh so rewarding, because I get to share my writing with you.

So, without further ado, thank you to YOU! My amazing reader. You motivate me to keep putting stories out there, especially this story of Rosemary's.

Nick, I could not do this without you. You pick me up when I'm down and carry me when I no longer feel like I can go on. You are why this writing career of mine is possible. Look at how far we've come! I'm so happy to be spending life with you. I truly cannot thank you enough in this acknowledgements section, so I'll just spend the rest of my life giving you all the love I can.

Rebecca, thank you for sitting on the phone for hours with me while I tried to figure out what the heck is going on with this story. Your input from the very beginning has been so invaluable, and I treasure our friendship without end.

Kristine and Sam, thank you for always having faith in me as a writer! Your words of encouragement and honest feedback make me a more confident woman and author. How have I been so blessed with such amazing friends?

Lauryn, seriously one of the best beta readers I could ever ask for! Your opinions and take as a reader truly shaped *Of Deceit and Snow* (and *Of Legends and Roses*!) into what it is today. Thank you!

Gina, thank you for being the best editor ever! *Of Legends and Roses* and *Of Deceit and Snow* shine because of you. Your dragon's eye catches everything. Seriously, everything. (Not to mention your knowledge in archery! Such a huge help with this one!)

Lena, thank you again for an absolutely amazing book cover! I knew the moment after you created the cover for *Of Legends and Roses* that I had to have you create *Of Deceit and Snow*'s cover as well. Your work is beautiful, and you are so talented. Thank you for giving the books of The Crowned Chronicles a stunning and eye-catching face.

Shannon with R&R Book Tours, thank you for helping indie authors like me gain traction among the reading community! Your enthusiasm is truly a gift.

Kseniya, thank you for creating breathtaking character art for the beloved characters in this series. I'm so amazed at your ability.

Lori and Amy, thank you for tirelessly spreading the word of my books and always showing so much excitement for me. You guys really get me through some slumps with your enthusiasm and support. I love y'all so much!

Len, Lynsey, Hilary, Aunt Maranda, Aunt Lisa, Susan, Aunt Beth, Aunt Teenie, Kaitlyn, Judye, and the rest of my family and friends who have shown so much support to me throughout the writing and publishing process, thank you for always believing in my capabilities! Your interest in my work emboldens me to keep going!

Mom and Dad, how to even sum up everything you have done for me? Pep talks, advice (story advice from Mom and business advice from Dad), and genuine interest in my writing career are only the start of it. Thank you both for teaching me to keep reaching for my goals, no matter how far away they might seem, and to take one step at a time when things get too overwhelming. Thank you for instilling in me a work ethic absolutely necessary to achieve this dream of mine. You set examples for us to work hard, pray harder, and love without end.

I thank God above all for blessing me with each and every one of these people and for gifting me the ability to write stories that I can share with you. Only through Him am I able to feel like I can conquer any obstacle in front of me. I'm so grateful for the passion and patience He has given me that makes being an author possible.

READ ON FOR THE FIRST CHAPTER OF

OF REIGN AND EMBERS

BOOK THREE OF
THE CROWNED CHRONICLES

(Contents following this page are not finalized. Subject to change
after editorial revisions.)

3

CHAPTER ONE

STILL CLINGING TO sleep in the early hours of the morning, I felt Zeke's stubble tickling my cheek as he kissed me goodbye.

His soft voice was low in my ear. "No wolves this time."

"No," I murmured. "No wolves this time." As I buried my head back into my pillow, the inn room's door quietly latched into place.

That had become our routine in the little inn in Flecte, from the very first night I screamed myself awake. If I let myself fall to the edge of sleep, I only saw the wolves prowling through the woods of Tarasyn, fur white as death. Only, rather than amber, their deadly eyes were crystal blue, bursting with red flecks. Their snarling teeth glinted in the moonlight, threatening to claim me as their next meal the moment I put my bow down.

My only reprieve was if Zeke stayed with me through the night.

So, it was either wake myself up every hour of the night with wailing—along with anyone else staying on the same floor of the inn as me—or let Zeke hold me steady. After he and two other guards rushed into my room two nights in a row, we both chose the latter.

I felt so silly, letting night terrors weaken me. I'd *survived* the wolves, hadn't I? I'd survived so much.

Still, the fact that I'd survived did not mean I was not haunted.

Especially by those red-flecked blue eyes.

For the past three nights, Zeke had stayed with me. Nothing more than sleep, and he always left before dawn. I knew my duties, and he knew his, but that didn't mean I wasn't disappointed every time the door closed behind him. And I was even more disappointed that his nightly stays would have to stop when I returned to Hillstone.

Which was a journey I would be starting today.

I rolled over in my sheets and kept my eyes closed, ignoring the light of the rising sun pooling on the floor through my window. Too soon though, a knock on my door called me to reality.

"Your Majesty?"

"I'm awake, Roger."

The door creaked, and the shadows shifted behind my eyelids. "They're readying the horses."

"Thank you. I'll be ready."

As the door closed, I peeked over at the dress draped over the bronze claw-footed mirror that had been brought in for me. Burgundy satin over gold-threaded cotton, the bodice laced with shimmering silver ties. Quite the change from my leather cloak and undergarments. After surviving for a week in the woods, this felt a bit extravagant.

Finally accepting that my bed was no longer an option, I got up and quickly slid the gown over my chemise. Though the innkeeper's daughter had offered her services as my chambermaid, I'd declined, for doing something with my hands had become essential for my sanity. The laces in the back of the dress were a struggle, but I managed. And I'd braided my hair enough to be able to throw something together, a pleasantly simple little weaving of my waves at the nape of my neck. In four days' time, Hazel would be in charge of my hair once more. She was lucky I hadn't cut it all off in the forest.

My bag of what little belongings I'd had with me—my leather clothes, relics, and book for Isabele—had already been packed and taken out of my room, probably by Zeke early this morning. Still, if I could've laid my eyes on the relics, made sure they were safe . . .

I shook my head. No matter. Zeke took care of them.

One final look in the mirror, and I was ready.

With Roger at my right side, I descended the stairs and found the innkeeper laying a breakfast down, large enough to feed three Rogers. A roast pig, poached eggs, sausage, a loaf of warm rye, fresh strawberries and peaches. When he saw me, he rushed over and gestured to the table, sweat glistening on his brow. "Might I offer you something to eat, my queen?"

Ever since I'd arrived at the little inn, the innkeeper has gone above and beyond for me. "Not often we have royalty in our accommodations, Your Majesty," he'd said while frantically sweeping my room. And as much as I'd reassured him that his inn was wonderful, especially after a frozen forest floor, he's fretted over every detail. The fireplace, the warm water for a bath, the plywood tucked into the baseboards in front of the tiny mouse hole (but I uncovered it every night—I've been as small as a mouse before).

"Oh, sir," I exclaimed, eyeing the table laden with food. "You're too kind! Preparing all this?" Really, all I'd wanted was an apple for the road. But I would never let his efforts go to waste. This was his hard-earned food, time, and work. "Where's your family?" I asked. His eyes widened. "Invite them down. We'll all eat together."

He stuttered his thanks and disappeared into the kitchens behind the bar top.

And sitting there with his family, his wife feeding their young son by the forkful and their two daughters jabbing each other in the shoulders with their spoons, reminded me of why I'd fought so hard to return home. Their laughs, their happiness. These were my people.

But the need to return to Hillstone pressed on my soul harder than the roast pig. After expressing my thanks and stuffing a few fruits in the pockets of my dress, I followed Roger out through the back entrance of the inn.

Down at the stables, Zeke had already hooked up a wooden and iron carriage to the great big horses lent to us by one of Flecte's chauffeur services. Roger's horse was saddled up and ready to go, and a coachman sat on his bench at the front of the carriage, reins in hand.

"Your Majesty," he said, tipping his hat to me in greeting as we approached. I smiled at him and made my way to Zeke, who was cinching up his stirrup strap on Hugo.

"What's all this for?" I asked. "I can ride like the rest of you."

But Zeke shook his head. "You're not traipsing through the woods anymore, Rose. You're our queen, and you'll travel like one."

I narrowed my eyes at him. "And what'd you do with the chestnut I rode here from Pruin? Surely she can't be left here."

"Gave her to the innkeeper's daughter as payment for us staying here. Quite a horsewoman, her father said, like yourself." He nudged my shoulder with his, wearing a little smirk.

Hm. I was starting to like that little chestnut. She was spunky.

But there was more. I could feel a tension in the air between the coachman straightening his vest, Roger tightening his saddlebags.

"Zeke, what's the real reason I can't ride?"

He looked out the stable doors toward the hilly horizon. "We'll be passing close to the Hiddon-Lecevonian border. A carriage is safer." He opened the door for me. "Now, will you stop arguing and get in, Your Majesty?"

I rolled my eyes and jabbed him in the ribs. "So tense." Gripping the sides of the wagon, I hauled myself up and settled onto the wooden bench. My bag from my rooms had been placed underneath the seat, and I couldn't stop myself from sliding it out and unlatching the top.

I took a deep breath, instantly relaxed. The emerald-hilted dagger and the golden bangle were nestled inside, and the bow, still unstrung, had been tied to the outside strap of the bag with a leather cord. I stroked a finger across the bow's intricate wooden carvings.

Find them.

That voice again. Just as I'd heard five days ago, and every day since. Filling my ears, yearning and beckoning, and then disappearing as quickly as it'd come. The low, reverberating hum of the bow beneath my fingertip was impossible to ignore.

I latched the bag shut and shoved it back under the seat with my foot.

Then Zeke swung himself into the carriage and onto the bench beside me, and the coachman lurched us into motion. His hand grazed the back of my neck as he rested his arm around my shoulders, sending goosebumps down my spine.

"Hugo?" I asked as he stuffed a hand into his pocket and pulled out an apple.

"Tied to the back," he replied. Then, he leaned in close to my ear and whispered, drawing out every word, "I've volunteered to be your personal guard." His fingers played at the satin neckline of my dress. "Eyes on you day and night." He leaned back, a smile pulling at one end of his lips, and took a bite of his apple.

"I don't need a personal guard." Though my flushed face told a different story.

Zeke laughed. "Sure you don't. You've never needed one. Not when you were almost killed by an archer in the woods, not when you were stolen right from under us . . ." His smile turned tight. "Not when wolves were after you for food."

The flash of teeth and white fur made me cringe into the seatback behind me.

"And not when you fell into a river," he continued. "No. Not even then."

The memory of the freezing current, so strong as it had whipped around my body, sent sharp icicles through my veins. I found myself leaning into him for warmth. "I got myself out every time."

"Except the river."

"Yes," I allowed. "Except the river."

I heard the buzz of a crowd, and I straightened as the first throngs of people appeared outside my carriage window.

My people cheered and waved as we rode through the streets of my kingdom's beautiful river city, with sturdy buildings and stained-glass windows, light cobblestone roads and dark mortar. Some people had even made colorful banners and waved them through the air. I heard a few voices through the crowd shout, "Welcome home!" "Safe travels!" Their joy brought a beaming smile to my face as I leaned out the window and waved back, and my smile lingered long after the heavy doors to the city rumbled shut behind us.

Good mood restored, I laid a hand on Zeke's knee.

"I still don't need one, but I suppose having a personal guard won't be so bad."

He placed his hand on top of mine and squeezed it, a devilish grin playing at his lips. "That's what I thought."

"It's a far cry from 'scout' though," I said, side-eyeing him. "Won't you miss it? Slinking your way through the woods and cities, being the first to know all the tantalizing news?"

He chuckled halfheartedly and was quiet for a moment, looking out the window to the Riparia River. Then, he sighed and laced his fingers through mine. "My ultimate goal is to keep you safe." His words sent an excited jolt through me, until he continued, "And seeing as you can't do that yourself, well—"

I slapped him in the shoulder.

One day carried into the next, bouncing along in the carriage. When we'd stopped for the night, I'd slept on the carriage floor, and at some point Zeke had switched off with Roger to get some rest of his own. In the morning, the coachman—Gibson, he was called—cooked us a breakfast better than anything I'd ever eaten on the move, eggs and salted pork and spice buns from his wife, and we were on the move again.

As afternoon came, however, the tension among the group returned. Gibson drove a little faster. Roger rode close. Zeke stared out the window intently.

"See anything, Gibson?" he called through the window.

"Not a thing, sir."

Outside the window, I caught my first glimpse of the war of my countryside militiamen.

Our carriage bumped and rolled over splintered wood trailing from the small collection of buildings that had been decimated, flattened to the earth, charred edges on what was left of the thatched roof that laid some yards away from the stone foundations. A house, a stable, a few sheds. Not a village, just a small piece of what was once working family land. With a family now nowhere in sight.

War was a revolting thing.

The desolation only got worse as we continued along the road, and with each destroyed home and workshop I saw, my anger surmounted.

Gryffin let his military do this.

Gryffin caused this destruction to my kingdom, my people and their land.

It would never happen again.

"We're approaching Cliva," Zeke said quietly. "The base of militia operations."

His words hurt my soul. The border village of Cliva had become a militia base, and I hadn't been there for them. I'd been an entire kingdom away.

We rode into Cliva as evening set. I'd visited when I was younger, and it'd been a village bustling with its modest shops and inns, giving travelers between Lecevonia and Hiddon a place to rest and restock. Now, it was alight with lanterns outside tattered tents, the shops transformed into kitchens or stables, the inns into refugee housing or healing quarters. No one even glanced at the carriage as we passed, either too preoccupied or too tired to care as to who was inside.

As soon as Gibson parked the carriage on the outskirts of town, I stood to exit the carriage. But Zeke threw his arm out, blocking my way.

"It's best no one knows you're here," Zeke said, ignoring my indignant stare. "Being so close to Hiddon, well, word might spread to their king." He spit the last words.

"He's not their king," I responded darkly. But I took my seat once more on the bench.

"Gibson sent Roger to get us some food." Zeke stretched out his legs and crossed his arms behind his head. "Just two more days, Rose, and you'll be home."

Two more days. Then I'd see Isa and Lisette and Clara, and Hazel and my advisors. I even missed Lord Castor. My hotheaded advisor always kept me on my toes.

After night had encroached, darkening the inside of the carriage, Roger knocked on the door and slid in two bowls of soup. Zeke lit the lantern inside and hung it on a hook above our heads.

I picked up my bowl and stirred around its contents with a moan of happiness. "Mmm, dumplings."

Zeke chuckled. "I don't think I've ever heard you say even *my* name with so much pleasure."

"I don't take food for granted anymore," I said, spooning one of the soft meat-filled dumplings into my mouth. The creamy broth they sat in was just a bonus. And I savored every last drop of it.

After dinner, Zeke extinguished the lantern, and I curled up on the floor with my blankets. "Good night, Zeke."

I felt his hand gingerly smooth my hair away from my face. "Good night, my Rose."

I laid there with my eyes closed for what felt like hours. Then, I heard Zeke's soft snore. I peeked an eye open and through the dark saw him sitting on the bench, head back against the wood, mouth slightly open and face lax.

As quietly as I could, I felt around for my bags underneath the seat and unlatched it, groping until my hand closed around my leather cloak. After fastening it around my neck, I opened the carriage door, shrinking back as it squeaked on its hinges. I stole a glance at Zeke, but his head still lolled against the back of the carriage.

I slid out through the door, and my feet landed on the dewy grass with a soft thud. Around me, Gibson snoozed on his perch, our big draft horses lazing at the nearby water trough. Roger's horse was with them, and Roger had taken up his sleeping post against a tree.

I carefully closed the door behind me, hinges squeaking again, and padded away across the road.

Ha! "Personal guard" my boot. Did Zeke truly think I wouldn't want to see the state of my kingdom's border?

My little escape success made me light on my feet. Hugging my cloak tightly around me despite the heat of the night, I began heading down the road back toward town, toward the firelit tents.

Until a hand clamped down on my arm.

"Where are you going?" Zeke growled. His disheveled hair made a halo of curls around his head in the moonlight.

"Zeke, I have to see what these people are dealing with."

"It's too dangerous for you to be out here." He began pulling my back toward the carriage.

But I yanked on my arm, and he let me go. "No, Zeke. *This* is where I'm needed." I waved my arm around me. "*This* is what I need to know."

And he knew I was right, though he could never fully understand, for it was not anything anyone but a ruler could understand. Part of being a ruler was knowing in what kind of state your people were living, what their struggles were, what their needs were.

He stood there, fuming, eyes dark. "Why don't you ever just listen to me?"

"I wouldn't be the same Rose if I did that." I winked at him in the dark. "Besides, I'm not the one who fell asleep."

He glared at me. Once again, I was right.

"I shouldn't let you go alone."

"Then come with me." I began walking again without waiting for his reply, and soon, his swearing and footsteps followed behind me.

"If you breathe down my neck one more time, I promise Haggard, I'm going to demote you."

But my threat only made him laugh and inch closer, so close I could feel the heat from his body against my arm. I rolled my eyes and slinked along in the shadows of the first tent. Men and women were gathered in the light of the swinging lanterns, drinking cider and shouting remarks.

"The village simply can't take in any more refugees!"

"Oh come now, they're living out here in tents—"

"We can't *feed* all these people!"

"It's only temporary, Helena! Just until they get on their way to Equos—"

"We're struggling to feed our *own*!"

I suddenly felt very guilty for the dumplings I'd eaten earlier.

Then a new voice. "Wouldn't you want the same if this had happened to our kingdom?" she asked. "The basic possibility of survival?"

Nodding to Zeke, we continued down the row of tents, keeping to the dark. Most tents had extinguished their lanterns or closed their tent flaps at this hour of night, but still others allowed me a glimpse of life for the Hiddon refugees. Through one tent's open flap, a mother hummed to her three little children dozing in her lap. Another, an elderly man clung to what looked like a hairbrush, knuckles white and shoulders shaking. In another, two men pored over maps splayed out in front of them on the grass. One of the man's cheeks was glistening in the low light. Still another, a father showed his little girl how to nock an arrow with a tiny bow. All of them gaunt, cheeks sunken. All of them with tired rings under their eyes.

"They've started trickling in to Equos," Zeke murmured. "We saw our first wave of them a month ago."

"And Isabele and my advisors have been handling it?" I peeked through at the little girl, tongue sticking out in concentration as she held her bow steady.

Zeke chuckled darkly. "Yes, handling it, as best as they could. Once Lord Brock was thinking clearly enough to take charge, Roger, Terrin, and I left for Tarasyn. Maybe their system's gotten better since then."

I looked at him sharply. "What was their system?"

He shrugged. "Let them set up their tents outside the city. Lord Brock started a sort of food distribution for them."

"Well that's good. The way you said it made me think—"

"Shh!" He pushed me into a space between two dark tents and wrapped his arms around me.

"Zeke, what—"

His lips against mine stopped any further words.

I didn't know why or to what end, but I let myself fall into his kiss, melting into his arms like wax. One of my hands found his hair, and the other gripped his arm, pulling him closer. He responded with a groan and pushed us farther into the shadows, almost tripping over the stakes in the ground holding the tents. His breath was like chicory and fire.

Then I heard the voices walking past our little hiding spot, hushed as night and indecipherable until someone chuckled and muttered something about wild love.

As the voices moved farther away from our little hideaway, Zeke's kiss softened from urgent to tender, lips soft and sweet.

When he pulled away, I was gasping.

"There," he said, his voice barely a whisper. I saw his half-smile through the dark. "Safe."

Part of me wanted to ask if that had really been necessary, but another part of me didn't care. Necessary or not, I loved it. I loved *him*. Here with him in the dark, his arms holding me to him and brown eyes shining mischievously, I could almost forget who I was. *What* I was.

But I couldn't completely forget.

"Thank you for your service to the Crown, oh good and faithful sir," I whispered, teasing, tapping the tip of his nose with my finger.

He grumbled something as I sidled past him out of the dark space and back into the row of tents. It had gone darker than before, more lanterns extinguished for the night.

"Have you seen what you needed to?" he asked, following me back through the darkness.

"Yes. We can go."

Zeke took the lead this time back toward the main road. But as we passed that first tent, I stole a peek inside. Only one person remained seated in the lantern's glow. Her disheveled blonde hair had fallen out of its bun bit by bit as she nursed her cider and shuffled between the papers in front of her, shaking her head and sighing. I recognized the look. Stressed, frustrated, hopeless.

I peeked back at Zeke, who already knew what I was thinking and was shaking his head profusely.

"Let's go," he mouthed.

But I offered him only a grimace of apology before turning back toward the tent and walking through the open flap.

The woman jolted upright at the new presence in the tent, hand resting on the hilt of a dagger at her waist. Now that I could see her better, I noticed she wore a set of leather armor.

I held out my hands peaceably. "I'm weaponless. At ease, miss. Please."

When the flash of recognition crossed her eyes, her hand left her weapon immediately. "My queen," she said, eyes wide. "I-I didn't realize you were passing through. I'll go get the others—"

"No, no, that's alright," I said. "The less people that know I'm here, the better." Though I disagreed, I gave Zeke the benefit of the doubt.

I straightened my shoulders. "I've heard the concerns of the people of Cliva. Is food the main issue?"

"And space," she answered firmly. "There are just so *many* of them."

My mind returned to Lord and Lady DeGrey at Snowmont's banquet, the state they'd said Hiddon had been in. The smoldering city of Vena, villages ransacked, forests destroyed. "I'm grateful they're alive."

"Me too," the woman said quickly. "Don't get me wrong. I had family in Hiddon when things went south. I helped them cross over into our kingdom. But Cliva is simply overwhelmed."

"I give you my word that I'll send aid. Once I return to Hillstone, I'll see what I can do. But I will do *something* for Cliva." After eyeing her armor, I asked, "Were you a part of the militia?"

She sat up a bit straighter and smiled. "Led a party alongside my cousin, Your Majesty."

"Thank you, sincerely, for protecting our border. And our neighbors." I bowed my head to her. "What's your name?"

"Helena Gardstone."

I held out my hand to her, and after a second of hesitation, she took hold of it. "Helena, you have my promise. Relief will be sent to your village."

"Thank you, Your Majesty."

With a final nod, I took my leave. I found Zeke standing outside the tent, arms crossed and expression fuming.

"Why don't you ever just listen to me?" he asked.

"I do listen! When you're right."

He rolled his eyes with a grunt and walked off, throwing his hands in the air. But as he sauntered down the road, me following quietly behind him, he seemed to cool off. Finally, he turned back to me.

"How did it feel? Acting as queen again?"

How did it feel? It felt so *good*, so *right*. It felt like I'd returned to actually where I belonged, what I was born to do.

My face must have given him enough of an answer, for he smiled and turned forward again. "I'm glad, Rose."

And for a moment, a wonderful moment, our walk through the moonlight felt content.

Until we saw the orange blaze rising from Gibson's carriage.

IF YOU ENJOYED THIS BOOK, PLEASE CONSIDER LEAVING A REVIEW ON GOODREADS AND/OR THE WEBSITE OF PURCHASE.

REVIEWS ARE INVALUABLE TO AUTHORS. REVIEWS INCREASE EXPOSURE OF LITERARY WORKS YOU LOVE AND ENABLE AND ENCOURAGE THE AUTHOR TO CONTINUE CREATING STORIES. AUTHORS APPRECIATE EACH AND EVERY REVIEW THEY RECEIVE ON THEIR WORK.

THANK YOU FOR YOUR CONSIDERATION IN LEAVING A REVIEW.

PRAISE FOR

OF LEGENDS AND ROSES

"I'm officially committed to this series! [...] Ashley has built an amazing world that I can't wait to visit again, in Book Two of The Crowned Chronicles!"
Amber Bunch, Author of the Goddess of Death series

"Of Legends and Roses was a great debut novel and really made me interested in continuing on with The Crowned Chronicles series. This book has lots of great world building and character development, along with mystery, secrets and plenty of political intrigue. [...] I am completely intrigued and pleasantly surprised with some of the twists and turns that were present in the book."
Michelle G., Blogger at BookBriefs

"The writing is fabulous—fully-fleshed out characters, good pacing, engaging writing, great character development, magic, romance, and political intrigue! I read it all in one sitting! [...] Now I'm dying for the next book!"
Heidi Hiatt, Bookstagrammer

"What a debut! Ashley Slaughter has a way with making you fall in love with all her characters. [...] I found myself going through emotional turmoil alongside the admirable Queen Rosemary. I cannot wait for the next book!"
Cheyenne Reyes, Goodreads Reviewer

"Of Legends and Roses by Ashley W. Slaughter is a FANTASTIC fantasy novel that I really had trouble putting down. I almost read this in one sitting, the only thing that stopped me was sleep!"
Jessica Belmont, Author and Bookstagrammer

MORE WORKS BY ASHLEY W. SLAUGHTER

THE CROWNED CHRONICLES

Of Legends and Roses, Book One
Available Now

Of Deceit and Snow, Book Two
Available Now

Of Reign and Embers, Book Three
Forthcoming

Short Story Anthologies

Eumonia's Monody and Five Other Stories
Available Now
Exclusive to Amazon and Kindle Unlimited
Read it for free on KU!

JOIN ASHLEY'S MAILING LIST FOR EXCLUSIVE CONTENT, COVER REVEALS, AND UPDATES!

(Don't worry, she won't spam you. She's still figuring out the whole *mailing list* thing.)

Visit Ashley's website to join:

https://www.ashleywslaughter.com

Visit Ashley's Social Media Pages for the Most Up-to-Date Publishing News!

Instagram: @ashleywslaughter
Facebook: Ashley W. Slaughter, @AWSwriting
Twitter: @AWSwriting
TikTok: @ashleywslaughter

Follow Ashley on Goodreads!
https://www.goodreads.com/awswriting

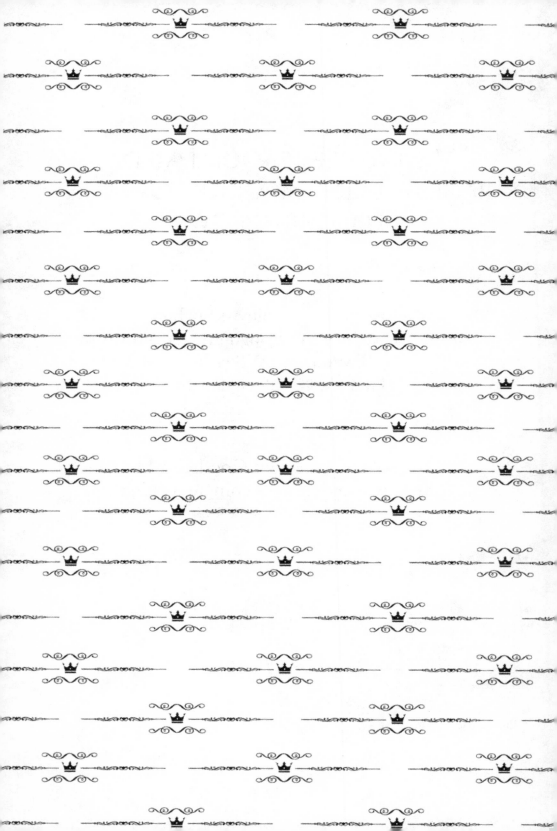

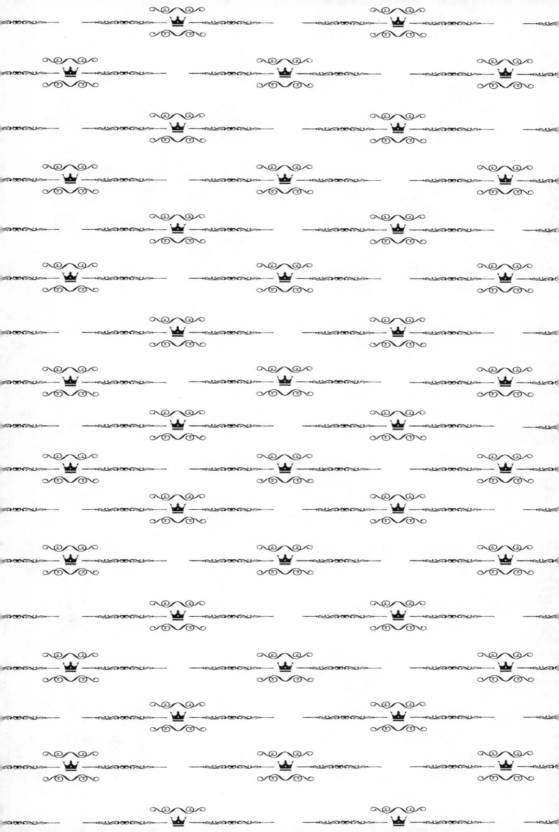

CPSIA information can be obtained
at www.ICGtesting.com
Printed in the USA
LVHW111401041122
732365LV00006B/62/J